Praise for

"Get in, sit down, shut up, and hold on."
—Lynn Viehl,
USA Today bestselling author, on *Red*

"Dark, action-filled, and hot! This heroine is a wolf
dressed in Little Red Riding Hood's clothing."
—Jeaniene Frost, *New York Times* bestselling author

"Clever and gripping, *Red* kept me guessing at
every step. Jordan Summers spins a dangerously
exciting tale with a mind-bending twist."
—Cheyenne McCray,
USA Today bestselling author

"Dark and dangerous and shivering with
possibility, *Red*'s a temptation worth indulging."
—Melissa Marr,
New York Times bestselling author

Tor Books by Jordan Summers

Red
Scarlet
Crimson

Crimson

Jordan Summers

TOR®
paranormal romance

A TOM DOHERTY ASSOCIATES BOOK
NEW YORK

This is a work of fiction. All of the characters, organizations, and events portrayed in this novel are either products of the author's imagination or are used fictitiously.

CRIMSON

A Tor Book
Published by Tom Doherty Associates, LLC
175 Fifth Avenue
New York, NY 10010

www.tor-forge.com

Tor® is a registered trademark of Tom Doherty Associates, LLC.

ISBN 978-0-7653-5916-2

First Edition: November 2009

Printed in the United States of America

0 9 8 7 6 5 4 3 2 1

To my family and friends—thank you for believing.

Crimson

chapter one

Red Santiago crawled out of the dark tunnel straight into the jaws of hell. Something growled near her ear and the hair on the back of her neck rose. She swallowed hard, then chanced a glance over her shoulder. She saw Morgan Hunter and Demery Wilson frozen in place. They were staring at something behind her. Red followed their gaze and her heart stammered in her chest. She had never seen so many carnivores. Something primal rose inside her as the mixed pack of canids closed in around them, their jaws snapping in anticipation of an easy meal.

Morgan began to peel his clothes off. His movements were deceptively unhurried. Demery's dark eyes took on a red glow and his fangs lengthened. Out of habit, Red reached for her laser pistol.

Before she could pull the weapon, Morgan shook his head. "We don't want to give away our position."

They'd removed their identi-chips so satellites couldn't track them, then they'd slipped across the boundary fence that divided the republics from no-man's-land. They'd done all this to remain undetected. And they'd succeeded so far. One shot from a laser pistol would change that.

Red cursed under her breath at her carelessness. She knew how the International Police Tactical Team operated and what guidelines they followed. As an officer with IPTT, it had been her job to enforce those rules.

But there were no rules here. Her tactical team training was useless. The sound of canid paws scrambling over the sand grated on her already frazzled nerves, leaving her edgy. Red flexed her hands, easing them away from the pistol. Why didn't they just attack already?

Morgan was naked now, poised for the pack's next move.

The largest canid, a coyote hybrid, stilled, sensing the change in its prey. Something in its bloodline had given it added size and darker coloring from the rest. Saliva dripped from its powerful jaws. It yipped, which in turn spurred the whole pack on. They all started baying. Starvation overrode the alpha's naturally cautious nature as it broke away from the pack to attack.

Morgan shifted, his scream fracturing into a pained howl. His amber eyes gave off a predatory gold glow as talons sprouted from his fingertips and his canines lengthened. Blood painted the sand crimson as his bones broke and muscles reshaped. His hair thickened, along with the skin on his chest and abdomen, which now formed a protective covering for his vital organs. Standing on two legs, Morgan was more wolf than man.

He was already moving by the time Red glanced around to judge the distance of the pack closing in behind them. He'd targeted the alpha male, his challenge for supremacy clear.

Demery hissed a warning to a few of the coyotes, wolves, and wild dogs that'd gotten too close. He swiped at them, his movements graceful and swift, but they remained out of reach.

Morgan tackled the alpha, his teeth going for the coyote's ruff. They tumbled upon contact, end over end. The hybrid was quicker. It leapt to its feet. Teeth bared, its head snapped back. Powerful jaws found Morgan's arm and bit down—hard. Blood welled in the canid's mouth as it shook its head, attempting to tear off bits of flesh. Morgan cried out, then slammed the heel of his palm down on the animal's muzzle, trying to break its grip. Red could tell that despite the pain he had to be in, Morgan was trying not to hurt the starving canid.

The coyote released its hold, licking the blood and bits of flesh from its teeth as it did so. The hackles on its back rose higher and its tail stiffened as the alpha prepared for a second attack.

Pain seared Red's hands as claws shot out of her fingertips, ejecting her short nails in the process. It couldn't have hurt more had she been playing with razor blades. She screamed, drawing the alpha hybrid's attention away from Morgan. He lunged, rolling the animal beneath him.

He placed his forearm over the alpha's throat. The other hand held the coyote's body to the ground. Morgan sunk his teeth into the animal's neck. It stopped struggling. He held the coyote and growled, until its tail tucked between its legs. The hybrid exposed its abdomen and whimpered in defeat. Morgan slowly let the animal up. The coyote dropped its head and slunk away. The excited yipping stopped. The silence made the hair on Red's arms stand on end. Was it over?

Morgan stood and made eye contact with each animal. In turn they ducked their heads and kept their gazes averted. A few tried to challenge him, but all it took was a rumbling growl from Morgan to bring them into line.

"That's more like it," Demery said. "Way to go, wolfman."

Blood smeared his skin. Morgan could smell its coppery tang. The aroma filled his nostrils and stimulated his senses, nearly making him drunk with desire. His mouth watered for a taste. He knew it would be hot, sweet, and sticky. Morgan licked a blood drop from his bottom lip and his gut clenched. What was happening to him?

He knew without looking that his eyes were glowing. They did anytime the wolf came out to play. But would they still be gold or had they started turning red—thanks to the vampire blood Raphael Vega had given him. Morgan had almost been killed that night in Nuria, fighting his cousin Kane for the alpha position. If Raphael hadn't come to his aid, Morgan had no doubt he would've died. But living came with a cost. One Morgan wasn't sure he could pay.

He'd lived so many years with his wolf. Through war, pain, and triumph. The feral nature of the beast was as natural to him as breathing. Morgan didn't know what he'd do if it went away. The wolf was what kept him bound to Gina, his little Red. If he lost that tie, then everything they'd sacrificed, everything they'd worked to protect would be for naught.

The thought that he might lose himself to the blood pulsing through his veins scared him more than he cared to admit. Without his wolf, who was he? There were no easy answers. Morgan would have to settle with knowing that for now he was still a wolf and Gina was still his mate. And he'd fight to his last breath to keep it that way.

He threw his head back and howled. The heart-pounding sound wasn't animal and not quite human either. When he finished, the pack scattered into the darkness and his gaze fell upon Gina. Morgan's nostrils flared and his cock began to rise.

"Come here." His guttural voice raked the air, scoring the night.

Gina's knees visibly quivered. She glanced over her shoulder at Demery.

"I'll be waiting for you three dunes over. Make it fast," the vamp said, grinning with more fang than usual. Demery hadn't fought, but he appeared to be worked up thanks to the blood dripping down Morgan's arm.

A growl rumbled out of Morgan's chest. A warning and a promise, letting the vamp know he would fight to keep Gina and his blood. Demery's dreadlocks shook as he laughed. Morgan watched the vamp go and didn't stop until he'd disappeared over a dune.

"I said come here," he repeated. This time his words weren't nearly as garbled. Morgan's ironclad control was gradually slipping back into place.

Gina hesitated, then slowly approached. Morgan's gaze sharpened as he circled her, demanding her submission. He stuck his nose in her long, black hair and inhaled deeply. Under the dust and sand, he smelled warm, musky woman. His cock jumped at her quick intake of breath.

"Mine," he said, sounding more like himself. "Now take your clothes off before I rip them from you."

Gina's fingers trembled as she unbuttoned her shirt. She wasn't scared. Morgan would've smelled it had she been. No, fear wasn't fueling her reaction to him. It was anticipation. Gina wanted him, almost as badly as he wanted her.

She pulled at the last two buttons and they popped off, dropping onto the ground to be swallowed by the sand. They'd barely had a chance to share a kiss much less do anything else, since Demery had been with them hiding out in the remains of Kane's house for the past week.

But he wasn't here now.

The tension thrumming between them created heat waves, electrifying their nerves, while ratcheting their need. Morgan's breathing deepened and his muscles quivered. He was afraid to touch her for fear he'd ravish her.

Gina's gaze locked on his mouth and she licked her lips, her hunger palpable.

Morgan shuddered. "Take off the rest," he rumbled when she hesitated.

The air rushed out of his lungs as Morgan's world narrowed to those luscious hard peaks hidden beneath a wisp of synth-material. One taste and he knew he'd be lost. He inhaled, catching the sweet scent of moisture gathering between her thighs as she seductively shucked her shirt and slipped her boots and pants off.

He hadn't bothered to shift entirely back into his other form. Morgan remained perched somewhere in between the animal and the man. He tongued his long, sharp canines in anticipation. Morgan couldn't wait to taste the delectable treat in front of him. By the way she was looking at him, Gina couldn't wait either.

"Get on all fours." He gently raked her with his claws. Gooseflesh rose on Gina's skin. Morgan needed this connection, this bond. It was what kept him alive when Roark Montgomery had him wrongly imprisoned and later tried to kill him. It was why he willingly crossed into lawless no-man's-land. And why he fought so hard to clear their names. "Please, Gina," he begged, laying his heart bare.

Morgan waited for her to drop, his breathing ragged from restraining his feral nature. The second Gina's knees hit the sand, he was on her. He pushed her onto her hands and swiftly entered her from behind. One thrust into Gina's tight warmth and Morgan was home. The only home he'd ever need. It seemed like forever since he'd last lost himself in her body. Morgan trembled, caught between savage need and emotional overload.

Gina moaned. The sweet sound coaxed him, drove him on to claim her. There was nothing gentle about his taking, though. Morgan's hips pounded her round bottom as he guided them toward hot, sensual bliss. He couldn't seem to get deep enough. He wanted to crawl inside her until they were one heart, one being.

His claws gripped her trim waist firmly, but managed not to puncture her skin. Morgan brushed a kiss against her neck and felt his canines lengthen into fangs. He was too far gone to stop. Along with the intermingling of their juices, he could smell the blood coursing in her veins. *Just one taste.*

Morgan's mouth began to water and revulsion filled him. He'd promised himself he wouldn't bite her again. Gina's delicious scent wafted in the air. Desire swamped him, demanding the ultimate release. Morgan might as well have been trying to hold back the moon. "Please forgive me."

His gaze fastened on his mark at the curve of her neck. He began to tongue the spot, licking the salty sweat from her skin. Gently at first, then growing in fervor. Morgan needed to mark her again, reinforce his claim while he was still able. He kissed Gina once more and she quivered, her body clamping him tight. Morgan growled, then latched onto her shoulder, biting deep where he'd bitten her the first time they'd made love.

Gina mewed and her legs nearly gave out, but he held her up. He wasn't done yet and neither was she. Morgan could feel the desire growing inside her. It throbbed in time with the pull of his mouth.

He rumbled deep in his chest, his rough tongue lapping at

her tender flesh while his hips continued to piston. Skin slapped heated skin. Bonding two bodies. Repairing wounded souls.

A chorus of grunts and moans punctuated his movements as Morgan conquered Gina's flesh and laid siege to her heart. His love deafened him to the world around them.

"Mine," he ground out, pressing his lips to the side of her neck and drawing deep. "And I'm yours."

"Always," she said.

In the whirlwind of frenzied coupling, they mended their relationship, erasing all the pain that had come with the separation they'd experienced thanks to Roark Montgomery's machinations. With Gina's blessing, Morgan had been able to lay his past to rest, no longer haunted by the wife and child he'd lost in the last war.

Morgan reached under Gina's body and stroked her sensitive flesh. By the third caress, she exploded on a long, drawn-out gasp, her body gripping his erection like a vise. His movements lost rhythm and became even more frantic as he rushed to follow her into oblivion. "I don't deserve you." The hot brush of his breath bathed her neck as tears silently fell from his eyes. He lost focus. Morgan jerked three more times, then he bellowed in release.

They both collapsed onto the sand. Morgan lay on top of her, licking the blood he'd drawn from biting her shoulder. His fingertips glided over her skin, loving her, memorizing every inch. He couldn't believe she was really real and not something his desperate mind made up to soothe the beast. His claws were gone now. So was the extra hair and skin that had covered his body. He pressed his lips to her nape.

"I'm sorry I bit you. I promised myself I wouldn't, but . . ." his voice trailed off. How could he explain to her that he couldn't control himself? The excuse sounded lame in his mind.

Gina looked over her shoulder. "You know I love it when you bite me."

Morgan frowned. She didn't understand. How could she, when he barely understood it himself? "It's different now. I'm not sure what's happening to me. Raphael's blood has changed me somehow. I'm a wolf, but my desires have altered."

Her eyes crinkled at the corners. "You are still the man I love. I'll take you in any form I can get you," Gina said, her voice a rich husk.

Morgan didn't deserve her. He'd meant what he had said. He was a hard man to love and he knew it. There was no denying his nature, but he was still grateful to have her. "I've missed you so much. I didn't think I'd ever see you again after Roark locked me up," he said, sliding off her.

The loss of warmth was acute.

Gina rolled over to meet his amber gaze. "Don't ever leave me again." She touched his cheek.

"I won't." Morgan pressed his lips to her palm.

"Promise?" she asked.

"On my life," he said, tenderly brushing the hair off her forehead. He'd die before he would allow them to be separated again.

"Good." She smiled. "Because I'll kill you myself if you do."

He laughed, a big belly of a sound that eased the last of the tension taking refuge in his shoulders. Morgan pulled her close. "I wish we could stay here like this forever."

Gina snuggled against him. "Me, too."

"But I doubt Demery will wait for us much longer and we don't want to lose the cover of night."

"Are you guys about done?" Demery called out from nearby as if on cue. "I'd like to walk for a few hours before we make camp."

He didn't sound three dunes away. If the shifting sand was any indication, he was on the other side of the dune they were lying on. Morgan tried not to smile.

"You better have just walked back," Gina warned. She gave a quick look around. "Or I'm going to kick your ass."

Demery was silent.

Morgan chuckled and began to gather his clothes. He slipped on his pants, then picked up Gina's clothes and handed them to her.

"Are you two coming or do I have to come over there and get you?" Demery asked, amusement in his voice.

"He wouldn't dare." Gina's eyes widened as she looked at Morgan.

He grinned. "I learned a long time ago never to encourage a vampire."

chapter two

They'd been walking over sand dunes for two days and hadn't come across a soul. Red had thought the Republic of Arizona was barren. It had nothing on no-man's-land. This place made the back side of the moon look subtropical. She wiped at the sweat clinging to her face. It had already started to slow. Soon she'd be completely dehydrated.

She glanced over at Demery, who was wearing a white protective suit that glowed in the emerging sunlight. He looked nice and cool despite the hideous temperature. For a second she was jealous, then she brought herself up short. His body didn't change temperature unless it was exposed to the sun. In which case, he'd explode and die, thanks to the genetic alterations he'd received during the last war.

She looked at Morgan, who was trudging along on her right. The heat didn't appear to be affecting him either. At least not as much as it was getting to her. Of course, he was used to living in Nuria, which had never had a protective biodome. Red had always considered herself prepared for anything, but nothing could've prepared her for the harsh, unforgiving desert landscape that lay before them. She'd never seen so much sand.

"Maybe we should seek shelter before the sun gets too high," she suggested, hoping they'd take the hint without her having to acknowledge she was tired.

Morgan looked around. "That would be fine, but I don't see anyplace we could hole up for the day. Do you?"

Red squinted into the retreating darkness. There was nothing for miles but dunes. "I guess we keep walking."

Demery signaled them on. "We might find something over the next rise," he said.

"Where did you rest the last time you crossed?" Red asked, licking her chapped lips.

"I didn't come this way. Too barren," Demery said.

Red stopped. If the place was barren, then why in the hell was he taking them this way? Red glanced around, her senses alert. "You do know where you're going, right? There's no shame in admitting you're lost."

"I'm not lost." Demery chuckled. "I know where I'm going . . . more or less. We went this way to throw off anyone who might be following. They wouldn't think to look for us here. They'd assume we'd head west where supplies are more plentiful." He pulled out a canteen and tossed it to Red. She caught it without thinking. "Take a drink. It'll make you less grumpy. I've enhanced the water with minerals."

"I'm not grumpy!"

Morgan and Demery laughed.

She was uncomfortable. There was a difference. Red took a drink. When she finished, she secured the lid and tossed it to Morgan, who took two big swallows before sealing it and handing it back.

"We have to find someone we can trade with. We need more provisions," Demery said.

Nothing turned out to be over the next dune but more sand. The grit covered Red's face and hands until it seemed a part of her skin. They walked through the heat of the day and into early evening. Red was ready to drop by the time they spotted fire light flickering in the distance.

"Am I seeing things?" she asked. It had been two days with no signs of human life. Hallucinating wasn't out of the question.

"No." Morgan stepped forward. "I see it, too." He sniffed the air. "I smell a lot of purebloods."

"Get down," Demery said and they all three hit the ground without question. "We need to figure out if these are squatters, drifters, or Sand Devils."

Horned creatures with forked tongues and red skin flashed in Red's mind. "What are Sand Devils?" she asked.

"They are bands of outlaws who rove the dunes in search of unsuspecting squatters and drifters."

Red reached for her pistol. Demery noticed the movement. "Relax. Let's find out who we're dealing with before we go in shooting. Okay?"

"Just want to be prepared." Red shrugged and looked over at Morgan, whose entire body was tense.

"If they're squatters, they'll have two lookouts. One stationed on each side of the group. They check in by signaling each other. The signal changes from group to group, but we should be able to catch something within the next few seconds," Demery said.

Red watched the inky horizon, waiting for a sign to tell them they wouldn't have to fight their way past this group. She was tired and hungry, and doubted she'd have the energy to put up much resistance if the situation called for it. Patience had deserted her long ago.

The silence was tense as they waited. An orange fireball exploded against the night sky with a boom. It was followed by another a second later. Demery released a breath and grinned.

"Looks like we've found our first band of squatters," he said, rising. "They should have sufficient supplies to trade. At the very least, we should be able to get enough supplies to make it to the next encampment."

Red and Morgan were slower to rise, since they weren't in a hurry to become an easy target for a nervous lookout.

"How do you want to do this?" Morgan asked Demery.

The camp sat a hundred or so yards away. Circular tents and lean-tos were huddled like melted marshmallows in the center of a ring of fire. Morgan couldn't tell what they were using for fuel, but the flames burned steady and were a good barrier moat between the inhabitants and any intruder that might wander by.

"What are they wearing?" Gina asked.

Morgan squinted. "Looks like whatever they could find."

Loose rags covered the people who were by the firelight, leaving very little skin visible. A few wore big cat and coyote hides. Morgan had seen similar clothing before. It had been worn in the Middle East by nomadic tribes. It was one of the few things that had survived from that area after the last war.

"Doesn't seem practical," Gina said.

Morgan looked at her. Gina's hazel eyes were wide in wonder. Despite the danger they were in, she was absorbing it all like a kid who'd just spotted her first flying shuttle.

"Actually, those outfits are great for this harsh climate. It cools you during the day and keeps you warm at night. The key is layers. They can be removed or added as needed," he said.

Demery watched the people. "Hey mon, I think I know this group," he said.

"Is that good or bad?" Morgan asked. The last thing they needed after their long trek was to run into hostiles.

"It's good. The Sand Moles welcome traders. You both stay here and I'll make contact." He approached the ragtag group without waiting for an answer. "If anything happens, head south."

They ducked back down to watch. Morgan didn't like it. The idiot was going to get himself killed. Could he lead Gina across the desert without a guide? Morgan knew the answer to that question. No. Without Demery they'd be wandering blind.

"What do we do if they kill him?" she asked, following the same train of thought.

"It won't come to that," he said.

"But what if it does?" she asked.

Morgan slanted Gina a glance. She'd gone from amazement to fear in record time. Her skin paled despite the heavy amount of sun it had received the past couple of days. Her dark hair was disheveled, torn loose from the clasp that held it.

"We run," he said. "And eventually head south like he said."

They watched Demery slowly approach the encampment. He held his hands in the air so the lookouts could see he wasn't armed. A horn sounded. It was followed by the blast from another. People filed out of their tents, guns, bows, and pipes raised.

Morgan took a quick look around. Other than the ridge of sand they were perched on there was no cover. If he and Gina had to make a run for it, they'd be easily picked off if the lookouts were a half-decent shot.

"What are they holding?" Gina asked. "They look like weapons, but I've never seen anything like them."

"Those are rifles."

"Laser rifles?"

Morgan shook his head. "No, those are antique rifles. They're made out of wood."

"Like the kind that used to fire metal?" she asked, inching forward to get a better look.

"I wouldn't do that if I were you." Morgan reached over and caught her leg, pulling her back. "The metal they carry is called bullets and can fire quite a distance. Getting hit hurts like hell."

"You've been shot with one of those." Her tone was incredulous.

"Not that exact model, but yes. It's an experience I'd like to forget." He rubbed his shoulder where he'd taken a bullet. It still ached when it rained. Fortunately, that didn't happen often.

"How did they get a hold of them? The International Police Tactical Team confiscated all of the weapons after the war. Houses were checked, buildings were scoured," she said, sounding bewildered.

Morgan grinned. "They obviously missed a few."

"Are our laser pistols any match to those weapons?" Gina asked, pulling her gun out of its holster.

"Yes, but those have us on distance. We'd need a laser rifle to compete."

Gina slumped against the dune. "I knew I should've brought a rifle."

Morgan kissed the tip of her nose. "We could only carry so many weapons. We had to leave room for food and water."

"I know," she said, sounding dejected.

Demery reached the group and stopped. He held his hands out in front of him, palms up.

One of the men in the group stepped forward and patted him down. "All clear," the man said, then quickly rejoined the group.

The murmur of voices rose.

"I'm here to trade, but I also seek shelter," he said. "My name is Demery Wilson. Does anyone here know that name?"

There were more murmurs. This time louder as his name rumbled through the crowd on a tide of voices. Finally a single voice rose above the rest.

"I do." An older man with silver at his temples stepped forward. He wore similar clothes as the rest and had a scruffy beard that started at one ear and ended at the other in a smile of hair.

"Gray?" Demery asked, stepping forward.

The guards notched the rifles against their shoulders.

"It's okay," Gray said. The man smiled, showing a gap in his teeth. "Been a long time, dread man. Didn't think I'd see you around these parts after your last encounter with Reaper."

Demery shrugged casually, but Morgan could see the tension in his large frame. His scent changed, too. It was subtle, but the sour tang was still there.

"You know me, mon. Nothing can keep me away from a good trade." Demery grinned, showing the dimples in his dark cheeks. His body relaxed as he slipped on the jovial, happy-go-lucky mask he used freely around others.

Morgan wondered—not for the first time—what the *real* Demery was like. It had taken him fifty years to understand Raphael and what motivated him. It had only been a week and change with Demery. A long way to go before the word "trust" would enter the picture.

"This man is known to me. Show him Sand Mole hospitality." Gray stepped forward and lowered his voice. "For your sake, I hope you brought Reaper what you promised."

Demery patted his shirt. "I have it right here."

Gray frowned in confusion, then threw his head back and laughed. "It's nice to know your sense of humor survived intact." He clapped Demery on the back.

"What's he talking about?" Gina asked.

Morgan shook his head. "I don't know. Now shh, let's listen to see if we can find out," he said.

"Do you know where I can find Reaper?" Demery asked Gray. "He still has something of mine."

"We don't run with the likes of him. You know that," Gray said, his brow furrowing at the mere suggestion of association. "We are a peaceful people unless we're provoked or deceived."

Demery smiled. "I know, mon, but you always seem to know where the devil hides."

Gray grinned back. "That I do. That I do. Speaking of which, tell your friends they can come out now."

Morgan tensed and Gina started to slip backward into the darkness.

"Could never get anything past you, old man. It's okay," Demery called out. "They won't harm you. Come on out."

"What do you think?" Gina asked, thumbing her pistol.

Morgan looked at the darkness squeezing in around them. "I think we don't have a choice. We need provisions and shelter or else we won't get far tomorrow."

She grasped his arm. "I don't like it," she said.

"I know, but down here Demery's the expert," Morgan said.

She shook her head. "It's not Demery I'm worried about."

Gina stood and put her gun away. Morgan followed, positioning his body between her and the armed men.

When they got close, Morgan said, "My name is—"

"Hunter," Demery provided, cutting him off. "And this is Red." He reached out and pulled Gina close.

The gesture was both friendly and possessive. Perhaps a warning. Morgan couldn't tell, so he said nothing, even though his first instinct was to rip the vamp's arm off and use it for a chew toy. *We are outnumbered,* he reminded himself. If Demery's little act would protect Gina, then he'd go along with it . . . for now.

"I'm Gray. And these are the Sand Moles. Welcome."

The group turned out to be quite hospitable. They offered Red and Morgan food, shelter, and water in exchange for a laser pistol.

Red was hesitant to give up one of her weapons, but it wouldn't do them any good if they died of thirst. Despite the circumstances, she was fascinated by the people and their customs. Women danced around a crackling fire in the center of the compound to music that was created using scraps of metal and wires. Red had never heard anything like the high-pitched pings and pops, but found herself tapping her foot and swaying to the music.

One woman with a thick braid of blond hair approached. She tried to coax Red into joining the other women, dancing. Red begged off. She'd never danced a day in her life and wasn't about to start now. But she was tempted. It looked like fun. At least the women seemed to be having fun.

The men watched, their eyes taking in every sensual movement. Morgan seemed entranced, too. He'd finally stopped staring at one of the digital diaries they'd found hidden in Kane's home. As far as Red knew, he hadn't listened to any of the recordings yet. The loss of his cousin was still too fresh in his mind.

"Why don't you put that away and try to relax?" Red pointed at the digital recorder in his hand.

Morgan looked at the device and pain momentarily hardened his austere features. In a flash, it was gone. He shoved the recorder in his pocket, then went back to staring at the fire.

Red glanced at the women once more. Maybe when this was all over she'd learn how to dance. She continued to watch as activity went on around them. The Sand Moles seemed so poor, yet moved with such freedom that for a moment Red envied their lot in life. That thought brought her up short. These people were criminals. She'd have shot them if she had come across them on patrol with IPTT. Now she was relying on their generosity and goodwill. Shame warred with duty, weighing heavily on her conscience.

She was so distracted by her thoughts that Red nearly missed Demery as he passed her on his way to a nearby tent.

"Where are you going?" she asked. Red thought it prudent to know where everyone was just in case they had to leave in a hurry.

His brown eyes sparkled mischievously and his dimples deepened. "To get a little refreshment." Demery nodded at the woman who'd just poked her head out of the flap.

She'd momentarily forgotten all about his need for blood. "Sorry," Red said.

He started to leave.

"Wait, I have a question for you."

Demery paused, his impatience showing.

He must really be hungry. Or maybe he was just horny from watching the women gyrate seductively around the flames. "What did Gray mean earlier when he asked if you brought the item for Reaper?"

Demery's cheerful expression faded a little. "Nothing, mon. Just old business that needs tending to while I'm here," he said, then kept walking.

Morgan waited for him to enter the tent, then leaned over to whisper in her ear. "What do you think?"

Red kept her eyes trained on the flap. "His scent tells me he's being untruthful. He's not lying exactly, but he damn sure isn't telling us everything."

"You want to go after him?" he asked.

"No, I am willing to give him the benefit of the doubt. He may just be overly hungry. Besides, I'm too exhausted to pursue it tonight. Unless it involves us directly, it really isn't any of our business what he does on his own time."

"You're right. I'm just being paranoid," he said, nuzzling her neck.

Red pulled back so she could look at him. "What's going to become of us, Morgan?" she asked softly.

His brow furrowed. "What do you mean?"

A couple strolled by within earshot. She closed the distance between them, hoping the music would help mask her voice. "We are fugitives. How are we going to prove our innocence if we're on the run and don't even know if we'll make it out of here alive?"

Morgan brushed her cheek with his palm. "I will figure something out once we locate a communications device and find out what Roark Montgomery's up to. I won't let anything happen to you."

"I don't need you to protect me. I need you to make sure nothing happens to you," Red said. She could handle anything no-man's-land threw at her as long as Morgan was by her side.

He was silent for a moment while his molten gold eyes searched her face. "I'm sure that Raphael and the others are working on a way to help us."

Red shook her head. If only that were true. After what she'd experienced in Nuria during Morgan's absence, she had her doubts. Raphael, Takeo, and Juan may be trying to help, but what of the rest? They were only three men, not enough to take on Roark's army. If the politician decided to have another go at Nuria, they'd be massacred.

She thought about Raphael's brother, Michael Travers. What would become of him? As Roark's assistant, he'd been their only chance to keep one step ahead of the politician and he hadn't succeeded. If Morgan was correct, Roark had gotten to him. Hell, for all she knew Michael was dead.

The thought saddened her. Not over the loss, but what Michael's death would mean to poor Raphael. He'd just found his brother after years of separation and believing he was dead. Now he may have lost him all over again. She closed her eyes and tried to mentally call him.

Can you hear me? Raphael, it's Red.

Silence met her.

Red tried again.

Still nothing.

She opened her eyes to find Morgan staring at her.

"Did it work?" he asked.

"Did what work?" she countered, feeling self-conscious.

"Calling Raphael," he said as if it were obvious.

Had he heard her thoughts or guessed? Red could live with guessing, but she wasn't sure how she'd handle an invasion of mental privacy. It was bad enough knowing Raphael could hear her thoughts whenever he felt like it. "How did you know?" she asked.

"I've been trying to contact him, too," Morgan said.

"I take it, it didn't work."

He shook his head. "No."

Her shoulders slumped. "I think we're too far away and I'm not entirely sure I am doing it correctly."

"Me either," he said quietly. "But I'm going to keep trying." Morgan looked away, his gaze growing distant. "I need to know how Nuria is holding up."

Red nodded, then went back to watching the dancers twirl this way and that, their skirts flowing out away from their bodies. After a few minutes, she tuned out the music.

Raphael where are you?

chapter three

It was late. Roark Montgomery sat behind his desk in his expansive office located in the center of the Republic of Missouri in what used to be the states of Illinois, Kansas, and Missouri. He stared out the window at the illuminated biodome that kept everything bright lush green on the inside and darkly shriveled on the outside.

Despite his being put in a healing vat, his sides were still tender from where Gina Santiago, or Red as she was known on the International Police Tactical Team, had sunk her claws into him. He could still recall the shock of discovery. Up until that moment, Roark had thought she was a pureblood. His mistake nearly cost his life. He'd been lucky. The bitch had missed his vital organs. Whether on purpose or by chance, he didn't know, didn't care. The only thing that mattered was that she pay for her treachery.

He spun his chair away from the window to face his assistant, Michael Travers, who stood nervously clasping his hands. His pale skin was more pasty than usual and his black eyes never stopped shifting. "What do you mean they haven't found them yet?" he asked, his thumb hovering above a small green button. "I told you to double the IPTT patrols."

"I did as you asked. Please," Michael begged, his gaze darting to Roark's hand. "I've done everything I can. It's like they've disappeared off the planet."

His oily black hair normally molded his scalp like a second

skin, but today it stuck out in random tufts around his head. He backed away, clutching his skull as fear contorted his expression into a macabre fleshy mask.

Roark smiled. "Obviously you haven't done everything or we'd have Gina Santiago and Sheriff Morgan Hunter by now. There are only so many places they can hide."

"I've had every place I can think of scoured, but they aren't there, and the satellites are no longer picking up their registration chips," Michael said.

Roark frowned. They should've been able to pick up the identi-chips. There were ways to mask the signals and temporarily block them, but it was impossible to stay hidden. So where were they? Why hadn't they found them? His hard gaze landed on Travers. "I will not tolerate incompetence," Roark said, pushing the button.

Michael Travers screamed and dropped to his knees. "Keep them away." He swatted at thin air, fighting off invisible attackers that only he could see.

"Are you going to try harder?" Roark asked. He chuckled as his assistant squirmed helplessly on the floor. This was more entertaining than an underground clone fight. He should've implanted the frontal lobe A.I. chip long ago. If he had, Roark would've never had to worry about his assassin turning on him. It would have saved him a lot of sleepless nights. Had Roark known from the start that Travers was a bloodsucking Other, he would have.

"I will. I promise," Mike pleaded, curling into fetal position. "Just make them stop. They're everywhere." He covered his head with one hand while the other scratched the air.

Roark lifted his thumb and Travers stopped screaming. He lay on the floor, his body trembling. A cold sweat covered his pale face.

"Get up. You're embarrassing yourself," Roark said.

Michael lay there, his hands still clutching his head.

"Don't make me ask you again or I'll give you something to whine about," Roark said. "And you better not have soiled my rug. You know how much it costs to get it cleaned."

Michael unfurled, then reached out to grasp a nearby

chair. He pulled himself to his feet. "I'll try harder," he said, gasping. "The rug is fine. See?" He stepped away so Roark could look.

"The next time you come in here to report you'd better have some news or I'll keep that button down until you pray your brain explodes."

"Yes, sir." Michael backed away, his gaze wary and unfocused.

"From this moment on, I want you to conduct the search yourself. I don't trust Commander Robert Santiago to send out his best men to find his granddaughter. Oh, and Travers, if you don't find them, do not bother coming back," Roark said. "Now go before I change my mind."

Michael rushed out of the room, shutting the door behind him.

With any luck Travers would die soon and save Roark the trouble of killing him. *It was so hard to find good help these days,* Roark mused. When he'd first found out that Michael Travers was an Other, Roark had been outraged. How dare he come so close to ruining his political career! He had done the only thing he could think of and had Michael's brain chipped. With the touch of a button, a small electrical current would stimulate his frontal lobe, causing delusions, paranoia, and best of all, pain.

According to the people he'd paid to do the procedure, a person would slowly be driven insane as the artificial intelligence linked to the brain and began to make its own demands. The scientists had told him the chip would eventually cause erratic behavior and eliminate impulse control.

Until then, Roark had to use the remote to trigger the chip. Travers had already begun to deteriorate mentally and it had only been a little over a week. Roark just needed him to hold it together until the election was over. After that, he could stay in his imaginary world where shadow people lurked around every corner.

Roark opened his desk drawer and pulled out an unmarked navcom. He punched in a series of numbers and waited. The second the transmission was answered he stared speaking.

"Scarlet," he said, praying the influ-gas he'd administered to Private Catherine Meyers and Lieutenant Bannon Richards nearly a month ago was still working.

"Yes," a sleepy voice said.

Roark grinned. "I have a job for you to do. I need an insurance policy."

There was a pause. "I do not understand."

"Just listen," Roark growled. "I want you on standby. When the opportunity presents itself, you are to assassinate the woman known as Gina Santiago. Got it?"

"Kill Red. Understood, sir."

"Good," Roark said. "Have you recovered from your trip?"

"Not yet, sir."

"Well be sure that you do. I need you in top shape for this mission. I'll be in touch."

Roark sat back in his chair and stared at the digital map projected on the wall. "Where are you hiding?" His gaze scanned the areas that had already been searched. It was possible that Travers had missed his targets, but Roark didn't think so. He was thorough when it came to hunting, even under duress. His eyes dropped to the boundary fence. Would Morgan and Gina be stupid enough to cross into no-man's-land?

Roark considered what he'd do if he were being hunted. First he'd remove his republic identi-chip and store it inside something that blocked the signal, then he'd disappear. There was no better place to disappear than into no-man's-land. Satellites didn't even track movement there. It was the one place Morgan and Gina could go where they'd be sure the IPTT wouldn't follow. Fortunately for Roark, he wasn't with the International Police Tactical Team anymore.

He activated the comlink. Michael Travers answered on the first ping.

"Get your gear together. I know where you need to go," Roark said. "But first, I want you to send out a communiqué."

"What should it say?" Michael asked.

"Grant immunity and registration to the first *unknown*

who brings me Gina Santiago or Morgan Hunter. If they can get them both, I'll add an additional fifteen-thousand-credit reward. I can't have them turning up unannounced before the election. We're in the home stretch."

With his backup plan in place, Roark wasn't feeling nearly as stressed out.

"Where do you want the message sent? The Northern Hemisphere republics? Southern Hemisphere republics? Or both?"

"I want it sent to no-man's-land. Better yet, tomorrow you can take it there yourself."

Michael was silent for a moment. "Do you really think they've crossed the boundary fence? That would be suicide."

"It's what I'd do," Roark said.

"Very well, sir. Should I add anything else to the communiqué?" Michael asked, his voice sounding small, like the man.

"Such as?" Roark asked.

"Do you want them dead or alive?"

"Glad to hear you're thinking ahead, Travers. Have the unknowns surprise me." Roark grinned. Having unregistered individuals, *unknowns,* pursuing Morgan and Gina was a stroke of genius. Even if they succeeded, the unknowns would have no recourse if he decided not to pay because in the eyes of the republics they didn't exist. "You might want to think about getting to them first, if you ever want that chip out of your head."

"Sir?" Hope filled that simple question. "You'd really take it out?"

Roark let the silence stretch, then he disconnected the comlink. He'd never remove the chip, couldn't now that the A.I. had started to attach itself to his brain, but Travers would work harder if he believed that were the case. He looked back at the map. Gina and Morgan thought they could hide from him by crossing the boundary fence, but they were about to learn nothing and no place was out of his reach.

* * *

It was getting worse. Michael didn't know how much longer he could go on before his mind simply refused to return. The power inside of him was building. He could feel it in his limbs, a sort of itching pressure that never subsided. Michael had no idea if he'd be able to control it. He feared for his safety and that of those around him.

"Raphael, my brother what will become of me?"

As usual, there was no one here to answer. A flash of movement caught Michael's eye. Gray, amorphous, and threatening, the shadows taunted him. They were growing weary of waiting on the fringes, lurking in the corners of his mind. Soon they'd become emboldened. A few more presses of the button and they'd have him. He'd be too weak to fight. What would happen then? Everything he'd worked for, everything he'd recently found would all amount to nothing. Then what?

Michael knew the answer, of course. Madness and death. The question was how many would he take with him before they silenced him forever? A dozen? A few hundred? A thousand? Death would be preferable to the guilt he'd feel.

Perhaps he should spread his arms and welcome death now. Save it the trouble of courting him. Death would make a most fascinating lover. There'd be no lies or deception. Only truth. Michael found its whispered promises of pain-free peace more seductive than any human caress. Not that he had many to compare it to. A few brief encounters where credits were exchanged could hardly count as having relationships.

He knew that said a lot about the choices he'd made in his life. Existence more like it. Michael had stopped living a long time ago. His brother, Raphael, was the only thing that kept him in this world. Without him, he'd be lost.

chapter four

Raphael Vega sat in his rented room located above the water trader bar in the town of Nuria. The plush room lay in shadows thanks to the heavy burgundy drapes covering the windows. It had been a week since he'd tried to find his brother, Michael Travers. He'd searched his home and attempted contact multiple times to no avail. He was more than a little worried.

Red and Morgan should be across the boundary fence by now, if Demery had kept his end of the bargain. He'd checked the remains of Kane's house to be sure they'd gone. Raphael didn't fully trust the vamp; not that Demery had given him any cause not to, but there was just something off about him.

For one thing, he was too damn cheerful. It wasn't natural to be that happy. Not after the war. In addition to that personality flaw, it was dangerous having another genetically engineered vampire bouncing around town. Vamps were territorial. It was part of their bioengineering. The governments had wanted solitary sniper assassins when they created vamps and they'd gotten them. Raphael should know—he was the most territorial of them all.

He rolled his shoulders. He had other things to worry about. Morgan would take care of Red. Not that Red couldn't take care of herself—she could, but she was out of her element. She'd gone from a world of rules to one of utter chaos. Red would need her inner wolf now more than ever.

A smile flitted over his lips as the word "chaos" crossed his mind. Raphael glanced over his shoulder at the shadowy naked figure lying in his well used rest pad. Catherine Meyers' hair was a tangle of short red curls as she lay on her stomach, giving him a tantalizing view of her pale back. She made soft snuffling noises while she slept.

Raphael could make out the curve of her luscious spine as it snaked down to reveal the arc of a ripe rump and a firm thigh. Those same thighs had clutched his hips as he slid inside of her. The room still held the scent of sex and hot, moist woman. His abdomen clenched and he groaned.

He'd taken his little Chaos, as she was nicknamed, an hour ago, but Raphael wouldn't know it by his body's eager response to her nudity. He thought by now he'd be tired of the woman. Instead, his need had only grown, along with his hunger, which was now a constant throbbing ache. He'd derived great pleasure in memorizing the location of every freckle and secret spot on her. The urge to do so again had him rising from his chair. He forced himself to sit back down.

If he were prone to worry, Raphael would be concerned over his building attachment to the woman, but he'd learned a long time ago to take life as it came.

Raphael's gaze caressed her once again. Possessiveness welled inside him. He couldn't keep her. Logically, Raphael knew that, but he wasn't quite ready to let her go. He stood and gathered his clothes. Raphael dressed silently, then slipped out of the room while Catherine slept.

He pressed his palm to the door and punched several buttons. When he was done, the only way the door would open was with his code and handprint. A twinge of guilt tugged at him. Raphael quickly squashed it. It was too late for guilt, too late for a lot of things.

Raphael made his way down to the bar. Evening kept the shadows in the water trader long and deep. Its faded walls and pillars showed its true age. A few tables had been scattered throughout the room and were mainly used for customer overflow. He looked around at the last of the patrons bellying up to the long bar to fill their orders as if nothing had changed in Nuria. Raphael didn't know whether to be glad or upset. He settled on the latter.

The least Nuria could do was mourn the loss of its sheriff—their alpha. Morgan Hunter had led these people well. Protected them with his very life. In the end, he'd given up his freedom. And so had Red. Did anyone in here acknowledge their sacrifice?

Raphael stared at the people standing around the bar laughing and visiting. His scowl deepened as the answer became apparent. He was about to head back upstairs to his room when Juan Sanchez and Takeo Yakamura entered. They had taken over responsibility for training a new Nurian Tactical Team in Red's absence. Juan, an average-sized man with dark cropped hair and an unnerving ability to divine the future, gave him a wave, then indicated an empty table near the back. Raphael hesitated, then joined them.

"Any news?" Takeo asked, his almond-shaped eyes narrowing on the crowd in suspicion. He'd dumped his trench coat onto a chair and tied his long, black hair into a tight queue. His powerful Asian frame practically vibrated with unused adrenaline—thanks to the chimera living inside him.

"Nothing yet," Raphael said. "But I think we would've heard if they'd been captured."

"How can you be so sure?" Juan asked. "Roark has done a good job of controlling the news thus far."

"They would've tried to mentally contact me or at least send out a distress signal. I don't think Morgan and Red would go quietly this time," Raphael said. "Not after what they went through. Their bodies would've turned up by now if Roark had found them."

The men's gazes met in silent agreement.

"When are you going to let Chaos go?" Juan asked.

Raphael stiffened. "When I get good and ready."

"You can't keep her forever," Takeo said, absently flipping his long, black hair over his shoulders. He nodded to the man standing behind the bar, then held up three fingers. Three synth-beers arrived a minute later.

Raphael's jaw clenched as he waited for the man delivering the beers to leave the table. "Don't you think I know that?" he snapped. He didn't want to talk about Catherine. She wasn't their business. She was his responsibility.

"IPTT will eventually send in a squad to look for her. It's been over a week. I'm surprised it hasn't occurred already. Do you really want them raining down upon Nuria again after what just happened?" Juan asked.

The International Police Tactical Team had swarmed the town looking for Red and Morgan. They'd arrested Red, claiming she'd been behind Morgan's escape from prison. It had all been an elaborate ruse organized by Roark Montgomery in hopes of leveling the town. If it hadn't been for Red's peaceful surrender, he would've succeeded.

Raphael reeled in his temper. He wasn't mad at the men— he was mad at himself. "Have you seen that in your visions?" He didn't take much stock in psychics, but Juan had been right about some things, so he couldn't dismiss him outright.

"No." Juan stared at Raphael with a pained expression. He picked up his beer and took a drink. "Nothing like that," he said, but didn't elaborate further.

Raphael watched him closely. There was something the psychic wasn't telling him. He could see it clearly in Juan's eyes. He opened his mouth to ask, but then closed it and exhaled loudly. Truth was Raphael didn't want to know what the future held. He'd already considered all the possibilities, including IPTT intervention. None of the scenarios he'd spun in his mind had been a big enough concern for him to let Catherine go. "I'll make sure she's returned," he said.

"When?" Takeo asked.

"I told you I'd handle it! Now enough with the questions." Raphael shoved his chair back from the table. It hit the wall behind him with a bang. Everyone in the bar stopped what he was doing, and gazed toward the commotion. Raphael glared at the weathered faces around him. Wariness overrode their initial curiosity and they went back to chatting, but the volume had dropped considerably. Satisfied, Raphael turned his attention to Takeo and Juan. "You both worry about building the new tactical team and let me handle the woman."

Juan and Takeo looked at each other. Then Juan held up his hands. "You know we wouldn't say anything, if the circumstances were different, but you've kidnapped an IPTT member. It'll be a miracle if you aren't arrested on sight."

Raphael's gaze cooled to a slow burn. "Don't you think I know that? It couldn't be helped. She'd been sent to kill Morgan and Red," he said. "Hell, she tried to kill me. If I hadn't subdued her, she might have succeeded."

"We know." They snickered. "What we don't get is why you slept with her, when you should've killed her and dumped her body near the boundary fence."

Raphael's gut clenched at the thought of any harm coming to Catherine. He flashed his fangs and hissed.

"Knock it off, dumbass," Takeo said. "You aren't the only one in the room with fangs." He opened his mouth wide enough to expose his large feline incisors.

A deep sound rumbled out of Raphael's chest.

"Terrific," Takeo snapped. "You've woken the chimera. You happy now?" A hiss punctuated his words as the viper uncoiled from his back. A forked tongue slashed the air and its head shot up over his shoulder in preparation to strike.

"What's next? You going to whip off your shirt and show me the goat's head poking out of your rib cage?" Raphael said, dismissing the threat.

"The only goat trait I have is in the form of my libido," Takeo said, smirking.

"I'm sure it's just as quick, too." Raphael snorted.

"Fuck off," Takeo shot back.

"Children, children, children. Play nice," Juan said. "Or you can't sit at the big kids' table."

"Put your toys away, chimera." Raphael wiggled his fingers. "I'm in no mood to tangle." He pulled his chair away from the wall and dropped into it. He wasn't mad at Takeo for stating the obvious. Raphael had been asking himself the same question since he'd found out the truth about Catherine's murderous deeds. She'd killed two people and tried to frame Red.

Why hadn't he killed her? She was trouble in more ways than one. His nature warred with his compassion and his nature had lost. Badly. It was a first. Which was why he'd resorted to picking fights and grasping at straws for answers.

"You started it," Takeo said.

Raphael sipped his beer as he gathered his thoughts. "She helped us break Red and Morgan out of Roark's prison. I don't think she's going to be quick to turn me in for detaining her, since she'd have to implicate herself."

Takeo shook his head. "I wouldn't bet it on it. She tried to kill you once. What makes you think she won't do it again?"

Raphael considered his question. "A feeling."

"You're joking, right?" He snorted. "Do you really think you should base your future and the future of this town on a feeling?" Takeo asked.

"No, but I'm going to anyway," Raphael said.

"You are *kurutta,* man," Takeo said.

Juan quietly watched the exchange, then glanced at Takeo to silence him. "He's not crazy, but I do believe our vamp has a case of bloodlust happening."

Raphael flushed. Not an easy feat for one such as him. "I do not . . . I-I am not . . . It's preposterous," he denied. Lust was definitely involved in his decision to detain Catherine, but there was more to it than that. An elusive *more* that didn't have a name as of yet. Whatever it turned out to be, Raphael knew he wouldn't be discussing it with the likes of these two. "I'd better get back to the room," he said, rising to his feet. "I don't want her to wake without me being there."

Takeo's brow rose. He glanced at his watch. "She's still in bed?"

Raphael grinned. "Where did you think I was keeping her?"

"I wouldn't know. I'm a goat, remember?" he said.

Juan and Takeo laughed, then quickly covered the sound with coughs as people at the bar looked their way. Raphael left them to it. Let them have a laugh at his expense. It didn't matter. They did not understand that the situation called for care and finesse. Raphael snagged a canteen of water off the bar and headed upstairs.

When he was out of view, Takeo turned to Juan. "Man, he has it bad."

He nodded in agreement. "Vamps are normally detached from their food," Juan said.

Takeo chuckled. "She means more than food to him. Did you see how he nearly took my head off at the mention of killing her?"

"Yep." Juan played with the label on his beer. "I've seen this in the wolves. Not a surprise, considering they are pack animals. But never in a vamp."

"Seen what?" Takeo asked. "Insanity?"

"Some may call it that. Others call it the drive to bond— to mate."

Takeo looked back toward the stairs. "Do you think he knows?"

Juan laughed. "Nope, but I do think he's beginning to suspect something is up. He's wound pretty tight."

"What'll happen if she leaves him?" Takeo asked.

"Depends," Juan said, shrugging. He finished his beer.

"On what?"

"On where she goes and if she plans to come back. I'm pretty sure he'd be able to track her blood anywhere on the planet, now that he's tasted her essence. And if Raphael is bonding to her like I suspect, he won't let her go easily."

Takeo shook his head. "Better him than me," he said, as a shiver sliced down his spine. If he were a gambling man, he'd say it was a sign. Lucky for him he wasn't, but it still took several seconds for the sensation to fade.

Raphael was a fool to let a woman get under his skin. He should know better given how many years he'd walked this planet. Takeo lifted his beer to his lips. No thanks. He didn't want any woman sinking her claws into his hide. He'd avoided feminine traps thus far. He should be able to hold out for another fifty years or so.

Juan canted him a glance. "I hope I'm around to see you fall, big guy. From the look on your face, it won't be long now. That woman won't know what hit her, and neither will you, when it happens," he said.

Takeo glared at him. "Don't hold your breath. It hasn't happened yet and there's been plenty who've tried to tie me down in the past." He held up two fingers. "Tender, bring us another round of synth-beers," he shouted.

Juan's dark eyes sparkled knowingly.

Takeo didn't like the way Juan was looking at him. It was as if Juan knew something he didn't. Damn psychic! They could be wrong sometimes. Right? Right! "Damned if I'm going to end up like Raphael. Miserable bastard."

Juan laughed softly.

"What's so funny?" Takeo asked.

"I'm sure Raphael is thinking the same thing."

chapter five

I held the navcom in a white-knuckled grip, unsure of what had just happened. Couldn't seem to put the device down after receiving the message. Conflicting images. The pictures didn't make sense. What was right? What was wrong? I didn't know anymore. My mind was a blur of crimson as the orders tumbled round and round in my head.

Kill Gina Santiago.

There was no mistaking the directive. Couldn't just sit here resting. Needed to move. My body was restless. Full of unused adrenaline. Had to find the target. The urge to hunt ate at my insides, churning like acid.

The world would be better off without Red in it. She'd brought shame to my home at the International Police Tactical Team. And continued to spite what the team stood for by forming her own second-string force in Nuria. What a piss-ass excuse of a town. It's crumbling down before everyone's eyes and no one is doing a thing about it. The desert blight should've been leveled long ago.

Gina doesn't deserve the rank of lieutenant. It should've been stripped the second she handed in her resignation. That was normal procedure for anyone processing out of the IPTT. If it hadn't been for her grandfather, Commander Robert Santiago, I had no doubt the rank would've been removed. He protects her at every turn. Ignores her mental incompetence and the deaths that have occurred on her watch.

Maybe he was the key to finding her . . .

A plan started to form, the details still amorphous and too general.

A direct approach wouldn't work. The IPTT commander—like Roark Montgomery—was too smart to fall for any obvious ploys. Robert Santiago would be suspicious, as would anyone in his situation. Divided loyalties can be easily toppled.

Fortunately, he wouldn't suspect me. I am the kind of person who's easily overlooked. I'm not saying I am above reproach. I'm not. No one is at IPTT. But I am underestimated. And because of that, I'd be able to get him to drop his guard. Convince him it's in his best interest to trust me.

If he knew or even suspected where Red was hiding, I'd find out. I'm good at uncovering secrets. I've learned to make myself useful. I take my responsibilities seriously. And once I get out of here, I intend to prove my loyalty to the team.

My fists clenched in frustration. It was the waiting that was difficult. I preferred action. Always had. Always would. It was one reason I was so good at my job. I glanced around, unseeing. Nothing seemed familiar or real. Yet I knew it was. This room. The furniture. All solid, not a dream, nor were they figments of my imagination. They were as real as the orders I intended to carry out.

In my present predicament, accomplishing them would be difficult, but I'd figure out a way. I had before. I would again. No man, no matter how powerful and intimidating, would stop me.

Catherine was sitting on the rest pad, wrapped in sheets, clenching her navcom. She slowly set aside the communicator as Raphael stepped over the threshold. He paused, his attention split between her actions and a distant voice whispering in his mind. It was too faint to make out. So faint that Raphael wasn't even sure if it had been real. Was he hearing things? Had his brother, Michael, tried to contact him? Whatever it was, it was gone now. He shook his head.

"Are you going to give me my clothes back? It's been one week, two days, and . . ." She glanced at her watch. "Nine hours. But who's counting?"

He shut and sealed the door behind him. "You weren't in a hurry to have them an hour ago."

Catherine blushed and ran a hand through her tangled hair. "I'd like them now," she said, ignoring his statement.

"Who did you call on the navcom?" he asked casually, feeling anything but.

"I didn't contact anyone, but I did receive a call," she said as if it were of little importance.

"From anyone I know?" Raphael asked, shocked by the surge of jealousy pounding in his blood.

She shook her head, tossing red curls everywhere. "I'd rather not discuss it," Catherine said. Her gaze dropped to the rest pad and color rose up her neck.

Raphael wondered how long he had before IPTT showed up. "We need to talk," he said, stepping deeper into the room. "I think you and I can help each other."

Catherine scooted back, exposing a pale thigh in the process. Raphael's gaze locked on the skin he'd lavished with attention and he felt himself harden. She must have noticed because Catherine flipped the sheet over to cover herself.

"I could talk better if I were clothed," she said.

"That's unfortunate," Raphael said, "because I like you naked. Preferably under me."

The pink in her cheeks deepened in color. "That's not going to happen again."

Raphael arched a brow. "Are you sure?"

"Very," Catherine said, tightening the sheet. "What occurred earlier was a mistake. You overwhelmed me."

Her words were as effective as a slap across his face followed by a quick dunk in freezing water. Raphael flinched, then his mood darkened. "Are you saying that I forced you?"

Her green eyes widened. "Not exactly."

"It's a simple yes-or-no question," he said. "You cannot preface your answer." If it were possible for his blood to boil it would be doing so now. How dare the little minx accuse him of forced seduction? He'd never raped a woman in his life. He'd never had to. They'd all come willingly to his rest pad. Catherine might have protested in the beginning, but she never once uttered the word no. "I'm waiting," he said, trying to remain calm.

"No, you didn't," she said. "But I was at a disadvantage. One you were more than happy to press."

"Disadvantage?" Raphael snorted. "Was this before or after you tried to kill me?"

"I was doing my job," she snapped, but her voice squeaked, giving away her nervousness.

"So was I," he grit out. "I recall subduing you with minimal force. As for the rest, I believe we both achieved mutual satisfaction, or were you screaming my name for show?"

Catherine crossed her arms over her ample chest. "There's no need for vulgarity."

His eyes narrowed. "You're the one who accused me of rape."

"I did no such thing. All I said was that you had the advantage. You know, being a vampire and all."

He threw his arms up in frustration. "It was daylight. I had very little sunscreen on. My skin was frying and my strength was compromised." Raphael waved his hand in the air. "You'll forgive me if I disagree with your assessment."

She rolled her eyes. "Whatever."

"Juan and Takeo seem to think that I should let you go." He wasn't about to tell her they'd wanted her dead.

"You should listen to them. It'll go easier on you during your tribunal sentencing."

Raphael's brows rose to his hairline. "I'm afraid I can't allow that to happen," he said casually. He caught the fear in her eyes before she masked it and immediately set out to reassure her. "Don't be ridiculous, woman. I have no plans to harm you."

"You threatened to kill me," Catherine said. This time she sounded petulant . . . and utterly adorable.

"And you tried to kill me. I'd say that makes us even."

"I was drugged with influ-gas and given orders I couldn't resist."

"Are you sure it's out of your system?" he asked.

Her forehead crinkled. It was easy to read her concern, but Catherine ignored the question. "You kidnapped me. Tied me to a chair and seduced me, then spent the week doing more of the same."

"I detained you for murdering several people and trying to frame Red. Not to mention killing any Other you happened to find. As for the rest, I was distracting you from your mission." He smirked.

"Distracting me! Of all the arrogant, self-centered, egotistical things I have ever heard, that one takes the synth-tart." She scowled, her nostrils turning white with anger. "As you recall, I didn't have control of my actions when I killed those people. Had I been in my right mind, I would've never tried to frame Gina Santiago. She's the commander's granddaughter. It would be career suicide."

"Can you prove it?" Raphael asked, watching her closely. "I mean if you could, then I'm sure Commander Robert Santiago would be more than happy to listen."

Catherine huffed. "Did you not hear a word I said?"

"I heard you clearly, now answer the question," he said.

Catherine's expression soured a second before her body sagged against the wall. "No." Just as quickly, her chin rose in defiance. "Can you prove that I did?"

Raphael shook his head. He was enjoying their bickering far too much. He kept his expression bland. "No, but that does put us in a similar bind, you and I."

She scowled. "How do you figure?"

"You claim that I kidnapped you. I don't see it that way," he said. "I was protecting the alpha and his mate. I know that you murdered those men. I saw it in your mind the second I tasted your tainted blood. Then there's the little fact that you tried to kill me."

"But—" she said.

He held up his hand. "I'm not finished," Raphael said. "You

claim diminished capacity. Perhaps a few of the tribunal members will take pity on you and believe you, but I wouldn't count on it since the influ-gas isn't detectable in your system. The tribunal must uphold the law for the sake of the republics. Add in the fact that Gina Santiago is the IPTT commander's granddaughter and it doesn't look good for either of us."

She crossed her arms. "They won't believe a vamp," Catherine said defiantly.

"Silly girl, vampires don't exist." Raphael grinned, flashing his fangs. "Do you really want to stand before a tribunal and blame an imaginary creature for all your woes? You'd have to reveal the little secret you've been keeping in order to prove it."

Catherine chewed on her bottom lip, drawing Raphael's eyes away from her gaze. He'd kissed those lips, drank from the sweetness like a man lost in the desert. And he'd do so again, if he had anything to say about it. She couldn't deny what had occurred between them. The room crackled with sexual tension. Raphael had never thought anything could taste better than hot, sweet blood, but he'd been wrong.

"Would you *out* me?" she asked, drawing into herself. Catherine's green eyes widened.

"I wouldn't have to," he said. She'd do that herself by talking. Catherine must have realized the same thing because her expression turned bleak.

"Can't we make a deal?" she asked after several seconds of silence.

Raphael glanced at his hands and made a show of thinking about it. "Depends." He shrugged. "What do you have in mind?"

"You let me go and I forget all about the whole kidnapping thing."

"That sounds reasonable, but do you think kidnapping—which you can't prove—is comparable to murder? Seems like I'm on the losing end of this deal." He stepped closer to the rest pad.

Catherine sighed loudly. "Shouldn't Roark Montgomery factor into all this? I mean, he's the one who gassed me with the mind control drug, Scarlet. He's the one who sent me on my murderous rampage. And let's not forget, he imprisoned your friends. I'd say the blame rests firmly on his shoulders."

Raphael's voice grew cold. "Roark will be dealt with, but not until *we* can prove Red's and Morgan's innocence. Until then, it's just you left to hang in the desert wind for his deeds."

"Terrific." She balked. "I guess I have no choice but to help." Catherine clasped the sheet and scrambled to the edge of the rest pad.

"Everyone has a choice, including you," he said, tonguing the tip of his incisor. Raphael needed her help. Catherine could get into IPTT headquarters. She could meet with the commander and ask for his assistance, if need be.

"Not this time," she said, shivering under his regard.

He could smell her body beginning to ripen. Raphael swallowed hard and shoved his hands into his pockets to keep from reaching for her. "That is a matter of perception," he said.

"Are you going to tell me what you want me to do or do I have to guess?" she asked.

"So cute, but so short tempered," Raphael said. "You must've been a handful for your parents."

For a second, Catherine looked pained. He wasn't sure what he'd said to upset her, but Raphael had no doubt he'd struck some kind of chord. Her hurt expression vanished, quickly replaced with a dagger-shooting glare. "I'm waiting." Her tiny foot tapped the floor angrily.

"You want to know what I want you to do. Fine," he said. His gaze flicked to the thin material covering her. "You can start by losing the sheet."

Raphael's smile turned feral. He even flashed both fangs. Chaos had no doubt he'd done it on purpose. The move should've repulsed her, but instead, it ignited her blood. She hadn't expected the quiver of anticipation to course through her body or the rush of renewed heat that moistened her core.

Damn him.

She'd promised herself she wouldn't sleep with him again—no matter how pleasurable she'd found it to be—after he began locking her in the room. And it had been pleasurable. She'd never experienced anything like their lovemaking. It took great sex to a level few could achieve.

Chaos glanced down in time to see the sheet hit the floor. She looked at Raphael, who hadn't moved. His black eyes simmered with hunger, scorching her flesh wherever they roved. Her nipples hardened under his perusal, turning a bright rose.

He reached for his shirt and began to undress slowly. The man was magnificent. Long and solid with dark, brooding looks that drew her forward. He was comfortable in his sexuality and rightly so given his talent in the carnal arts. He'd brought her to release three times with his mouth and tongue before he'd ever entered her. And from the look on Raphael's face, he planned to do it again and again, even though he had nothing to prove.

Chaos squeezed her thighs together and kept her expression blank. She didn't want him to know how much she looked forward to this. How much she wanted this. Wanted *him*. A girl could get addicted if she wasn't careful. She'd entered Nuria with no clue that Others existed. Now she was willingly sleeping with a vampire. She should be committed. Most people would be screaming right about now, but not her. No, she went looking for trouble and had found it—all six foot two of it.

He tongued his fangs sensually and she felt her neck and thigh tingle where he'd bitten her earlier. This was so wrong. Wanting him was wrong. The logical side of her knew that, but the tactile being didn't care. It wanted another taste of this man, this creature, who could infuriate her one minute and seduce her the next.

What was the matter with her? She wasn't thinking clearly. Chaos needed some space. Yep, that would take care of everything. She opened her mouth to tell him. At the same moment, Raphael dropped his pants, revealing his straining erection. Veins corded the thick length, leading up and up to a flushed crown. Her mouth went dry.

Nope, nothing to prove.

It would be easy to blame Raphael for the predicament Chaos found herself in, but he hadn't been there the day she went to Roark Montgomery's office with Lieutenant Bannon Richards. She'd gone on her own accord. Raphael also hadn't drugged her with influ-gas and programmed her to kill. That had been Roark, too. And he wasn't forcing her now to lie back on the rest pad and open her legs in preparation for him. Nope, she was doing that all on her own.

Raphael gave her a triumphant grin. He'd won and he knew it.

chapter six

Miles and miles of sand and not a drop to drink. The sun rose less than thirty minutes ago and already Michael could feel his brain baking inside his skull. Sizzle. Pop. He didn't know how far he'd walked since crossing the boundary fence. Probably not far. Too bad his body didn't agree. It felt weighted, sucked down by the sand pooling around his feet. For all his strength, there was an underlying frailty.

Michael knew this firsthand, even without the chip in his frontal lobe to remind him.

He gazed out at the barren abyss. It stretched as far as the eye could see. He glanced down. Footprints were impossible to follow. The sand swallowed them up in one bite, greedy for more. Michael inhaled. Hot air singed his nostrils, burning his sinuses. Red's and Morgan's wolf scent remained elusive. Like the sand and the sun, the air's aroma toyed with him, whispering promises it had no intention to keep.

A shadow slipped past Michael in his peripheral vision. He turned, but there was nothing there beyond vast emptiness. There was never anything there, yet Michael continued to see them. The shadows followed him, waiting like vultures for him to drop so they could pounce and pick his bones clean.

Once again Michael wondered if he should make it easy on them. The vampire inside of him roared in defiance.

"Stay the fuck away from me." He swung his fist wildly, contacting with nothing but hot air.

Michael refused to sit down. That's what the shadows wanted. He'd be damned if he would give in. His gaze locked on the horizon. Waves of heat rode the dunes, surfing them into oblivion. He focused on putting one foot in front of the other.

"Where are you?" he shouted.

He'd put out the bounty just like Roark had asked. Michael hadn't wanted to do it, but he'd had no choice. Roark would've found out had he not and he would've pressed the button. Couldn't afford for him to press the button again. The button was bad. Bad button. Made Michael hurt.

He needed to get the chip out. That was the only way to prevent the pain and madness from taking over. He could feel the chip digging in, anchoring itself somehow. Michael clawed at his skin until blood ran down his face, blinding him. It was no use. The bone wouldn't give. The only way he'd succeed was if he found Morgan and Red first. Then, and only then, would Roark remove the blasted chip.

Michael stumbled and dropped to his knees. For a second his hands looked as if they'd been dipped into a scarlet puddle. Splashy. Splashy. Licky. Licky. He blinked, clearing the mirage. All that remained was dried blood. Fighting the urge to shove his fingers in his mouth and suckle, Michael forced himself to stand. He needed to find shelter before the sun evaporated the last of his sanity. His clothes wouldn't protect him during the worst heat of the day, not with his telekinetic power drained.

Scanning the area, Michael spotted a dark mass in the distance. He couldn't tell what it was from here, but anything beat the endless sand.

Forging on, Michael climbed dune after dune until he lost count. The dark form was beginning to take shape now. At least he hoped it was. He couldn't afford for his shelter to be a figment of his imagination.

The sand had been talking to him for the last forty-five minutes. It beaconed him to rest like a siren luring weary sailors to their death. Michael plugged his ears and screamed to drown out its insidious voice.

Not much farther now.

He was almost there.

Michael could see the rock up ahead, its corpulent noggin protruding from the sand in defiance. A giggle burst from his parched throat, morphing into a hacking cough. He threw himself against the rock grateful for the tiniest increment of shade. Michael patted the giant mammoth and crooned to it, stroking its hard surface. So pretty and welcoming, almost like it had been left here for him.

He plopped down, putting his back against the rock face and dug into his pack for the canteen. The water did little to quench his thirst. Only fresh blood could do that now. Michael decided to wait here and rest until the early evening. Night would make traveling much easier. With any luck, Morgan and Red would do the same.

chapter seven

"I'm going to take you back to International Police Tactical Team headquarters today," Raphael said. He buttoned his shirt before fastening his pants.

Chaos sat on the rest pad not sure she'd heard him correctly. "Why?" There had to be a reason for his sudden change of heart.

"It's what you wanted, right? Or have you changed your mind?" Irritation grated his voice as he yanked his dark hair back into a tight, painful-looking queue.

"No, I haven't changed my mind. I need to get back to IPTT before they send a team after me. I'm just curious, what changed *your* mind?" Chaos asked.

Raphael's jaw clenched. "Just be happy I did. I do not need to remind you about our agreement."

Chaos' heart sank. He was only doing it because of their agreement, not because there was anything else going on between them. She should've known. *You tried to frame his friend for murder and would've killed her given half the chance. Did you really think he'd developed feelings for you? Your own parents didn't want you. Why would he?* Chaos looked away when her eyes started to burn.

She wouldn't turn him in for kidnapping no matter how tempting the thought. She'd go back to IPTT headquarters and do damage control. While she was there, she'd check on Bannon Richards. He'd been with her when Roark

Montgomery gassed them. Perhaps he was suffering the ill-effects of the influ-gas, too. That was the first time she'd ever been to the politician's office in the Republic of Missouri. The visit hadn't been memorable and now she knew why.

Chaos had gone with Raphael and the Nurian Tactical Team to help break Gina Santiago and Morgan Hunter out of Roark's secret cell below his office. Not that she'd had much choice at the time. Raphael had made it abundantly clear she had to go. Partly so he could keep an eye on her and partly to pay for the lives she'd taken while under the gas's influence.

She hadn't seen the filth, but she'd heard the cell described by the other men. Chaos shuddered at the thought of being locked away without a fair tribunal hearing. She'd watched the history vids and knew it had taken place in the past, but Chaos had thought that the Dead World had moved beyond that stage in its evolution.

"Are you going to get dressed or am I going to have to dress you?" Raphael asked. The bite in his tone caught her off guard. What was he mad about? Chaos had given him her word last night that she wouldn't have him arrested.

"I can do it myself," she said. "Just give me time to use the cleansing unit."

"Don't take too long or you may find yourself walking. I've asked Jim Thornton to take you and I'm not sure how long he'll wait."

Chaos stopped halfway to the cleansing unit door. She'd thought when he'd said he was letting her go that Raphael meant he'd be taking her back. "You're not coming," she said, confused and more than a little disappointed.

Disappointed? She should be happy. She'd be out of here soon. Isn't that what she wanted all along?

Raphael's harsh expression softened a fraction. "I have to go find my brother. He works for Roark and I haven't been able to contact him."

She bit her lip. "Do you think what Morgan and Red said about the A.I. chip was true?"

"I don't know and I won't know until I talk to him. Their

word combined with your experience with the influ-gas has given me many reasons to be concerned."

She nodded and continued into the cleansing unit. Chaos didn't know why it bothered her so much that Raphael wouldn't be the one returning her to IPTT. She'd wanted nothing more than to see the backside of him for the past week or so. Maybe she'd developed Stockholm syndrome. Could great sex cause that?

Chaos didn't really have a point of reference. She'd had decent sex in the past, but nothing like what she'd experienced with Raphael. Chaos wasn't sure what she was more surprised about, the sex or the fact that she'd stumbled upon a town full of Others.

She'd never met anyone like herself. Not that she was like Raphael or the men and women she'd encountered here. Her ability to disorient and disrupt human thought was rare even for this town. She wasn't an Other—at least she didn't think she was, but Chaos definitely understood the need for discretion. She had spent her entire adult life hiding her powers and running from a past that she neither understood nor cared to explore.

Chaos showered quickly and got dressed. She didn't think Raphael would change his mind about releasing her, but she didn't want to take the chance that he might. When she opened the door he was gone. Her belongings had been placed on a chair in the corner. The same one he'd tied her to right before bringing her pleasure that she'd never known existed. Chaos could still smell sex and his manly scent wafting in the air, but the musk was fading quickly. She inhaled, trying to store the memory.

You're pathetic.

She shook her head in disgust, angry she was even thinking about what they'd shared. There was something seriously wrong with her if she believed there was more to their romp than manipulation. "He's moved on already. Deal with it," she muttered under her breath.

The door to the room was open.

Chaos poked her head out and looked around, but the

yellow hall with flowers painted on it was empty like the ache growing inside of her. She stepped out and shut the door behind her. All the other doors remained closed as she picked her way down the hall, her footfalls silent on the fur-covered floor.

Raphael was waiting at the water trader bar with a portly redheaded man whose thick glasses made his brown eyes look enormous. He motioned her over when her foot hit the bottom step.

"Catherine, this is Jim Thornton. He's the director of the local dissecting lab," Raphael said. He sounded so normal. Nothing like the man who'd had her stripped bare an hour ago and crying out for release.

"Nice to meet you," Chaos said, frowning at the about-face.

Raphael placed his hand on the man's shoulder and squeezed. "Jim is going to take you back to IPTT."

Jim eyes widened and his gaze shot to Raphael, who casually released him. His attention turned back to her and he smiled broadly. "It'll be my pleasure, my dear."

"Thanks," Chaos said. She opened her mouth to ask Raphael if she could have a word with him, but he beat her to the punch.

"I'd better get going," he said. "Like you, I have a long ride ahead of me." Raphael barely glanced at her before he strode toward the door.

Chaos stared at his retreating form as he put his sunshades on and slipped out into the early morning light. She waited to see if he'd look back. Just one glance to confirm that last night wasn't just another blip on his sexual radar, but he didn't. The sting of rejection burned strong.

Fine, two could play that game, Chaos thought as she pushed past the pain. "I hope I didn't keep you waiting long," she said.

Jim adjusted the thick glasses perched on his nose. "Not at all. I like to start my patrols early. Got to get to the bodies while they're still fresh."

Chaos inwardly grimaced, then gave the water trader one more look around before heading out the door. She knew there was a very good chance she wouldn't be back. Nuria held too many memories, some she'd rather forget.

Raphael stayed in the shadows, watching as Catherine and Jim climbed into the hydrogen car. Her head was down and she looked determined, if not a little lost. Other than a few covert glances out the window, Catherine showed no emotion whatsoever. *What did you expect? You've been holding her against her will. Not exactly the way to a woman's heart.* His body shook as Raphael forced himself to remain rooted where he stood. Every fiber of his being wanted to go after her. Stop her. Keep her.

The last thought brought Raphael up short. He didn't *keep* women. He bedded them and then he moved on. If they were donors, then he'd visit them a few times, but he always broke it off before an emotional attachment could form. It had been easy. An ingrained habit that was second nature . . . that was until Catherine came along.

The closest he'd come to breaking his self-imposed rule was with Red, but Raphael realized that what he'd felt for Red was nothing compared to the riot of emotions raging through him now. And it was all due to a short, voluptuous redhead who'd tried to kill him. Life did have its surprises.

Raphael could still taste her essence on his tongue, feel the squeeze of her body as she gripped his cock, milking him until he'd collapsed. He'd loved every inch of her body, but her mind truly fascinated him. Raphael had never encountered anyone who could do the things she could. His brother, Michael, was the closest and even he couldn't cause the confusion and memory loss Catherine was capable of. Raphael was going to miss his little Chaos. The question was, now that he'd finally released her, would she ever return? The thought of never seeing her or touching her again made him uneasy. If Catherine didn't come back, would he be man enough to forget her and let her go?

Chaos waved good-bye to Jim Thornton as he drove off. He'd left her at the entrance to the International Police Tactical

Team Headquarters. He was a pleasant enough man, if you could get past the hours of dissection lab shop talk. At least she'd been able to tune him out long enough to formulate a plan.

She'd made up her mind to keep her word, even though Raphael had coerced her into doing so. She'd help him find Red and Morgan as she agreed. He may not believe in keeping his word, but she did. She'd been betrayed many times throughout her short life by people who promised one thing and delivered another. Chaos didn't take giving her word lightly. She also wasn't stupid enough to believe that everyone else in the world felt the same.

If Raphael decided to go back on his word and turn her in for her crimes, Chaos hoped by then she would have a get-out-of-trouble-free card she could play. She prayed it didn't come to that, since it would mean choosing between her freedom and her job.

Chaos cursed the sexy vampire under her breath. It was his fault she was in this mess. It was easier to put the blame on him than to look too deeply in the mirror at the real culprit.

Now if only she could garner the commander's cooperation without having to expose her secrets. Chaos didn't want to lose her job. It was all she had, but there was no way the commander could let her keep it if the truth about her nocturnal activities in the town of Nuria came out. Even he couldn't look the other way when it came to murder.

Chaos had to convince him that she believed in Gina Santiago's innocence. She didn't, not entirely. The evidence of her guilt was overwhelming. They had her on video visiting Morgan at the Taos detention center minutes before he broke out. But she supposed it wasn't that far out of the realm of possibility that Red had been framed given what Roark had done to her in one office visit. Ultimately, it didn't matter what Chaos believed. All that mattered was that the commander be convinced of her sincerity by the time she left his office.

Chaos rolled her shoulders and groaned at the stiffness, then glanced at her watch. She had time to go back to the dorm and grab some shut-eye before heading to the commander's office. Chaos wanted to be sharp when she presented her highly unethical and slightly illegal proposition to Red's grandfather.

If all went well, she would secure her job, garner her get-out-of-trouble-free card, and not have to worry about the deaths in Nuria coming back to bite her. The last thought caused a tingle in her neck. She reached up and touched the spot that Raphael had been so fond of nibbling. Chaos' body flooded with heat and she shivered.

"Get your head in the game," she muttered under her breath. "Stop mooning over the vampire. He doesn't give a shit about you. He just did those things to get his way. It's time you look out for yourself."

Chaos found Bannon Richards at the main building of headquarters. A pyramid-shaped structure built to withstand car bomb blasts. Sunshine filtered through the sloped windows as she walked to the security check point. Chaos was quickly scanned for contaminants and explosives, then ushered forward. She'd managed to get a few hours of sleep, so her head wasn't quite so fuzzy. Bannon sat at his metal desk, his shoulders hunched, writing reports. He glanced at her, then looked back at the compunit screen. Catherine diverted from her course and stopped in front of his desk.

Bannon didn't immediately acknowledge her. His blond head glinted from being shaved so close to his scalp. "It's about time you graced us with your presence and checked in," he said, glancing up. "I thought I was going to have to report you for being AWOL."

Chaos bristled. "I've been on the job for the past week. You were there. You know that."

He snorted. "Yeah, sure you have. Most team members put in their time without checking in regularly."

"Roark ordered me to seek out enemies, while you were strong-arming Gina Santiago. You didn't notice because you were too busy getting your rocks off."

His blue gaze darkened. "Watch your tone, Private, or you may just find your bags packed with a one-way ticket home."

She flinched at the threat. Chaos had no place to go. Her parents had dumped her on the steps of a cloning lab as an infant. She had no family. No home. No one. Chaos checked her temper and tried again. "I'm not here to fight. I stopped by to ask how you're feeling."

"What are you talking about?" Bannon's face flushed. His eyes dropped away for a second, unable to meet her gaze. "I'm fine. Why are you so concerned all of a sudden?"

Chaos studied his expression. He didn't seem fine, if the sudden tremor in his hand was any indication. And why was he getting so defensive? She'd asked a simple question. Maybe like her, Bannon had experienced bouts of missing time. What had Roark ordered him to do? She glanced around as unease set in. Bannon was around headquarters and the commander. Chaos opened her mouth to ask him about missing time, but closed it as his expression turned murderous.

Screw him. Bannon could take care of himself. "I was just curious," she said. "Thought I'd come down with a bug after leaving Roark Montgomery's office. The illness left me a little confused, but if you're fine, I guess I caught it somewhere else. Probably just something going around."

For a second, fear flashed in Bannon's ice-blue eyes, but he quickly extinguished it. He leaned back, angling his body away from her. "If you're sick, don't give it to me," he said, covering his nose and mouth with a beefy hand.

She coughed in his direction. "I wouldn't dream of it," Chaos said, then strolled away as he muttered under his breath about crazy rookies.

Chaos stood outside of Commander Robert Santiago's office with her eye pressed against the optical scanner. A moment passed, then the wooden door slid open.

"What can I do for you, Private?" he asked.

She started to answer, but stopped short when she took in his appearance. His white hair was disheveled as if he'd been running his hands through it repeatedly. His normally sharp eyes were bloodshot and his chin held growth that hadn't seen a razor in at least a couple of days.

"Sir?"

"Are you going to stand in the doorway or are you going to come inside?" he asked, his impatience clear.

Chaos stepped into the room and waited for the door to close behind her. She'd only been in the commander's office once before and not much had changed. It was still filled with creepy holograms of dead species and the scent of musty old books—made out of paper of all things. She'd suffocate if she had to stay in here all day.

"I won't keep you long, sir," she said, trying to avoid the holographic animals, which to her always looked hungry. Their eyes seemed to follow her no matter where she stood in the room.

"Are you here to give me your report on Nuria?" he asked, looking up from the synth-documents in front of him.

"No, sir. There's nothing to report," she said unable to meet his all too knowing gaze.

"You've been gone over a week. What have you been doing all this time?" Robert Santiago asked.

"Searching the Nurian water trader depot, sir." It was almost the truth. She had searched Raphael's room, when he'd stepped out to feed or to pick her up something to eat. Chaos blushed to the roots of her red hair. She pictured Raphael and all the carnal things they'd done. There was no way she'd discuss that with the commander. She swiftly changed the subject. "I have reason to believe that Gina Santiago is innocent. I'm here to make you an offer."

His white brows shot up. "Exactly what kind of proposal do you have in mind?" he asked, sitting back in his chair. He placed his hands casually over his still firm abdomen, but his expression remained leery.

"I'd like permission to seek proof of her innocence and retrieve her for you," Chaos said quickly before he tossed her out of his office and off the tactical team.

"Why would you want to do such a thing? What's in it for you?" he asked, watching her closely. His red eyes narrowed.

"Are you looking for a promotion in rank? Or are you after something else?"

Chaos shook her head. "Not rank, sir. I know it has to be earned. No one on the team will respect you if you're bumped without putting in your time." Chaos thought carefully about what to say next. She did not want to upset him before he agreed to her terms. She didn't know if it would be enough to keep her job in the end, but it was a better chance than she had at present if the truth came to light.

"I'd appreciate it if you'd consider giving me a get out of trouble free IOU for future use if I succeed."

His heavy brow thickened like fat thunder clouds above his dark eyes. "An IOU seems like an odd request. What would you need such a thing for? What have you done?" he asked, seeing through her.

"Nothing," she said in haste. Calm down. He doesn't know anything. He's just guessing. Chaos twisted her fingers. "I am hoping I never have to use the IOU, sir, but I'd like it all the same—just in case."

His gaze assessed her. "Why should I trust you?" he asked. "For all I know you're working with Roark."

Chaos' chin shot up and a flash of anger warmed her cheeks. "That will never happen," she grit out between clenched teeth. *Again* was left unsaid.

"Do you want to tell me what's really going on here?" Robert asked. "This seems a little sudden."

What could she say to him? She'd been drugged and used as a weapon to frame his granddaughter, then forced to break Red out of Roark's prison? Yeah, that would go over really well. She could see it now: *Commander Santiago I broke one law to cover up my other crimes.* Chaos choked and quickly covered it with a cough. She wouldn't believe that story if she were in the commander's position. And if by chance he did believe her, Robert Santiago would arrest her on the spot.

Chaos would need proof to convince the commander of her innocence, which was something she didn't have against Roark.

Raphael seemed pretty positive that influ-gas was undetectable in her bloodstream. There was no reason for him to lie. It would end up being her word against Roark Montgomery's and Chaos had no doubt who would come out on top if she sought legal action. She sighed. The only way she'd make it out of this mess was if she stuck with lies and half-truths.

"Given Gina Santiago's record with IPTT and the fact she was the highest-ranked female officer, her behavior seems uncharacteristic. It casts a negative light on the remaining female tactical team members." Chaos knew there were still a lot of people in the world who believed the tactical team should be made up solely of men. She knew the commander was well aware of that, too. It had to have crossed his mind. And if it hadn't, it didn't hurt to remind him. "I believe there may be proof out there that hasn't been uncovered yet. I'd like the chance to find it. That way we can clear Gina's name and protect the future of female IPTT officers at the same time."

If there was a Hell, she'd be going there for sure with that whopper.

He considered her for several beats. Chaos toed at the floor with her boot. What if he turned her down? What would she do then? Would she still go after Red or would she stay in the barracks and pray that Raphael kept his word and no one found out the truth?

"I can respect your need to protect your job, since I know Lieutenant Santiago would do the same. You know I can't sanction your actions, if you choose to investigate and try to locate my— Lieutenant Santiago. You'd have to do it on your own time," he said. "The International Police Tactical Team is on strict orders to apprehend on sight."

"I understand, sir." Chaos nodded. "I would take a personal leave and keep a low profile."

"How low?" he asked.

"Low enough that only you and I would know what I was up to," she said.

Robert Santiago steepled his fingers under his chin and rocked back in the chair. "If you're trying to set me up so Roark Montgomery can come in and take over IPTT, you'll be sorry. Getting rid of all female officers would be his first order of business."

Chaos' mood blackened. She could feel the power inside of her starting to rise. She tamped it down. The last thing she needed was for the commander to forget why she was here. *Breathe, he's agreeing to your plan. Stay calm just a little longer and you'll be out of here.* "As I said before, there's absolutely no chance of that happening, sir."

The commander must have seen something he liked in her expression because he nodded and a smile hovered over his thin lips. "Where do you plan to start?"

Chaos hadn't thought that far ahead. She knew Gina and Morgan weren't in Nuria. They'd talked about hiding out at Kane Hunter's home and possibly no-man's-land, but Chaos didn't know where they'd ended up going. They may have said that just to throw everyone off their scent. She would've in their position.

She considered contacting Raphael, strictly for information—not because she wanted to hear his voice. That would be ridiculous, since he'd just let her go. Chaos doubted very much he'd willingly share that kind of information with her. He may have fucked her, but he damn sure didn't trust her. Raphael would've never made her agree to help him absolve Red and Morgan otherwise.

Robert Santiago must have correctly read her panicked expression because he tapped his cheek and said, "I don't know about you, but I've heard Roark and Gina had been traveling north in a shuttle when Sheriff Hunter *attacked* them and helped Gina escape. Shuttles aren't small and they're difficult to hide. I wonder how hard it would be to find that vehicle outside of the Republic of Missouri."

Chaos cleared her throat. "I'll let you know," she said, then pivoted on her heel and strode out the door.

I t was going better than I'd expected. I watched as tactical team members brushed by me on their way home or off to patrol. Once again the urge to go with them swept over me.

Gina Santiago was out there somewhere, hiding, mocking IPTT.

Several officers gathered in the entryway near the mammoth fountain. They stood next to the sloped walls that glittered in the sunlight like lethal incisors. The team checked their weapons and verified their patrol routes, then marched in unison out of headquarters. Their black boots echoed under the pyramidal-shaped roof. Each thump sounded in my chest and I found myself picking up the pace. I had to force my feet to slow before anyone noticed. No need to hurry. The commander still didn't suspect a thing.

I slowly made my way to my work space, winding through a maze of steel desks. Some were still occupied, while others now stood empty. The air held a hint of vanilla. The aroma should've soothed my nerves, but it didn't. Nothing would until I got out of here.

"Be patient. Everything is going according to plan," I whispered under my breath.

I needed to log in to my compunit. Make sure I hadn't received any new intel. The chances were slim, but still possible. A few heads turned as I neared. The officers seemed surprised to see me. I ignored the curious stares from the worker drones and sat down.

A quick press of the screen showed that the files in my compunit were empty. I tried not to let my disappointment show, but a curse slipped past my lips before I could stop it. A couple of officers at nearby desks looked at me, then quickly went back to work.

They didn't understand. How could they? No one had ever tasked them with something as important as saving the reputation of the International Police Tactical Team. I knew what my duty was and was proud to be tapped for such a job. Not everyone was trusted with this kind of sensitive information.

My chest puffed out. I wouldn't let the team down. I'd find Gina Santiago and silence her once and for all.

chapter eight

Raphael stood outside of the Republic of Missouri biodome and attempted to hail Michael via their mental link. Static filled his mind. He couldn't tell if the crackles and pops were interference or the sound of Michael's thoughts. The latter brought a shiver to his spine. It was impossible. No one was powerful enough to control his brother—not even with an A.I. chip implanted in his brain.

He thought about the drugs that had been administered to Catherine. No, not even influ-gas was strong enough to control Michael. Perhaps Morgan and Red were wrong. They had to be. They'd only seen Michael for a few minutes. Not nearly enough time to assess his condition.

Raphael climbed back into his maglev shuttle. The sun was beating down on him, but the military-grade sunscreen kept his sensitive skin protected. He wouldn't burn, but it didn't stop the pain. Of course he'd take the pain over the other option any day, since most vampires exploded when exposed to sunlight. He glanced at the sun and winced. Raphael knew he couldn't stay out here any longer.

He'd wanted to avoid entering the biodome city, but with Michael not answering Raphael didn't have much choice. The soft blue dome glowed as he approached the gates. He wondered not for the first time if Catherine or Roark had bulletins out for his arrest. Raphael took a deep breath and released it slowly. He'd find out soon enough.

The clean-cut guard at the gate perked up as Raphael's hydrogen fueled vehicle approached. He pressed a button so the maglev shuttle would hover in place. "I.D. please," the guard said, giving Raphael a bored expression as if he could barely be bothered to do his job.

Raphael knew it was a ruse. Even now the man was taking in details about his appearance just in case his chip and I.D. came back stolen or invalid. He handed over the paperwork and exposed his neck. It took a minute for his Republic of Arizona chip to register. By the time the light turned green and the guard waved him through the gates, Raphael was sweating.

That was twice he'd been caught perspiring. First with Catherine and now here. He'd have to check himself into the emergency care center if it didn't stop. Vamps shouldn't sweat, especially ones as old as him.

Raphael drove past the green manicured parks and rising skyscrapers straight to Michael's home. It was a modest two-room unit—inside a multistory steel and concrete building—that had a private cleansing room attached for convenience and comfort. The amenities were rare given the communal bathing facilities located throughout the city. He couldn't afford to stop by Michael's office in case Roark Montgomery was in. Raphael wasn't sure if the politician could identify his face as being one of the men who'd come to break Red and Morgan out of his prison, but he had no doubt he'd recognize him as Michael's brother. Raphael would just have to try to contact Michael via comlink if he wasn't home.

He used the code his brother had given him after their reunion a couple of months ago. Reunion probably wasn't the correct term to describe their encounter. His brother had been about to assassinate Morgan Hunter when Raphael came upon him in the desert.

Until that point, Raphael had thought Michael was dead, along with the rest of their family. It had been a happy moment and one of utter disbelief. So much pain endured and years lost, but that was over now. They'd found each other once again and Raphael wasn't about to let anything or anyone tear them apart.

The lights were off when he entered Michael's living quarters. Normally obsessively neat, his home lay in disarray. More like ransacked. Clothes and rest pad linens lay strewn across the floor. Empty blood bags had been tossed haphazardly next to toppled furniture. Had Michael been robbed? If so, the thief was probably buried out in the desert by now. Michael had little patience for thieves or anyone else for that matter.

Raphael stopped and looked around, but didn't immediately see any broken items. He inhaled, but noted no scent of Michael's blood or of strangers. What had occurred that would make Michael do this to his home? Was it the chip? And why hadn't he contacted him if he was in trouble? Raphael had tried to find him after the impromptu prison break, but had been unable to locate him. He realized now he should've tried harder.

Morgan had said that he'd heard screams when Roark chained him to the wall. He'd also told Raphael that Michael seemed different. He walked over to the storage bins under Michael's mini–water dispenser where he kept his equipment bag as he called it. Raphael knew the assassination kit contained a laser rifle, a knife, and at least one pistol. He opened the bin. The bag was gone.

There was no need to call Roark's office now. Raphael knew for certain Michael wasn't there and he had a pretty good idea where he'd find him. He pictured Morgan and Red running for their lives. There would be nowhere safe they could hide. Not with his brother on their trail.

Michael was an efficient hunter, and Raphael had no doubt that he was a deadly assassin. The old military had trained them well, but Raphael's skill was nowhere near his brother's. Working for a man like Roark had only honed Michael's awesome skills. Couple that with his telekinetic abilities and he was unstoppable.

Panic and fear gave his gut a one-two punch, leaving him

breathless. After everything they'd been through and all the time they'd lost, only one question remained.

Why?

It took the whole afternoon, but Chaos finally located the maglev shuttle wreckage. Someone had gone to a lot of trouble to keep it out of sight. Whether it was Roark, Red, or Morgan she didn't know. The craft was half buried in the sand and from a distance resembled a boulder. No wonder IPTT hadn't been able to find it.

Twisted metal radiated heat. She approached, weapon drawn. A hole the size of two laser cannon blasts gaped obscenely at the desert sands, its metal teeth frozen in a perpetual roar. Chaos ducked inside with her pistol raised, but the shuttle was empty. She holstered her weapon, then began a slow search.

At first glance, the only damage appeared to be the hole in the side of the shuttle, but upon closer inspection Chaos found that the navigation system had been carefully removed, not yanked out like she would've expected if someone were trying to disable the vehicle. The instrument panel and tracker cell were also missing. Almost like the parts had been harvested to sell.

Why would someone take the time to do that, when the whole point of the attack was to escape or at least make it look like Red had escaped? Did they need credits? Who would they take the parts to if they did? It wasn't like Red or Morgan traded in this area. It didn't make sense. She pushed charred pieces aside with the toe of her boot. They crumbled under the pressure.

After several minutes of futility, Chaos was convinced she was on the wrong track. No one had left any clues behind, only an empty shell filled with more questions. She was about to leave when an exposed wire caught her attention. Chaos brushed the debris aside and found the remains of a navcom buried beneath. It was an old model and severely damaged, but definitely IPTT issue.

Chaos carefully picked up the pieces and placed them into a preprogrammed courier pouch. She punched her I.D. number into the side of the pouch and addressed it to Commander Robert Santiago. The courier would fly directly to IPTT. He'd have to put in his I.D. number and thumbprint to get it to open, which would keep it from falling into the wrong hands once it arrived at headquarters.

The pouch also generated its own electromagnetic field to prevent it from being shot down outside of IPTT. Every security measure had a countersecurity measure to ensure the contents' safety.

Chaos stepped outside of the shuttle. It was only then that she noticed the sun was starting to set. She shook the contents of the pouch to make sure it was secure. The bag was silent. It may not be anything, but it was all she'd been able to recover. Chaos set the courier pouch on the ground and pressed a button on its side.

The pouch took off like a guided missile, which was apt, since that's where the technology originated. She watched the pouch rocket through the air, leaving a fiery contrail behind. When it was out of sight, she turned back to the shuttle to reexamine the hole.

What had Morgan used to make it, since a laser cannon was far from portable? He'd been on the run, so he'd had to travel light, but there wasn't anything out there to her knowledge besides the cannon that could do this kind of damage. Was that when Roark had captured him or had he already been imprisoned? She should've asked when she helped Raphael break them out.

Chaos ran her finger over the edge of the opening. It wasn't sharp. It had been fused, which meant heat. Roark should've had this hauled in as evidence when he reported the incident. It would've backed up his story and been damning to IPTT. Unless he didn't want it to be found. It was one thing to show a vid of the damage. It was quite another to produce examinable proof. Nothing would surprise her at this point.

"What are you up really to?" she said aloud.

She reached for her backpack and took out her solar light

to disperse the growing shadows. With a twist, it glowed to life. Chaos went back to examining the blast pattern. There was no way Morgan could've done this on his own and Red wasn't known for her demolition skills.

Besides, now that she'd reexamined the hole it was clear from the edges that the blast had come from the *inside*. No wonder Roark hadn't wanted the vehicle to be found. The portable equipment IPTT held in its vault wasn't capable of this kind of damage. The only thing that could've made a hole this size was a blast cannon and they weighed two hundred pounds. Chaos looked around, but didn't immediately spot anything that could hide a weapon of that size.

Roark had obviously caught them at some point or they wouldn't have ended up inside his personal prison. But where? And how? She really should've asked Raphael. It's not as if Red and Morgan were easy targets. They'd know how to hide in the desert. It was part of law-enforcement training.

Heck, Roark even had the same training, although it had been a long time ago. Chaos stilled. If he was willing to drug her, a total stranger, how far would he go to get Red and Morgan back? She shivered as the answer stared her in the face in the form of a manufactured hole. Chaos punched the shuttle coordinates into her navcom and sent them to the commander. He could decide how to proceed.

What did Morgan and Red have on Roark that made him so desperate to silence them? Chaos wished she knew. It would go a long way to solving this mystery. Despite her assurance that she'd find the commander's granddaughter, Chaos wasn't entirely convinced she could do it. She hadn't mentioned that when she asked for the commander's IOU or when she'd given Raphael her word that she'd help him. Didn't think that confession would aid her cause.

She just wanted to keep her job and avoid arrest. If finding Gina Santiago guaranteed that, then she'd travel to hell to do it.

She'd heard whispers during training about the woman nicknamed Red because of the blood she spilled on the job at IPTT. Those rumors included a lot of dead rookies, who'd been killed trying to provide backup. How many recruits had she lost? Chaos didn't know, but Red's kill rate on unknowns reached legendary status.

Chaos didn't lend the stories much credence given what the other recruits said about her. She thought about the cruelty she'd been subjected to since joining IPTT.

Her given name was Catherine, or so she'd been told at the cloning labs before they put her to work with the manufactured labor force. She'd jacked an unused I.D. and escaped on her twenty-third birthday, joining IPTT shortly thereafter. The recruits had called her Catherine in the beginning, but it didn't take long for that to change. A couple of slips of power on her part and she'd become *Chaos*. Like Red, she'd turned the name into a badge of honor.

Fortunately, the recruits hadn't known exactly what happened. They'd been left confused, disoriented, and with short-term memory loss. They had been lucky. It could've been much worse. Chaos had seen what happened when her power went unchecked for long periods of time and it wasn't pretty.

The blank faces of the mindless haunted her dreams. Memories of their existence erased in a blink never to be recovered. Those faces never let her forget her past. Maybe she and Gina Santiago had more in common than she thought.

She bent over to examine the entry one more time and a warm breeze washed over her, raising the fine hairs on her arms. Her hand automatically moved to her weapon, and in that instant Chaos knew she wasn't alone. She also had no doubt about who was with her.

Chaos couldn't see Raphael, but she felt him like a caress of fingertips across her bare skin. She glanced over her shoulder and scanned the area. Nothing stood out. The desert remained quiet. Abnormally so. Like it knew a predator hunted in the area. She wasn't sure how Raphael had found her. Chaos was positive he hadn't followed them to IPTT. The motion sensors and radar at headquarters would've detected a shuttle stationed nearby.

The sensation of being watched occurred again and she

unconsciously reached for the spot on her neck where Raphael had bitten and drunk from her. The thought sent a delicious shiver down her spine.

Despite her resolve to forget about him and the whole incident in Nuria, Chaos' body remembered with a vengeance. Even now she could feel an ache building, where moments ago there'd been none. She growled in frustration and glared at the darkness.

"Come out where I can see you," she said. "There's no point in hiding. I know you're there."

The shadows shifted and suddenly Chaos found herself staring at her seductive kidnapper. His dark hair lifted from his broad shoulders as a warm breeze caught it. His black eyes seemed flat until they landed upon her, then they took on a predatory glow that she felt all the way to her . . . soul.

"As you wish," Raphael said, his gaze scrolling over her.

Her breath caught. "I don't appreciate being followed," Chaos said. Ire and desire mixed to form a volatile cocktail inside of her.

"Hmm, I was thinking the same thing. If you wanted to see me again all you had to do was comlink me," he said smoothly.

Her eyes widened. He had not just accused her of chasing him like some lovesick moppet. She did not chase men and she especially wouldn't chase him. Chaos hadn't even known he was there until a minute ago. "Your ego is astounding." She huffed. "I'm amazed there is room to stand next to you."

"It's funny, I don't recall you complaining about my . . . *ego* last night or the night before or the night before that and the night before that—"

"Enough! I get it." Chaos felt a flush of heat fill her face. "We're not discussing that anymore."

"If you don't want to talk about our . . ."

"Raphael," she growled his name in warning.

"Nocturnal activities," he continued, "then perhaps you'll tell me what you're doing here out in the middle of nowhere. Anyone could've come upon you. You left yourself vulnerable."

Why was he suddenly angry? It wasn't like she'd snuck up on him. "I'm armed," she said, tapping her laser pistol.

Raphael moved with blinding speed, quickly disarming her. "Weapons are of little use, if you're caught unaware," he said, handing her pistol back to her. "Now I'll ask you again, what are you doing here? What were you looking for?"

Chaos tensed. She didn't want to discuss why she was here. She'd given him her word that she'd help. That should be enough. As for her other reasons for being here, those were none of his business. Chaos didn't want him to know she was trying to work around their agreement. She wasn't sure how Raphael would respond to the news. "I'm on patrol."

"You aren't dressed for patrol."

"How would you know?" she asked.

"Do not play me for a fool, my little storm." He stepped closer, crowding her, and inhaled. "I can smell the truth— and the lies before they leave your succulent mouth. If you like, I can steal them off your lips with a kiss."

She saw his eyes close and his face relax. Almost as if being near her calmed him, which was ridiculous, since they'd just met and not under the best of circumstances. She smiled as she recalled their hand-to-hand combat. It had been fun, albeit dangerous. Raphael could've easily hurt her, but he hadn't.

The battle had ended in a bite. Chaos had never been so surprised in her life. Despite the savagery, there'd been something overwhelmingly erotic about the moment. Not that she'd ever tell him. She looked over and realized his eyes were open. Raphael was watching her, a smile playing on his sinful mouth.

Chaos broke eye contact first, then cleared her throat. "A kiss won't be necessary." She was *not* disappointed. She glanced at his mouth, taking in his savage lips. *Nope, not disappointed at all.*

She knew she'd have to tell him the truth or at least some version of it if he could detect a lie so easily. Chaos still wasn't sure how he could do it, but the *how* wasn't nearly as important as the fact that he could. She'd tried confusing him and look where that got her, fanged and banged. She sighed in resignation. "I'm going to find Red."

Raphael's expression changed from flirtatious to suspicious in a breath. "Why?"

"It's what we agreed to, remember?" she asked. "Find proof of their innocence."

"Yes, I recall, but I doubt that's what brought you out here in the middle of the desert." He cocked his head and looked at her, studying her as if she were a new species. Chaos couldn't tell what he was looking for, but after a while, he relaxed. "Whose orders are you following?" he asked, straightening the sleeves of his shirt casually while he waited for her answer.

Chaos scowled. His question left no doubt that he could smell a lie. "The commander's orders. Well, he didn't exactly give me any orders. More like permission."

"I see." Raphael didn't say anything else, only slowly looked around as if someone might be listening.

"I'm alone," she said.

"I know you are," he said, as if it was obvious to anyone who wasn't a simpleton.

Chaos rested her hand on her hip. "Are you going to tell me what you're doing here? Because I'll be honest, this whole conversation is beginning to bore me." She glanced at her short nails. She'd definitely have to stop biting them when she returned to IPTT headquarters.

Raphael gave her a withering look. "Nothing has changed since we last spoke. I'm still seeking my brother. I'd like to find him before he gets into trouble."

Disappointment washed over her. That wasn't the answer she'd expected—or hoped for. Chaos had thought he'd say he was out here looking for Morgan Hunter and Red. Or better yet, he was searching for her. But Raphael hadn't. He was after his wayward brother. Jealousy burned through her, unwelcomed and unwanted. Chaos knew it was wrong to feel that way, when Raphael was only looking out for his family. So why did she?

And why in the hell was she disappointed? It wasn't like

she wanted him here. He was already in the way. Raphael would only impede her search further once he found out she didn't care what happened to his friend Morgan Hunter.

The fact that Raphael was after his brother only reminded Chaos of what she lacked in her own life. If she went missing tomorrow, no one, not even IPTT, would look very hard for her. No one would care.

chapter nine

Red turned over to find Morgan gone. The tent flap was closed, keeping the light at bay, which was probably why she hadn't noticed. She stretched, then glanced down at her watch: six o'clock.

Red jolted out of bed. How had she managed to sleep so long? She never slept all day, especially surrounded by strangers. The Sand Moles had kept their word and provided shelter for the night. They'd even shared their food, although Red still had no idea what she'd eaten. She'd been so hungry and so sick of nutri-bars she didn't care. Whatever it was had tasted good and managed to stay down despite the oppressive heat.

Even now her body lay covered in a fine sheen of sweat and grit. She dressed quickly, strapping on her laser pistol before untying the flaps to the tent entrance. The sun and the heat smacked her in the face, causing her to flinch.

She squinted, cupping a hand over her eyes, and scanned the encampment. She spotted Morgan seated next to Demery at a makeshift table under a lean-to not far from a cooking fire. It wasn't much shade, but it was better than none.

Demery was back in his white protective suit. He waved when he saw her and motioned for her to come over.

"Why did you let me sleep so long?" Red asked.

Morgan looked up from his steaming drink and grinned. "You needed it after last night's hike and exercise."

Red opened her mouth to ask what exercise, then quickly shut it. Heat flooded her face and she cleared her throat. "What are you drinking?" She nodded in the direction of the cup.

Morgan's amber eyes twinkled, but he allowed the change of subject. "It's some kind of tea, or so Gray told me. Tastes more like gasoline."

"Gas what?" Red asked.

Morgan shook his head and laughed. "I forgot that you were born after the gas disappeared." For a second his rugged features showed his true age. He wiped a hand over his face. "Years ago cars and just about everything else ran on a fuel called gasoline. It was made from oil. Wars were fought over it. Countries destroyed. Races obliterated. That's how the last war started, but it quickly morphed into something bigger. It's not important." He brushed his dark thoughts away with a wave of his hand. "The only thing you need to know is that gas burned and tasted like shit, if you happened to get it in your mouth."

"Thanks for the warning," Red said. "I'd still like some."

Morgan chuckled. "Sure. Take a seat." He patted the bench beside him and poured her a cup.

Red took one sip and nearly spit it out. Fire shot down her throat and out her nose as she breathed in sharply and exhaled. Her face puckered and she coughed. Morgan slapped her on the back until she stopped.

"I tried to warn you," he said.

"Yes, you did. I should've listened," she said. "It'll definitely take some getting used to." Red raised the cup to her lips, but this time tipped it slowly. "Find out anything while I was asleep?"

Demery leaned forward. "Gray thinks he may know of a place that might house the type of equipment we're looking for."

"May? Might? Either he knows or he doesn't," Red snapped.

"Someone woke up on the wrong side of the tent today," Demery said.

She ran a hand through her hair. "Sorry, I'm just used to having solid intel. I don't like guesses."

Demery nodded. "Understood. Unfortunately, we won't know for sure until Gray's scout returns."

Red met Morgan's gaze. "And exactly when will that be?" she asked.

"This evening," Morgan said.

"I don't like the idea of losing that much walking time," she said, glancing around at their hosts. "I wouldn't want us to overstay our welcome."

"I don't either, but we'll lose a lot more if we go off on a wild boar chase," Morgan said. "This is the last place you want to get lost."

"Agreed." Demery grinned through his faceplate. "No sense in wandering around in this heat, mon. Won't get far if we're baked. Sun will be down soon enough."

Red nodded and finished her drink. Morgan handed her a plate of food, none of which she could identify. "What is this?" she asked. She wasn't as hungry today as she'd been last night, so the food didn't look near as appetizing.

"It's better if you just eat it and try not to think about it," Morgan said.

"Okay." She shrugged. It couldn't be worse than some of the things she'd eaten in her life. She'd gnawed on a few bodies when she was in her Other form and didn't even know it.

Red picked up a piece of mystery meat and plopped it in her mouth. It was dry. Really dry. She poured herself another cup of tea in order to wash the food down. She doubted the drink was the real thing, considering how rare and expensive tea was these days. Good thing, too, since this beverage would likely kill any bacteria lingering in the food.

She took a sip to knock back the flesh clogging her throat. "It doesn't get better," she said, swallowing hard. "So what are we supposed to do until the scout arrives?"

Morgan's smile turned seductive. "I can think of a few things."

Red snorted. "Not going to happen. The tent was hot when

I left. I can't imagine what it's like now that the sun's hitting its side."

"Spoilsport." Morgan teased. "I guess we'll just have to occupy ourselves by trading for more goods."

"What are you going to do, Demery?" she asked.

"I have some business to take care of. Plan to make a few trades of my own. Need to locate Reaper if possible. Still hoping Gray knows how to find him. After that, I'm going to entice a few of the men into playing a game of zigzag quartz." He pulled out a worn deck of metal cards. "I'm feeling lucky."

"Is the man you seek nearby?" Morgan asked.

"Probably not. He doesn't get along with Gray's group or any other for that matter. I'm hoping he'll be camped on the way to the next place we journey. If so, we can drop in for a quick trade."

"We'll see," Morgan said. "Don't have a lot of time for side trips."

"It's important that we make time," Demery said. He didn't elaborate further.

Morgan shook his head. "That wasn't part of our agreement."

Demery stilled. "I didn't realize we had one, mon." He left them sitting at the table, staring at his retreating back.

"Looks like we'll be stopping," Red said.

Morgan met her gaze. "Looks like."

While they waited for the scout to return, Red and Morgan managed to trade extra charges of ammo for a few canteens and a portable food storage case. Red hoped they weren't out here long enough to make use of the case. She wanted to find someplace to get a communiqué out, not learn survival tips for no-man's-land.

Morgan went back to the tent to rest. There wasn't much else to do. Red found Demery under a lean-to collecting what looked to be valuable stones from a couple of the Sand

Mole men. They didn't look happy, which meant Demery had obviously won the zigzag quartz game.

"Did you find out about your friend?" she asked.

"Friend?" Demery frowned. "You mean Reaper? He isn't my friend. He's the most vicious snake I've ever encountered and a hell of a zigzag quartz player. Far better than me." His brown gaze dropped to the metal deck in his hand and his full lips thinned.

"I thought—" She stopped midsentence. "Then why are you looking for him?"

"He has something of mine. I told him the next time I was down here I'd stop by and pick it up."

"Sounds serious," she said, keeping her voice light.

Demery gave her a strained smile. "Not really," he said. "With all the tactical team training, I haven't had the chance to return and retrieve it."

"What is 'it'?" she asked. Red couldn't imagine anyone leaving anything of value in this place.

"You could say it's a family heirloom. It's of *personal* value to me, but wouldn't mean much to anyone else," he said. "Reaper's been keeping it safe for me, while I've been away. I don't want to impose on his hospitality any longer."

"Makes sense." If someone had something that was dear to her, she'd want it back, too. Of course if it were something really valuable, Red wouldn't have let it go in the first place. So why had Demery?

Night descended on no-man's-land, bringing the predators with it. Red caught glimpses of movement by the sand dunes, but the fire moat surrounding the Sand Mole encampment kept them at bay. The scout arrived shortly after eight. He was a wiry man with a thin beak of a nose and small dark eyes that took in everything, but gave little away. His scraggly brown hair curled at odd angles around his head, making him look as if he'd been hit by lightning more than once in his lifetime.

He entered the encampment after giving a two-bark signal followed by one clap. One of the women broke away from the group and rushed forward with a canteen in her hand. She threw herself in his arms and kissed his cheek repeatedly.

"Welcome home, Jeb," she said, leading him over to the center table, which turned out to be the communal gathering place for the Sand Moles.

"I bring news," he said, exchanging greetings to those he passed. People gathered close so they could hear what he had to say.

"Do tell," Gray said, clapping him on the shoulder. "We could use some good tidings."

"Word has arrived that—" The words caught in his throat at the sight of Red, Morgan, and Demery, choking him into silence.

Gray frowned. "Jeb? What's wrong?"

"Who are they?" Jeb stabbed a finger at them accusingly.

Gray motioned for them to approach. "This is Hunter, Red, and you know Demery."

Jeb nodded at the vamp, but didn't acknowledge Red's or Morgan's presence. "Have they joined our group?" he asked, his gaze taking in their clothing.

"No." Gray shook his head. "They are just passing through. They've been enjoying our hospitality, while awaiting your return."

Jeb blinked, then his beady eyes narrowed. "Why were they waiting for me?" he asked. His wiry body coiled, ready to spring. Morgan couldn't tell whether he was set to attack or retreat.

"They hope you can help them. I fear I've bragged about your extensive travels. I told them that if anyone knew where communiqué equipment could be found, it would be you."

An uneasy smile touched Jeb's face. "Why thank you, brother. I do believe I can be of assistance to the strangers. I know of such a place south of here."

"That's wonderful," Gina stepped forward before Morgan could stop her. Waves of excitement poured off her, flowing onto the group.

Morgan didn't want to dampen her enthusiasm, but he knew something was wrong. He could smell it in the little man's sweat. It stank of deceit and lies. Jeb's body twitched and Morgan closed the distance between him and Gina.

"Where is this place?" she asked, inching nearer, not noticing the change in his demeanor.

Jeb watched her closely, his eyes cold and calculating as if he were waiting for the perfect opportunity to strike.

Morgan's muscles tensed, ready for an impending attack.

Jeb noticed Morgan's close proximity and casually shrank back. "It's two days' journey to the southwest about an hour from the old coast," he said.

The move was casual. Morgan doubted anyone noticed but him.

Gina turned to Demery. "Do you think you can find it?"

"Are you talking about the ruins near Verde?" Demery asked.

"No." Jeb shook his head. "You'd need to head an hour south of there."

"Okay," Demery said. "I know the general area. I think I can find it." His attention was caught by the woman he'd slept with the previous night. "Be back in a minute," he said, not waiting for an answer.

"Who do we contact once we arrive?" Gina asked.

The man looked at her as if he were considering his answer carefully. "You need to speak with Razor. Tell him Jeb sent you. That should at least get you past the towers."

Gina smiled. "Thank you."

"Don't thank me yet," Jeb said, before turning back to Gray. "Mind if I have a word with you in private?"

"Of course," Gray said. "Excuse us a moment. Feel free to continue to enjoy our hospitality until I return to see you off." He nodded in the direction of the musicians, who began to play.

Morgan watched the two men walk several yards away. He couldn't hear everything they were saying with the music playing, but he could make out a few words. He caught enough to confirm his suspicions. There was definitely a problem. Jeb knew who they were and why they were here.

"What's the matter?" Gina asked, brushing a hand over his arm.

"You need to start using your senses," Morgan snapped, staring at Gray and Jeb, who kept their backs to them.

Gina slowly drew her hand away. "Why? What's happened?"

"That man, Jeb. He was lying about something. I could smell it reeking from his pores. Even if he hadn't, his body language screamed deception. He knows who we are and he's up to no good."

"I—" was all Gina had a chance to say before he cut her off.

"No excuses," Morgan said. "Our lives are in danger. Don't let their hospitality cloud your judgment."

Gina's jaw clenched. "Do you think he's lying about the location?

"No." Morgan stared at the men, who were now looking back at them. "It's something else." He ran a hand through his hair, disheveling it. "Something having to do with us."

"But no one knows we're here," she said.

"I can't hear them over the blasted music." Morgan's hands shook in frustration. How was he supposed to protect Gina if he couldn't even hear himself think?

She stepped closer. "Do you think Gray made them play louder on purpose?"

"Maybe." Morgan took a deep breath. The scent of the people nearby hadn't changed. Whatever was happening was coming directly from Jeb, and now Gray. "Get your things together. We may need to leave in a hurry." Morgan kept his attention on the men and the group around them. He sniffed the air every minute to make sure nothing had changed.

With luck, they'd be able to leave without any problems. So what if Jeb knew their real names? It didn't mean anything. Or at least it shouldn't.

Jeb and Gray glanced back once more, their gazes moving assessingly from him to Gina. This time there was no mistaking the speculation in their eyes. Something Jeb said had changed Gray's opinion of them, and not for the better.

Red watched the exchange for a moment, then walked off toward the tent they'd stayed in the night before. Demery caught her right before she stepped through the flap.

"What's going on?" he asked, wiping his mouth as he exited from a nearby tent.

Red pressed a hand to her chest. "Not sure. Morgan is spooked about something. Said Jeb was lying. He knows who we are."

Demery glanced over at Morgan. "Did you pick up anything?"

Red felt a blush of embarrassment. "I didn't think to try."

Sympathy filled Demery's chocolate brown eyes as he tore his gaze away from the men. "It takes time," he said. "You'll get it eventually." He cupped her elbow and squeezed, then released her.

Would she? Or would she end up dying before she learned how to use her abilities? Red didn't have a terrific track record when it came to embracing the wolf inside of her.

"What are you doing?" He nodded toward the tent she and Morgan had shared.

"Morgan said to pack up our things. We may need to get out of here in a hurry."

"Right." Demery slipped around the back of her tent toward his own. He returned in minutes, bag in hand.

"That was quick," Red said, shoving the supplies into the extra tote they'd brought along for this purpose. She filled the food case next.

"If Morgan says we may need to leave in a hurry, I'd like it to be with my things. Wouldn't want to get caught without my protective suit." He grinned.

"I'm going to find out what's going on."

Red shoved the rest of their belongings into the bags and dragged them to the center of the compound. She placed them on the ground near her feet and nodded to Morgan to let him know they were ready.

Gray and Jeb had returned to the group. They were now seated at the long metal table, while Jeb ate. Something in Gray's demeanor had changed. He still wore an easy smile, but it didn't reach his eyes, and tension filled his lean shoulders, making them stiff beneath his baggy clothes. Morgan was right. Something was wrong. What had Jeb said to him? Red had never seen the man before today. Yet she was detecting hostility. They needed to get out while they still had the chance.

"We're leaving now," Morgan said to no one in particular. "Thank you for your hospitality."

Red watched Gray and Jeb pause as she hoisted two of the bags onto her back. Everyone around them seemed to notice the change, too, because the music stopped abruptly.

Gray rose slowly from the table. "I'm afraid we cannot allow you to go," he said.

Red's ears were ringing from the blood pounding in her head. Her hand slipped to rest on the pistol strapped to her thigh.

"We aren't asking," Morgan said, his voice raspier than it was moments ago. His fists were clenched at his sides.

The wolf was riding him hard. Even now his eyes were changing color and his hair was beginning to thicken to a rough mane.

"The situation has changed," Gray said, nodding to the people around them, who slowly pulled out their weapons.

Red stepped forward. "We don't want any trouble."

"I appreciate that, Ms. Santiago. It is Gina Santiago, isn't it?" Gray asked.

Red felt the blood leach from her face. She glanced at Morgan, who'd stiffened at the sound of her name being mentioned aloud. He'd been right, when he'd said Jeb knew their true identities.

"I don't know what you're talking about," she said calmly. "My name is Red."

"No." Gray shook his head. "Your name is Gina Santiago and that there," he pointed at Morgan, "is Morgan Hunter."

"You're wrong," she said, sounding desperate.

"There's a fifteen-thousand-credit bounty on your heads that says I'm right."

Red couldn't have heard him correctly. Did he say bounty?

Who would've placed— She stopped short. Roark. Only Roark would do something like this, which meant he'd figured out where they'd gone. Red fought the urge to vomit. Now not even no-man's-land was safe. Safe? She laughed to herself. They'd been anything but safe from the second they crossed the boundary fence.

"Jeb here says news of the bounty is spreading fast. The Sand Moles deserve those credits more than most. We're the ones who've put you up and been hospitable."

"Yes, you have," she said. "So why stop now?"

Gray shrugged. "Credits are credits. Besides, you owe us."

"We traded in good faith," Red said. "We owe you nothing."

"That's not how we see it," Gray said.

"That's your problem," Morgan said. "Not ours."

He sighed. "Did I mention that the credits are good whether you're dead or alive?" Gray asked.

That was all Red needed to hear. She drew her pistol before she could reconsider and fired. The laser shot out, dropping Gray where he stood. A cauterized hole smoldered where his heart had beat only seconds ago. The smell of burning flesh and intestinal waste polluted the air. Someone screamed and there were a few muffled cries, but no one moved.

"We're going to gather our things and leave now," Red said, hoping the shock of her actions kept everyone in place for a few minutes longer. "Anyone tries to stop us and they'll end up like Gray, with their blood watering the ground."

Demery's brown eyes were wide, but he didn't say anything. Like Morgan, he'd drawn his weapon and pointed them at the lookouts before they could raise their rifles. He quickly gathered his tote and slung it over his shoulders.

"Let's go." Red reached for Morgan.

They retreated into the desert, keeping their eyes and guns trained on the small group until they cleared a big dune, then disappeared out of sight.

"What were you thinking?" Morgan asked when they were a safe distance away.

"I knew we weren't going to get out of there without a

firefight. The way we were placed, there was a pretty good chance we'd end up shooting each other in all the commotion. I didn't want to risk it, which meant that either Jeb or Gray had to die."

"You're crazy, mon." Demery shoved his dreadlocks away from his face. "You could've gotten all of us killed."

"I took a calculated risk. I knew the loss of Gray would shock the group and prayed it was enough to keep them from acting. Jeb's loss wouldn't have been as great. Gray would've ordered his people to fire. In the end, it was an easy decision." Red said the words dispassionately, but inside she was chilled at the ease with which she'd taken the man's life. When she shot, she hadn't felt anything but the need to survive. Like a trapped wolf ready to gnaw its own leg off, she'd acted quickly and without remorse.

"Gray was good people, mon," Demery said. "As good as people get on this side of the fence."

Red's eyes narrowed. "He was a threat and planned to turn us over to Roark. You heard him. We're wanted dead or alive. Personally, I'm partial to breathing."

Demery slowed. "You don't know Roark was the one who put a bounty on your heads, mon."

Red rounded on him. "Don't be naive. Who else would've done it? My grandfather?" she shouted. "Doubtful. Not many people can afford to part with that many credits. But Roark can. He's amassed a fortune while he's been in politics."

"Point taken," Demery said. "I still think we could've worked something out with the Sand Moles. Now I'm never going to be able to trade with them."

"I'm sorry we messed up your commerce opportunities," she said sarcastically. "Fifteen thousand credits hanging over our heads make me a little twitchy on the trigger. Who knows how many people have heard about the bounty by now. We aren't going to be safe anywhere."

Morgan came over and put his arm around her. "It'll be okay," he said. "All we need to do is reach the encampment Jeb spoke of."

She gave a pained laugh. "It stopped being okay a long

time ago. And who's to say that Jeb was telling the truth? I know you didn't sense deception, but he could've been lying."

"He wasn't," Demery said. "I know the place. It's real. I've been there or at least been by there on my travels. I've never actually stopped."

"Let's hope they weren't the ones who told him about the reward," Red ran a hand through her loose hair. She'd been in such a hurry to pack and leave that she'd forgotten to tie it back. Maybe she should cut it. Long hair wasn't meant for these conditions. Like compassion, it only got in the way.

chapter ten

"I'm going to take off now," Chaos said, gathering her things to head back to her shuttle. She'd spent most of the night scouring the area, but hadn't turned up anything else. The sky would be lightening in a few hours.

"Where are you going?" Raphael asked.

"I have some more things to check out," she said. If she was lucky, he wouldn't notice that she hadn't answered his question.

He lifted her tote onto his shoulder. "Perhaps I can come along and help?" Raphael suggested.

"You said you were looking for your brother," she said. "I don't want to keep you."

"I am. If we are going in the same direction we could keep each other company." His hand brushed her arm, the move casual but intimate. A subtle reminder of what they'd shared this past week.

His warm scent washed over her and Chaos' breath caught. When Chaos realized what she'd done, she growled in frustration. "I work better alone," she said hastily.

"If I make you uncomfortable, all you have to do is tell me," his voice teased, but there was no mistaking the challenge behind his words.

"You don't," she snapped, knowing it was a lie. Truth was Raphael had her coming out of her skin. "That would require feeling something for you."

"Exactly." Raphael flashed her a grin that made her knees weak.

Chaos didn't know how she felt. One minute she wanted to punch him. The next she had to fight to keep from throwing herself in his arms. "You are impossible!" She groaned in frustration, then jumped into her maglev shuttle and started the engine. "I better not see you following me or I'll shoot you out of the air." Chaos slammed the shuttle into gear. It rose two feet off the ground and took off. She arced to the left, purposely traveling in the wrong direction to confuse him. She'd circle back soon enough and head to the boundary fence crossing.

"You won't see a thing. I assure you," Raphael murmured as she drove away. He didn't know what the little minx was up to, but he'd find out. Raphael hadn't asked her to contact the commander of IPTT about Red and Morgan. He'd only planned to do so as a last resort. She'd taken it upon herself, which knowing how Catherine's mind worked didn't bode well for him. He thought he'd come up with a clever trap, one that would work out for the both of them, when he'd gotten her to agree to help him. But he obviously hadn't been clever enough. Raphael had considered reading her thoughts, but he wanted Catherine's trust. For some reason her trust was important to him.

Raphael was torn between the need to locate Michael and the need to go after Catherine. He hopped into his shuttle and started the engine. Thanks to the eye replacements he'd had during the war, with a blink he could see as well at night as he could during the day.

Catherine zoomed farther east. Raphael threw the shuttle into high gear and killed the lights. She'd never see him back here. As long as he kept a couple of miles between them, the sensors on her shuttle would never detect him.

Raphael followed at a steady pace, sipping on a packet of blood. Catherine had turned south ten minutes ago and seemed to be on a direct course for the boundary fence. The thought of her crossing into no-man's-land alone curdled the blood in his stomach. What was she thinking?

She may be powerful, but Catherine was no match for no-man's-land. It didn't matter that he'd intended to go there himself. She had no business putting herself in danger. He had the overwhelming urge to turn her over his knee and paddle her delectable bottom. His body liked that idea far too much. Raphael shifted to ease his burgeoning erection.

Catherine stopped at a lot a quarter of a mile from the official boundary crossing station and parked her shuttle. Raphael had hoped he'd been wrong about her destination. She disembarked from the shuttle and gathered a pack that was almost as big as she was, then tossed it onto her back. He shook his head as she nearly toppled from the weight.

He should just go back to Nuria and leave her. That was the smart thing to do. It wasn't as if he was prepared for a trip into no-man's-land. Raphael stared out the window as Catherine stumbled toward the crossing checkpoint. He hit the wheel in frustration, cracking it, then scrambled out of his vehicle. Stubborn woman. She'd get herself killed if she wasn't careful.

"Wait up," he shouted.

Catherine ignored him and kept walking. Raphael secured his vehicle and jogged over to the crossing. She had thrown her pack on the table and presented her neck for scanning.

"State your purpose," a guard wearing a navy quadrant inspector's uniform said.

"Business," Catherine said.

"Pleasure," Raphael added.

The guard looked at him askance. "Anything to declare?"

"She's insane," Raphael said, glancing at her.

The guard snickered. "Move ahead." He ushered them on.

"You are the most bullheaded human being I've ever met," Raphael said, grabbing her arm and yanking her around.

Catherine looked down at his hand and waited for him to remove it. Raphael pried his fingers open and glared at her.

"I thought I told you not to follow me," she said, showing her I.D. to the next set of guards at the checkpoint. "What are you doing here?"

"I told you. I'm looking for my brother, Michael Travers."

Her green eyes narrowed in suspicion. "What would he be doing here?" she asked. "This isn't exactly a travel destination."

"Probably the same thing you are," Raphael said, exasperated. "I thought you said you were looking for evidence."

"Who said I'm not? You don't know what I'm doing," Catherine said, before quickly lowering her voice. "Unless you've read my mind."

He rolled his eyes. "I don't have to read your mind to know what you're up to. It's written clearly on your little cherub face." Raphael pulled out his I.D. He had expected to have time to return to Nuria to retrieve supplies before crossing into no-man's-land, but Catherine had blown that plan into space. Now he'd have to buy what he needed from the trader store and they always marked things up.

She shook her head. "You're seeing things that aren't there," she said.

"Am I?" he asked, ushering her forward.

"Yep."

"Fine, have it your way." Raphael exposed his neck to the scanner. Two beeps later he was walking down the long gray, sparsely lit corridor that would eventually open up into no-man's-land. Catherine strode in front of him, her pack swaying from side to side like stacked plates ready to fall.

"It seems to me," he said, breaking the silence, "that we'd probably get a lot further if we worked together."

"I told you I'd keep our bargain and I meant it," she said. "I don't need your help."

"I have no doubt that's true, but I could use your help finding my brother. You must have met him when you went to Roark's office."

Catherine stopped dead, her shoulders tense. "He showed Bannon and me into a waiting room. I never saw him after that. He certainly wasn't there when we left. Do you think he had anything to do with us getting drugged?"

She asked casually, but Raphael heard the apprehension in her voice. "No," he said. "I'm sure that was all Roark." There was no doubt in Raphael's mind that had Michael participated in something like that he would've let Raphael know. That knowledge should've stopped doubt cold, but it kept crawling forward, whispering insidiously in the back of his mind.

"Why would he be in no-man's-land?" she asked. Catherine's expression told him she hadn't quite believed his assurances.

"That's what I'm here to find out," he said. Raphael dropped into the outfitting shop and picked up a pack, canteens, food, a tent, industrial-grade sunscreen, and protective clothing. His credit account took a major hit, thanks to Catherine's impromptu trip, but it was necessary. He could stay out in the sun fairly long for a vamp, but he didn't think he'd make it all day. He did have his limits, although Raphael rarely copped to them.

Despite all her protests, Catherine had followed him into the store and was browsing the items. She picked up a hat and an extra canteen. He noticed that she bypassed the tents, so either she had one in that enormous pack of hers or she didn't anticipate being out here long.

It was too much to hope that she planned to share his tent with him. Raphael had never cared for camping, but he could get used to it if Catherine were his tent mate. He looked at her as he considered the possibility.

She scowled back.

Perhaps it would be better if they had their own space.

Catherine hadn't told him what she was doing here. Sure she'd mentioned getting permission from the commander of IPTT, but permission for what? It was one thing to look for proof, quite another to pursue fugitives. Raphael didn't know what Catherine planned to do once she caught up with Morgan and Red. It was just one more reason he needed to go with her.

Raphael shoved his supplies into his pack and stared longingly at Catherine's bare neck. What he wouldn't give for a canteen full of blood. Just looking at her stoked his hunger. Thanks to her nearness and the need she evoked, he'd finished the last of his supply on the ride down here.

Catherine tipped her head and he glimpsed his teeth marks on the side of her nape. They looked more like love bites in this artificial lighting. He licked his lips as his incisors lengthened. The material on the front of his pants strained under his growing erection as he inhaled her feminine musk. He'd just have to improvise, when it came to feeding. The thought of what that would entail had his temperature rising. Catherine caught him looking at her and flushed bright pink. Obviously his expression had been patently transparent.

"All done," Raphael said.

"About time," she countered.

He laughed. "I didn't realize you were waiting for me. Had I known, I would've hurried," Raphael said to get a rise out of her, since her actions had been blatantly obvious. "I take it you've reconsidered my offer."

She shrugged. "We can travel together and hope to find your brother along the way, but we go in the direction I want," she said. "No arguments."

"Of course," Raphael agreed, since he knew they'd be heading in the direction he needed to go. That didn't stop him from hoping he was wrong about his brother, Michael. Maybe Roark had sent him somewhere else. It would explain his absence. Even as the thought flitted through Raphael's head, he knew it was unlikely.

He hoisted the pack onto his back and indicated for Catherine to lead the way. She did, but stopped when they reached the final gate. There she hesitated.

"Having second thoughts?" he asked, in hopes she'd call the whole thing off.

"No, just adjusting my pack." Catherine made a show of shifting her pack, then she stepped forward and pressed a button on the wall. Nothing happened for a second so she pressed it again harder.

"Give it time. You are so impatient, my little storm," Raphael said. "Don't you know good things come to those who wait? Besides, the sun will be up soon. We'll have to camp at the crossing until dark."

Catherine rolled her eyes. "Shut up, cliché man."

The final door slid open with a hiss. A blast of warmth greeted them with a dry embrace. The gaping maw that was the endless desert stretched out before them, waiting to swallow them whole. There were so many directions to go in. They could be anywhere.

Raphael tried to ignore Catherine's delicious scent as they proceeded into the fleeting darkness. It was difficult given the lack of distracting odors. The sand gave under his booted feet. This would not be an easy journey—his gaze fell upon his petite traveling companion—for either of them.

Good thing she had a day to reconsider her folly.

Chaos felt him behind her watching. Raphael did that a lot. She didn't know if he was waiting for her to attack again or if he was sizing her up as a snack. She didn't want to think that it might be sexual. It was hard enough walking this close to him without her body betraying her at every turn. Did he have to look so good?

They waited at the gate for the rest of the night and all through the next day. There'd been nothing to do but sleep and talk. Raphael had regaled her with stories from his childhood. He'd charmed her, weakening her resolve to remain aloof. It seemed to take forever for the sun to set. Even after the fiery ball sunk below the horizon, it was still unbearably hot. The heat didn't seem to affect him like it did her. Chaos was already sweating and they'd only been walking a few minutes. She'd be a puddle by the time an hour had passed.

It didn't help that her pack weighed a ton. She'd wanted to be prepared, so she'd requisitioned everything required for outdoor survival. Chaos had no idea what they might encounter on this side of the boundary fence, but she was determined to be ready.

Her hand moved to the pistol strapped to her thigh. Its weight was reassuring. In the distance, a big cat yowled. The hair on her neck prickled. She glanced back at Raphael to make sure he was still there. He was, but his expression remained deceptively placid. So either he hadn't heard the cat or he wasn't bothered by its presence.

Fine, two could play that game. Chaos straightened her pack and kept her hand on her weapon as she scanned the area around them. She wasn't afraid of any animal. Even one that might turn out to be four feet high and five hundred pounds.

The lights from the checkpoint were a dim memory glittering in the distance. If a predator lurked behind a dune there was no way they'd make it back to the gates before it attacked. She took a deep breath and let it out slowly. No reason to be concerned. It was more afraid of them than they were of it.

Raphael touched Chaos and she jumped, letting out a startled yelp.

"I'm sorry. I didn't mean to frighten you."

"You didn't," she shot back. "Now what do you want?"

His lip canted, but he didn't contradict her. "I wanted to tell you that the cat we heard earlier is stalking us from the west."

Chaos spun around so fast the weight of her pack teetered, sending her crashing into the dune. She struggled out of the straps and came up with her pistol in her hand. "Where? Do you see it?" She tried to look everywhere at once.

Raphael started laughing and couldn't seem to stop. His shoulders shook and he clutched his flat abdomen.

"What's so funny?" Chaos glared at him, giving Raphael her best withering glance.

"You," he said, pressing his lips together, trying to keep from laughing again. He didn't succeed.

Chaos brushed her clothes off. "You said a cat was stalking us. I don't think that's a laughing matter."

"Yes, it is," he said, trying to catch his breath. "You should've seen yourself, jerking your gun this way and that way. I'm lucky you didn't shoot me."

"I wanted to be ready," she ground out through clenched teeth.

"It would help if you were facing the right direction," he said, casually pointing to a spot over her shoulder.

Chaos turned and searched the darkness for movement.

"You need not worry," Raphael said. His lips brushed her ear, sending goosebumps down her spine.

Chaos hadn't even heard him move, his footfalls were so silent. Like the cat that was determined to have them as a meal.

"I will not let the feline touch you. You are mine—*to eat*."

Heat flooded Chaos' face as his words singed the panic out of her mind. She shivered and swallowed hard, forcing herself to meet his black gaze. He was smiling at her, his white teeth glowing in the darkness. At that moment, she didn't know which was the more dangerous predator, the cat or Raphael.

"Don't make me shoot you," she warned. "I only agreed to allow you to tag along because you said we were headed in the same direction. At least for a while. I can easily change my mind and send you on your way."

Raphael snorted, but quickly covered it with a cough. "Whatever you say."

"Let's get moving," Chaos said, lifting her pack from the sand dune and brushing it off. "I don't want the cat to get any closer. I'd hate to have to kill it."

"You are absolutely right." Raphael dropped his pack and raced to the top of a nearby dune so quickly she barely tracked his movements. When he reached the top, he slowly turned his head to the west. When he spotted his target, he stopped. A rumble rose from inside of him, building in ferocity. When he released it, the sound came out as a primal roar.

Chaos heard a feline's answering snarl closer than she would've cared for it to be. Raphael spread his arms wide and hissed, exposing long, sharp fangs. There was another growl, but this one seemed less sure than the previous one.

The cat was having second thoughts about attacking. Hell, *she* was having second thoughts. Raphael roared again and strode off in the direction the snarl had come from. Chaos frowned. What was he doing now? Surely he wasn't crazy enough to confront the animal unarmed.

He disappeared into the darkness. Chaos listened carefully, but couldn't hear much over the pounding of her heart. She charged her weapon with the press of her thumb.

"Raphael?" she called out.

He didn't answer.

Chaos dropped her pack and climbed to the top of the dune. It was so dark that she could barely see her hand in front of her face. Damn him. Where had he gone? The thought that the cat might have gotten to him and drug him off stilled her movements. The disturbing image was followed by a wave of sadness that nearly upended her.

"Raphael, this isn't funny. Where are you?" she said in a hushed tone in case it decided to hunt her next.

She squinted into the darkness as if that would somehow help. Chaos raised her pistol and pressed a tiny button on the side of the barrel. A night-vision scope popped into place. She put her eye up to it and slowly scanned the area.

There was no movement or heat signature lingering anywhere. For a second, she couldn't breathe. Her hand went to her chest as she tried to calm down. What if something had happened to him? What if she never saw him again? Panic and something akin to fear overwhelmed her.

"Where are you damn it?" Her voice broke. She swallowed back the sudden grief.

"It's nice to know you missed me."

The whisper was so soft it barely registered. When Chaos did, anger flooded her. She spun around and slammed her tiny fist into his face. The punch must have caught him off guard because Raphael rocked back on his heels and fell onto the sand.

Chaos bent over him, her finger jabbing him in his chest. "Don't ever do that again. Do you hear me?"

"Loud and clear, ma petite."

Not even the blood on his lip could detract from the stupid grin he wore on his handsome face.

"What are you smiling about?" Chaos shouted, getting

madder by the second. She'd been so scared that she'd lost him it hadn't crossed her mind that he might be playing with her.

"You wouldn't have hit me if you didn't care." He stood gracefully and brushed off his clothes.

"You're making too much out of it," she said, hoping to misdirect him. "I just didn't want to have to fill out a report listing cause of death."

"If you say so." The smile refused to leave Raphael's face. He knew the truth. In a flash of anger, she'd as good as shouted her feelings for him.

"I swear." Chaos growled, her fists clenching at her sides. "If the cat doesn't get you next time, I will."

chapter eleven

The sun had drained Michael more than he realized. Somehow he'd lost a day, sleeping in the half-shadow of the rock. Without the sunlight, he could move more quickly. Not that the sand sucking at his shoes helped. He'd emptied them twice already, but had finally given up on ever getting the tiny granules out of his socks.

A slight breeze picked up from the south. It wasn't cool, but it did relieve the stifling heat that still air created. Michael moved steadily, trying to sense Red and Morgan. He hadn't picked up their scent, but was convinced they'd come this way.

Going to either coast was useless. Nothing survived near the poisoned seas. The boundary fence lay to the north, which left only one direction: south. Roark was convinced they'd gone to no-man's-land. Their desperation was even greater than Michael's if they had.

Deciding to give it a few more days, he trudged on. Michael scanned the dunes for any sign of life. Nothing moved but the sand, forever shifting and reshaping, erasing all trace of those who dared tread upon it. Seas of beige cascading waves, tumbling, tumbling down.

A mile farther Michael came upon a pack of wild dogs eating what appeared to be a small deer. It was only when he got closer that Michael realized it was a child, not a doe, wrapped in brown clothing, its tiny limbs ripped from its body and spread across the desert floor.

His senses went into overdrive. If a child was here, then that meant people couldn't be far off. Michael picked up his pace, the thought of fresh blood driving him. Licking his dry lips, he skirted by the ravenous pack. If the kill hadn't been old, he would've joined in on the feast or taken it from them. Nothing like a feeding frenzy to remind him that he was alive.

It took another four and a half hours, but eventually Michael stumbled upon what looked to be a nomadic settlement—tents huddled in the middle of a rise surrounded by a flaming moat. There was one walkway that led in, but Michael was sure there had to be another. No one was stupid enough to trap themselves without the possibility of escape, especially people living in no-man's-land.

Dropping to the sand, he began to belly-crawl forward. People were rushing from place to place within the compound, their movements frenzied. Had they been recently attacked? He thought of the dead child lying in pieces. Tension gripped him as he inhaled deeply. The last thing Michael needed was to be caught off guard by an unseen enemy.

A flash of movement to his right had his head turning. The shadow disappeared before he could get a good look at it. Not now. Michael slammed his eyes closed, squeezing until the lids hurt. The pain helped him focus. Reminded him of who he used to be.

"Go away," he hissed under his breath. Michael's head began to throb and he felt movement under his skull once again. The chip was burrowing deeper. An impossibility, so it had to be his imagination.

A shock zapped him, painfully contorting his muscles. Michael gasped. Roark was nowhere near. He would've sensed him. That meant the chip had acted on its own. It took Michael a moment to digest the gravity of the situation. He didn't like the conclusion he came to. What had Roark done to him?

Michael watched the shadows retreat, but how long they'd stay gone was anyone's guess. Shaken, he started forward again, dropping lower in the sand. The gentle shoosh as his clothes brushed the grains would be lost to human ears. He didn't want them to see him before he was ready. He licked his chapped lips. So thirsty. The raw ache for blood burned his insides, demanding to be filled.

Guards flanked the encampment, their eyes alert, almost fevered. The faint coppery scent of blood tickled Michael's nose, teasing him with the promise of sustenance. The blood was old, but Michael's body didn't care. His stomach growled loud enough for the guards to notice. They both turned, weapons raised.

"Come out," the one nearest him shouted, unable to pinpoint his exact location.

Michael considered not complying for a moment, then slowly rose to his feet, putting his hands in the air. It was all for show of course. He could kill them both in a blink and not strain a muscle. The chip in his brain flared at the thought, flooding his body with endorphins, encouraging him to act on the impulse. Michael fought the urge and a wave a pain swiftly followed. He gulped in air and staggered forward.

"I'm unarmed," he said. It was the truth and a lie, since Michael had dropped his assassination kit on the ground where he'd been hiding moments ago. The real weapon lay within him dormant, but ready for use at a moment's notice. It was the reason he'd survived for so many years. The reason Michael had found his brother, Raphael. And the reason Roark had him chipped.

"Come forward and don't try anything or we'll shoot," the guard shouted. That wouldn't happen, since Michael was quite capable of stopping a bullet.

He did as the guard asked because it suited his purpose. Michael needed to find out whether Red and Morgan had passed this way. The only way to do that was to get closer.

"Do you have any water?" Michael asked. "I ran out an hour ago." It wasn't water he needed, but he figured they'd be far more accommodating than if he'd asked for their blood.

"Keep your hands where we can see them," the guard said, not answering.

Michael walked across the small entryway while flames licked at his flesh from both sides. Sweat beaded on his forehead. Unusual, but not unheard of for his kind. The fire crackled, fed by some kind of liquid fuel and rags.

"I could really use your help," Michael said, repeating his request for water. His meek act slipped easily onto his narrow shoulders. Once again he became Michael Travers, lowly assistant.

One of the guards nodded to a woman, who placed a canister of some sort on a table. She pointed to it and then stepped away.

"Thank you," Michael said, reaching for it. The water burned his raw throat, causing him to choke. He wasn't even sure it was solely water, but at least it was wet. Michael put it down and took a couple of deep breaths, while forcing himself to remain as unthreatening as possible. It wasn't hard. He was not a big man. Despite the changes in him, Michael had small hands and delicate features. Most people didn't see him as dangerous until he killed them. It was one of the many reasons he was such a good assassin. Michael took another drink of water. This time it soothed.

The guard stepped forward when Michael finished, weapon raised. "State your business."

Michael watched him, paying special attention to the slight tremor in his hands and the laser pistol strapped to his thigh. It looked new, unlike the weapon in his hands, which had seen better days. Despite the varnish, the wood of the rifle had rotted from age. The inside of the barrel looked clean, but rust dotted the outside in red freckles.

"I told you. I ran out of supplies and need assistance," he said.

"You don't look like a trader. Where did you come from?" the man asked.

"The boundary fence."

"You're registered?" He sounded surprised.

"Yes." Michael didn't bother to ask him if he was since anyone living on this side of the fence had chosen not to or couldn't afford the credits it took to go through the process.

Michael turned his head to show the man where his chip was implanted.

His brown eyes narrowed in suspicion. "Why would so many *Regs* want to suddenly journey into no-man's-land?"

Michael arched a brow. Why indeed? He took another deep breath and caught a familiar scent. It was wild and feminine just like its owner. "Where is she?" he asked

The guard stilled, his gaze growing wary. "Where's who?"

"Don't play dumb with me," Michael said, starting toward a tent not far from the table.

"Stop or I'll shoot," the guard shouted, then fired. A blast landed near Michael's feet.

He stopped, anger and energy rising inside of him. "That was a mistake," he said softly, turning to face the man. So softly Michael doubted he heard him.

"The next shot will be in you," the guard warned. His bravado was admirable, but it did little to wipe the stink of fear from his skin. The man knew now that he was staring at death.

Michael watched the other guard off to the right raise his weapon. He was still a good distance away. Smart man. Too bad it wouldn't help him.

"The last man who pulled a gun on me didn't live to take his next breath," Michael said. The chip in his brain pulsed in approval. Suddenly the need to resist the impulse to kill didn't seem all that important.

"Huh?"

Michael reached out with his mind to the nearest guard and yanked the gun from him, tossing it into the fire beyond. The man stood dumbfounded, gawking at his empty hands. Before the other guard in the distance registered what had happened, Michael mentally grabbed his weapon and slowly turned the muzzle on him. It became a battle of wills. Michael's was stronger. When the muzzle rested against his chest, Michael blinked and the gun fired, sending a loud crack rumbling through the air.

Screams filled the night as people ran out of their tents and lean-tos, weapons drawn.

Michael became a killing machine, disarming them all at once. He smashed their bones and piled the bodies up near the fire like human kindling. The physical drain was immense. Michael's power weakened, but no one seemed to notice. When there were only two people left, the first guard and a woman, he stopped his rampage. Once again the chip in his brain flooded his body with endorphins. A reward for a job well done.

"Now, I'm going to ask you again. Where is she?"

The woman whimpered. Tears streaked down her grit-covered face, leaving clean trails behind. She glanced at the corpses of her people. "They killed Gray and left," she said.

The man shot her a censorious look meant to silence her, but the woman was too far gone to notice.

"Where did they go?" Michael asked, barely containing the urge to taste her throat.

"Southwest," she said, then dropped to the ground and started rocking.

"You come here." Michael summoned the guard.

The man shook his head. Defiant to the end. "Go to hell," he ground out between clenched teeth.

"I'm not going to ask you again." Michael raised his arm, directing his telekinetic power toward the guard. The man's feet left the ground and he began to float toward him. Michael's power faltered and the man's toes dug into the sand.

The guard shrieked, the fear inside of him exploding like a cork under too much pressure. He struggled against Michael's mental bonds, but it did him no good. He may be weak from lack of blood, but he was still stronger than any being currently walking on the dead world.

Michael set the man down in front of him and looked into his leathery face. His gray eyes were wide and he'd wet himself. The acrid odor of urine nearly overpowered the scent of blood coming from the bodies.

"Bring me the canteen," Michael said to the woman. For a second, she didn't move. Her mind had created a safe haven for her to escape in.

"I said bring me that canteen," he repeated, but this time louder. Michael pointed to the object on the table.

She blinked as if waking from a dream, then rose to do as he bade. The woman handed him the canteen, then quickly backed away. Her fingers shook violently as she plunged them into her pockets.

"Thank you," he said. Michael's fangs lengthened in anticipation.

The man's eyes got even wider if that were possible and his struggles increased. Michael brushed his scraggly hair away from his neck. His skin was dirty, but it mattered not, because what Michael was after wasn't found on the outside.

It was difficult to hold the guard with need riding him so hard, but somehow Michael managed. He stared at the man's neck and concentrated, watching his pulse jump beneath his skin. The movement was hypnotizing.

A small tear opened the guard's throat, gradually growing larger and larger, then deeper and deeper, until it reached the carotid artery. The man's cries had turned into terrified whimpers. Michael mentally plucked at the vein and it opened, exposing glorious fountains of crimson. They showered him, covering his face, blanketing his clothes. Michael closed his eyes in ecstasy and licked his lips. So warm. So salty. So delicious.

Michael placed the canteen against the man's neck and waited for his heart to do its job. It didn't take long to fill. When it was finished, he sealed the lid.

"Do you have any more?" Michael asked the woman, but she didn't hear him. She was already going into shock.

The man's color began to fade. Michael moved quickly and covered the opening with his lips, sucking hard. The coppery taste exploded on his tongue. So good. So sweet. More. He needed more. He drank and drank until Michael was convinced his stomach would burst. The man tasted so fresh. If Michael didn't stop, he'd be blood sick. But the thirst remained, driving him to gluttony. Or maybe it was the chip.

Michael released the man and he fell. Deceased before he hit the sandy floor.

The woman was staring in his direction, but Michael didn't think she could see him. He searched the tents and found two more empty canteens. The rest were full of water. He'd take as many as he could carry. Michael returned to the woman. She hadn't budged. The merciful thing to do was to kill her.

He plucked her off the ground. She didn't struggle or cry out. She simply lifted her matted blond hair off her neck and tilted her head, so he'd have better access. Fang marks glared back at him. Someone had fed from her before. Michael didn't recognize the vamp's earthy scent. A twinge of guilt hit. It was wrong to poach on another vampire's food source, but guilt had no place in no-man's-land.

"Thank you," he said, then clamped onto her throat with his teeth and ripped.

She didn't make a sound as Michael filled his canteens and then left her to bleed to death. It seemed like such a waste of blood, but he couldn't carry anything else. Michael's power surged, striking her heart. By the next beat it stopped and the woman was dead . . . just like the rest of her people.

He went back into the tent where he'd found Red's scent. It mingled with Morgan's. They'd stayed here, and not long ago. A day perhaps, two at the most. The scent was too strong to be old. At least now he knew they were still alive.

Michael left the tent and its contents behind and gathered the canteens, making his way back across the entrance and out where he'd left his weapons. He added the canteens to his supplies, then climbed the ridge of the nearest dune and looked out at the ever lightening horizon. The black had been steadily replaced with light gray. The sun would be coming up in a matter of minutes. There was no time to waste.

The breeze increased, bringing with it a familiar odor wafting on the air. It stopped Michael in his tracks. He turned his face into the wind. The scent was there again, stronger, closer. Michael inhaled deeply to be sure he was not mistaken. He wasn't. He was still far away, but the wind confirmed Michael's fears.

"Raphael, what are you doing here?" he asked the night, not expecting an answer. The spicy odor of his brother taunted him. Made Michael long for his company, when he needed no man. Raphael's scent was tangled with a lighter one, sweeter almost. One that seemed vaguely familiar. His brother wasn't traveling alone.

Michael debated for a moment whether to contact him, but decided against it. There could be only one reason Raphael was out here. And that was to stop him. Michael went back into the compound and grabbed a lean-to to take with him. The thought of burning the remaining tents crossed his mind, since it would eliminate his scent, but the flames would draw Raphael straight to this location. If he didn't burn the place, there was a possibility his brother might miss the compound. Michael decided to leave it standing.

The best thing his brother could do was stay as far away from him as possible. Michael loved Raphael, but right now he was a danger to him and anyone who might be traveling with him. And he would remain so as long as this chip stayed in his head. Raphael's blind devotion prevented him from seeing the truth. For both their sakes, Michael prayed that never changed.

chapter twelve

They smelled death before they saw it. Raphael and Catherine approached the camp, spotting the pile of bodies immediately. The fire burning in a deep trench was almost out. It wouldn't be long before the predators approached.

Catherine put her hand over her nose and mouth. "What in the hell happened here?" she asked, gagging.

Raphael could tell she wasn't really looking for an answer. He inhaled, catching his brother's scent. It was faint due to the decomp, but strong enough to let him know that he'd been here recently. Michael had certainly been close enough to hear his call. Raphael made his way around the pit and walked into the middle of the tents. He picked up three more familiar scents—Red, Morgan, and Demery. Every muscle in his body clenched. Had they all been here at the same time? Were they among the dead? If not, who was responsible for these deaths?

"This one's throat has been ripped out," she said, standing over the body of a woman. "And that one's been slashed." She pointed to a man lying nearby. "I don't see any marks on these others. It's like they just died."

"I doubt very much that they all laid down in a pile and died. Have you spotted Red or Morgan?" he asked.

"No." She shook her head. "Not yet. I'll keep looking."

A wave of relief hit. "Let me know if you find anything," Raphael said.

She scowled. "Other than Red and Morgan, what am I looking for?"

"Signs of trauma." Raphael wasn't about to share his insights into what had happened here. This carnage wasn't the work of shifters. The only creature he knew of who could kill like this was a vamp, which meant either Demery or his brother, Michael, had been behind the killings. The question was why? Had these people tried to attack Red and Morgan? There was no reason to assume so. Yet this was no-man's-land. They didn't exactly operate by the rules, nor did they need a reason to kill.

After a few more minutes of searching, Catherine approached him, looking paler than she'd been only moments ago. The sun had barely peeked over the horizon. Soon it would be beating down upon them and they'd have to take shelter. This place was as good as any.

"Are you okay?" He reached out to stroke her cheek.

She swatted his hand away. "I'm fine. What are we going to do with the bodies?"

"Move them out into the desert, so that the predators don't come in here while we're sleeping."

"I'm not staying here." Catherine gaped, looking around at the destruction. "This is a dead zone. We don't even know what happened. What if whatever killed them comes back?"

"It won't." Raphael had no doubt the killer or killers were long gone. "The sun is coming up. We won't get far in the heat. This place has shelter and probably a few supplies we can make use of. It's not like they'll need them anymore. Rigor has come and gone in all the bodies. They've already begun to decompose."

"What if something in their supplies killed them?" she asked. "We have tents. We should go."

He hadn't thought of that, but this clever woman had. Raphael walked over to the pile of bodies. He hated to do this, but he had no choice. He leaned over them and breathed deep. The scent of decay hit, rolling his stomach, but beneath that he smelled nothing unusual.

Raphael reached out and lifted one of the victim's arms. It crumpled, bending in an abnormal way. He started at the wrist and felt up to the elbow. The bones were like gravel beneath his fingertips. He dropped the limb. Definitely a vamp's work.

"I don't think they were poisoned," he said, slowly backing away from the bodies.

"Then what killed them?"

More like who, he thought. "I'm not sure what happened here." That was the truth. Raphael had seen only one sign of shots fired and the slug was still in the ground.

"Do you think Red and Morgan did this?" Catherine's green eyes were wide as she looked around cautiously. Her hand moved unconsciously to her pistol.

He shook his head. "No, I'm certain they didn't have a hand in this slaughter."

"If not them, then who? Do you think your brother came this way?" she asked casually. "You said you were following him."

Raphael tensed, but kept his features calm. "I doubt we'll ever know what was behind this massacre. Now help me with the bodies before the sun gets much higher," he said. "My eyes are watering from the stench."

"Why don't we burn them?" she suggested.

He shook his head. "The animals we encountered are starving. These bodies could keep them fed for a week or more."

Catherine frowned. "But they're people," she said, as if that explained everything.

"Yes, they were, but they're dead now. They won't feel a thing and their deaths will help ensure the survival of others," he said softly. "I know you find this distasteful, but I could really use your help."

Raphael looked at her. He could see the battle raging behind her soulful eyes. She wanted to fight him on this, but part of her understood and agreed with his reasoning. In that moment he realized how young Catherine really was, and he'd never felt so old.

"Fine, let's get this over with." She marched toward the bodies. Catherine grabbed the smallest one and began to drag the corpse over the walkway that led out of the compound. Raphael didn't speak. He walked over, picked up two of the bigger bodies, and followed.

They drug the bodies out fifty yards from the moat of fire and scattered them over a forty-foot area. Raphael took out a knife and sliced through the corpses' clothes, wrenching them off.

"What are you doing?" Catherine shouted, her color high. She was out of breath and itching for a fight. He knew it was her way of dealing with the death surrounding her.

"I'm making it easier for the animals. This way they won't have to eat their way through clothes. And if anyone wanders by in need of clothing, they'll have it readily available."

Catherine shot him a look of disgust. "You're creepy some-times, you know that?"

"I know," Raphael said quietly. Her assessment hurt more than it should. "Now come here and stick out your arms."

She did as she was told. Raphael cut the clothes away and piled them in Catherine's arms. When the pile reached the top of her head, he told her to go back to the compound. He fin-ished what he'd started and collected the remaining outfits.

He could already hear the predators approaching. They were silent, but not silent enough. There was a pack heading in from the east and a big cat coming from the north. Maybe even the same one they'd encountered earlier. It wouldn't matter. There was enough food here for all of them.

Raphael straightened and headed back to the compound. He could feel the sun's needlelike rays begin to sting his skin. He hadn't bothered putting on sunscreen because he'd planned to be inside by now. He hurried, dropping the rest of the clothes on a table near the center of the compound.

He found the fuel the group used to keep the fire in the pit going, a combination of rags and various flammable liquids that Raphael had never seen before. He wondered where they'd gotten their hands on such a thing, but quickly released the thought as the pain in his skin intensified. He replenished the moat until the flames once again rose high, then grabbed their packs and slipped into a tent.

Chaos watched Raphael rub his arm and seek shelter. She glanced out over the horizon. The sun was higher now and so was the heat. It was like someone had tossed flame onto the ground and set everything alight.

She missed the climate-controlled dome at IPTT. Hell, even the shuttles were cooler than this and the air only worked half the time in them. She started to turn away when movement caught her attention.

A pack of canines had found the bodies and began to feed. There were coyotes with them, which let out excited yips before joining in. A big cat with black and gold stripes came in from the opposite direction. The pack tried to run it off, but didn't succeed.

Despite the bones sticking out of its sides, the cat was large and powerful—easily big enough to kill every canine. Chaos rubbed her arms to ward off the chill skating over her spine. She couldn't think about what the animals were eating or she'd scream. She gave the horizon one last look and followed Raphael into the tent.

He was lying down, holding his arm when she entered. Raphael sat up quickly and dropped his hand.

"Let me see your arm," Chaos said.

"It's nothing," he said. "Just a little burn. It'll be gone by nightfall."

"I'll be the judge of that," she said, pushing his hand away so she could roll up his sleeve. Blisters covered his arm where it had been exposed to the sun. Chaos gasped before she could stop herself.

"I'm fine." He winced.

"Like hell you are, this is bad." Chaos looked around the tent for her pack. She saw it perched against the wall and left him to retrieve it. She dug into the bottom and came out with a white tube.

"Really, it's nothing." He sighed. "At least it will be in a few hours."

"Yeah, you're a big tough guy. I get it. This should help," she said, opening the lid and squeezing some of the clear substance onto her fingertips. "It'll hurt a little at first, but it should take the pain away."

Raphael watched her, his dark gaze unwavering. He didn't try to stop her when she reached for his arm and drew it onto her lap. Chaos dabbed the medicine on his skin and carefully smoothed it over the burn and the worst of the blisters. When she was done, she popped the lid back onto the tube and dropped it into her pack.

"Try not to move. It takes a couple of minutes to set."

He nodded.

She ignored the heat she saw banked in his black eyes and rose to explore the tent. The space wasn't big, about fifteen feet across, but there were hides and rags tossed around that indicated at least eight people slept in here. Chaos wondered which of the bodies had called this place home.

Raphael lay on the center mound facing the entry flap. Even in repose, he was watchful. "Get some rest while you can," he said, patting the empty spot beside him.

"I can sleep over here," she said, ignoring the heat rising inside the tent.

"Suit yourself." Raphael grinned, then rested one arm over his eyes.

Chaos waited for a moment. When she was sure he wasn't peeking, she took the time to really look him over. She hadn't been able to do so before because he was always watching her. Now she looked her fill.

He had a lean body, made for swift movement and stealth. He'd walked up on her so many times without her hearing him that she was convinced Raphael somehow floated. His fingers were long, pale, and tapered. She knew firsthand that he could do wicked things with those hands. He'd brought her pleasure unlike any she'd ever experienced with just the brush of his thumb.

Even now she could feel his hands caressing her flesh,

seeking out the hidden places in her body, exploring moist openings. She allowed her gaze to venture down his long, hard length.

Chaos paused at the bulge protruding at the juncture of his thighs. Raphael may have a lean body, but he was a big man. She'd nearly fainted at his size, convinced there was no way he'd ever fit inside her. But fit he did . . . repeatedly.

The bulge seemed to grow before her eyes. Her gaze swept to his face, where a smile danced over his sensual mouth. Even resting, Raphael toyed with her like he knew her every thought, her every fantasy. Maybe he did. Maybe that bite delivered more than orgasmic release. Maybe something entered her blood, even as he feasted.

Her nipples hardened under her shirt and Chaos nearly groaned aloud. Her body ached—and not from the long hike they'd made. She wasn't going to let her hormones get the best of her. She punched her pack before settling against it. It was going to be a long day.

Raphael kept still, although it pained him to do so. He could feel Catherine's curious gaze, studying him. He wanted her to look. Liked that she'd spent so much time doing so. His cock ached and he wanted nothing more than to strip those dirty clothes off her and give her a tongue bath, starting at her toes and working his way up.

He could smell her need. It permeated the tent, making the hot air even more stifling. He thought about reaching out to take her, but he'd done that enough. It was her turn to do the taking. She needed to be the one in control, even if it was an illusion. That would be the only way they'd ever move past him *detaining* her against her will.

Raphael waited, but still she didn't move. What was taking Catherine so long? The ache in his groin had intensified to out-and-out pain. Damn it, at this rate he'd have blue balls before she ever got the nerve to act. He peeked out from under his arm, opening his eyes just wide enough to see. She was propped against her backpack, arms crossed over her chest . . . *sleeping*?

Raphael sat up abruptly. What the hell? He looked at her

again. Catherine's eyes were closed and her mouth had fallen open. Her knees were bent to keep her upright. She had to be toying with him. Surely she hadn't gone from lust to sleep that fast. He leaned closer, expecting her to yell "gotcha!" Catherine snuffled, then she let out a loud snore.

Raphael fell back onto the rags. So much for a romantic afternoon rolling on furs.

chapter thirteen

They had kept their pace throughout the night. Demery took the lead, while Morgan brought up the rear. All watched for potential ambushes.

Demery slipped his white protective suit on as the sun peered over the horizon. "It'll take another day or so to reach the outpost the scout spoke of," Demery said. "Do you want to keep going or rest?"

Red looked at Morgan. He tilted his head as if to say it's up to you. "Let's go a little farther. I want more distance between us and the Sand Moles."

Demery nodded and strode on.

Movement to the left caught Red's attention. Something brown scurried over the dune, leaving an S shape in the sand behind it. "What's that?" she asked, pointing.

Morgan came forward as Demery stopped. He smiled when he saw what had caught her attention. "It's a lizard."

"I didn't think there were any of those alive outside of captivity," she said.

He grinned at her. "I guess someone should've told the little guy."

Red watched in fascination. She'd read about lizards and all the other creatures that used to live on Earth before the last war. Most were extinct. The ones that weren't either lived in captivity or struggled with starvation. But not this small one. It was wild like the animals her grandfather told her stories about. She followed it up over the ridge and watched it disappear inside a tiny hole in the sand.

"He went in a hole," she said.

Morgan laughed. "That's what they do when a predator is after them."

"A predator?" She frowned and glanced around, but didn't see anything that would eat the small lizard. Red looked back at Morgan, whose smile had grown.

"Oh, you mean me." She laughed as she stepped off the dune. It felt good. She hadn't done much laughing lately.

He hugged her. "You are amazing," he said. "You know that?"

"Why?" she asked.

"Even in the middle of this hellhole, you can still find time to be fascinated by the simplest thing."

"Thanks." She squeezed him back. "I guess I've spent enough time terrifying lizards."

They trudged on. Sand filled their boots and abraded their faces. They journeyed for another hour without spotting any other signs of life.

"Do you think they'll have the equipment we need?" Red asked Morgan as they sat to rest in the shade of a dune.

"I don't know. I'm not expecting much," he said, looking grim. "The good thing is that even if the equipment is old school I should still be able to do something with it."

"Old school?" she asked. "I don't understand."

"From my time," he explained.

Once again Red was reminded that despite appearances, Morgan was older than her grandfather. "Let's hope it still works," she said tartly.

He grabbed her side and squeezed. Red wiggled away from him before returning to rest her head on his shoulder.

Demery watched them with something akin to envy in his eyes. "You better get some sleep, mon. We have a lot of miles to travel before we reach the outpost."

Red nodded and closed her eyes.

Morgan waited until Red's breathing had deepened, before propping her against the pack. He stood stretching his legs and back. Despite exhaustion, sleep evaded him. He'd pulled out Kane's diaries, but still couldn't bring himself to listen to them. He was too distracted, too worried.

The scene from the previous night kept replaying in his head. Gina had shot the leader of the Sand Moles with little to no thought. Something she wouldn't have done outside of patrol a month and a half ago. Was the wolf changing her or was he to blame?

The latter thought disturbed Morgan. He'd brought her into a hostile world. She'd been naïve in so many ways, her life sheltered by IPTT. Morgan didn't want Gina changing because of her association with him. He loved her the way that she was, even before she knew what lurked inside of her. Gina was a brave, fearless, sensual woman. His match in every way.

Morgan leaned down and pressed his lips to her forehead. She murmured, but didn't wake. The wolf lurked close to the surface. So close it was a wonder Gina had been able to control it this long.

Part of him longed for her to let go, allow the wolf free rein for a while. The wolf in him wanted its mate. Another part of him feared it. What if she couldn't control herself in her other form? She'd finally controlled a partial shift. It had taken months and Roark trying to kill him to do it, but she'd managed. He'd been so proud of her.

Morgan didn't want to take that away, but there was more to being a wolf than just controlling the change. There were responsibilities she'd have to accept if they ever returned to Nuria. Responsibilities he wasn't sure she'd be happy about. The biggest one would be stepping into the position of alpha female and eventually bearing his young.

The thought of Gina carrying his child hit Morgan in the gut and slowly rose to sit comfortably on his heart. If he closed his eyes, he could almost picture her rounded belly and heavy breasts, her body bursting with new life. Morgan choked on unexpected emotion and had to walk away. The thought was too overwhelming for him to contemplate, when there was a very good chance they wouldn't make it out of here alive.

He scanned the horizon. It wasn't the first time he'd wondered why they hadn't been followed. It could be that killing the leader of the Sand Moles had scared the group into inaction, but it didn't seem likely.

People living in no-man's-land didn't scare easily. They were used to death hanging around, patiently waiting for one of them to make a mistake. So where were they? Where was the scout? Morgan knew Jeb wasn't following. He would've smelled him.

"Is there a problem, mon?" Demery asked, lumbering up beside him.

Morgan rolled his shoulders and squinted behind his sunshades. "Something isn't right," he said.

Demery tilted his head and slowly made a 360-degree turn. "I don't sense anything," he said once he'd finished.

"That's just it. Why aren't they following us?" Morgan asked. "We shot their leader. They should've at least sent the scout out to keep an eye on us."

Demery frowned behind the mask of his protective suit. "You're right. I haven't sensed anyone out there. No one behind or up ahead."

"Me neither, which is odd." Morgan scratched his head. "We should be able to sense someone or something. I realize this place is dead, even more so than the republics, but this is something else." He stared at the sand until his eyes watered.

Demery continued to scan. "It's like we are the only living creatures for miles around."

Morgan nodded in agreement. "I don't like it. Feels wrong. Could be a trap."

At the word "trap," Demery stiffened. "You're being paranoid, mon."

"You heard what the scout said. We have a bounty on our heads. I realize that doesn't include you, but I doubt that would stop anyone from shooting first and asking questions later," Morgan said.

"You're right. I am in danger as long as we're traveling together." Demery glanced at Red.

It was Morgan's turn to tense. "Is that your way of telling me that you're going to leave us out here?" he asked.

"No, mon. I won't be leaving you yet." Demery grinned. "Maybe it's a coincidence we haven't run into anyone. Try not to look a gift lizard in the mouth," he said.

Morgan laughed, but his stomach continued to churn.

It was late afternoon by the time Red woke. The light had begun to turn the sand crimson and orange. Morgan and Demery were huddled beside her in the shade, sleeping. She stood and stretched, reaching her arms above her head before rolling her shoulders. She crawled to the top of the dune, keeping her head down, so she could peek over and scan the area. There was no movement. Red squinted in the direction they were heading.

"Hey guys, I think it flattens out over there," she said.

The two men came awake with a start.

"What?" Morgan asked.

"I think I see a flat area in the direction we need to go." Just the thought of being out of these dunes made Red giddy. She had sand in her boots, pants, hair, and teeth. Pretty much any bit of exposed flesh was covered in grit.

The men rose and joined her on the ridge of the dune. "Have you spotted anything?" Morgan asked.

"No, no movement."

"Then let's go. The sun will be setting in a few hours," Morgan said.

They gathered their equipment and started walking. Just as Red had thought, the dunes gave way to a flat desert valley landscape. The skeletal remains of cactus dotted the area like sentries from the past, their ghostly white bodies a reminder of the fallen. She'd never seen anything more beautiful or more frightening.

Red stopped to empty her boots. Morgan did the same. Demery didn't have to worry about it, since sand couldn't get into his suit during the day. Night was a different story.

She turned to the vamp. "How much farther?"

"Another day's walk from here. We can probably get to within a few miles of the outpost if we walk through the night, but I don't think it's a good idea to cross the mountains in the dark. The hiking trails are treacherous and there are a lot of places for people to hide."

The craggy ridge of sienna-colored mountains stood majestically in the distance. They appeared small, but Red knew they'd be imposing once they got closer. At this pace it would still take several hours to reach them. "We better get going," she said. Maybe they'd get lucky and make good time without being spotted. She judged the time before sunset. There was no way they'd make it to the foothills before dark, which meant they'd be sleeping out in the open. Red didn't like that idea. It left them vulnerable to attack.

They were two hours into their walk when Red spotted a puff of dust rising in the distance. She squinted, watching the plume grow as it drew closer.

"Something's coming," she shouted, glancing around for a place for them to take cover. There was none. "Stay down," she said, rushing them toward the mountains.

She judged the distance between the plume and the mountains and realized they wouldn't make it, but they had to try. They sprinted, keeping low to the ground. Red had hoped they'd blend with the terrain, until she glanced over at Demery's white protective suit. It glowed like a beacon against the flat beige desert floor.

Morgan followed her gaze and cursed under his breath, then ran faster. "We may have to shift," he shouted over his shoulder.

Red nodded in understanding, even as her stomach protested. She'd have to stop in order to shift. She wasn't like Morgan, who could shift in midair. Her process took time and concentration. It must have dawned on Morgan at the same moment because he looked back at her, then around, searching for a place to stop that wasn't quite so out in the open. There wasn't one.

The cloud of dust grew larger. Red could see a glint of metal reflecting off some kind of vehicle. She could also see something else—there was more than one vehicle. There were many, traveling in a convoy. She looked up at the mountains ahead of them. They were closer, too, but not close enough.

"Shift and get out of here," she shouted to Morgan.

He looked at her like she'd lost her mind.

"We may need your help when these people catch up with us."

Demery looked over at the approaching band. "I think I know these people."

"You said that last time and look where it got us," Red said, panting to catch her breath.

"We were doing fine until you killed the leader," Demery retorted. He was slower in his suit, which made him still faster than Red and any pureblood around.

She shot him a sharp glance. "I saved our asses from getting turned over to the authorities."

"Well there are a lot more of these guys. We're out-manned, out-gunned, and out-maneuvered. If this is who I think it is, running won't help," Demery said, starting to slow.

"Who are they?" Red asked, fear coiling in her gut. The vehicles seemed to multiply by the second. Even Morgan looked worried as he pumped his fists harder. His hair had already started to thicken and the muscles in his back and legs began to cord as the change ripped through his body. His clothes tore away, leaving flesh exposed and vulnerable to the unforgiving sun.

Red's lungs burned and her side ached like she'd been kicked by a tactical drill sergeant. She wasn't sure how much farther she could run before she collapsed. Between the heat and the weight of the pack, her body was dehydrating at an astonishing rate. Soon her muscles would cramp and the race would end.

Don't give up now, you're almost there, Red chided herself. *Just a little farther.*

She reached for her pistol and pressed her thumb to the stock. It wasn't much, but Red found the weapon's presence soothing. Children had blankets, she had her gun. She heard a beep and knew she had enough time to charge it, but did she have enough ammo to take out an entire band of armed enemies? The answer was clear. No, she did not.

Red tried to focus on the change, calling to it. Her hands burned as claws forced their way through her fingertips. A burst of energy shot through her, but didn't give her enough added speed to beat the motorized pursuit.

"Demery," she shouted. He didn't answer her immediately. "You said you knew them. Who are they?"

He stopped to face the approaching vehicles. "It's Reaper and the Sand Devils," Demery said, smiling. "We found them at last."

Red looked at the dark cloud of dust that the vehicles were kicking up in their wake, then back at Demery. Why in the hell did it feel like that wasn't a good thing?

chapter fourteen

Raphael awoke to something tickling his stomach. His first reaction was to swat it away. Only when it happened again did he realize what the tickle was . . . Catherine's lips.

He stayed very still, waiting to see what she'd do. She pressed her mouth to his abdomen and slowly made her way down to the front of his pants. Raphael's breath caught.

"I was wondering when you were going to wake up," she said.

His lashes fluttered open to half mast so he could see her. She was straddling him, her knees resting next to his thighs. Her lips were slightly swollen like she'd been kissing him for a while. The fact that he hadn't woken was a testament to his exhaustion and the level of trust he had in her.

"Don't let me stop you," Raphael said, licking a fang.

Catherine's full lips quirked and she leaned forward to lay another open-mouthed kiss on his chest. Her tongue peeked out, tasting his flat nipple through his shirt, hardening it instantly. Raphael gripped the rags and furs beneath him to keep from reaching for her. This one was for her. Catherine needed to be in control. Needed to realize that there was more going on between them than bargains and threats.

Raphael dropped his head back and tried to relax, but her sensual mouth wouldn't let him. Catherine teased his flesh, biting, nibbling, and licking like he was covered in synth-honey. His body bowed beneath her as she reached the waist of his pants.

He wanted her to open them and take him deep into her mouth. Raphael wanted to feel Catherine's lips surround him. Her tongue stroke him. The suction of her mouth, when she drank from him. He was so hard he felt near bursting. One touch, one caress, and he'd spend himself like a teenage boy next to his first naked woman.

Her warm breath caressed the hairs leading into his waistband. Raphael's stomach clenched as she slipped her tongue beneath the material and slowly stroked. He gritted his teeth and grasped the rags tighter. They ripped.

Catherine giggled. "Like that?" she asked.

"You know I do," he said between ragged breaths.

She leaned down and kissed him again, trailing her lips along his abdomen. His eyes followed her every move. Her fingers deftly found the opening to his pants and unfastened them, spreading the material wide. Warm air hit his cock and he gasped.

"What do we have here?" she asked. His erection pulsed, growing under her hungry gaze.

"Damn it, woman," Raphael growled. "Are you trying to torture me?"

"Yes," Catherine said, laughing. "I figure it's only fair, given what you've done to me."

She had a point, but he didn't have to like it. "Fine," Raphael said. "Do what you wish. I am yours for the taking."

That throwaway statement stopped her. Catherine blinked in surprise and looked at him, her gaze searching. The vulnerability he sensed rocked him, shattering what little protection he'd had around his heart. Raphael meant every word and hoped she could see the sincerity in his expression.

"Why would you say such a thing?" she asked.

He met her green eyes. They shimmered with such intensity that it nearly stole his breath. "Because it's the truth," he said softly.

Chaos stared for a moment longer, then reached for

Raphael's shirt. She pulled it over his head, exposing his firm chest. The same chest she'd been kissing seconds ago. He had such a beautiful body, all strong lines and firm walls.

In clothes or naked, he oozed sexuality as easily as most people exhaled. She'd wanted to touch him on her own terms for some time now, but didn't think that was ever going to happen.

She still couldn't believe she'd gotten up the nerve to do so while he was sleeping. Chaos splayed her small hand over his chest, running a finger down the length of dark hair that led to his impressive erection. She longed to taste him there and she would, in a moment, after she'd had her fill of exploring the rest of him.

Chaos stood and stripped the boots off Raphael, taking his pants along with them. When she'd finished, he was lying against the makeshift rest pad, gloriously naked. She allowed her eyes to feast, taking in every inch of him. He lay back so erotically male, waiting to be worshipped.

A smile played on his lips as he watched her. He looked to be getting as much pleasure from this encounter as she was. Why that surprised Chaos, she didn't know. Maybe she'd thought he only got off while using high-handed tactics.

His expression said otherwise. Raphael was a creature of pleasure—both giving and receiving. He wasn't selfish as she'd initially thought. She'd misunderstood his earlier actions. Chaos wondered what else she'd misunderstood about the man.

"Don't move." She slowly undressed.

Raphael's eyes darkened, heating in the low light, and his breathing deepened. The muscles in his arms quivered, but he didn't move. He only watched. His hunger was palpable.

"What are you planning to do?" he asked, his voice a rough rasp that puckered her nipples.

His eyes followed her body's responses, taking in every change, every subtle nuance as her need grew. Like a predator, he was clocking her weaknesses, waiting for a chance to pounce.

Chaos dropped to her knees and straddled his thighs once

again. His cock bucked against his abdomen causing pre-seminal fluid to leak. She began at Raphael's neck and slowly kissed her way down his body. He gasped when Chaos bit his collarbone, then groaned as she soothed the sting with a swipe of her tongue.

His cock rose with every embrace to brush the moisture gathering between her legs. By the time Chaos reached his shaft, she was drenched and his body was covered in sweat.

She grabbed him at the base, then met his gaze before slowly sucking him into her mouth. His nostrils flared as she drew on him deeply before releasing him and repeating the whole process again. Raphael let out a strangled cry. His hands bit into her shoulders as he clung to her.

"Your mouth is amazing," he said, rolling his hips to chase her retreating lips. "So hot. So moist." He groaned. "And so damn good. Please," he said, breathlessly, his entire body tense with desire.

Chaos giggled around his cock, then ran her tongue along the underside until she reached his balls. She sucked one testis into her mouth while gently palming the other. A small amount of fluid shot out of Raphael's shaft and his entire body trembled as he fought to stave off release. A sense of power washed over Chaos, knowing she had—at least for now—this extremely powerful man under her control and craving her touch. She reveled in the feeling, even though it made her body ache.

Arousing Raphael had backfired. Chaos ground her clit into his hard thigh to get some relief. It was the wrong thing to do. Instead of easing her need, the small movement made it worse. She whimpered around Raphael's sac then gradually released him.

Raphael's eyes were clouded with desire, his gaze locked on her hand as she encircled his length. Chaos rose, positioning her body over his cock, and then slowly lowered herself onto him.

His lungs heaved, bellowing loudly as Raphael disappeared into her entrance only to reappear seconds later.

She rode him slowly, rocking her hips, so she could grind her clit between thrusts. He felt so good, so big and hard, filling her completely. Chaos couldn't remember a better fit or a sexier man than Raphael. He was slowly but surely erasing every man from her memory and she was letting him. But could she trust him with more than her body?

She rose to her knees. The heated glide of his shaft was exquisite as it stroked in and out. The need built inside Chaos until she couldn't take it anymore. She reached for her clit and plucked at her swollen flesh while she bounced up and down, faster and faster. The wet sound of skin slapping skin filled the tent. The world narrowed between them as the primal dance continued.

Their eyes met and what Chaos saw shimmering in Raphael's black depths stole her breath. A moment later, she was plummeting. Falling further, faster, and harder than she'd ever tumbled before. Power rushed out of her body, encircling them in a cocoon of chaotic energy. Raphael convulsed beneath her, his hips rolling up, driving his cock deep. A cry wrenched from Chaos' throat and her body jolted on top of him, dimming her vision and deafening her.

By the time the wave allowed her to come up for air, Chaos was sprawled across Raphael's chest and he was stroking her back. Her breathing was coming in great pants and she noticed one more thing—he was still hard as a boulder.

"I thought you . . ." she started, trying to get her thoughts together.

He smiled. "This one was for you." He continued, caressing her with his short nails.

"But I wanted you—" Chaos began.

"And you had me," Raphael said before she could finish.

"You didn't climax," she said, frowning.

Raphael smoothed her brow. "I need a little something more," he said, without clarifying.

"More?" She was worn out. Chaos didn't think her body could handle more after that orgasm. It took her a moment to realize what he meant. Raphael hadn't taken her blood this time. His words came back to her. *This time was for you*. He'd purposely held off biting her so she could be in charge. Something in Chaos' heart melted. Something she thought would never thaw. She reached up and brushed her short hair aside.

Raphael's heart stuttered in his chest as Catherine bared her neck to him. He licked his lips before he could stop himself. "No." He shook his head. "This one was for you. If I take your blood, it'll change everything."

"Not if it's freely given," she said, tilting her head a little farther until the muscle bulged.

Raphael's nostrils flared as he fought the urge to yank her to him. Instead, he made S shapes up her back with his fingertip, then threaded his hands into her short red hair. He pulled her mouth to his and kissed her deeply and passionately. Tasting, touching, stroking, and coaxing her tongue to tangle with his. She'd done a good job of avoiding the intimate act earlier. Perhaps she thought it would somehow protect her. But Raphael would have none of it. He wanted all of her, demanded nothing less than complete surrender.

Catherine was tentative at first, as if she wasn't used to being kissed. Her style was clumsy and endearing. He vowed that would change under his tutelage.

He pulled back, letting her take charge and set the pace. Raphael waited for her to relax. They clanked teeth and mashed lips in a clumsy mating that made his heart melt with its purity and sheer innocence. When things fell into a natural rhythm, Raphael deepened the embrace, tasting her once more with his tongue, worrying her lips with his teeth. He made sure to keep his fangs retracted. He didn't want to accidentally cut her and send himself into a frenzy. Catherine followed his lead, then slowly took over.

Raphael could feel her body responding to the embrace. Her swollen nipples hardened as they brushed his chest. He pulled her close and kept kissing her. She tasted so fresh, so clean, utterly wrong for him, but that didn't stop him from taking what she offered.

He wanted her. Hell, he needed her. And Raphael hadn't needed anyone for a long time. He knew he was in trouble as Catherine's weight settled on top of him. He released her hair and ran his hands down her body, grasping her ass. It was small and compact, much like the woman. He squeezed, grinding her hips into him. His cock thickened as it surged toward release.

Raphael broke the embrace, trailing kisses over her eyes and cheeks. Catherine's breath was coming out in great gasps as he made his way to her ear. He nibbled on her lobe, before dipping his tongue inside. She gasped, her body clenching him tight. Raphael knew in that moment that he wasn't the only one anticipating the bite.

"Do you want me?" he murmured in her ear.

"You know I do," she said, rolling her hips.

"All of me," he asked, running his fangs along the column of her throat.

"Yes," Catherine hissed, slamming her body down on his erection.

Raphael groaned. "You're not playing fair," he said, biting her lobe before returning to nuzzle her neck.

"I never do," she said. "You of all people should know that by now."

Raphael growled and bit down. Catherine exploded on contact, her body riding another orgasm. Her hot blood rushed into his mouth. His senses came alive, cataloguing the moment like a voyeur. The musk, the sweet taste of her essence on his tongue, the tight grip she had on his shaft, and the need that kept building and building inside of him. Raphael pumped his hips, driving her down until she was locked tight.

Damn it, he couldn't get enough traction. Without thought, he rolled them, never breaking contact. He tongued her neck, while drawing from the wound. God, she tasted and felt so good. His hips rocked, then pumped hard as the fucking became animalistic in its fervor. Raphael threw his head back and roared in triumph.

He was half out of his mind and blood drunk by the time he followed Catherine into oblivion. His body emptied for what felt like an eternity. When he was finally spent, Raphael collapsed to the side, pulling her close and tucking her small frame against his chest.

It took some time, but her breathing finally leveled out. Soon she'd be asleep. Raphael stroked Catherine's hip, trying to maintain consciousness, but it was a losing battle. She'd sapped his strength, leaving him deliciously spent in every way.

"That was the most amazing thing I've ever experienced," Raphael said, knowing now he'd never be able to let her go.

They rose in the late afternoon. Chaos gathered her pack, struggling to get it on her shoulders. Raphael walked over and plucked it out of her hands. He handed her his smaller pack, then tossed hers onto his back.

"Let's switch for a while," he said, securing her pack into place.

Chaos opened her mouth to protest, but closed it quickly, secretly grateful. She shrugged into his pack and then flipped up the tent flap. The fire in the moat had died down, but was still enough of a deterrent to keep the predators away. Not that it would matter, since they'd be leaving the safety of the fire ring soon.

She stepped through the opening and scanned the area around them. Chaos didn't see anything, but waited for Raphael to confirm her observations before going any further.

He followed her as she walked past the tents toward the thin strip of sand that acted as a safe crossing spot.

"Do you think we'll ever catch up with them?" she asked.

Raphael looked at her, then at the empty area surrounding them. "Yes, as long as they don't encounter any trouble."

"What about us?" she asked.

Raphael caught her chin in his fingertips, his black gaze burning in the fading light. "I won't let anything happen to you," he said with such conviction her heart clenched.

Chaos swallowed hard. "I'd appreciate if you kept yourself out of harm's way while you're at it."

His expression softened, but before he could say anything they might both regret, she said, "Let's go. We have a lot of ground to cover before dawn."

He nodded, but the knowledge she saw in those black eyes unnerved her.

Raphael followed Catherine feeling more content than he'd ever felt in his lifetime. He still wasn't sure what that meant, but he was happy to wait for the answer.

Once they reached a rise atop a particularly high dune, Raphael closed his eyes and inhaled deeply.

Michael, can you hear me? he asked, using the psychic channel they'd used as children.

Silence met his call.

Michael, I know you can hear me. You're close. I can sense you near. Why do you not answer?

A breeze picked up, rustling his hair.

Brother, please don't play this silly game. We've been apart long enough. He pleaded.

Raphael? The voice was quiet, hesitant, almost unrecognizable.

Michael, it's me. Where are you? I searched everywhere after Morgan said you were injured. Your silence concerns me. Let me see with my own eyes that you are well.

I'm camped to the south. Where are you?

I just left a nomadic settlement. Raphael paused, wondering whether he should mention the dead. Michael would sense it if he held back anything. *There were bodies. Lots of bodies.*

Michael ignored the mention of bodies as if they were of no consequence. Or perhaps it was because he already knew. Raphael's unease grew. He knew he'd protect Catherine with his life, but what if the person he was trying to protect her from was his brother, Michael? Ice filled his veins.

"Are you okay?" Catherine asked. She'd stopped when he hadn't followed. "Is something wrong?"

"I'm fine," Raphael said eventually. "I am trying to contact my brother, *using the method I spoke to you with.*" He finished the last half in her mind.

"Still not comfortable communicating that way. I'll be over here. Come get me when you're done," she said, pointing to a spot not far from where she currently stood. It was enough space to give him privacy—not that he needed it.

Michael, are you still there? Raphael called out again.

Yes, you were about to tell me who you are traveling with, he said.

It was Raphael's turn to pause. He hadn't mentioned he was traveling with anyone.

Come now, brother. Don't be shy, Michael teased. *Who is she?*

Her name is Catherine Meyers. She's a member of IPTT.

The news was met with more silence.

We've reached an agreement. I take full responsibility for her. I think it would be best if we met up and traveled together.

How did you know I'd be here? he asked.

Raphael thought about it, then decided to once again answer truthfully. *I searched your home. When I saw your bag was missing, I had a pretty good idea of where you were headed. The only question I have is why?*

Michael sighed mentally, but Raphael heard it.

It's a long story, brother. Much has happened since we last saw each other.

I've heard some troubling news, but the full story remains murky. Care to clear things up for me? Raphael asked.

I won't wait long. Michael ignored his request and sent him a mental picture of his surroundings.

We'll hurry, Raphael said, breaking the connection. They needed to reach Michael. He could feel it in his gut. His brother was on the edge of being lost and Raphael was determined to save him.

"Did you talk to him?" Catherine asked, rising from the spot she'd been sitting in.

"Yes." Raphael nodded.

"And?"

"He is waiting for us to the south. I've seen his small shelter. It's tucked between the dunes."

Catherine looked around and laughed. "Everything here is tucked between dunes."

Raphael smiled. "I've seen what he can see from the top of the dunes surrounding him. I'll know it when we get close." He looked around to get his bearings.

She hesitated. "It's none of my business, but are you sure this is a good idea?"

"Meeting up with Michael or traipsing out in the middle of no-man's-land without an army?" Raphael asked.

She snorted. "The prior. I mean the guy hasn't exactly gone out of his way to speak to you. And I know you've been trying to contact him."

She had a good point and Raphael knew it. These were all questions he'd asked himself and had yet to come up with satisfactory answers. What had Roark Montgomery done to his brother to create the screams that Morgan had heard? Why had his brother been avoiding him? Why was his brother after Morgan and Red, when he'd sworn to help them? All good questions that Raphael had no real answers for.

"It would be safer traveling with my brother," he said quietly, hoping it was the truth.

"No offense, but your brother didn't look like much of a fighter when I met him," Catherine said.

"In this instance, looks can be very deceiving. Michael is the most dangerous man I know."

Her face scrunched. "I thought you owned that title."

Raphael laughed, the sound painful to his ears, and shook his head slowly. She had no idea how very dangerous his brother could be. And he prayed that remained the case for her sake—and his.

Her world was swathed in shades of black and white. There was no gray, only right and wrong. Catherine had no clue how violent a human being could become when survival was on the line, but Raphael and his brother did. They'd lived in hell and walked out the other side, brushing flames off as they went. "You should know, little storm, that even though I'm extremely dangerous, I am defenseless compared to my brother, Michael."

"Good thing you brought me with you." Catherine grinned.

"If only it were a joking matter," Raphael said softly.

Her expression grew pensive. "How can you love him if he's such a monster?" she asked, her eyes the size of synth-steaks.

Raphael slipped into her mind and saw she hadn't meant to offend him, so he answered her query with one of his own. "I think the better question is, can you learn to love a monster?"

chapter fifteen

aphael and Catherine found Michael Travers exactly where he said he'd be waiting. His campsite was packed up and he was pacing like he could bolt any second. His skin was paler than usual and Raphael noted a slight tremor in his hands.

Raphael put an arm out and stopped her. "Wait here." He needed to see how his brother was doing. Michael didn't look well.

"If you need me, yell." She patted her gun.

"I'll be all right. He's my brother," he said, not sounding as confident as he would've liked. "Michael," Raphael called out.

Michael stopped pacing and turned to face him. For a moment, it was like they'd never been apart. Happiness showed on his face, reminding Raphael of the boy who had followed him to school every day. The joy was gone as quickly as it appeared. His eyes narrowed when they landed on Catherine.

"It's me, Raphael."

"I know who you are. Do you think I would not recognize my own brother?" Michael continued to stare at Catherine, his gaze cold and assessing.

Raphael waved his arms, drawing his brother's attention away. His heart was hammering in his chest, threatening to batter his lungs into jelly. He stopped a few feet away from

Michael, noticing for the first time the dark circles under his eyes.

"What are you doing out here?" Raphael asked.

"The same thing as you, I suspect," Michael said.

"I doubt it." Raphael replied. "What happened to you?" he asked, taking in Michael's torn clothing and scraped knuckles. He looked as if he'd been on the losing end of a fight. Raphael thought about the dead nomads they'd encountered.

Michael glanced at him. Cold swept over Raphael despite the heat.

"Michael, tell me what's happened so I can fix it," he said, sounding desperate. He needed to reach him. He hadn't found his brother after all these years only to lose him again. Michael was his only family.

Raphael glanced over his shoulder at Catherine. Her hand rested casually on her weapon, but there was nothing casual about her stance. He willed her to stand down, even though she was only trying to protect him. Something in his chest softened. It was evidence of how shaken Raphael was that he'd forgotten he could mentally communicate with her.

"I can smell the woman on you. Her scent covers you like cologne," Michael said. This time his gaze was assessing. "She is prepared to shed blood in order to protect you."

"So? A woman's scent on me is nothing new." Raphael shrugged and kept his expression placid, even though he was feeling something akin to panic inside. Catherine was his. He wouldn't share her body or her blood. Brotherly love wouldn't change that fact.

"She looks familiar."

"You've run into her in passing."

Michael grunted in response. "When do you plan on dumping her?" he asked. "She won't be able to keep up the pace we set."

"I'll release her when the time feels right," Raphael said. *It would never happen.*

"Typical," Michael said.

Raphael shook his head. His brother wouldn't understand. "There is nothing typical about this one," he said.

That got a rise out of Michael's left brow. "You'll have to tell me all about it, brother, especially what makes this one so special. She doesn't seem like your . . . *type*."

"I have a type?" Raphael asked.

Michael laughed. "Not that I recall." He opened his arms and walked forward.

Raphael stepped into the embrace. "I've missed you," he said, relaxing. Michael seemed normal enough. Contrary to Morgan's assessment, he wasn't showing any signs of distress. Maybe things weren't as bad as Raphael thought.

"Me, too," Michael said. "Now tell your woman to get her hand off the gun stock. I'm not going to bite."

Raphael shook Michael's hand, then waved to Catherine.

Chaos came forward cautiously. Raphael's expression was one of relief. She wished she could say the same for his brother's. Something about Michael Travers left her cold. She didn't know whether it was his black eyes or his pale gray complexion.

She glanced at Raphael, who had the same features, but somehow less defined. Raphael was a rough draft to Michael's polished finish. Chaos continued to stare, cataloguing each man's features. She decided it wasn't the color of the eyes that told the real story; it was what she saw in them. Death.

If Michael Travers felt anything, he didn't show it. Looking into his eyes was like staring into the abyss. Chaos didn't like what she saw reflecting on the calm surface. A shiver traversed her body despite the heat of the evening. He was everything Raphael described and more. How could she have ever thought he was incapable of murder?

Michael practically vibrated with barely leashed violence.

Raphael said they'd be safer traveling together, but Chaos wasn't so sure now that she'd gotten a good look at his brother with his tattered clothes and wild eyes that burned with madness.

"Come here," Raphael said. "I know you've met my brother briefly, but I'd like to introduce you properly."

"Catherine Meyers, I'd like you to meet my brother, Michael Vega," Raphael said.

"I thought you said your name was Travers," she said, staring past Raphael to meet Michael's black gaze.

"It is. I changed my last name long ago, when I thought . . ." his words trailed off as he looked at Raphael.

"We thought we'd lost each other," Raphael said. "We only recently reunited. It was a joyous day for us both."

Love shined in Raphael's face. It was so bright that its brilliance nearly blinded Chaos. She'd never had any siblings or parents for that matter. She'd never had anyone to call family besides the clones she was raised with, and even then, she knew she'd never really be one of them. Chaos hadn't been created, she'd been born. Her parents just hadn't wanted her. She'd gotten over it, but every once in awhile, when she witnessed this kind of love, it drove home all she'd missed.

Chaos stuck out her hand. "Nice to meet you," she said.

Michael grasped her fingers and she felt a mental push that didn't feel like Raphael's gentle presence. *You don't have to pretend,* the voice said. *I sense the truth.*

She knew it was Michael, but didn't understand how he was able to speak directly in her mind. *Yes, I do,* she said, responding in kind. *For Raphael's sake.*

His lip canted into what Chaos guessed was supposed to be a smile. "It's a pleasure to see you again." *I know you don't care for me,* he added mentally.

Do you blame me? The last time I saw you I ended up drugged out of my mind. She didn't add that she went out and killed people afterward. *Your boss is a real piece of work.*

I had nothing to do with that, I assure you.

Raphael said you'd say that, she said.

But you don't believe him.

Now that I've gotten a look at you, no. She shook her head.

It's the truth. I don't act in such covert ways. Once you get to know me, you'll find I'm quite direct. It was said nonchalantly, but the threat was apparent.

Really? Then what are you doing here? Chaos asked. *Taking in the sights?*

Michael gave her a real smile this time. "She's clever, brother," he said. "You'd better watch her closely. I know I will."

Raphael's grin seemed forced. He pulled Chaos close. "I rarely take my eyes off her."

"That's evident," Michael said, acknowledging their embrace. "I've never seen you quite so taken. She must *really* be special."

A slash of red covered Raphael's cheeks. He released Chaos as if she had singed his fingertips. "Well, I . . ." he stammered.

"Eloquent as always." Michael slapped him on the back and chuckled. His warm gaze moved from his brother to Chaos, where it quickly cooled. *You better not hurt him,* he warned.

Funny, I was about to say the same thing to you, she said.

The dust continued to grow, its ominous brown plume billowing up as the vehicles barreled toward them. The sound of the engines rumbled like thunder.

"We have to make a stand," Red shouted to Morgan.

"There's no cover," he said. "It would be a slaughter."

"I'll try to talk with them," Demery said, giving Red a quick smile. He kept approaching the Sand Devils.

"What if they aren't in the mood to reason?" Red asked. "They may know about the reward, too."

"Probably, but it doesn't matter. The sun will be down soon." Demery said. "We aren't going to make it to the rocks in time and even if we did, they know this area ten times better than I do. It's where they hunt. Besides, they have something of mine."

Her heart stuttered in her chest at the thought of being hunted and she tripped as she turned back to Morgan. Red barely kept from falling. She'd always been the predator, never the prey.

Morgan's gaze fell to her. She was the reason they couldn't

make it to the mountains before the Sand Devil vehicles reached them. Red knew it and could see the blame clearly in his amber eyes. Once again her inability to control her Other was putting them in danger just like back in Nuria. Despite all her progress, nothing had changed.

I'm sorry, she mouthed, then looked away unable to meet Morgan's gaze for fear she'd see condemnation. Red turned to face the group approaching from the west.

They didn't have much left to trade with, but they could part with a few items. She hoped that would be enough, because they didn't have the firepower to fight their way out.

The Sand Devils came to a halt thirty yards away. The windows had been replaced with metal, leaving slits for the drivers to see out.

Red couldn't spot any of the people. They remained tucked in their vehicles like turtles inside of metal shells. Demery stepped forward in his protective suit and held his arms wide. Morgan moved closer to Red, positioning his body between her and the group.

"Who's in charge here?" Demery shouted through his suit.

No one in the steel convoy replied.

"My name is Demery. Perhaps some of you know me," he said, loudly. "I seek Reaper."

A door to one of the vehicles in the rear popped open and a long-limbed beautiful woman with skin like the night sky poked her head out and looked at them.

"Demi, is that you?" she cried and bounded out of the vehicle toward him. She wore a long skirt and top that matched the desert. It flowed around her slim frame. Her feet were bare and callused from walking on the sand.

"Melea?" Demery rushed forward and caught the woman as she leapt into his arms. "I've missed you so much," he said, holding her close.

"I knew you'd come back for me." She hugged him like she'd never let him go.

Demery pulled back and brushed her long braided hair

away from her face. "Are you well? Has he been—" Demery's voice broke. He glanced at Red and Morgan as if remembering that they were still there.

"I'm fine," she said, tears filling her big brown eyes.

"Melea, time to return to your rightful place," a baritone voice boomed. "Your blood and I have business to discuss."

Red and Morgan looked at each other as a massive man stepped out of the same vehicle Melea had been in only moments ago. Standing head and shoulders taller than the roof of the vehicle, the man's body was corded with muscle. A snake tattoo started at his neck, then curled down around his arm before its head ended at his closed mallet-sized fist. Metal piercings twinkled in the fading sunlight, protruding out of his shaven head like horns. He was not a handsome man. From his pulverized appearance, Red could tell he had participated in plenty of fights. The altercations had left his nose winding like a potholed road down his face.

"I'm not going to ask you again, Melea," the man growled, flashing teeth that had been filed into sharp points.

Demery held the woman tighter. "We had a deal, Reaper," he said.

"And I've kept my side of the bargain," Reaper said. "Your woman is in more or less the same condition you left her in."

Demery pulled Melea back to have a good look at her.

The woman was a little underweight and scraped up, but otherwise appeared fine as far as Red could tell.

What in the hell was going on? Who was this woman? Was she the item he'd needed to pick up? What had Reaper meant by blood? Red didn't like the sound of that, considering that a vampire was involved. "Demery," Red called out.

He shook his head, warning her to remain silent.

"Who are your friends?" Reaper asked.

"No one of consequence," Demery said. "I believe we have business to discuss."

Red didn't like this, and from the tension pouring off Morgan, neither did he. Demery obviously knew these people, but why had he left this woman with Reaper? Did he have a choice? She thought about everything Demery had told her at the Sand Mole compound. He hadn't shared much beyond his love for zigzag quartz. He'd made the arrangement with the Sand Devils sound casual. Yet if the woman was involved, their business here was anything but casual.

Morgan reached back for her hand. "We may have to make a run for it," he whispered under his breath. He'd obviously been thinking the same thing as she had.

"What about Demery?" Red asked.

"He can take care of himself," he said.

"But he's the only one who knows where the outpost is located," she reminded him. "We can't leave him with these people."

From his sour expression he must've forgotten and hadn't appreciated the reminder.

"We can't outrun these vehicles," Red said, judging the distance to the foothills of the mountains.

The man approached Demery and plucked Melea out of his arms. Reaper shoved the woman back toward the vehicle and demanded she get inside. She fell to her knees. Her shoulders were slumped and it looked as if she were about to cry. Demery tensed like he wanted to stop him, but he didn't act. His hands curled into fists until his knuckles popped under the pressure.

Red's free hand moved slowly to her laser pistol.

"I wouldn't if I were you," Reaper said, indicating to the armed people who'd left their vehicles and taken up position behind him.

Red flexed her fingers and forced her hands to relax.

"Let's talk," Demery said, stepping forward. The movement took Reaper's attention off Red, whether by accident or on purpose, she didn't know. "I'll be right back," he said.

Morgan and Red watched Demery disappear into a far vehicle with the big man following behind.

"What do you think they're discussing?" Red asked.

"No idea, but I wish like hell I did," Morgan said.

"Do you know what Reaper meant when he called Demery blood?"

"No," Morgan said, but that wasn't entirely the truth. He

had an idea of what "blood" meant, but didn't want to say anything to Gina until he was certain.

He'd known a few vamps over the years, but other than Raphael Vega, they'd kept mainly to themselves. Morgan had heard rumors about blood bonds, but they were rare from what he could gather. Not because of any kind of fear on the donors' part, but because a bond was rumored to make a vamp vulnerable to attack.

Morgan didn't understand how they worked, but knew it was some kind of symbiotic relationship. Hurt the donor, hurt them both. He looked at Gina. He may not understand a blood bond, but he was well aware of the pain he experienced when he'd thought he had lost his mate.

"What do we do now?" Gina asked, looking at him as if he held all the answers.

Times like these Morgan wished he did. "We wait," he said, taking a seat on the ground.

"That's it?" she asked.

He grabbed her hand and pulled her down next to him. "That's all we can do until Demery comes out."

Demery sat next to Reaper and waited for the big man to settle. It was difficult to be in the same space with the beast. Even inside his protective suit he could smell the taint of cruelty wafting from the behemoth's skin.

"It's been a long time," Reaper said.

"Yes, it has, mon," Demery agreed. "I tried to get back here sooner, but I had to locate the goods for holding up my part of the bargain."

"And have you?" he asked.

Demery's gut twisted over what he was about to do, but what choice did he have? Melea wouldn't last much longer out here with the Sand Devils, and if something traumatic happened to her while he was so near, Demery would experience it, too. He had to get her away from Reaper so he could get his life back. He just hadn't had time to broach the subject with Morgan and Red yet. He was sure once they understood the seriousness of the situation they'd be more than happy to help. "Did you notice the man I'm traveling with?" Demery asked.

"I miss nothing," Reaper said, eyeing him cautiously.

"He carries what you need, mon," he said, hoping he could at least keep Red and his blood safe. Demery didn't want to leave the sheriff behind, since he'd been kind to him, and wouldn't if he could avoid it, but this was no-man's-land. The rules of survival were different here.

"Are we talking wolf blood?" Reaper asked.

He nodded. "Yes."

"He was a wolf soldier?" he asked.

"Yes," Demery repeated. "He's one of the originals, mon."

"What about the woman?" Reaper asked. "She looks like she holds some potential."

Demery kept his expression blank. His protective visor helped conceal the tension thrumming through him. "She is a pureblood I picked up for feeding purposes only."

"Pity." Reaper smiled, his sharklike teeth menacing. "Does the wolf know about our deal?"

"Yes," Demery lied, ignoring the bile rising in his throat. He forced his thoughts back to Melea. Soon the sun would be down and he'd be able to remove this tiresome suit and feel his blood's skin in his hands. Taste her essence on his lips. The moment would be bittersweet given the price of the privilege.

"The wolf doesn't look like someone who'll readily give up his blood," Reaper said, anticipation lighting his features. "I may have to take it."

"Since when has that ever stopped you?" Demery asked.

"Never!" Reaper threw his pierced bald head back and laughed. "Force makes the blood taste better. It makes a lot of things better." His gaze flitted over the women standing nearby.

Demery's stomach pitched. He did not envy Morgan. He needed to talk to the sheriff. Convince him this small sacrifice was their only way out of this situation. "This concludes our deal," he said. "Melea comes with me and so does the other woman."

"Getting greedy in your old age," Reaper said, watching him carefully.

"No," Demery said, sadly. "Just hungry."

chapter sixteen

Raphael watched Michael as they made their way south. He'd been looking for any odd behavior. A twitch, a flash of anger, anything to explain his brother's reluctance to be near them. Thus far he'd seen nothing. Had Roark lied to Morgan? It wouldn't be the first time.

Michael hadn't said much since they joined him on his journey. Not that he had ever been chatty, but this was too quiet, even for him. Michael was thinking and that made Raphael nervous. When his brother focused his thoughts, people died.

"Do you have any new information on Red and Morgan?" Raphael asked. He had no doubt his brother would know more than him and Catherine. Roark was nothing if not thorough.

Michael glanced over his shoulder. "Nothing beyond the reward for their capture," he said, but his expression told a different story. Even as kids, Raphael had always been able to tell when Michael was lying. His brother had gotten better at deception over the years—they both had in order to survive, but his eyebrow still twitched when he lied. Or in this case, withheld the truth.

Raphael stopped as Michael's words registered. "There's a reward? What kind of reward?" And why was this the first time he was hearing about it?

His dark gaze flicked to him. "Roark had me issue a bulletin before I left," Michael said without further explanation.

Dread seeped into Raphael's bones. If people in no-man's-land knew there was a reward for Red and Morgan, then no place would be safe. He thought about the dead nomads they'd encountered. Had they known about the reward? Was that why they were dead?

Raphael quickly dismissed the idea, since bulletins weren't issued in no-man's-land. The fence wasn't the only divide between the republics and this area; communications were also kept out. For all intents and purpose, no-man's-land was perpetually in the dark. "What exactly did the bulletin say?" Raphael asked.

"Fifteen thousand credits for the person or people who bring in Red and Morgan." He shrugged as if the whole conversation was boring him. Maybe it was. Michael always was a little different. Even as a child he'd been detached.

"If you needed credits, all you had to do was ask." Raphael frowned and looked at his brother with fresh eyes. He peered beneath his disheveled appearance to the heart of the man.

"Stop staring at me," Michael said. "I don't need your pity or your credits."

"Red and Morgan aren't in the republics," Raphael said, instead of asking the question he wanted to ask. He'd have to wait until he could get his brother alone. "Why would Roark send that message out? It doesn't make sense."

"The notification wasn't for the republics. It went out to no-man's-land," Michael said.

Raphael flinched. "That's impossible. Not even Roark can broadcast to this area without permission."

"When are you going to learn?" Michael laughed, an ugly grating sound that hurt to listen to. "Roark can do anything he wants and there's not a damn thing anyone can do to stop him."

He shook his head in disbelief. "What are you really doing here, Michael?" Raphael asked, watching for the telltale sign to indicate a lie. He'd asked him before, but his brother had brushed off the question with a nonanswer. Raphael had planned to wait, but now it seemed imperative to know.

"Like everyone else in no-man's-land, I'm trying to collect." Michael's voice nearly gave Raphael frostbite for all the emotion it held.

"You've never cared about credits," he said.

"Things change," Michael said. His brow twitched, exposing the lie.

Chaos wasn't concerned about rewards or Morgan Hunter, but she'd sworn to the commander that she'd do her best to bring his granddaughter back and that's what she planned to do. Roark putting a bounty on their heads didn't help her cause. The job had already been difficult. Greed made even the sanest person crazy.

She realized it was a good possibility she'd have to go through Michael to fight her way out of this place. Chaos had no doubt she'd lose Raphael if she did. So much for future relationship plans—not that she'd made any. Or even thought about making any plans with Raphael. But they had shared a few precious moments.

Chaos looked at Michael. He avoided her gaze. Something was amiss in his story and she was determined to find out what. "Why would Roark send you in, when he could wait for someone to bring Morgan and Red to him?" she asked, genuinely curious. "I mean credits are nice, but there has to be more to it." Roark struck her as someone who loved to delegate duties. Without Michael around he had no one to order around.

"I suppose it's because I'll bring them back alive," he said, not sparing her a glance. "Can't say the same for the people who received the bulletin."

Chaos' heart did a nosedive to her knees. What if Red was killed before she could reach her? What would she do then? She couldn't exactly bring Gina Santiago's body back to IPTT and expect the commander to understand.

Raphael grabbed Michael's arm and hauled him to a stop. "Why does Roark want them dead?"

"They're a threat to his political campaign. Now if you'll

excuse me, I have to check in." Michael reached into his pack and pulled out a navcom. He pressed a button and spoke into a small microphone. "Target is still at large," he said. "Repeat, target has yet to be located."

Roark's voice crackled. "You know what needs to be done. Let me know when you find them."

"Affirmative." Michael turned the device off.

"We could've used that earlier," Chaos said. It would've come in handy, since her navcom hadn't worked since they crossed the fence.

"Doubtful," Michael said. "It only works with its twin. It would have to be rewired to send a message out anywhere else."

So much for contacting the commander to warn him about the bounty. The navcom wouldn't do much good if all it could do was contact Roark. Of course, she might get some personal satisfaction from telling him exactly where he could go.

"Do you plan to kill them when you find them?" Chaos asked.

"No," Michael said. "I already told you, I intend to bring them back alive."

Chaos watched Raphael tense. "Back to what exactly? Prison? A tribunal? Will the law be involved in any way?" Doubtful given Roark's actions to date. Chaos had the overwhelming urge to shoot something or someone. Her gaze landed on a likely candidate.

"You ask a lot of questions," Michael said.

"And you aren't exactly forthcoming with answers," she said. "You did say you planned on bringing them *both* back, correct?"

"Are you deaf or are you just trying to annoy me?" Michael asked. "I'm taking them both to Roark. That's clear enough for even you to understand. Honestly, brother, I don't see what you see in this woman." He gave Raphael a censorious look.

Chaos couldn't let him have Red. Before she could tell him so, Raphael reached out and squeezed her arm, silencing her.

He looked at Michael. "We'll decide what to do with Morgan and Red, when and if we find them."

They traveled on in tense silence. No one felt the need to speak, but there was no doubt plans were being made. Even the closeness she'd felt with Raphael before meeting up with his brother had somehow fractured. A wedge by the name of Michael Travers Vega had been driven between them. She missed the connection, missed their bantering. And wondered if they'd ever get it back.

Demery exited the vehicle with a grim expression on his face. The sun had gone down, so he carefully removed his protective suit. He approached Morgan and Red, debating how to tell them the truth. Perhaps, if he had sufficient time to explain, Morgan would voluntarily give up some of his blood. Demery was sure he could convince Reaper to take less, if he had the time and Morgan's cooperation. He opened his mouth to ask, but caught the sheriff's narrow-eyed expression. His wolf was suspicious—not that Demery could blame him. He'd be if he were in Morgan's position.

"What's happening?" Red asked. "What did Reaper want?"

"It's taken care of," Demery said in lieu of explanation. He couldn't exactly blurt it out and take the chance that they'd bolt. He needed a drink. Maybe after a few games of zigzag quartz, he'd come up with the right approach.

"What does that mean?" she asked, looking at Morgan.

Reaper exited the vehicle behind him. "It means you will be our guests for tonight," he said. It wasn't a request.

"Demery?" Red asked. "What is he talking about? I thought you were going to get the item and we'd be on our way."

"We will. Later I'll explain everything." He clasped her arm and their gazes met briefly. "You just have to trust me. I promise we'll be out of here by tomorrow." Demery didn't look at Morgan. He grabbed his pack without explaining further and went toward the vehicle containing Melea. What else could he say to Red that wouldn't upset her? Nothing.

So he said nothing. She'd forgive him eventually. They both would once they learned why he'd agreed to the deal. Yet even as the thought crossed his mind, Demery knew it wasn't the truth. Red would kill him the first chance she got. That's what an alpha female did when faced with the threat of losing her mate. And Red would definitely never forgive him. Fortunately, she was in good company.

"I have a bad feeling about this," Morgan said.

"So do I," Red said. "What do you think he did? It's not like Demery to be *this* cagey."

He shrugged. "Whatever he's up to doesn't bode well for us," Morgan said. "The scent of the big man has changed to one of anticipation. I can smell it and depravity in his sweat. He practically vibrated with excitement when he said we'd be staying the night."

Red inhaled. The rancid odor remained trapped on the hot breeze. "He's not an Other, is he?"

Morgan shook his head. "No, he's something far worse."

"Is that why he smells funny?" Red asked.

"Yes. He reeks of perversion and violence."

Her grandfather had warned her that there were worse things out there than unknowns. She hadn't believed him at the time. She'd thought he was just being overly protective. Red realized now she should've listened. Her life was in shambles. They were severely outnumbered by Sand Devils, whose pure-blood leader went out of his way to appear animalistic. She didn't know how he'd accomplished such a feat, but she had no intention to stick around and find out. They needed to grab Demery and get out of here.

Her attention turned to their dreadlocked guide, who'd disappeared into another vehicle. Demery was up to something. She could tell by the way he carried himself and the fact he hadn't been able to look her in the eye since they met up with the Sand Devils. She trusted this man, this vamp, with her life. Had grown to like him and depend on him as any tactical team member would. He'd stood by her when Nuria had turned on her. It hurt Red's heart to think her trust might have been misplaced.

Morgan was right. The change in Demery did not bode well for them. His explanation had better be a good one.

Red glanced at the shadows of the mountains in the distance. With the sun gone, they looked almost purple against the sky. People began to set up camp, using the vehicles as both homes and protective walls against the elements. She'd read about circling the wagons, but she'd never witnessed it until now. Except these weren't wagons and this wasn't the Old West. The Old West was civilized compared to this place and these people.

Music played from somewhere on the other side of the makeshift settlement. Women started to sway. This music wasn't like what the Sand Moles had played. It was deeper, more primal. It rattled Red's chest with its thumping beat. The women continued to dance, then one by one they shed their clothes. Some playfully hid their nudity, while others boldly flashed their curves.

Red's mouth dropped open at the brazen display.

The Sand Devil men watched the dancers, their eyes aglow. Some had already started to strip, baring their bodies so they could join the dance. They were less graceful than the women, but no one seemed to notice. Other men simply touched themselves, while the women shimmied seductively in front of them, bending at the waist.

"What's happening?" Red asked, as the tone of the dancing turned carnal. The men who'd taken their clothes off were stroking their shafts suggestively. Red had seen plenty of naked men in her time. She wasn't bothered by the nudity, but she didn't care for what they were doing.

One of the men grabbed a swaying naked woman and slung her over his shoulder. His muscles bunched as he twirled her around and laughed. The woman screamed, but not in fright. He slapped her bare bottom, then probed it with his thick fingers. She squealed loudly and squirmed, but didn't try to push him away. If anything, it looked as if she was enjoying the attention.

"You'll do," he said.

The man strode off to lie in front of one of the vehicles.

Rags had been tossed in a pile to form a makeshift rest pad. He dropped the woman onto them and mounted her without prelims. She didn't seem to mind, if the moans coming from her were any indication.

Red flushed and looked around nervously. "What are they doing?" she asked, as couple after couple paired off. No one sought privacy. They simply dropped where they felt like it and began rutting.

"It's called an orgy," Morgan said. "It's when couples have sex in a group." He sounded like he was speaking from experience.

"Have you ever participated in one?" she asked.

Morgan blanched. "No, not exactly my style, but I have witnessed them before."

Red was silent for a few moments. "I don't think I like the Sand Devils," she said, then scooted closer to him. "They're not like Gray's group." Red wished they were back with the Sand Moles. It didn't matter that she'd shot their leader. They were still preferable company to these people.

Morgan placed his hand on her waist and pulled her close, then leaned in to nuzzle her ear. She thought he was trying to comfort her, until he whispered, "If the situation deteriorates, we may have to leave in a hurry. There won't be a lot of notice. If I tell you to run, I want you to head straight for the mountains and don't look back."

chapter seventeen

Why must they look so fucking happy? They were in the middle of nowhere; roasting and still they looked at each other like lovesick buffoons. Catherine's scent was all over Raphael and his covered her. It was impossible to discern where one began and the other ended. Which made being around them unbearable. Michael questioned his brother's sense of loyalty. Raphael swore he was all about family, but was he? It didn't appear so, if Raphael was challenging his intentions.

Michael wanted to tell his brother the truth. Had tried on many occasions, but each time he opened his mouth the chip in his brain sent pain cascading through his body. By the third time it happened, Michael knew it was a warning of some kind. Somehow the chip had figured out a way to protect itself and was behaving like a cornered animal. His gaze moved over his brother.

Oh, Raphael, my dearest Raphael. Notice me.

At least Michael would no longer have to worry about Raphael. He'd be well taken care of, if this trip didn't turn out as Michael planned. He wanted to trust Catherine Meyers, but like him, she had an agenda. Michael could sense it, even though she tried to hide it from him. *Little girl, little girl, don't you know it's not nice to trick a vamp?*

Get back! Stay away!

The shadow slunk out of view, but its laugh rumbled like

thunder in its wake, hurting his ears, clouding his mind. Pretty colors, dancing and twirling out of sight. Michael tried to follow, but his eyes refused to focus.

The wind shifted, erasing the rainbow, bringing contempt and deceit. Michael raised his head and inhaled. His mind cleared enough to ascertain that enemies lurked up ahead. There were three—no, five. They hoped to surround them. They thought because their clothes were not rags that they'd make easy victims. Michael grinned to himself. Fresh blood was so much better than the hot, rancid brew floating in his canteens.

A bark of laughter escaped before he could stop it. Michael clasped his hand over his mouth to hide his fangs. "Excuse me," he said absently.

"What's so funny?" Catherine asked, her delicate features pinching in distaste.

She'd probably make the same face if he pulled her head off and drank from her skull. The chip pulsed, urging him to act. Michael's fingers twitched, but Raphael was watching. Always watching her. If he didn't know better, Michael would think his brother didn't trust him. Raphael was so focused on her every move that he didn't notice the real threat, gliding in over the dunes.

"Inside joke. You wouldn't understand," Michael said, wondering how long it'd take her and Raphael to realize they were being hunted.

It was probably wrong not to say something, but Michael was disappointed that his brother's senses had dulled to such a degree. There was a time when he'd have located them first.

Oh, Raph, stop thinking with your dick for a moment and open your mind.

He didn't of course. Raphael always had odd priorities. Fortunately for him, Michael *always* focused on the details. The shadows skipped through his mind, a none-too-gentle reminder that that was not the case anymore.

Damn phantoms! Leave me in peace!

A cackle was their only reply.

The delusions were getting worse. The phantoms' visits had increased. Their time spent with him grew longer every day. Roark didn't need to press the button for the A.I. chip to do its job. It continued to act on its own. Roark had probably had it specially developed at one of his research labs. A bio-weapon, if Michael were to guess.

Green button, green button go away. Come again some other day.

The threesome continued their journey as the band of thieves closed in. They were quiet, but the sand gave their location away. It whispered their impending arrival in a time-weary voice.

Catherine stopped. "Did you hear something?"

Michael wanted to say yes, but the chip flared. He shook his head no. Raphael listened. Nothing but the sound of wind and sand answered.

"Let's keep going," Raphael said, his gaze now moving cautiously over the dunes.

Michael prepared for the upcoming battle by dropping his cumbersome pack onto the ground. The attack came from the left. The pureblood moved faster than expected. Michael had a split second to call out a warning before the man slammed into Raphael, sending them both sprawling into a dune. Pain pulsed through his skull. Michael gasped and nearly crumbled to the ground.

Catherine screamed as another assailant came storming out of the darkness like a demon without the virtue of fire. She spun, throwing the pack off in the same movement as a blade sliced the air where she'd stood only seconds before. A wave of power burst out of her, sending the man to his knees. If Michael hadn't experienced it with his own senses, he wouldn't have believed it possible. His head swam and for a moment Michael was dangerously disoriented, leaving him vulnerable.

My, my, my, aren't we just full of tricks. What are you, little girl?

Michael clutched his head, trying to clear it. There was no time for answers. Three more men sailed in from atop the nearby dunes. They swooped down upon them like scavengers, ready to pick their bones and pockets clean. Raphael's fangs extended and he viciously tore at one of the men attacking him. The other stayed just out of range, waiting for an opening.

Catherine made a grab for her weapon, but she wasn't fast enough. Whatever power she'd had began to dissipate. The man who'd tried to knife her was closing in for a second go, while the other rushed Michael.

His mistake.

It only took a thought to stop the man's heart. The look of surprise on his face was priceless. Too bad Michael didn't have time to enjoy the moment.

Michael rushed forward to aid Catherine. His brother would never forgive him if he allowed her to die, when it could easily be prevented. Raphael may not know he loved the woman, but Michael did. It was etched clearly on his brother's face and verified by deed. The pain of the emotion cut deep and he nearly faltered. Michael had just found Raphael only to lose him again. It would've been easier if they'd never reunited at all.

Michael grabbed the thief, shaking his hand off Catherine's throat, then twisted his neck until something popped. The sound was loud enough for all to hear. *Pop, pop. Twist, twist. Crackle, crackle. And they all fall dead.*

The third man turned away from Raphael and saw his comrades lying at their feet. He hesitated as he looked at Catherine, then headed toward Michael. Perhaps the man thought he could avenge the dead. He obviously believed Catherine was helpless because she was a woman. A stupid mistake that was about to cost him his life. Catherine pulled her weapon and fired, dropping the man next to his dead friends.

Boom! Out goes the lights.

Raphael was doing a fair job at fighting the two remaining thieves, considering his teeth were locked on the one man's neck, slowly draining him, while punching the other man in the face.

"Need any help?" Michael asked. Catherine rushed forward.

He caught her before she could do anything foolish like get herself killed.

"Let go," she shouted, struggling to break free.

"No!" Michael's arms locked, restricting her movements. "Raphael will be fine. There are only two of them. What did you do to me?"

"What are you talking about?" she asked, refusing to tear her gaze away from Raphael.

One of the men managed to chuck Raphael under the chin, but his brother didn't budge.

"He needs help." Catherine pried his fingers, applying moves Michael had no doubt she'd learned at the tactical team training facility. They'd probably be effective on someone who'd never been tortured.

Her movements tickled him. Raph didn't need her help dispatching those two. The one in his arms had just died. The other man simply hadn't realized yet that he'd soon follow. Michael could speed the process up, but what fun would that be? Besides, this scuffle would serve as a lesson to his brother to pay attention to his surroundings.

The remaining thief drew a knife and lunged at Raphael's chest. Raphael twisted, putting the dead man in his arms between the attacker and himself. The man impaled his partner to the hilt, then screamed in outrage. He probably thought he'd killed him.

Raphael dropped the dead guy and swiped his leg out, depositing the remaining man on his ass.

"Enough!" he shouted, bringing everyone to a standstill. "Brother, are you hungry?"

Michael smiled. He knew him so well. "I could use a nip."

"He's all yours," Raphael said, shoving the man toward him.

The thief tried to scramble up a nearby dune, but Michael stopped him by mentally lifting him off his feet and bringing him back. From the fear in his eyes, Michael could see it had finally dawned on him just how large a mistake he and his friends had made by attacking them.

His fangs extended, the familiar length tickling his tongue as Michael licked them in anticipation. The sensation sent delicious gooseflesh dancing along his spine. He angled the man's neck, while keeping his arms pinned to his sides. His mouth watered as he sank his fangs into the thief's artery and began to feast.

He was yummy. Michael had expected something less appetizing from his worn appearance.

He would've bitten him elsewhere if he'd wanted the man to live, but Michael didn't. As he drank, Michael watched Catherine's expression change from one of curiosity to out-and-out revulsion. Her red hair was tousled from the fight and her clothes were covered in sand. She was sweating and out of breath.

Michael waited to make sure he had her undivided attention, then he smiled, allowing the blood to dribble down his chin onto his shirt. The coppery sweetness stuck to his skin, teasing his nostrils with its heavenly scent. Normally he wasn't what one would call a messy eater—far from it actually—but Michael hadn't been able to resist the urge to rattle her. He wanted to scare Catherine off before she could take Raphael away from him.

He liked having her off balance. It made them even for that stunt she'd pulled earlier. Catherine watched for a few more seconds, eyes rounded and mouth gaping, then slowly turned away. Raphael reached for her, but she jerked out of his grasp.

"Leave me alone," Catherine said and kept walking.

She didn't look back as she disappeared into the night.

"Catherine, where are you going?" Raphael frowned like a child who'd lost his favorite toy.

How Michael wished that were true, but he'd never been that lucky. He considered the woman threatening to come between him and his brother. He pictured the blood running down his chin. With the vision clearly in his head,

Michael closed his eyes and sent a thought slamming into her mind.

Welcome to the family, Catherine Meyers.

Chaos couldn't seem to get the picture of blood dripping down Michael's chin out of her mind. Every time she tried it came back in even more vivid detail, along with Michael's sinister welcome. She had no problem killing if the situation called for it, but she didn't take joy in the act. Not like he did.

She could see it in his black eyes. They'd sparkled as he'd drained the man in front of her. He'd enjoyed it. Reveled in the act of killing. The whole thing had been performed like some twisted dance with Michael as the star. He'd wanted to shock her and it worked. She was shocked—not by the death, but by the method.

Sure, Raphael was a vampire. And yes, he'd killed, too, but she hadn't seen the same gleam of satisfaction in his eyes. Raphael had killed because he had to. Yes, he'd drank from one of the men, but it had come more from hunger and control than from pleasure. He didn't get off by sucking people dry.

Chaos stopped walking. Was she rationalizing Raphael's actions? Possibly, but she hadn't mistaken the joy she'd seen on Michael's face. Killing was second nature to him. He loved it and he was very, very good at it.

She wondered if Raphael had seen the gleam in his brother's eyes, or had he been too blinded by love and devotion to notice. Was this the fate that ultimately awaited Red and Morgan? He could have Morgan on a platter if it made him happy. Let Michael snack on him or take him back to Roark, but she wouldn't let him have Red. Gina was hers to return safely to IPTT. The sooner Michael Travers Vega knew that, the better.

He saved your life, a little voice in Chaos' head reminded her. It knocked the self-righteous indignation right out of her system. Michael had saved her from being choked to death, when he didn't have to bother.

Was she being too hard on him? Maybe she'd misjudged him just as she'd done with Raphael when they first met. Let's face it—when she tried to kill him. Was she any better than they were? Chaos had killed without mercy in Nuria. It had been under Roark Montgomery's compulsion, but she had carried out the murders. Suddenly the answers weren't nearly as clear as they'd been a moment ago.

Raphael watched Catherine until she disappeared. Her shoulders were stiff and she held her head high. Waves of anger and disgust radiated off her tiny frame. He'd warned her that Michael was a dangerous man and now she finally believed him. He should be relieved that the blinders had been removed from her naïve eyes. So why did he feel like shit?

He turned back to Michael, who finished drinking, then dropped the dead man onto the ground.

"Good to the last drop," he said, smacking his lips for emphasis.

"Why did you do that?" Raphael asked. His brother had never been a messy eater. He was fastidious by nature. Dripping the blood had been for show.

"Do what?" Michael asked innocently.

Raphael's eyes narrowed. "You know what I'm talking about. You turned into a movie cliché. Since when do you waste blood by letting it drip on the ground? You practically rubbed that body in her face."

"Oh that." Michael shrugged. "I thought she should know what we really are, not what we present to the world," he said. "She needed to experience the truth firsthand and not romanticize it."

His jaw clenched. "She already knows. Shocking her was overkill, but then again, you know that. You smelled me on her. You know I've tasted her. Hell, you've seen my mark on her neck."

Michael sighed as if the conversation bored him. "I don't want to see you get your heart broken by a woman who can't handle a little blood."

Raphael stiffened. What did he mean by that crack? His

heart wasn't in any danger of being broken by Catherine. A myriad of emotions filled him. Raphael opened his mouth to issue a denial, but the words tangled in his throat and came out sounding like a snarl.

"What is she anyway?" Michael asked, wiping the blood off his face with the back of his sleeve. "I don't sense Other in her."

"I told you, she's unique," Raphael said, thinking of Catherine's smart mouth and fiery temper. He'd kiss that mouth right now if she'd let him. Thoughts of Catherine took his mind off the glee he'd seen on Michael's face as he'd killed the men. Raphael had never enjoyed killing, but he'd accepted that it had to be done on occasion. What he'd witnessed moments ago had frightened him more than any surprise enemy attack.

"She almost knocked me on my ass when that one guy attacked her. My head wouldn't stop spinning. I've never felt that kind of power from anyone," Michael said.

"It's why they call her *Chaos* at IPTT. She's like a microburst waiting to descend. I'm not sure she even knows where her power comes from or how to control it completely. We haven't discussed it in detail. We've had more important things on our minds," Raphael said, already losing interest in the conversation. He didn't want her to get too far ahead of them. What if another predator came upon her? His heart had nearly stopped when he had seen that thief go for her throat. If it hadn't been for Michael, she'd be dead.

"I have to go after her," he said, gathering his gear. "Thank you for saving her."

Michael snorted. "She really has you whipped, doesn't she? Do you ask how high when she says jump?"

Raphael stilled, his hands clutched at his sides. He had the overwhelming urge to punch his brother in the face. "What are you implying? Out with it!"

Michael toyed with the strap on his pack. "There was a time when this woman would've been falling at your feet, trying to figure out ways to please you. Not the other way around. She has you bowing and scraping before her."

He scoffed. "You don't know what in the hell you're talking about," Raphael said.

"Don't I?" Michael asked. "When we met up, you implied Catherine wasn't special. You let me believe you'd get rid of her once you grew tired of her company. But that's not going to happen. Is it, brother?"

Raphael's body tensed. Through the years he'd been an ass to a lot of women. Oh, he'd left them satisfied. He wouldn't have been able to call himself a man otherwise, but he'd still used them. Sometimes for shelter, other times for sex, but mostly he'd used them for blood. A woman in the throes of passion tasted better than anything on the planet. He should know—he'd sampled a veritable smorgasbord.

It wasn't until he'd met Red that Raphael realized something was missing. She was so strong and powerful, yet naively vulnerable. The wolf inside her was beyond alluring. He'd made his move on her and she'd been tempted, *very tempted*, but in the end Red had turned Raphael down. Her heart belonged to another. The rejection had hurt, but he'd respected her all the more for it. That's when Raphael knew for sure she was the right woman for Morgan.

The trouble was that now he wanted more. The thought of a quick roll on the rest pad for blood and sex had left him cold. The afternoon he'd made love to Catherine had turned his world upside down. She'd brought him to life, when Raphael hadn't known he was dead inside. Catherine, and only Catherine, had filled the emptiness swallowing him whole. He couldn't lose her. It had taken too long to find her.

His gaze returned to his brother. "Times change, Michael. And so do people. You should know that better than anyone. Now I'm going to walk away before I say something I truly regret," Raphael said.

Michael's lip curled in disgust. "I do know better, brother. I'm staring at the proof and it nauseates me. You've gone from a proud warrior to a groveling snit. You should see yourself."

"You just don't get it, do you?" Raphael shook his head and felt a pang of regret. Michael never would understand what it felt like to give his heart to another. To want to be with that person as much as possible because the time apart made you ache. No, his brother would never understand. He was too caught up in the chase, in the kill. It was all a game to him. To be won at all costs. "I'd better go find her before she gets lost," Raphael said softly.

"Do you want me to bring her back?" Michael asked. His tone implied he'd be perfectly happy to let her wander the desert forever. "It would be quite easy to lift her. It's not like she weighs a lot. Might even be funny to see the look on her face, when invisible hands pick her up and carry her over the desert." He chortled.

Raphael glanced over his shoulder. "Thanks, but I think I can handle it." He looked at his brother. Really looked at him. He ignored the blood-stained skin and the rumpled clothing. Looked past them to the face beneath the civil mask. His true face.

Michael wasn't the same man Raphael had known and loved a lifetime ago. The years of torture and the assassinations he'd performed had eaten away at his humanity and changed him. The question was into what?

chapter eighteen

Red awoke to a callused hand covering her mouth. She struggled until her eyes managed to focus in the pre-dawn light. Morgan stood over her with his finger pressed to his lips. She nodded in understanding and he released her. Red stood, trying not to make a sound. The group had been drinking and partying all night. They'd only stopped as dawn approached.

She'd never seen anything like the wild dancing and cavorting taking place. This was nothing like the first encampment they'd encountered. These people were savage. Demery had stayed close to Reaper and his blood for most of the night. He'd pulled out the metal deck she'd seen him playing with at the Sand Mole compound and gambled until she couldn't hold her eyes open. That was the last she'd seen of them. Red looked around, but didn't immediately spot him.

She turned to Morgan and mouthed, *where's Demery?* Morgan shook his head and shrugged. He pointed to the mountains, which had turned gray from the fast-approaching dawn. He splayed his fingers and mimicked a running movement.

"Time to go," Morgan said.

Everyone appeared to be asleep or passed out from the revelry. Red didn't see Demery or his white protective suit anywhere. She also didn't see Reaper or Melea. She leaned in close to Morgan and pressed her lips to his ear.

"He didn't get a chance to explain what's happening."

Morgan met her gaze with a sharp one of his own. "He had all night. We gave him every opportunity. At one point, I even cornered him after a game of zigzag quartz. Demery didn't say a word. He just gave another excuse, then went off to relieve himself behind one of the vehicles."

"We can't just leave him," Red said. "He wouldn't leave us."

"After what you witnessed last night are you sure?" he asked.

She hesitated as she thought about it. "Yes, I am."

His brow furrowed. Morgan scrubbed a hand over his face, his frustration evident. "I looked all over, but I couldn't find him. I don't like the idea of leaving him any more than you do, but now is our chance to get out of here unscathed and we're going to take it. Demery is a big boy. He knows these people. He'll be fine."

Red shook her head violently. She wouldn't leave anyone behind. It had been drilled into her since day one at IPTT.

"We don't have time to argue." Morgan grabbed her arm and tugged her away. "We have to make it to that outpost before anyone else hears about the bounty. Do you really think these people will let us go once they do?"

Her heart sank. He was right. Red knew Morgan was right. If they didn't make it to the outpost and try to contact the outside world for help, they could end up dying here in no-man's-land. Red didn't want to die in this place.

"Okay," she said. "But promise me we'll come back for Demery when we're done, if he hasn't reached the outpost by then."

Morgan kissed her. "Agreed," he said. "Now let's go."

They crept out of the campsite as silently as possible. Red's heart was pounding so hard she doubted she'd hear it if anyone sounded an alarm. When they got a hundred yards away, they ran for foothills, reaching them in minutes.

"Keep going," Morgan said, as he began to climb.

"I'm really worried about Demery. What if they kill him when they find out we're gone?"

Morgan frowned. It was obvious from his expression that it hadn't occurred to him. "I don't think they will. He has some kind of deal going with them, remember? He was the one who wanted to find Reaper. It was sheer luck that they found us first."

"Bad luck," she muttered.

Red understood, but she still wasn't convinced that the deal was enough to keep him alive. She had no doubt the situation involved Melea. What she couldn't figure out was where they'd factored into it. They didn't have anything to bargain with other than their pistols, and the Sand Devils had plenty of weapons. They didn't need more.

Damn it, Demery! You should've explained the situation you were in.

The mountains grew rapidly steeper and Red had to pull herself up to reach the next outcropping of rocks.

"You doing okay?" Morgan asked. Sweat dripped down his rugged face, leaving his hair curling into his neck. His amber eyes watched her closely as he gave her a leg up here and pulled her up there.

"I'm fine. Just a little winded. Not used to this altitude. Do you have any idea where we're going?" It had dawned on her an hour ago that Demery was the only one who knew the exact location of the outpost. The thought of wandering around the desert for days, weeks, or months in search of it was decidedly unappealing.

"The Sand Moles had said it was located southwest of their position. I figure as long as we keep traveling in that direction we'll run into either it or another group who can help us pin down the location," he said.

"Those are a lot of ifs," Red said, straining to climb.

"What choice do we have?" Morgan asked.

"We could've located Demery and found out what was really going on. He'd said we'd be leaving today. I don't think he meant without him."

Morgan sighed and ran a hand through his hair. "I'm sorry. I really tried to find him. I told you. I snuck all around that place and didn't see him anywhere. The suit would've stuck out against the sand if he'd been there. Maybe he went off with one of the women."

"Without telling us? Seems unlikely," she said.

"Not sure if you noticed, but he wasn't exactly acting normal once we ran into the Sand Devils."

She grasped the rock above her. "It was obvious that it had been awhile since he'd seen Melea, his blood. Maybe he was nervous."

"Possibly, but we gave him every opportunity to come clean. Nerves alone do not explain his odd behavior. He was up to something. I don't know what, but I smelled deception on his skin when he took the protective suit off. Staying in the Sand Devil camp any longer was not in our best interest," he said. "Now keep climbing."

Red scowled, but did as he suggested. It was too late to turn back. By now they would've discovered them missing. She hoped that Morgan was right and that Demery would be okay. If not, she'd never forgive herself.

Morgan struggled to pull himself up onto the next cliff face. He hated mountains. He'd been camped in them, when his wife and child were killed. He could still remember the helpless sensation of trying to get down from the ridge he'd been on and reach his family in time. It had taken so much longer than it should have. That mountain had been covered in trees, back when real forests still existed. It hadn't been dead like this one. He'd been too late. They'd died waiting for him to arrive. He wouldn't go through that with Gina.

His hand slipped, slicing his palm on a jagged rock. Morgan grunted, then forced his arm to change. Claws and fur appeared, then disappeared quickly, leaving a pink line where the cut had been. He continued climbing.

"We'll stop at the next outcropping of rocks," he said. "Make sure no one is following us."

"What if we spot Demery?" Red asked.

Morgan grunted. "As long as he's not with friends, we'll wait."

She looked over her shoulder at him. "And if he is?"

"Then we'll keep moving and pray we can outrun them."

They reached a small ridge that gave them enough flat space to stand on, but there wasn't room for much more. The sun was higher now, but the mountain kept them from being exposed. That would change once they reached the top and had to make their way down the other side.

"How long until we get out of here?" Red asked.

"No idea," Morgan said. "I'm not sure how wide this range is."

"Do you think we'll make it out before dark?" she asked. Red looked at the tiny ledge they were standing on. It was a sheer drop on one side and a rough slide on the other. Both would ensure injury if they fell. There was nowhere to sleep and no way they'd be able to traverse the terrain in the dark.

"I sure as hell hope so," Morgan said.

They had at least thirteen hours of daylight to make it to the other side. "Let's get going. No time to lose."

Red and Morgan reached the top of the final mountain. They stood looking out at the valley below. Much like the one they left, the desert had taken over everything, leaving slopes of sand behind. At least these dunes didn't seem quite as high as the ones they'd traversed.

A warm breeze blew over them. Red closed her eyes and inhaled, taking in everything around them. The mountain had an earthy smell, almost as if water clung to it, when there hadn't been rain in months. She didn't scent any people or death, even though it waited for them around every corner.

She opened her eyes. In the distance, something glinted, flashing in the sunlight like a diamond faceted by fire.

Red shielded her eyes and peered at the object. "What's that over there?" she asked. It flashed again, bursting with life in the valley of the dead.

Morgan grabbed a monocular and pointed it at the shiny object. "It doesn't look like much. Hang on." He adjusted the lens. "I think we may have found the outpost."

"Are you serious?" Red asked, clapping her hands and squealing, unable to contain her enthusiasm. They'd made it. Somehow they'd managed to find the elusive outpost.

She almost wept in relief. Her body ached from all the hiking and climbing. She never realized how easy she'd had it at IPTT. Given another opportunity, Red would never take her boring life for granted again. They'd still have to get down and hope the place held the equipment they needed, but at least they'd made it this far.

"Don't get too excited," Morgan said, squashing her enthusiasm. "That's a lot of open space to cover. A lot can go wrong. We still have to get from here to there without being spotted by the Sand Devils."

"Do you think they're following us?" she asked, glancing over her shoulder at the route they'd taken through the mountains. Her muscles trembled from exertion.

His lips thinned. "If they aren't yet, they will be soon. We just haven't spotted them yet."

Demery awoke on the ground, sprawled out next to the woman he'd fucked the night before. Her blood had fed him, while he sated her needs. She was naked. Her ripe nipples stabbed skyward, a bountiful offering if he'd ever seen one. Too bad the suit prevented him from taking advantage. Light splashed her skin, making it appear striped. She was making tiny snuffling sounds each time she exhaled. Demery smiled in remembrance, then stretched, rolling his stiff muscles.

The ground was harder here. He'd gotten used to sleeping on the sand. His head ached from the Sand Devil wine, leaving him woozy. Demery couldn't remember the last time he'd drunk so much. He'd spent time with Melea, making sure she was okay. He had only taken a little of her blood. Just enough to test their connection. It was still intact, even though he'd hoped otherwise.

Demery hadn't wanted to be greedy, so he'd sent Melea away before his body could make further demands and found another willing donor. She was now lazing in the sun like a satisfied cat. He'd even managed to win a few hands of zig-zag quartz. Luck had been on his side.

All and all it was a good night with the Sand Devils. Reaper had been surprisingly hospitable given the debt he owed him. He supposed he would be, too, if someone laid a gift of powerful blood at his feet. He knew he had to find Morgan now and explain before Reaper got to him.

Demery inhaled deeply and froze. No, this couldn't be happening. Not when he was so close to gaining everything. He inhaled again, seeking the slumbering wolves, but his senses didn't lie. Red and Morgan were gone, leaving him and Melea as good as dead.

chapter nineteen

Staring at the endless sand only brought home how vast the world was and how many places there were to hide. Red was out there somewhere. Perhaps shielded by misguided individuals who'd fallen prey to her lies. I feel helpless. It doesn't matter that I'm doing everything I can to find her.

Surrounded as I am by curious eyes, I can't make any sudden moves. The men are skilled and could easily stop me. Even if I managed to lose them for a time, they'd eventually catch up with me. I wouldn't be able to travel fast enough over the terrain to outrun them.

It was definitely hard to wait. Seems like all I've been doing these past few days was bide my time. My hand moved to the laser pistol strapped to my thigh. My palm itched to pull it. I caressed the stock with my fingertips. So cool and deadly. It would be easy to pick them off. I drew back appalled by the direction my thoughts had taken. The guilt didn't last long.

Soon, I thought, picturing Gina "Red" Santiago in my mind.

If I concentrated hard enough, I could see myself pulling the weapon, taking aim at her chest, and firing. I could almost smell the seared flesh as the laser shot out from the muzzle and blew a hole in her body. Red wouldn't have time to respond because she'd never see it coming. She would never suspect a thing.

Robert Santiago sat behind his desk at IPTT headquarters blindly staring at synth-reports. He hadn't heard from his granddaughter, Gina. Catherine Meyers notified him she'd crossed into no-man's-land. Given the place's reputation, he didn't know if Gina was alive or dead. He shook his head, sending white hair onto his forehead. That wasn't true. He'd know if she was dead, but that didn't stop the worry or the fear of losing her.

He had to do something to clear her name. He felt helpless sitting behind his title, doing nothing. Robert thought about Private Catherine Meyers. He shouldn't have let her go after Gina. She wasn't experienced enough to head into no-man's-land alone. It was only desperation that had made him say yes and now he deeply regretted it. If anything happened to Meyers, it would weigh heavy on his conscience.

The door to his office chimed. He hit a button on his desk and an image of one of the tech support men came into view. Robert pressed another button and the door opened.

"Sir," the young man named Tucker said.

"Do you have anything for me?" Robert asked, dispensing with small talk. The tech department had the remains of Gina's navcom, Rita, for several days now, and surely they'd been able to come up with something in that time period.

Tucker looked pinched in the face like his pants had shrunk. "Nothing yet, sir."

"Then what are you doing here?" he asked, barely leashing his temper, which had gotten worse in Gina's absence. She was the only family he had left. The thought of losing her forever was unthinkable. He'd already lost his daughter due to her love of an Other. He wasn't about to lose his granddaughter, too.

He fidgeted. "We aren't sure we're going to be able to fix the navcom, sir."

Robert rose, towering over the much smaller man. "What do you mean you can't fix it? I thought you were the best."

"I am," Tucker said. "I mean we are. The thing is, the navcom is pretty banged up. Crushed really. Red has broken Rita plenty of times, but never like this."

"*Gina* didn't break Rita," Robert bellowed. "Not this time."

He swallowed hard. "If you say so, sir."

"I do."

Tucker shuffled his feet and looked at anything but Robert Santiago. "We have one more thing to try, but if that doesn't work, then there's nothing we can do," he said. "I'm sorry."

"Did you bring me *any* good news?" Deflated, Robert sank into his chair.

"We can tell there is something on it. We don't know what it is yet, since we haven't been able to retrieve the recording."

"I suppose that's better than nothing." Robert perked up, feeling hope for the first time in a week. "Keep working on it. Let me know when you have something."

"Yes, sir," Tucker said, then turned toward the door.

Before he could reach it, Robert stopped him. "Oh, and Tucker."

"Sir?"

Robert leaned forward. "This project is considered top secret. No one but you and the other tech guy working on the navcom are to know what you find. As soon as you have the information, I want you to come to me immediately. Day or night. Understood?"

"Understood, sir." Tucker nodded, then left the office.

Robert knew there could be anything on the navcom. It wouldn't necessarily be something they could use. He just had to hope that Gina had been smart enough to try to record her last moments with Roark and that Roark wasn't smart enough to watch what he was saying.

How likely was that? His head dropped into his hands. Those were a lot of ifs and maybes. Too many for his peace of mind. There had to be another way to catch Roark Montgomery in his lies. He just wasn't seeing it because he was too close to the situation.

Robert stacked the reports he'd been reading. The buzzer at his office door went off again. He looked down at the monitor and saw Bannon Richards standing outside.

"You may enter," he said, pushing a button.

Bannon strode in as cocky as ever, wearing a shit-eating grin on his face.

"Lieutenant, how can I help you?" Robert asked.

"I was wondering if you have any new orders for my team, Commander."

Robert tilted his head. "Such as?"

Bannon cleared his throat. "We still haven't located the fugitives. I thought maybe you had a new area in mind for us to search. Roark says he's covered everything to the west."

Robert's eyebrows shot to his hairline. "Since when do you work for Roark Montgomery? I had the impression that you were a decorated tactical team officer under my command. Did you resign from your post without my knowing it?" He clasped his fingers to keep them from shaking. Anger vibrated through him, tensing his muscles. Robert was well aware that some of his men moonlighted for Roark on their days off. He also knew that Roark's IPTT record garnered him a lot of respect and adulation. But he didn't like the idea that Roark had somehow infiltrated IPTT and had started taking command. He took a deep breath and slowly let it out, hoping to stave off a migraine.

"No, sir. I didn't resign my post." Bannon's jaw jutted. "I just thought that pooling our resources would allow us to cover more ground."

"You aren't paid to think, Lieutenant. You have your patrol orders. I suggest you get back to work, unless you want to find yourself busted back down to private."

Bannon's square face flushed and his blue eyes chilled to ice chips. "Yes, sir." The words dripped with so much venom that Robert Santiago found himself leaning back.

"Dismissed," he said, watching Bannon stride angrily to the door. He made a mental note to keep an eye on him.

The lieutenant slipped out, shooting him a dirty look before the door closed. Robert had known about the rivalry between Bannon and Gina. He'd had no idea that the animosity ran so deep until now. Bannon was a good officer, but he was going to be a problem, especially if he'd already started taking orders from Roark Montgomery. His ambition must have gotten the better of him. He still couldn't believe the gall of the man. How dare he come in here and question his orders. Who did he think he was? Commander?

His head began to pound. Robert pinched the bridge of his nose and rubbed his temples. This was one more thing to worry about on top of a mountain of others. He opened a drawer, brushing aside his toiletries, and took out a dissolving patch to slip under his tongue. The headache would be gone in a matter of seconds thanks to the medicine. If only his other problems could be remedied as easily.

Gina and Morgan descended, then kept to the base of the mountains, slowly making their way west. It had taken all day to get down. They'd double-checked coordinates and determined the exact location of the outpost. Now all they had to do was reach it without getting caught by the Sand Devils or shot by the people living in the outpost.

Morgan led the way, keeping Gina close to his back. He'd changed into his Other form to prevent a surprise attack. He felt like shit dragging her into this mess. Her life had been so orderly before she'd shown up in Nuria on the hunt for a killer.

Both their lives had changed that day, but neither could've anticipated how much. Morgan had lost his cousin, Kane, a man he'd loved like a brother, and Gina had lost her innocence. She'd discovered that her entire life had been built around lies. Her father had been killed because he'd been an Other. And now her life was in danger for the same reason.

And it was his fault.

Had Morgan just run her off when she came to town none of this would've occurred. She'd still be a lieutenant with the International Police Tactical Team and he'd still be sheriff of Nuria.

Morgan's heart wrenched. Who was he kidding? The thought of not having Gina in his life was too painful to contemplate. He loved her like he'd loved no other. Not even the woman he'd once called his wife. Their love was what brought them here, had them running for their lives. He hoped that in the end, she'd think it was worth it as he did.

"We should make a break for it," she whispered from behind. "We're about to run out of mountain."

Morgan looked around and saw the foothills up ahead. "Okay, but first, you need to change. We'll go a lot faster if you do."

Her eyes grew wide.

He knew she was afraid, but she had to do this. If for nothing else than to prove to herself that she could. They stopped. Gina removed her pack and shoes. Her clothes were loose enough that they shouldn't rip from the change.

"Ready?" he asked.

"Ready," she said, then stepped back.

Pain shot through Red, searing her flesh like someone was trying to skin her alive. For a second, she couldn't breathe, couldn't think. She heard bones snapping, then felt the agony of them reshaping into something that remained foreign to her. Claws shot out where her fingernails had been moments ago. Her teeth were ejected, replaced by longer fangs; canines that were made for tearing at flesh and devouring it.

She cried out before she could stop herself and dropped to her knees, clutching her abdomen. Blood spattered the sand around her, staining the rocks crimson. She closed her eyes as the world seemed to implode. When Red opened them again, it was complete sensory overload.

Despite the impending dusk, everything came alive. She could see scavengers prowling in the distance; hear their feet upon the sand. The air even smelled different, more savage than it had moments ago.

She sniffed, picking up something else. Guards. At least she thought they were guards, since the odor was coming from the outpost they were headed to in the distance.

"Can you stand?" Morgan rasped.

She looked at him through the eyes of a predator and her nostrils flared. A rumbling growl came out of Morgan's chest and she quickly lowered her eyes. Red nodded or at least she hoped she did, then scrambled to her feet. She lifted the pack, which now felt like it weighed nothing and struggled to get it on her back. Morgan helped, then gave her a quick lick when he was done.

"We must move. I can hear the Sand Devil vehicles in the distance. They are driving around the mountains."

Red's ears perked, twitching this way and that until she found what he'd heard. The low hum of the vehicles was a steady drone and they were getting louder. Their threat was imminent. She growled, her ears pinning back against her head. She wanted to find them and drag them from their transports.

"There's no time," Morgan said, his voice garbled due to the change. "Run now, fight later." He tugged at her arm.

Red followed reluctantly. The need to stand and fight was great. She didn't like being hunted under normal circumstances, but in her Other form, it was unbearable. She was a predator—not food. The Sand Devils would learn that if they kept coming.

They raced across the desert floor, running faster than she'd ever run in her life. The sights, sounds, and smells of the world around her kept distracting her and she nearly tumbled on a couple of occasions. Still she managed to keep her feet and continue.

Morgan was yipping in excitement and she joined in. It was the first time they'd ever had the chance to run together and they made the most of it by butting into each other's shoulders and nipping playfully. Red wished that the circumstances had been better. She'd prayed this would happen when she was in Nuria.

Night after night she'd stood in a clearing attempting to force the change and it had eluded her. Yet today it had embraced her, welcomed her with open talons as if it had anticipated her arrival. It was cause for celebration, when there was so little to celebrate.

"We're almost there." Morgan nudged her. Red could tell he was enjoying the freedom of running with his mate for the very first time. She prayed it wouldn't be the last.

chapter twenty

Morgan and Red approached the outpost cautiously. They kept their weapons holstered, but they'd charged them beforehand just in case. The outpost looked like an upside-down metal bowl with a door and three windows carved out of it. The windows didn't hold glass; instead metal had been pounded and tied together in primitive shutters.

Three towers with crude rope ladders formed a triangle around the outpost, giving the guards an unobstructed view of the area. Like the first group they'd encountered, a pit surrounded the whole compound. Unlike that first group, this pit was filled with razor-sharp glass and pieces of metal that had been molded into spikes. There was no way of crossing it without being cut to pieces.

"State your business," the guard to their left shouted.

Morgan and Red raised their arms in the air. They'd shedded their Other form to appear less threatening and to prevent panic.

"We are looking for Razor. The Sand Moles sent us. They said you might have some communication equipment we could use or barter for," Morgan said.

"Who told you such a thing?" the guard to the right hollered.

"Jeb," Red said.

The two guards looked at each other, then back at Morgan and Red.

"Jeb wouldn't do that," the guard on the left said. "He knows better."

"You must be Razor," Morgan said.

"I am," the guard on the left said.

"How else could we have found you, if not for Jeb?" Morgan asked. "We are traders who have never been to this area."

The guard on the right said, "Maybe we should ask Jonah."

Razor didn't look happy about the prospect. "What do you have to trade?" he asked, looking them over carefully.

"Weapons. A few supplies. We will pay for anything we use," Morgan said.

"With what?" the guard on the right asked, suspicion clear.

"Credits," Red said.

"Show me," Razor said.

"Let's see the equipment first," she said.

Razor pondered their proposition while the guard on the right waited.

"Okay," he finally said. "Drop your weapons and come across the bridge, but if you make any sudden moves, you're dead."

Red glanced at Morgan, who nodded for her to comply. She unbuckled her holster and let if fall to the ground. She felt naked without her laser pistol. They walked across the small bridge with their hands held high and stopped when they reached the other side. Razor had managed to scurry down the rope ladder and was waiting when they arrived.

"Remove your packs and drop them on the ground."

Red looked up and saw that the guard on the right had them covered from above. She shrugged and did as they asked, dropping her backpack onto the sandy flat. Morgan followed suit.

"Now can we please speak with Jonah?" she asked, hoping that he was more intelligent than the two guarding the entrance. She glanced up, noticing four more in the towers.

She squinted. Make that six guarding the back and the front entrances.

Razor motioned them forward with the barrel of his rifle. Morgan told Red to lead the way. It seemed the gentlemanly thing to do, but Red knew that wasn't why he'd offered. Morgan wanted to put his body between her and the gun.

They walked to the reinforced metal door and waited. Razor hit a spot on the ground with his boot heel and something clanged. Red looked over her shoulder at Morgan and frowned. His expression was placid. Deceptive under the circumstances. He waited patiently for the door to open.

They didn't have to wait long. The big metal door slid open with a scraping noise that Red had no doubt came from sand buildup. Darkness greeted them.

"Get inside," Razor said, nudging Morgan with the rifle.

Morgan looked at the gun, then grinned at the man. Razor's eyes widened and he took a step back, forgetting he was the one who was armed. Red faced the darkened entry and stepped over the threshold. She waited for her eyes to adjust before going any further. It didn't take long. The place looked like a warehouse of some sort, but for what she couldn't tell. Morgan walked forward and stopped at her side.

"Where's this Jonah you spoke of?" he turned to ask Razor, but he was gone, shutting the door behind him.

Morgan rushed forward, but couldn't stop it in time. "Damn," he said, pressing his hand all over the door. "I can't feel a handle. There doesn't seem to be a way of opening it from the inside."

"Is this a trap?" Red's skin began to itch at the thought of being stuck in here. The wolf suddenly wanted out. She rolled her shoulders and tried to relax.

Morgan inhaled. "No, I don't think so. I smell a pureblood. The scent is fresh, but he's not in here with us."

"Sure it's not Razor?" she asked.

"Positive. This scent isn't malodorous."

She looked around. "Then where in the hell is he?" Red asked, inching forward, her senses on high alert.

Morgan sniffed and she did the same. Despite the dust clinging to the metal crates, the air smelled clean, like it was blowing in from outside. They didn't spot any vents, nor did they see anything out of the ordinary.

"There's something about this place that's familiar," Morgan said.

"You're not saying you've been here."

"No, nothing like that," he said.

"Then what do you mean?" she asked, looking at the shadows. From what she could tell the warehouse was full of nothing but junk.

He began to examine the area. "I've seen this type of building before."

"A warehouse? I have, too, and they pretty much all look the same," Red said.

"Shh—" Morgan said, moving in circles around the room. "I think I hear something."

Red listened, but didn't immediately hear anything. She listened harder and caught a whirling sound coming from the floor. It was followed by a strong vibration. "What is that?" she asked, backing toward the door they'd come through.

"If I'm not mistaken, it's an elevator."

"Here? In the middle of no-man's-land?" Red asked. He might as well have proclaimed this place a hydrogen car factory. How could a dilapidated warehouse hold a working elevator? It wasn't possible. There was no power here. *You hadn't thought there'd be vehicles here either,* a little voice in her head chided.

Morgan studied the floor some more, tapping his foot here and there.

"What are you doing?" Red asked.

"Looking for the door," he said.

Maybe the heat had gotten to him. It was possible he was suffering from heat exhaustion, even though they'd made an effort to remain hydrated. He continued to bounce and tap on the floor.

"Morgan, you aren't making sense. There's nothing here but mechanical ghosts. Demery was wrong. The guards were just trying to trap us with that talk of Jonah. He probably doesn't even exist." They'd left Demery for nothing. Her heart sank as she realized they'd finally run out of options.

The whirling sound grew louder and Morgan stepped back. Red moved closer to him.

"It's coming," he said, a smile flitting across his lips.

Red stepped into his arms as the floor opened up. She gasped, her eyes widening as the hole grew larger and larger. Would it swallow the room and them with it? She looked up to judge the distance to the beams that ran along the ceiling. Could they jump and reach them in time?

A platform appeared a moment later. A blond-haired man stood in the center, holding a device in his hand that had a red button and a green button on it. A large pistol was tucked into a holster and strapped to his leg.

"You must be the traders Razor spoke of. Don't get many around these parts outside of the Sand Moles. At least not any who aren't out to cause trouble. Are you looking for trouble?" he asked, his gaze sliding to Morgan.

"No," he said.

Red said nothing.

"I prefer the lady's response," he said. "It's more honest."

"But I didn't say anything," Red said.

"Exactly. You don't talk. You can't lie." The man smiled and beckoned them forward with one tanned hand. The other held the device tight as if he were afraid they'd rip it away.

Morgan placed his hand on the small of Red's back and guided her onto the platform.

"What is this thing?" she asked.

"If I'm not mistaken, it's an old missile silo," Morgan said.

"You are correct, Mr. Hunter," the man said, pressing the green button once they'd joined him.

"You know my name?"

The man grinned mischievously. "Everyone around here knows your names. Bounties tend to make their own kind of introductions." The man turned to face Red. "And you must be Gina Santiago. I can't wait to hear all about what you've done to warrant such a high price."

Red's stomach dipped from his words and the sudden descent.

"Where are my manners? My name is Jonah. No call for surnames out here." He held out his hand, which was surprisingly clean given the conditions of the warehouse. So were his clothes, come of think of it. Red felt a twinge of jealousy. She'd give her left boot for a cleansing unit.

Morgan shook his hand. Red just looked at it, then at him. He seemed courteous enough, but she still might have to kill him. Like the elevator, Jonah was an anomaly. Red didn't like anomalies. They made her nervous. Jonah wiped his hand on the side of his gray pants and nodded.

She couldn't see the bottom of the shaft. Red could barely make out the top. The doors slowly slid shut, leaving them in complete darkness. Her heart leapt, then slammed into her ribs. The darkness felt like it was closing in, taking all the oxygen with it. She fought the panic clawing at her throat. She couldn't breathe.

"Morgan?" she called out.

His hand found hers with ease and he pulled her into his body. "It's okay. Take a deep breath. We're almost there," he murmured.

"How can you tell?" she asked.

"Most of these things are around 176 to 200 feet deep. Just large enough to accommodate a missile, a well, kitchen, rec area, storage space, living quarters, and a command center. At least the ones I've been inside of."

"He's right, you know," Jonah said. "We've arrived."

On cue, the platform stopped with a slight jerk. Red could hear Jonah patting the wall in search of something. She was afraid to move for fear she'd fall off into the abyss.

"Here it is," he said. Something clicked and lights came on all around them.

Red blinked, temporarily blinded. A door stood five feet away. It had a round handle of some sort. Red had never seen one before. "What is that?" she asked Morgan.

He smiled. "It's called a hatch. You spin the wheel to open and close it."

"Really?" she asked. "Why doesn't it just open when we approach?"

Jonah chuckled. "I fear we're a little old-fashioned around these parts. Don't have the modern amenities found in your dome cities."

Red watched him spin the wheel. There was a loud clank and the door swung open on creaky hinges. Jonah stepped through and waved them forward.

"This way," he said.

Morgan went through the door next. Red followed, but stopped to examine the wheel. It appeared to move in only two directions, left and right. She spun it back and forth, using one hand, then both. It was kind of fun.

"Does it do anything else?" she asked, turning it again.

"Nope," Morgan said, prying her fingers off the hatch. "Let's go. You can play with it later."

The hallway had lights like she'd never seen affixed to the walls about every twenty feet. She could see Jonah moving ahead of them. He didn't seem too concerned about his safety. He had a pistol on his thigh, but he wasn't even watching them—or maybe he was. Red looked around and immediately spotted digital recorders.

The hall was bare with thick concrete walls and a matching floor. Sound traveled, but quickly muted.

"How thick are these walls?" she asked.

"Very," Morgan said. "The shaft we just came down was used to launch missiles. These walls had to be thick enough to contain the blast."

"What are those?" She pointed to the balls stuck on all the doors.

"Those are called door knobs. You turn them to open and close the doors just like the hatch."

Red approached one cautiously and tried to turn it. The metal felt cool to the touch, but nothing happened. "I think this one's broken," she said.

"Why?" he asked.

"Because it doesn't turn," she said. "See?" She tried the knob again, but it merely rattled in her grip.

Morgan smiled indulgently. "It's probably locked."

Her lips pursed. "I keep forgetting that you're from this world," she said softly.

"I'm in your world now." He reached for her hand.

Instead of giving it a reassuring squeeze, Morgan laced his fingers through hers and held on as they walked.

"I've never been this far underground. Do you think Jonah will have what we need? And if he does, will the equipment work from here?" she asked.

"He should," Morgan said. "Most missile silos came equipped with communication centers. They were made to work underground. We just have to hope that no one looted this one before Jonah moved in."

Jonah waited for them at the end of the hall. He stood in front of another metal door.

"This way," he said, opening it and then stepping aside.

Morgan dropped Red's hand and walked forward to look inside. "It's okay," he said.

She followed. There was a decent-size room and another long hall, except this one had several doors shooting off from the main hall.

"Welcome to Eden," Jonah said after they were all in the room.

Red looked around at the sparse mismatched furnishings and the metal doors. Nothing about this place reminded her of the biblical Eden. Eden was supposed to be lush, green, and bursting with life. This place was just the opposite with its sterile gray walls, beige, green, and orange furniture, and steel doors. Her expression must have given away her thoughts.

"Don't let outward appearances fool you," Jonah said. He walked over to the nearest door and opened it, revealing a botanical wonderland.

Red gasped. "Is that real?" she asked.

Jonah grinned. "Every last leaf. Go ahead. Check it out."

Red couldn't believe her eyes. She'd seen the greenhouses

inside the biodomes. They were organized in neat rows to optimize growth. This place looked like the jungles she'd read about in school. Plants exploded from every direction, cutting off walkways and towering overhead. Bright lights dotted the ceilings. "But how?" she asked, gaping at the multitude of green. So many shades, so many different textures. The beauty was so overwhelming that it nearly hurt her eyes.

"Those are sunlamps," Morgan said from behind her. "They provide the light needed to grow these things. What I don't understand is how you managed all this without any water."

Morgan and Red turned back to Jonah, who looked like a proud father showing off his first child.

"It's spring fed," he said.

"That's not possible." Red sobered. "All the springs in the world were poisoned during the last war."

His brow quirked. "Not all of them," Jonah said. "I test the water daily. So far, it's clean. We even have enough to shower."

Morgan's body practically quivered. "You have showers here. With real water."

Jonah nodded and grinned. "Yep, we sure do. We use solar panels to heat the water."

"Do you have any idea the kind of gold mine you're sitting on?" Morgan asked.

Jonah's smile withered. "This is my Eden. I share it with whom I wish and no one else. A few people have tried to take advantage of my good nature and hospitality. They are buried out back in unmarked graves." The warning in his voice was clear. "Now let me show you where you'll be staying."

He stood at the door. Red didn't want to leave. There was something about this room that felt so peaceful, so relaxing. It reminded her of the photos in her grandfather's books. The green world he'd spoken about on so many occasions.

She reached out and touched the petals of a yellow flower. They were soft and dewy. The fragrance coming from the blooms perfumed the air. "Amazing," she murmured. This place truly was Eden. Red had the overwhelming urge to stay. Chuck her old life, leaving Nuria and Roark behind for good. The thought scared her. She released the plant and followed Morgan and Jonah through the door.

They were led farther down the hall to another set of steel doors.

"You'll find showers and extra clothes in there. Let me know if you need anything else. When you're done bathing, just come out and I'll show you to your room. The halls are monitored, so don't get any funny ideas. One blast of the alarms and the guards have orders to eliminate all outside intruders."

Morgan stopped him before he left. "We need to use your communication equipment, if you have any."

"Later," Jonah said, opening the door to a tiled room.

Red stepped through the doorway and looked around. The room was plain with white walls and metal benches bolted to the floor. Several showerheads protruded from the far wall. Metal cases of some kind flanked the row of showerheads. She ran her hands over the metal, examining the dials attached to the outsides.

"Those are called lockers," Morgan said after Jonah shut the door. "You put your clothes inside while you shower."

Red frowned, spinning the dial. "Why doesn't it open?" she asked. She spun the dial the other direction just like the door knob, but nothing happened.

"You have to pull up," Morgan said, showing her.

The door to the locker swung open, revealing towels. Red picked one up and placed it on the bench. "Do you think we're safe?" she asked, her gaze moving to the closed door. "He's been so accommodating—too accommodating if you ask me."

"His behavior is definitely unusual, but I think we're okay for the time being. I scented no deception. If Jonah wanted us dead, he wouldn't have bothered to give us the grand tour. He could've just ordered the guards to shoot." Morgan walked to the door and pressed a button.

"What did you do?" Red asked.

"Locked it," he said on his way back. He reached out and turned a knob. Water shot out of the showerhead. Morgan held his hand under the stream and adjusted the temperature. He played with the water, cupping it in his palm. "I can't believe this," he said, turning to grin at her. "I haven't had a real shower in years."

He started stripping his clothes off. Red watched the layers peel away, revealing bronzed skin. Within seconds he was gloriously naked. Her mouth went dry. She sat on the bench and gazed at Morgan as he dipped his head under the water, sloshing it down his back.

Sand and grit turned the water brown at his feet, but he didn't seem to mind. He was like a child experiencing his first chemical pool. He splashed and laughed, flicking water over his shoulder at her. Red giggled as moisture hit her. It felt incredible. She began to undress, watching the man she loved enjoy himself for the first time in weeks. It was good to see him smile. He hadn't done that in a while because there hadn't been a lot to smile about.

"Is the water still warm?" she asked, expecting him to say no.

"Yes," he said. "It's perfect." He splayed his hands, allowing the water to wash over his fingers.

"Save some for me," she said.

He was whistling now as he rubbed cleanser on his body. By the time she stepped near the spray, he was covered in foamy suds. Red ran her hands over his smooth skin, then dipped her head under the water.

"This feels so weird," she said. She'd spent her whole life taking chemical showers. Never once had she experienced water. It felt strange. It didn't immediately cleanse her parched skin. Instead, it slowly eroded the dirt, before washing it away.

Morgan cupped the water and let it rain over her head. Red laughed and closed her eyes as water splashed on her face. He grabbed the cleanser. "This is soap," he said. "It's what we used to use before they developed cleanser."

Red had heard soap used to come in bars, but she'd never

seen one. Morgan started rubbing the bar over her skin and she watched as bubbles began to form.

"This seems like an antiquated way of doing things," she said.

The words had barely left her mouth when Morgan ran the soap over her nipple, causing it to pucker.

"Antiquated, eh? I don't know about that. From here, it looks like we might've been missing out on the good stuff by using technology."

chapter twenty-one

Gina's breath caught as he swirled the bar of soap over her other nipple. Gooseflesh rose on her skin as he began a slow glide along her length, washing away the sand and grit, leaving clean skin and awareness behind.

Morgan couldn't take his eyes off her. She looked so beautiful with her long black hair hanging down her back. Her small breasts jutted proudly from her chest and her stomach quivered when he brushed a hand over it.

The soap left streaks of suds that were immediately washed away by the water sloshing over their bodies. He brought the soap to her head and began to lather his hands. When the suds were thick enough, he plunged his fingers into her hair and massaged her scalp.

Gina groaned. Her head fell back and her eyes closed as he scrubbed.

"That feels so good," she said, peeking out between wet lashes. Her body was flushed from the warm water. Morgan longed to taste her skin. She looked like a sprite playing in a fountain. Positively delicious. She shifted her legs, giving him tantalizing glimpses of her firm thighs and the black curls that hid something far more appetizing.

Morgan's mouth watered at the thought of dropping to his knees and tasting her. She'd be sweet. She always was when her juices flowed. Gina was everything he could ever ask for in a woman—a mate. He wouldn't lose her, couldn't lose her again. Not without losing himself in the process.

"Lower," she growled, shifting her head around so he could reach her fragile neck. His fingers slid down, guided by a force outside of himself. He could feel his body respond with every knead, every stroke. Round and round he rubbed, making sure he hadn't missed a spot.

"Relax, and let me lead," he murmured, trailing kisses over her collar bone, which were followed by gentle nibbles. "I'm just getting started."

Morgan guided Gina under the spray and rinsed the soap from her hair. It felt like silk in his hands. He ran his fingers through the length, carefully detangling it as he went. He continued his downward slide, even after he ran out of hair, until he was cupping the globes of her bottom. His strong hands began to mold her flesh, taking care not to rub too hard.

She groaned, resting her forehead on his shoulder as his lips once again found the curve of her neck. Her spicy scent rose above the fragrance of the soap, enticing his senses. Morgan reached lower, stroking her supple thighs. He loved her legs. They were so long and luscious. The feel of them wrapped around his body was as close to heaven as he'd ever get.

"Do you know how hot you made me when you shifted earlier?"

She shook her head, but didn't raise it from where it rested.

"I was so hard I nearly busted out of my pants. I was also incredibly proud of you. Still am. I always knew you could do it. You've given me a gift that I can't begin to repay." He clasped her thighs and slowly lifted. "I love you." The declaration branded her flesh. He wanted those words to sink so far inside her that she never forgot.

Gina instinctively encircled his neck, her taut breasts crushing into his chest. Morgan's knees locked and he leaned forward until her back made contact with the wet tiles.

She gasped.

"Cold?" he asked.

"Yes," she said, her voice a mere whisper.

"Won't be for long." Morgan nuzzled her neck, finding the spot where he'd claimed her.

Her hips rocked, brushing the top of his erection.

Morgan's jaw clenched as he fought for control. After a few swift breaths, he went back to the mark. His teeth grazed her tender flesh, followed by sensual laps of his rough tongue. He knew when he played with the spot it drove her crazy.

"You taste incredible. You've always tasted incredible. Is it any wonder I fell at your feet?"

"Mmm . . ." She rotated her hips again. The movement slotted his cock at her entrance. This time Gina wiggled, trying to lower herself. "I don't recall things going so smoothly."

"Honey, you had me the moment you sashayed into the dissecting lab." Morgan growled and bit down on her shoulder. Gina's head fell back and she mewed, her body shuddering in his hands. He couldn't seem to get enough of her blood. Like the finest liquor, she burned going down his throat and made him crave more. Morgan forced his mouth to release her.

He'd always liked the taste of blood during sex, a nibble here, a scratch there, but it had been more primal screwing than anything else. And he'd never marked anyone. Now he could hardly orgasm without blood being brought into the equation.

Red couldn't get enough of Morgan. His body was so rough and hot it nearly singed her. She still couldn't believe that she'd climaxed when he bit her. Even now her body rode a wave of sheer exhilaration, waiting to tumble once more. It helped that Morgan admitted to being proud of her. Hell, she was proud of herself. She'd finally shifted on command and it felt good. More than good. It felt natural.

She rocked her hips and Morgan slid an inch deeper. He was so hard and thick, she could barely catch her breath. Her eyes met his and froze. His amber gaze was shadowed and tinged with a ring of red.

"What's wrong? You're not thinking about the blood thing

again, are you?" she asked, brushing his forehead with her thumb to smooth the lines.

He didn't say anything as he licked the wound on her neck, then guided her under the warm cascading water.

"Morgan, talk to me."

He stared at her, his gaze seeking reassurance.

She held him close, comforting him the only way she knew how. Red knew he thought he was losing himself to the thirst for blood, but she knew better. Once an alpha wolf, always an alpha wolf. The vampire blood only enhanced his abilities.

He shook his head and the wariness faded. "It's nothing. I'm sure it's just the stress of being on the run."

She tilted his chin and kissed him, allowing her lips to linger. "Talk to me," Red said.

"You still feel connected to me, right?" he asked. "I mean your feelings haven't diminished since Raphael shared his blood." Morgan subconsciously brushed his thumb over the spot on her neck.

Red's eyes widened. How could he think such a thing after all they'd been through? She had to reassure him. "Of course not. If anything, the bond I feel for you has grown." Even now she yearned to feel his teeth in her flesh, the brush of his tongue, the gentle pull of his lips as he sucked her blood.

His smile came out lopsided and wolfish. "Glad to hear it's not one-sided."

"I know it seems silly, but I was concerned because my tastes have changed. I have cravings for things that I wouldn't normally—shouldn't crave. I know vampires can't turn people into vampires. It's not like in the entertainment vids. They aren't magical creatures. They're genetically engineered like I am. But that doesn't explain the changes I've experienced. It's like he somehow infected me."

Red listened, paying attention to what he wasn't saying. Raphael was a vampire, so naturally he needed blood. He could go outside, but most vamps couldn't. No wonder Morgan was afraid. But despite his fears, Red knew in her heart he hadn't changed. Now all she had to do was convince him. "You bit me and took my blood long before Raphael saved you," she said. "So the wolf part of you must be inclined to do that."

His eyes met hers and pain turned them molten. "That was different."

"How so?"

"Unmarked females aren't allowed to stay in Nuria. They disrupt the pack. I was marking you," he said softly.

Red tried to squirm out of his arms, but he wouldn't let her. "You only did it to keep me safe?" For some reason that thought hurt. She'd always assumed he'd done it for more personal reasons.

"No," he said, shaking his head.

"Then why?" Red asked.

"For me." The words were so faint that she barely heard them. "I wanted you so badly I never considered your feelings. I'm sorry." He brushed a hand over her arm soothingly.

"So you didn't mark me because of the rules?" Red asked, relieved to hear him say so.

"That's the reason I gave myself when I decided to do it." Morgan snorted. "But I was only trying to justify my actions. I hope someday you can forgive me."

There was a time when Red would've been angry after hearing his confession, but that was before she almost lost him to Roark Montgomery.

She sighed and gently stroked his hair. "There's nothing to forgive," she said. "We've both done things we aren't proud of. There's no changing the past."

Morgan tilted his chin. "You aren't mad?"

She shook her head. "No, but I am curious."

"About what?" he asked.

"You said you bit me in order to mark me as yours."

He nodded.

Red nibbled on her lower lip. "Does it matter that I never bit you back?"

A genuine smile played at his sensual lips. "Yes and no. To Nuria, you're still considered my mate. But *I* need more than their acceptance. I need yours."

The vulnerability she saw in his eyes was something Red had never witnessed from Morgan. He'd always been fearless and aggressive. Every inch an alpha werewolf. This moment was different. He was laying his heart in her hands to do with as she pleased. If she chose to, she could crush him and walk away. But if she did that, Red would be hurting herself, too. In the end, the choice was easy.

"Do you want me to claim you?" she asked.

"It must be your decision. I've disrupted your life enough. I will not take this choice away, too."

She started to lower her mouth to the spot where his neck met his shoulder.

"Wait!" Morgan cried out, halting her midmotion. "There is one more thing you should know before you bite."

Red nodded for him to continue.

"If you bite me, it's irreversible. You won't be able to take anyone else to your rest pad without suffering extreme discomfort. So think about it. You need to make an informed decision," he said. His eyes closed and the muscles in his body tensed as he waited for her to decide.

"I thought you said that vamps and wolves can't change regular people," she said.

"That's true, but you aren't a pureblood. You're a wolf. A biological human-wolf hybrid. You weren't created like me and the others. You were born this way. A medical impossibility, according to the scientists who created us. To me and to the creatures like me, you are rarer than the freshwater spring beneath this missile silo. That's why I want you to be sure. Really sure. Because once you do this there will be no escape for either of us." Morgan cupped her face.

She kissed his firm lips tenderly. "I've already made my decision," Red said. And she had. She'd made it the moment she'd broken the law and crossed into no-man's-land.

Morgan's eyes opened. "Are you positive?" he asked. She

could see the hope blossoming in his rich amber depths, but he kept it tightly leashed.

"I am," she said and continued her descent. Red's lips brushed Morgan's throat. Despite the soap he'd used earlier, his skin still held a hint of salt and a rich earthy aroma.

She licked the spot she intended to bite, then concentrated on producing fangs. Pain shot through her jaw and blood filled her mouth as her teeth were ejected by sharper incisors. She spit them out, rinsing quickly with water to cleanse her palate. She wanted to taste him and only him.

Red returned to the tendon bulging at the base of Morgan's neck. It strained beneath her lips, so enticing, so inviting. She could no longer resist. The world flashed brilliant colors a second before she bit down.

Morgan's body jerked, driving his erection deep into her body.

Red gasped at the sudden invasion as her channel adjusted to his size, but she didn't let loose. Instead, she drew deep, filling her mouth with his blood. Morgan's whole body trembled beneath her and he slowly sunk to the ground, still cradling her against him. Red rocked her hips, taking him deeper, while her tongue worked the tender flesh at his neck.

Corded muscle bunched every time she sucked, but Morgan made no move to stop her. His eyes were closed and his jaw remained clenched as he teetered on the verge of release. Red had never felt more powerful in her life. She rose up onto her knees, then slowly glided back down.

Morgan groaned, his hands curling into fists as he let her have her way.

Red swiped her tongue over the bite mark, then began to fuck him in earnest. He didn't touch her, but she could tell it pained him to do so. She rode Morgan steadily until they were both panting for relief. Red reached down between their bodies and stroked. Morgan's eyes were open now, riveted on her fingers. His rib cage cracked as his body attempted to shift.

Red smiled. It was the first time she'd ever seen him this

out of control. She ground her hips into him, nearly sending her over the edge. Morgan cried out as claws sprang from his fingertips. His eyes changed to a deep gold and his fangs came out. He tongued them and growled. The sound hardened her nipples and Red felt the first ripple of release rush through her system.

She squeezed him, refusing to orgasm without him. Morgan was so far gone that was all it took. He bellowed, his hands latching onto her hips without slicing her to pieces.

Red arched, feeling him thrust wildly before emptying inside of her. Her hands moved to her breasts to tweak her nipples as she milked his cock. Morgan placed his hands over the top of hers, the claws now gone, and gently squeezed. Red shuddered.

"I don't think I can move," he said, kissing her tenderly.

"Try, the water's getting cold," Red said.

They rose and rinsed, before shutting off the shower. Morgan grabbed the towels and began drying her.

"I can do that myself," she said.

"I know." He grinned. "But I can't seem to keep my hands off you."

Red brushed his scruffy face lovingly with her fingertips.

He finished drying her, then handed her the clean clothes he'd found in one of the other lockers. They didn't fit. The shirt was too tight and the pants were too loose, but they'd do until she could clean her others.

"Now let's go talk to our host," Morgan said, getting dressed.

They found Jonah waiting in a nearby room. He was staring at something that held wires and circuits. "I was about to send in the guards to get you two." He snickered.

Heat flooded Red's face and she looked away before he could see. "I'd never seen a water shower before," she said in way of explanation.

"I doubt all that groaning and moaning was due to the shower," he said, giving her a look that said she wasn't fooling anyone. "Relax, I'm teasing."

"What are you doing?" she asked, changing the subject.

He pointed to the flat board in front of him. "Trying to get this to work."

"What is it?" she asked.

"A circuit board," Morgan answered.

Jonah glanced at him and raised a brow. "How did you know? Most people these days have never seen a circuit board outside of a museum."

Morgan looked uncomfortable for a moment. "You make do with what you have," he said by way of an answer.

Jonah's gaze sharpened, but he didn't persist. "I think this one is shot, unless you can get it working," he said.

Morgan stared at it. "I can take a crack at it," he said. "Do you have a computer to attach it to?"

"What's a computer?" Red asked.

"It's like a compunit, but much, much more primitive," Morgan said.

Red stared at the equipment. Morgan had said they might be able to piece something together in order to contact the outside world, but now that she'd seen the circuit board, she was having doubts. Five years' worth of rust covered the flat board, along with a layer or twelve of dust. It would take a miracle to get it working and Red was fresh out of believing in those.

"My dear," Jonah said. "Perhaps you can help me gather some vegetables for a meal."

Red looked at Morgan. She could tell by his expression and the tension in his taut frame that he didn't want her to go, but she was of no use to him here. At least picking vegetables was something she could do. She hoped. Red had never actually picked anything that didn't come out of a food dispensing machine.

"Don't worry," she said, brushing a lock of dark hair from Morgan's handsome face. "I'll be fine." Her gaze swung around, pinning Jonah where he stood. "Besides, if he tries anything, I'll rip his heart out and eat it."

Jonah laughed, but Red didn't. She kept her expression neutral and waited for him to squirm. Great host or not, she meant every word.

chapter twenty-two

Red followed Jonah into the greenhouse. The room was hot and moist, a sensation she'd never experienced before. She was used to hot and dry, but the moisture was different. It clung to her skin, beading on her lip and forehead. Her clothes became weighted after a few minutes, clinging to her modest curves.

"What is this called?" she asked, feeling the air with her fingertips.

"Humidity," Jonah said.

"Is it always this sticky?"

"Always," he said, grinning. "The vegetables are over here. Once we gather some, we'll head over to the fruit trees."

Red glanced around, trying to take the place in. The space was so large that it was impossible to see everything from one spot. The air was rich, almost as if it couldn't be contained by the room. She'd seen pictures in the vids and read stories about the planet in its green years, but nothing could've prepared her for the sensory overload of this wild place. This place that was so foreign, yet oddly comforting.

"How long did it take you to grow all this?" she asked, touching a leaf. It was smooth and moist, its fine "hairs" tickling her fingertips. She laughed in awe of what he'd created.

"Years," he said. "We lost a lot of crops at first, then we worked out the proper temperature and environment. After that, things took off rather quickly. Now come over here and help me pick carrots."

Red walked over to where he stood. The tufts of green stuck out of the ground every few inches. "I've read about carrots, tasted synth ones, but I've never seen a real one. What should I do?"

"Follow my lead." Jonah reached down and grabbed one of the green stalks at the base and pulled. An orange root appeared. He dusted off the extra dirt and shoved it into a basket crooked at his elbow.

"This," he said, pointing to the orange bit, "is a carrot."

"You eat the orange part?" she asked, eyeing it like it might bite. Didn't look very appetizing. Synth-carrots were purple.

"Yes." He wiped off more dirt, then brought it up to his mouth and bit down.

Red watched him. The root crunched as he chewed. Jonah smiled, flashing orange teeth, then swallowed.

"Here," he said, holding out the carrot. "Give it a try."

Red hesitated, then leaned forward and inhaled. It didn't smell bad. Strange, but not bad. She stuck her tongue out and touched it. The texture was weird. Hard. Much harder than anything she'd ever eaten. She took a bite. The first taste was sweet, but it was quickly followed by a tang of bitterness. She chewed, allowing the root to crunch, then swallowed. She wasn't totally convinced that real carrots were better than synth ones.

"What do you think?" Jonah asked expectantly.

"Not bad." Red analyzed the taste that remained in her mouth. "It would take some getting used to," she said, not wanting to hurt his feelings.

"They're a lot better once they've been stir-fried. They soften up quite a bit and the bitterness goes away."

Red shook her head. The terms Jonah used were so foreign to her that she had no idea what he was talking about.

Her confusion must've shown because he added. "Cut up and tossed in a pan over a fire. It's one of the many ways we cook things out here."

No food dispensers or protein packs. Everything done by hand over a fire no less. It was almost too much to fathom. Could she live like this? Would she want to if given the choice? Red didn't know. "Why are you helping us?" she asked. The question had been nagging her since they'd met.

"You mean why help two fugitives?" he retorted.

Her stomach clenched, twisting the carrot she'd just swallowed. "Yes," Red said, wondering if she'd have to kill Jonah after all. If she did, who would tend the plants? She looked at the basket of carrots and frowned.

"As a rule, I've never liked politicians and I don't believe half of what I hear."

Red nodded. "Good policy, but there has to be more to it than that," she said, unconvinced those were the only reasons for his assistance.

His gaze grew distant. "I didn't always live here, you know. I had a wife and family once upon a time. Back in the days when they used to hunt you down and force the chip into your neck. Not everyone took the time to do it right. A lot of people died during the implantation process. People were afraid to help." Jonah shook his head to clear it. "I realize governing bodies are a necessary evil, but I don't have to like them. Never believed in folks being chipped for their own good. Thought it violated the basic right to privacy. Still do, but I'm in the minority."

"Morgan feels the same," Red said. Although he'd preferred to fight for changes on the inside before the trouble with Roark cropped up, instead of running away to live as an unknown. Red supposed these choices weren't as black and white as she'd once thought. She inhaled, smelling only leaves and earth. Red could detect no deception on Jonah's part. But she worried that the soil was fooling her senses. Or, maybe she was just seeing things clearly for the first time.

Jonah's eyes crinkled. "Smart man. I knew I liked Morgan. Now I know why," he said with a wink.

* * *

Morgan spent the next two days trying to piece together enough equipment to fashion a transmitter and receiver. It was difficult, given that most of the computers hadn't been touched since the early twenty-first century. There was no telling whether it would work. And if by some miracle it did, Morgan could only think of one man who might be able to hear them. He wasn't sure if Coleman Parker would listen after everything he'd done.

The Eye of God, as Coleman liked to be called, had welcomed him on his first day of work at the Santa Fe Cloning Lab Corporation. He'd invited him out for drinks and dinner, which Morgan had happily accepted. He knew the man wanted more than friendship and he'd used Coleman's attraction to get close enough to his electrical equipment to jam it.

At the time, Morgan had thought he was doing so in order to retrieve the DNA of his wife, Sarah, and son, Joshua, who'd died during the last war. According to false bulletins, they were to be cloned for pleasure use and cheap labor.

After the explosion at the lab that Roark Montgomery had arranged, Morgan realized that he'd been set up to take the fall. The politician had made sure he was spotted near the blast. Roark had arrived shortly after the bomb detonated and carted him off to the Taos Detention Center, while the Eye of God watched in disbelief.

Morgan ran a hand over his freshly shaven face. It wouldn't be long before the stubble returned. He sat back and stretched, trying to loosen the kinks in his back from being hunched over circuit boards.

Gina had gone to sleep hours ago. He should've joined her, but he couldn't keep his mind off the equipment. He'd put Gina through so much. She'd given up everything she'd ever worked for, and for what? To go on the run? Become a wanted criminal? To follow a man who abandoned her when she needed him most? Morgan vowed once again to be a better man. The kind of man Gina deserved.

The only way he was going to be able to keep his word was if he got them out of this mess. His eyes lit on the diaries he'd found at Kane's home when they'd been hiding out.

Morgan had thrown them into his pack, but hadn't listened to them yet.

The thought of hearing Kane's voice again was too painful to bear. He still had nightmares about killing his cousin and probably always would. Morgan hadn't told Gina about the dreams because he hadn't wanted to upset her. She had enough on her mind without tossing his guilt onto the pile.

He looked around the area that used to house the command center. So many memories, so much destruction. And for what? A planet that was barely able to sustain life. How long before their luck ran out?

The diaries were a constant reminder that life as he knew it was over. This may be his only chance to connect to the man he once loved like a brother. Morgan picked up the first digital diary and turned it over in his hands.

He stopped spinning it and pressed play. A hiss erupted. It was followed by Kane's deep baritone, discussing inconsequential things. At least at first. Morgan flushed and looked around to ensure he was still alone, as Kane had moved on to describing the last time they'd shared a woman. He fast-forwarded to see if there was anything else on the device, but it ended with Kane's thoughts about the evening and ideas for future encounters. Sadness welled. Not for their past, but for the future they were denied.

Even if his cousin hadn't died, Morgan had moved beyond sharing women now that Gina was in his life. He dropped the recorder and picked up another. There were thirteen diary entries total. Morgan hoped they weren't all like this one or he'd definitely have to go find Gina.

Unfortunately, he got his wish. The next ten recordings were barely comprehensible rants about Morgan's leadership or lack thereof and the need for a change. By the time he'd finished listening to the eleventh recording, Morgan's chest hurt as if he'd done twelve rounds in a ring with a prizefighter. They'd been so close at one time.

How could he have missed all the signs of his cousin's unhappiness? Maybe Kane was right. Maybe it was time for new blood to lead Nuria.

He glanced at the two remaining recordings and debated whether to listen or to just toss them in the trash. Morgan pushed them aside and went back to work on the transmitter. He got his first signal shortly after dawn. It was crackly and didn't sound like much, but he hoped it would be enough. The Eye of God had powerful equipment at work and at home. He'd talked about being able to pick up signals around the world. Morgan prayed he hadn't just been bragging to impress him.

He soldered two more wires together and tried speaking into the jury-rigged device. Morgan waited and listened, hearing only pops and squeals. He put his mouth to the mic.

"Eye of God, can you hear me?" he asked.

Static answered with an angry hiss.

"Coleman, I know you're always listening to rogue communications. Please pick up. It's Morgan."

More garbled signals came back, some so high pitched only his wolf could hear them. What had he expected? A welcome back? Glad to hear your voice? Oh, by the way, thanks for fucking up my equipment and making me look bad on the job?

Morgan sat back in his chair and ran a hand through his hair. It needed a cut. Maybe he'd take care of that before they left here. He'd been at it all night and for what? Static. Gina was still asleep. He decided to let her rest. No sense in waking her with the bad news.

Morgan continued to listen to the high-pitched whirls for another hour, hope fading. He picked up one of the two remaining diary entries his cousin had made. This time when he pressed play a different voice appeared. Kane's rich baritone had been replaced. Whether from lack of sleep or disbelief, it took Morgan a moment to recognize the voice. When he did, he nearly fell out of his chair. He grabbed the device and hit replay. No, he wasn't imagining it. The voice *was* Roark Montgomery's. Why did Kane have a recording of the politician?

Morgan listened carefully. He could hear the sound of the emergency care center in the background. Kane had been at work when he recorded this. It was the next words out of Roark's mouth that nearly shattered Morgan's composure.

I want you to take care of Gina Santiago. Morgan jumped back to the beginning of the recording to make sure his exhausted mind wasn't playing tricks on him, but the words were the same. This time Morgan let the recording continue, listening in horror as Roark ordered a hit on his beloved Gina and openly discussed the Others.

"We have you now, you bastard," Morgan muttered under his breath. He looked at the jumble of multicolored wires lying on the table in front of him. He picked up a few and started detangling them. If he could only get this blasted machine to transmit, they may just have found a way out of this mess. And their chance had come from the most unlikely source.

Demery struggled to keep to his feet as he tumbled down the short ridge. Reaper had beaten him for hours after discovering Red and Morgan missing. It was only his promise to return Morgan to the asshole that had kept him and his blood woman alive. Even now, he could hear Melea's screams tearing at his eardrums and see the tears streaming down her face as Reaper tied her facedown onto a battered old truck and sliced her clothes off with a wicked blade.

His chest clenched in pain as the memories flooded his mind. Demery had thought for sure that Reaper was going to kill her. Perhaps he should have. It would've been kinder than what he'd put them through. Demery would never forgive Reaper. Never forgive Morgan for causing it or for forcing Red to leave. And he had no doubt that Morgan had been behind her leaving without him. Red wasn't the type to leave a man behind.

He willed his body to rise, pushing past the agony to keep moving. They couldn't have gotten much farther than the mountains. Maybe Reaper already had them. He shook his head, knowing that wasn't the case.

There was no way Morgan would've gone down without a

fight, and Demery would have heard the laser fire crackling on the wind. Instead, all he'd heard was the drone of vehicles as the Sand Devils made their way to their other compound and the constant ringing in his ears from Reaper's right hook.

Demery swallowed hard, his throat parched from lack of blood. He should've been fine after feeding two nights ago, but trying to repair the beating had used up his reserves. He hadn't seen a living creature for the past three hours, but he'd seen plenty of dead ones. Fortunately, none of them had been Morgan or Red.

He could see the foothills up ahead. It had taken all night, but he'd finally made it through the mountains. He was too tired to celebrate the small victory. Too hurt to even shout.

He'd been lucky. Reaper had let him live. Barely. The only thing that mattered was that Melea was still alive. As long as she lived, he would. She'd pleaded with him to stay. Pleaded with him to save her when Reaper mounted her body and rutted in her bruised flesh like a mongrel dog.

Demery could still hear her muffled wails as she uselessly beat at the monster's sides. He felt her pain and humiliation, then the sudden invasion, tearing at his flesh as if it were he who'd been violated.

Damn the blood bond.

Reaper had laughed, his knowing gaze locked on Demery. "Enjoying it, vamp?" he'd asked, pumping harder.

Demery had closed his eyes and gritted his teeth, shutting out Reaper and the shocked pain of what was happening. He'd willed Melea to do the same. When the Sand Devil was finished defiling her and Demery, Reaper ordered Melea to be removed to their other compound.

The beatings had begun shortly thereafter. Demery had been grateful that Reaper had not forced Melea to watch like he'd forced him to do. Through the years he'd suffered worse physical injuries, but the blood had always been there to ease his pain. Now nothing outside of vengeance would.

Reaper was sadistic and knew that the best way to torture him was through his weaknesses, the need for blood and Melea. Demery tripped and fell halfway down one of the foothills before coming to rest against a boulder. Everything ached and it hurt to breathe. He laid there for a few minutes, then forced himself to his feet. Demery checked his suit to make sure it hadn't ripped in the tumble.

Anger pushed him on, fueling his muscles. He had to find Morgan and Red. He knew they'd have come through here at some point. This was the only trail leading over the mountains. The only track smooth enough to traverse.

The land was beginning to flatten out. The foothills became smaller and smaller the farther away from the mountains he got. The scent of blood caught his attention. Demery followed it, his senses springing to life.

He didn't know if an animal had been wounded or perhaps it was those he sought. Thirty minutes later he found the remnants of a small crimson puddle that had long ago dried in the heat. It had Red's essence all over it and the strong scent of wolf.

Demery glanced around the area, examining the clearing. Nothing else had been disturbed, which meant there hadn't been a struggle. He inhaled deeply. The blood was a day or so old. Had he really lost a day after the beating? It must be true if he was this far behind. Morgan and Red had shifted, which meant they were covering far more ground than they would have normally.

He cursed out loud, using languages he hadn't spoken since his childhood. They could be anywhere by now. But at least he knew where they'd been headed before the detour with the Sand Devils. Had they found the outpost? He'd been the one guiding them. He knew where it was located. They didn't. Had they gotten lost? They wouldn't last long if that were the case, especially with the Sand Devils on the move south. They were bound to come across them if they were caught out in the open.

Demery decided to follow his gut. It was leading him to the outpost. If Morgan and Red stopped there for supplies or to head to another location, he'd find out . . . or he'd torture everyone he encountered until he did. His blood was counting on him.

Demery came upon the compound several hours later. He dropped to his knees, half out of exhaustion and half to avoid being spotted. The outpost was heavily armed and situated in a location that gave them good visibility. They'd see anyone approaching no matter which direction they chose.

He stared at the three towers, gauging his chances of making it under one without being spotted. He decided they were nil. He'd have to take a direct approach and hope he got close enough to get his hands on one of the guards.

Demery looked down at his protective suit. He'd have to be careful. He couldn't chance one of them shooting a hole in it while the sun was up. He glanced around at the sand, its choking beige closing in on him with its oppressive monotony. How could anyone stand to live out here? At least in the towns and biodomes there was some green to look at. Out here there was nothing but death and sand relentlessly staring at you.

He burrowed deeper into the dune to plan his approach, trying to ignore the constant growl of his stomach and steady pain from his ribs. His dreadlocks were matted to his head where Reaper had kicked him, the lump that remained a reminder of the asshole's displeasure.

He'd sensed Morgan's Otherness when they'd first arrived in their camp. Luckily, he hadn't detected Red's. Reaper wanted a pet, one he could bleed when it suited him. Somehow he'd found out that drinking an Other's blood could give him strength. He'd been seeking them out ever since.

Demery had made the mistake of trying to trade with him. When that didn't work, he'd gambled and lost. Melea paid for that mistake with her innocence. Demery had promised to protect her and he'd failed. He'd never get over it and neither would she. By the time Demery was done, he vowed Morgan would feel every last ounce of pain they'd endured.

chapter twenty-three

Robert Santiago sat behind his desk, rifling through synth-paper reports. He'd tried to review them and sign off, but couldn't, his concentration too scattered to focus on the work before him. It had been almost two weeks since he'd heard from his granddaughter. It felt more like an eternity. He should've been there to protect her.

If he had, she wouldn't be in this predicament. But Robert knew it wasn't true. It had always been only a matter of time before Gina discovered the truth about her family history, about her true nature. There was no way he could've predicted the path that knowledge would lead her down. Unfortunately, it did little to stave off his guilt.

He rubbed his temples, attempting to fight off a headache. He should've gone home for the night and at least grabbed a couple of hours of sleep, but it was too late now. Morning had arrived. His navcom beeped, then immediately fired medication into his bloodstream. It wouldn't help. Hadn't helped the four previous times either.

The vidscreen on his desk activated. He dropped his hands and turned to the screen. Tucker, a man he recognized from the tech repair lab, was standing outside his office door, holding something.

Robert Santiago glanced at his watch to confirm the time, then pressed a button on his desk to open the door.

"Commander, I've found something," Tucker said, stepping

through the door. His clothing was rumpled and his brown hair poked out from all sides. Despite the early hour, excitement added lift to his gait.

Robert held a finger to his lips, immediately silencing the man. He pointed to the door, which hadn't closed yet. Tucker nodded in understanding and waited. The door slid closed with a hiss.

"You were saying," Robert said.

"You're never going to believe it." He rushed forward. "We found something on the navcom, but it doesn't make sense."

"Play it for me," Robert said.

Tucker did as he was asked. Roark Montgomery's voice came out of the small speaker.

You'd have been dead . . . now . . . Kane hadn't fallen for you and fucked . . . up. He had orders to kill you.

What you're doing is highly illegal . . . (Gina's voice) *If the tactical . . .* (static) *. . . found out, you . . .* (hiss) *. . . arrested.*

But . . . (pop) *. . . aren't going to find . . .* (static) *. . . I'll report your escape . . . like I reported . . . Hunter's.*

Roark's threat was as clear as if the politician was standing in the room with them. Robert Santiago trembled, not from fear for himself, but for what his granddaughter had gone through. She must've been terrified sitting in the back of that shuttle.

The recording stopped abruptly.

"What happened to it?" he snapped.

Tucker's face flushed. "I'm sorry. That's all we could recover. The crystals were crushed."

It wasn't a lot, but coupled with the shuttle they'd towed in thanks to Catherine Meyers' GPS coordinates it would be enough. "I want a copy of that before you leave this room," Robert said.

"I anticipated as much," he said, taking out a miniature digi-recorder. "It's already on there. What would you like me to do with the original?"

"Seal it in the vault as evidence, then repair the navcom. I want Rita up and running asap."

Tucker shook his head. "It's in so many pieces I'm not sure that's going to be possible."

Robert smiled at him. "I have complete confidence in your abilities."

Tucker grinned. "I'll do my best." He walked toward the door. "Sir?"

"Yes?"

"Was that Roark Montgomery on the recording?"

He debated whether to answer truthfully. "Yes, it was."

"But he's running for office on a reform and unity platform," Tucker said, unable to comprehend why the man would do such a thing.

"I know." Robert Santiago stopped him before he left. "Tucker, I trust you'll keep what you found in the strictest of confidence. Need I remind you this is an active case."

"Yes, sir." He looked stricken.

Robert had seen that look before. The last time had been on his own face, when someone he'd looked up to had fallen from grace. A man didn't get over that kind of thing, but he did learn from it. "Once you've placed the evidence into the vault, take the rest of the day off. You've earned it."

Tucker's expression brightened again. "Thank you, sir."

"Dismissed."

Lieutenant Bannon Richards ran into Tucker, the tech lead, coming out of Commander Robert Santiago's office. The man was distracted and didn't notice he'd stepped into his path. The tech guy ran straight into him as Bannon had planned.

"Heads up, Private Tucker," Bannon said. "A commanding officer is present."

The man's eyes widened and he stiffened to attention. "Sorry, sir. I didn't see you there."

"That's because you weren't paying attention. Where were you headed in such a hurry?" Bannon asked. He knew where Tucker had come from. He needed to know why the tech had been visiting the commander. The thought that the reason could be innocent was quickly dismissed when Tucker's expression grew wary.

Tucker took longer than he should've to answer. "Nowhere, sir. Just back to the lab." His gaze dropped, leaving little doubt that he'd lied.

Bannon nudged him, moving into Tucker's personal space. "What were you doing in the commander's office?" he asked, his tone demanding the truth.

"N-nothing. He'd wanted updates on some repairs I've been working on," Tucker said.

Bannon's eyes narrowed. What was the commander up to? He never asked about regular maintenance. "Repairs on what?" he asked, not expecting an answer.

"A junked navcom," the man said, his gaze darting down the deserted hallway. "If you'll excuse me, I'd better get back to work." Tucker swallowed hard and sweat broke out along his temples.

Bannon reluctantly moved aside to allow him to pass. Tucker had gone five steps when Bannon called out, "Did you succeed?"

He stopped and slowly looked over his shoulder. "Yes, I did." Tucker rushed off without another glance.

Bannon didn't know what was going on, but he figured the navcom must be pretty important if Robert Santiago was requesting the tech department to report directly to him. He thought about the talking navcom unit Red used to wear and realized he should've asked the tech guy more questions.

Roark had told him to keep an eye on things. Mainly to let him know if he'd seen any sign of Gina Santiago. He hadn't. But something told him that Roark would want to know about this.

He walked away from the commander's office and pressed a button on his navcom. He didn't want to be overheard. It took a few seconds to receive confirmation that the private connection had indeed been made. A moment later, Roark's voice boomed out of the tiny speaker.

"Sir, this is Lieutenant Bannon Richards. I may have something."

"Has Gina Santiago tried to contact her grandfather?" Roark asked.

He shook his head, forgetting Roark couldn't see him. "Not that I'm aware of," Bannon said.

There was silence. "Then why are you contacting me?" he asked. "I told you the only time you should call is if you spotted Gina or Morgan."

Bannon was beginning to think he'd made a mistake. He'd been so damned determined to earn a position at Roark's side that he'd acted hastily. If he wasn't so concerned about angering Roark further, he'd disconnect now. Instead, he brought his lips closer to the mic. "I just ran into a tech guy who was leaving the commander's office."

"So?" Roark said. "That's fairly common as I recall."

"Yes, sir. Normally it is." Bannon lowered his voice when a private walked by. "He said the commander had him working on a busted navcom. Seemed kind of odd, since the commander doesn't care about broken equipment beyond viewing repair request reports."

Roark was silent again. "Did this tech tell you where he got the navcom?"

Bannon experienced a flush of embarrassment. He hadn't bothered to ask, but he wasn't about to inform Roark of his incompetence. "No, sir."

A buzz sounded on the line.

"What was that, sir?" Bannon asked, fearing someone had intercepted their communiqué.

Roark didn't immediately respond.

"Sir?" Bannon repeated. Maybe he hadn't heard him. The buzz grew more insistent.

"It appears that your commander is trying to get in touch with me. I better see what he wants. Keep your eyes and ears open, Lieutenant. Good work."

Roark cut the transmission and straightened his tie. The vidscreen glowed, then buzzed again. He pressed a button on his desk and Robert Santiago's weathered face appeared on the screen.

"Commander, I was just on my way out," he lied. "What

can I do for you?" Roark asked, giving him his best bored expression. It was no coincidence that the commander contacted him now. He must have found something really important. Stay calm. No need to panic. Find out what he wants.

Robert's dark eyes sizzled with barely leashed fury. "It seems a navcom has been recovered from your old shuttle," he said.

"My shuttle?" Roark's heart began to pound. What kind of game was Robert Santiago playing?

"Yes, you know the one you said Morgan Hunter bombed in order to help Gina escape."

Roark forced a smile. "Ah, that shuttle. A total loss. I haven't thought about it since the incident. How did you find it by the way?"

Robert waved the question away. "It's not important. What is important is what was inside the shuttle."

"And what would that be?" Roark asked, tugging at his tie.

Surely there had to be more than a navcom if he was contacting him. Roark had thought his man had taken care of everything when he'd hauled the shuttle farther out into the desert and blasted a hole in its side. Obviously he'd forgotten to search the inside. Or maybe he'd thought the laser cannon blast would take care of any lingering evidence. He'd been a fool and Roark planned to make sure he never had the opportunity to repeat his stupidity—after he dealt with the commander.

"A navcom was recovered from the site."

"So you've said. Is that it?" Roark shrugged. "I thought perhaps you'd found a clue to your granddaughter's whereabouts."

The commander didn't rise to the bait. "The navcom recorded the most interesting thing," Robert said. "At least I found it interesting. I'm sure a tribunal would, too."

Roark was beginning to sweat. The man was bluffing. "I doubt there'd be much left on a destroyed piece of equipment," Roark said. His brain worked overtime as he tried to recall the conversation he'd with Gina Santiago.

The commander grinned and Roark's skin tightened to

the point of discomfort. "We've recovered enough," Robert said. "Certainly enough to raise a few questions about your version of what transpired."

"Is that so?" he asked. "Navcom recordings can be faked."

"True, but I believe under further examination this one will be easily authenticated."

Roark loosened his tie. "Mind elaborating?"

"Not over the vidscreen," Robert said, then sat back calmly, placing his hands on his abdomen.

"Then I suppose all that's left to do is for us to meet," Roark suggested. He had to find out what the commander knew. The election was too close for his character to be called into question now. If Robert Santiago somehow managed to find something to implicate him, Roark would simply have to have Bannon destroy it.

"Tell me where and when," Robert said, "and I'll be there."

"Today, at my office." Roark glanced at his watch, wondering if he'd have time to get things into place. He thought about his prison below the building. It wasn't as if it would need to be cleaned. "Let's say we meet at noon. I'll type you in for a couple of hours. That should give us more than enough time to cover the important points."

"See you then," Robert said.

"Look forward to it," Roark said, then disconnected. He had a lot to do before the commander arrived. He wished his assistant, Michael Travers, was around. He didn't want to get his hands dirty. Unfortunately, Roark had little choice. If Robert Santiago wanted to play games, he'd let him. One thing Roark would guarantee was that this would be a visit the commander of IPTT wouldn't soon forget.

chapter twenty-four

Jonah knocked and stepped into the room. "There's a man outside asking to see you," he said.

Morgan jumped, dropping the screwdriver he'd been using onto the floor. It clattered and rolled under his chair. He hadn't realized he'd dozed off. He scrubbed a hand over his face and yawned. "Did he give you a name?" No one but Demery and the Sand Moles should know where to find them. He pictured the hole Gina had left in Gray's chest and the shock on the Sand Moles' faces. He didn't want to bring trouble to Jonah's door, if he could avoid it.

"He's wearing a white protective suit and says his name is Demery," Jonah said.

Despite telling Gina otherwise, he hadn't expected to see Demery again. The Sand Devils were the type of people who didn't forgive mistakes. That was why he'd been so determined to get her out of there. Had Demery managed to escape, too, or were the Sand Devils waiting nearby? "Is he alone?" Morgan asked.

"Looks to be. I put the guards in the towers on high alert. If anyone is sneaking around out there, they'll spot them long before they get here. You expecting company?"

"No one I want to see," Morgan said. He debated how much he should share with Jonah. They'd been through a lot. Made some hard decisions. Morgan had no doubt that he'd understand, but would Jonah want to anger the other groups when he had to live here? "Have you told Gina about Demery?"

"No." Jonah shook his head. "I didn't want to wake her. Besides, he was asking for you. Didn't mention the girl."

The hair on Morgan's neck rose and his muscles tightened as his wolf brushed his flesh. "Did he say what he wanted?"

"Said something about needing your help." Jonah scratched his head. "Not sure what he meant by that. Do you know?"

Morgan ignored the question. "How does he look?" he asked instead.

"Can't tell." Jonah rubbed his whiskers. "Can only see his face in that suit he's wearing. Looks okay, I guess."

That was a good sign, wasn't it? Morgan thought. The Sand Devils wouldn't have allowed Demery to leave with his suit if they'd wanted him dead. But that didn't explain Melea's absence.

"You sure Razor and the others didn't see anyone else with him?" Morgan asked.

"Not unless they're invisible. My men have him covered. Mind telling me what's going on? I'm beginning to get that twinge in my side that tells me trouble's coming."

"It's a long and complicated story," Morgan said. "If I knew there was going to be a problem, I'd warn you."

"Appreciate it," Jonah said. He leaned against the door frame. "Is this fella really a friend of yours?"

"Not exactly, but we were traveling together until we ran into the Sand Devils. Parted company unexpectedly after that."

Jonah stilled, then let out a long whistle. "Never did care for that bunch. They have a camp about ten miles south of here. They leave us alone, but it's not by choice. We give them incentive to stay away." He patted the weapon strapped to his leg.

"Do they know about Eden?" Morgan asked.

Jonah eyed him suspiciously. "No, and I'd like it to stay that way."

Morgan's chair screeched as he scooted back to stand.

"Then I'd better get out there and see what he wants. If Gina wakes up, tell her I'll be right back, but do me a favor."

Jonah paused. "What's that?"

"Don't tell her where I've gone," Morgan said. He wanted to find out what was going on before he brought Gina into the mix. If it turned out he had to kill Demery, Morgan didn't want Gina to have to witness the vamp's death.

"Thought you said you weren't expecting trouble." Jonah's face pinched with worry.

"Nothing I can't handle." Morgan met his gaze fleetingly, then looked away.

A moment of silence stretched between them.

"Did you get that thing working?" Jonah nodded at the mass of wires and circuits that passed for a transmitter.

Morgan was relieved by the change of subject. "Don't know. I have a signal, but I'm not sure if I'm able to broadcast. Haven't received a reply yet." He stood and rolled his stiff shoulders. They popped. "If this takes longer than I anticipate, please give this to Gina and tell her to keep trying to contact the Eye of God. He'll know what to do with it." Morgan handed Kane's recording to Jonah. "I'll be back soon."

"Make sure that you do. I'm not going to be the one to break bad news to your woman. She's liable to take my head clean off." Jonah grinned and walked out of the room.

Morgan rode the lift up to the opening of the missile chamber, listening to the steady hum of the hydraulics. His nerves were taut. He'd gone over their encounter with the Sand Devils multiple times in his mind. He'd had no choice but to leave Demery and escape. Morgan hoped the vamp understood why. He would've done the same given the chance, or so he told himself as he stepped into the blistering heat.

The sun had barely poked above the horizon, yet the temps already soared. He took a deep breath and slowly exhaled, scenting the air for traps. When he was sure he wouldn't be ambushed, Morgan exited the dome.

Demery stood on the other side of the moat with the guns in the towers trained on him. His hands were in the air, and when he got closer Morgan realized Demery's hands were trembling. He knew it wasn't from fear.

Morgan waved to Razor and the other guards, then signaled Demery to lower his arms. They came down in a rush. The protective suit he wore was no longer white. Dirt and sand tarnished it, leaving only fleeting glimpses of the color it used to be. It looked as if he'd been rolled down a hill and then stuffed into a sand dune.

"Didn't think I'd ever see you again," Morgan said, approaching cautiously. Demery may be in a protective suit, but he was still a vamp.

"I'm not surprised, since you left me to twist in the sun, mon," Demery said. His words were hoarse, but they still held a bite.

"I looked for you before we left. Checked everywhere I could think of. You weren't in any of the vehicles."

He swayed and winced, clutching his side. "You mustn't have looked too hard, because I was there," he said. Demery's gaze flickered to the guards.

Morgan reached out to steady him. "I'm telling you, I looked everywhere."

"Don't touch me." Demery shrugged out of his grasp.

Morgan released him and held up his hands. "After what we'd witnessed the night before, I knew I had to get Gina out of there as soon as possible. You would've done the same," he said.

Demery laughed. "No, I wouldn't, mon. I would never leave a man behind. Every soldier knows that. It's the first thing you learn. Obviously you forgot, or maybe you were the type who saved his own hide and didn't worry about your men."

Morgan flinched. "You would if it meant your mate's life," he said. He'd already lost Gina once. It wouldn't happen again. He had felt bad about leaving Demery, but knew he wouldn't change a thing.

"Melea and I have a blood bond," he said.

"True," Morgan said, "but she's not your mate or you wouldn't have left her."

Demery's expression sobered. "I guess we'll never know,

mon. Did you find what you were looking for here?" He nodded at the dome.

"Maybe," Morgan said. He needed to know more about what happened before he shared information. For all he knew, Demery had come here to gather intel for the Sand Devils. "How did you escape?"

"Easy. I waited for Reaper to get bored with beating the shit out of me, then I grabbed Melea and ran, but not before he raped her in front of me. Since we are blood, I got to share the experience with her." He drew a pair of pants out of his pack and tossed them on the ground at Morgan's feet—the back was covered in blood.

Morgan winced at the savagery.

"You ever experience anything like that in the war, Hunter? Know what watching and feeling something like that does to a man?" Demery asked, his face contorted with anguish. He didn't bother to conceal his rage.

"My cousin Kane, a man I loved like a brother, attacked and killed three women. One of whom I had a relationship with. His intention was to go after Gina and force her to be his mate. He would've used any means necessary, including rape, to get what he wanted. If it hadn't been for Jesse Lindley, the owner of the water trader you were staying in, he would've succeeded. I found Gina beaten and lying on the floor with a sack shoved over her head." He took a deep breath as he relived the nightmare. "Jesse was an old wolf and was in even worse shape, since she'd fought Kane off. He killed her while she lay helpless in the emergency care center because he was angry that I'd claimed Gina as my mate. I didn't see any of these things happen, but I know how helpless I felt afterward. I imagine it was the same for you, not being able to help Melea."

"As you can see," Demery said, pointing to the pants. "It was so much more than a *feeling*. I experienced what she went through, thrust for thrust, tear for tear. Perhaps you didn't notice, but Reaper is *not* a small man."

"I'm surprised you let him live," Morgan said. He'd have killed the man, even if he died in the process.

"I didn't have a choice. It was leave or die," Demery said.

Morgan understood Demery's outrage. No, he'd never been sexually assaulted, but he had been repeatedly violated at the genetic labs, his body subjected to extreme pain and psychological torture. There were times Morgan had thought he wouldn't live through it, but he had. And had come out the other side a changed man. "Where is Melea?" he asked.

Demery indicated to the foothills in the distance. "I had to leave her against that outcropping of rocks. She was too exhausted to continue and my injuries prevented me from carrying her. That's why I came here. I figured if you'd made it, you would be able to help."

"And if we hadn't been here?"

"Then I would've asked the guards for assistance," Demery said.

Morgan glanced at the rocks and tried to gauge the distance. The wind moaned as it picked up sand, carrying it from dune to dune. "You left her unprotected? What if there's a predator around?"

"She's safe for now, but she won't be if Reaper finds her." Demery looked around. "As for you not being here, where else would you have gone?"

He was right. There was no place to go. Morgan knew that and so did Demery. Oh sure, they could've kept walking, but to where? The Sand Devil encampment? They'd only heard about this outpost. He supposed they could've theoretically been sent on their way by Jonah, but Morgan knew they were running out of options. Hell, they'd run out of them when they arrived here. It was either make this work or die trying.

"I heard the Sand Devils making their way around the mountains, when Gina and I hit the foothills."

"Reaper sent some of his men ahead to prepare the encampment south of here. Not sure where it is, but I saw my chance to escape then and I took it," Demery said, his dark gaze dropped to the sand at his feet.

"So they're not out looking for you?" he asked. "I find that hard to believe." Morgan scanned the horizon for movement.

"I'm sure they have scouts in the area, but the group has moved on."

Morgan glanced at the sun. It wasn't getting any lower. If there was even a chance that what he was saying was the truth, then helping Demery was the least he could do after leaving him. "We'd better get going before it gets too hot," Morgan said. It was difficult to get a read on Demery through his protective suit. He could be lying, but what if he wasn't? Did he really want to gamble on Melea's life again? The answer was obvious. No, he did not.

He debated for a moment whether to retrieve his pistol, but decided against it, since using the lift again might wake Gina. Besides, if Demery tried to pull anything, all Morgan had to do was grow a claw and rip a hole in his protective suit. "Lead the way," he said.

"Thank you." Demery turned and wobbled.

Morgan's hand shot, but stopped short of touching him. "Are you sure you're up to this trip?" he asked. "You can wait here. I can get Razor to come with me. Between the two of us, we should be able to carry Melea."

Demery's eyes narrowed and he shook his head. "You've left me little choice, mon. After what she's been through, Melea's unlikely to come to anyone but me. She knows to hide if she doesn't see the white suit."

Morgan's hackles rose at his tone, but he let it slide, given what Demery'd been through. He owed him that much. Contrary to what the vamp thought, Morgan had never left a man behind before.

If the circumstances were different, he wouldn't have in this case either, but it wasn't all about him anymore. He had to keep Gina's welfare upmost in mind. He'd noted the Sand Devil leader's predatory gaze when it fell upon Gina. It wasn't a matter of if he acted, but a matter of *when*. And Morgan would die before he'd let Reaper lay a finger on his mate.

They made good time crossing the desert floor, despite the sand sucking at their boots and Demery's injuries. It wasn't long before they reached the outcropping of rocks he'd pointed out. They were much smaller than they'd appeared in the distance. There weren't many places to hide.

"Where is she?" Morgan asked, inhaling in an attempt to catch Melea's elusive feminine scent. The hot oppressive air refused to give up its secrets. He walked a few more paces and looked around. "I don't sense her presence." Unease prickled Morgan's scalp. He looked around, preparing for a possible ambush.

"She's over there," Demery said, pointing to a cluster of boulders thirty feet away.

"I should be able to smell her by now," Morgan said. "Especially if she's injured."

"She's there," Demery said, taking the lead. "I cleaned her up the best I could. Can't exactly have her running around smelling of blood, when I'm in this shape."

Morgan followed, his senses alert. If this was a trap, as he was beginning to suspect, he needed to be ready. Claws sprung from his fingertips. He welcomed the pain.

"Melea," Demery called out, then ducked behind a boulder. Morgan frowned and approached cautiously. He still couldn't detect her scent. He sniffed again, finally catching a faint musky odor.

Demery was still hunched over. "It's okay, I'm here. You can come out now," he said.

Morgan waited.

A scarf appeared in Demery's hands. Morgan recognized it as being one that Melea had worn. His muscles relaxed and his claws retracted. Morgan thought getting him out here had been a ruse, when he'd been unable to smell her. Had been expecting one, which was why he hadn't wanted Gina to come along. He was relieved to be proven wrong.

"You know what I love about wolves?" Demery asked, laughing.

He shook his head. "No, why don't you tell me." Morgan's unease came back in an instant, along with his claws.

"It's that they rely on their sense of smell and ignore what's right in front of them." Demery turned, the material bundled in his fist.

Or at least Morgan thought it was material. He didn't register the laser pistol in the vamp's hands until it was too late. The shot rang out, catching him in the chest, knocking him onto the rocks. His skin burned as if a torch had been taken to it. Gina . . . He'd lost her for good this time.

Morgan glanced down, expecting to see a gaping hole where his heart had been. Instead of a fatal wound, his skin reddened and continued to burn. A stun blast. The son of a bitch had hit him with a stun blast. Morgan's body stiffened and a wave of pain rolled over him, then he felt nothing at all.

chapter twenty-five

D emery unzipped a pouch in his suit and pulled out a
short-range comdevice. "It's done," he said. "Come
and get your pet."

He put the comdevice away, then picked up the shackles
the Sand Devils had left for him. He shoved his blood's scarf
into his pocket, then went to work. Within a few minutes, he
had a collar around Morgan's neck and his limbs bound.
He'd removed his shirt and replaced it with a long silver
chain, which fastened at his neck and ran to his waist.

Demery tugged at it, testing the leash's strength. It clanged,
but otherwise stayed strong. Perfect for leading the wolf
around. If Reaper wanted a pet to bleed for sport, then he'd
damn well give him one.

The Sand Devils arrived quickly. Morgan was still out
and would remain so for at least another hour or more, since
he'd hit him at such close proximity.

"I've done as I promised, mon. Now give me my blood
and let me be on my way," he said with more authority than
he felt.

Reaper signaled to someone at the back of the caravan.
Melea was shoved out of one of the vehicles. She ran toward
Demery on shaky legs. Before she could reach him, Reaper
snatched her by her braids, stopping her.

"We had an agreement," Demery said, between clenched
fangs.

"I will keep my end of the bargain, but not until I'm sure that Other blood runs through his veins." A fat finger pointed at Morgan's unconscious body. It was followed by a swift kick to the ribs.

Morgan moaned, but did not wake.

"I gave you my word," Demery said.

"And look where it got me," Reaper said.

Demery growled in frustration. "I had no control over their actions," he said.

"Maybe that's true. Or maybe you helped them get away." He shrugged. "Your word doesn't mean much around here. You gave me your word before and you ran off to live on the other side of the boundary fence. If I hadn't taken care of your blood, she would've perished." Reaper cupped Melea's ample breast until she cried out in pain.

Demery shook with fury, feeling the discomfort, his gaze locked on Reaper's hand. "I didn't leave her. I went in search of what you wanted. You said specifically that you'd only accept wolf's blood in exchange for Melea, mon," he said. "Here's your wolf." He toed Morgan.

"If that's true, then our trade will be complete," Reaper said. "But if you've double-crossed me again, I will pass your woman around to every man while you experience her pain. Then I'll bleed her slowly in front of you and watch you thirst to death."

Melea's mocha skin paled at the threat. Blood roared in Demery's head, deafening him to everything but his rage.

"Or maybe if the wolf doesn't suit me, I'll have *you* take his place," Reaper said.

"Taste him and be done with it," Demery snarled. All this talk about blood and violence was making him hungry. "Stop wasting time."

"You forget your place." Reaper shoved Melea behind him and stood nose to sun shield with Demery. "I will taste the wolf, but not here," he said, glancing around at the mountains. "I'd rather be back in my encampment, instead of exposed to unseen enemies."

"How long will it take to get there?" Demery asked,

praying it wasn't too long. He didn't think he'd make it much farther without blood.

"Fourteen miles south of here. Now pick him up and put him in that vehicle. We don't have all day and I'm thirsty. I haven't had an Other since you left." Reaper pointed to a metal monstrosity that resembled a steel armadillo. Reaper jumped in the passenger side and pulled Melea onto his lap. He went back to stroking her breasts, all but daring Demery to stop him.

Melea stared straight ahead, her big brown eyes wide and unfocused. He'd seen the look before in the soldiers who'd experienced heavy combat. Given time she might recover from the trauma. Demery looked closer at her vacant expression. Then again, she might not.

Demery bit the inside of his mouth and tasted blood. He swallowed it, praying it would keep him going until he could feed properly and get Melea away from this madman.

The ride to the Sand Devil encampment took awhile, as the vehicles weren't made for speed. In the distance, he could see the outpost where he'd found Morgan. Demery was grateful that Red hadn't come up to meet him. He wasn't at all sure he would've been able to go through with it and lie to her face as easily as he'd done to Morgan.

He glanced down at the sleeping wolf, who'd been dumped onto the vehicle floor. He was snoring loudly, which was a side effect of the stun. The collar around his neck had already begun to turn his skin red. When Reaper finished with him, he'd be raw. He didn't envy him that, but Morgan had brought it on himself.

Demery hadn't intended to exchange any of them for Melea, but he had hoped to bargain for her using some of their blood. He'd almost worked out a deal when Morgan and Red left him. Reaper had been furious. Despite Demery's speed and added strength, they'd beat him. All it had taken in the end was a threat to Melea's life to get him to comply. After that, he hadn't bothered to protect himself when Reaper laid into him.

The big man had used everything in his arsenal: whips,

chains, fists, feet, and pipes. Demery had lost track of the number of blows he'd received. One thing he couldn't ignore was the pain. It had been constant and intense, radiating throughout his entire body until he was convinced that no uninjured spot remained.

Without blood to replenish him and repair his wounds, the healing had been slow going. Demery still ached, but not as bad as a couple of days ago. Soon he and Melea would be out of here and they'd leave this nightmare behind.

They hit a rock and Morgan groaned.

Demery looked at him, but he still wasn't awake. When Morgan did come around, he'd have one hell of a hangover, but the pain in his head would be nothing compared to what Reaper would do. The barbarian wanted the blood of an Other.

Demery had made the mistake of bartering his own blood when he'd first come to trade with the Sand Devils. It hadn't taken long for Reaper to discover the advantages of drinking an Other's blood. Soon he had added strength and speed without any of the drawbacks. Eventually Demery's blood wasn't enough. Reaper wanted more and greater variety. His thirst damn near unquenchable.

Demery had barely escaped with his life. He hadn't been able to save his blood woman, Melea. She would've slowed him down. Like a coward, he'd had her deliver a message, saying he'd return with a wolf, then left her with these animals. What survived was a shell of the woman he once knew.

They made it to the Sand Devil camp. Morgan was removed from the vehicle and chained to a metal spike that had been driven deep into the ground. His arms were pulled out to his sides to form a macabre cross. His lips were cracked and his skin had already started to burn from the sun.

Demery watched as he came around. He knew the moment Morgan woke because his head shot up and his amber gaze locked on him. A growl sounded deep within his throat, both promise and threat, then he yanked on the chains. They clanged loudly, but held.

"You have no one to blame but yourself," Demery said, brushing aside any second thoughts when Melea slid off Reaper's lap.

Morgan's eyes drilled him in place. "You will regret this, vampire," he said, his voice guttural.

"It won't do you any good to shift. Those chains are silver laced with steel and that post is sunk six feet into the ground," Reaper said. "You can't break them." He shoved Demery's blood toward him, then drew a large knife from the sheath at his thigh and approached Morgan. "This will hurt," he said, then sliced him across the chest. A line of red appeared as his skin opened, then began to drip.

Morgan winced, but didn't make a sound. His gaze remained on Demery.

"Someone get me a cup," Reaper shouted. One of the Sand Devils rushed forward.

He pressed the cup below the wound and waited for the blood to flow. It took some applied pressure to hurry the process along. When the crimson liquid neared the top, Reaper brought the cup to his lips and drank. Blood spilled out of the sides of the cup and down his face as he swallowed greedily.

His lips smacked when he'd finished. "Ahh," he said. "He'll do nicely." Reaper pressed the cup back to Morgan's chest, working the wound once more, then turned to Demery. Crimson sloshed over the sides, spilling onto the ground.

Morgan trembled in anger and his muscles tensed, which only made him bleed more. His taut abdomen was now slick with blood. The sweet coppery aroma filled the air.

Demery's mouth watered. He could smell the blood through his protective suit's air filter. It enticed him, lured him closer, when he knew he should stay where he was. He had Melea back. This was what he wanted. The smart thing to do was go. If they left now, they could be over the mountains by tomorrow night.

"Care for a sip?" Reaper asked, waving the cup under his face shield.

Demery's eyes followed the liquid's swirling movements,

mesmerized by the ebb and flow. He was so hungry. His mouth began to water and his fangs extended.

"Blood, let's leave," Melea pleaded, tugging on his arm.

He looked into her ashen face. Abuse at the hands of Reaper had faded her natural beauty. "We will soon," Demery said, brushing his gloved knuckles over her cheeks. "I promise."

She shook her head. "No, let's go now. I promise I'll feed you." Tears welled in Melea's big, brown eyes.

Demery knew she was right. They should leave immediately. But it had been days since he'd fed. His body ached from the hunger. He was too weak to go far. Demery knew he'd never make it over the mountains. Despite her offer, he refused to feed from Melea, not after everything she'd been through. His gaze locked on the cup and his stomach roared.

Reaper chuckled. "I see your body knows what it needs. As does mine." He slapped his firm abdomen. His hand bounced off the muscle with a loud thwack.

Melea tried once more to pull Demery away. "Please, let's go," she pleaded.

"You should listen to your blood," Morgan said, "while you can."

Demery's face hardened. He pried Melea's fingers off him. "All I need is a quick taste before we go," he said, looking at Morgan. "Then you can get to know your new friend."

Tears fell silently down Melea's cheeks as Demery stepped forward and grasped the cup. The smell of blood grew stronger, drowning his senses. Like Reaper, drinking Other blood affected Others, too. It was one of the few things that would get them drunk, which was why they rarely touched the stuff outside of the rest pad. He didn't plan on overdoing it. He just needed enough to squelch his hunger, regain his strength, and wipe that look of superiority off Morgan's face.

Demery unzipped a spot on his suit and pulled out a special straw that allowed him to feed during the day. He placed one end of the straw into the cup and sucked. The blood swirled, making a couple of loops before disappearing inside of his suit.

The first taste of the hot coppery substance hit his throat and he choked, nearly dropping the cup. His fingers tightened. Demery managed to hang onto it long enough to empty the container. His head swam and he shook it to clear it.

"Enjoy it while you can, vamp," Morgan said. "I plan to kill you as soon as I get loose."

Morgan had never been so pissed off in his life. He was angry at the vamp, but even more so with himself. He knew it had been stupid to follow Demery. If he hadn't been feeling so guilty about leaving him, Morgan would've listened to his gut.

Now he was strung up like a sacrificial lamb, waiting to be slaughtered pint by pint. His mind immediately jumped to Gina. What would she do when she woke up and found him missing? Would she come looking for him?

The thought chilled him. He couldn't let her. Somehow he had to warn her to stay away. Jonah would give her Kane's recording when he didn't return. She could take it and run for the boundary fence. At least that way she'd be far away from this place and out of danger. He glanced over at Reaper. The man's taste for blood ran far deeper than just drinking it. He wouldn't survive unless he could figure a way to escape.

Morgan's gaze moved to Demery. Hatred surged through his body and he tested the strength of the chains once more. With the right amount of pressure applied, they would break. But he wouldn't be able to do it if they kept bleeding him. Demery's white protective suit glared obscenely against the sand. The vamp was enjoying the blood, sucking it down in quick bursts as Reaper refilled the cup. Soon Demery's senses would dull. His reactions would slow. That's when Morgan would strike.

chapter twenty-six

Red awoke slowly, stretching her arms over her head as she groaned. She opened her eyes and jackknifed up. It took a few breaths to recall where she was and why she was here. The room was dark and quiet. She glanced at the bunk next to her, which hadn't been touched if the neat sheets were any indication. Where was Morgan?

She rose, grabbed her clothes, and made her way to the showers. She expected to find him splashing away, but the faucets were quiet. Red glanced at the floor, but it was barely damp. If he'd used them, it had been awhile ago.

She turned on the water and jumped under the spray. It felt wonderful, but she didn't have time to linger. She wanted to find Morgan and check on his progress with the transmitter. Red finished showering and threw on her clothes. She walked down the dimly lit hall. She couldn't be the only one up. She glanced at her watch in shock as the time registered. Why had he let her sleep so long? It was beginning to be a habit.

Red entered the room that held the spare scraps of equipment Jonah had collected over the years. Jonah sat at a desk opposite of where she'd last seen Morgan. Morgan's work space held a crude-looking compunit transmitter and receiver that was much larger than the ones they normally used. Red rubbed her bare skin, suddenly missing Rita.

"Where's Morgan?" she asked before he had time to turn around.

"Good morning to you, too," Jonah said, swiveling his chair to look at her.

"Sorry, good morning," she said, running a hand through her wet hair to detangle it.

Jonah smiled, then went back to reading the paper in his hands. "He should be back soon. Why don't you have some breakfast?" He pointed out the door in the direction of the food dispensing station, except that wasn't what Jonah had called the room. He'd called it a kitchen.

Red was hungry, but she wasn't about to eat until she found Morgan. "Where did he go?" she asked. And why hadn't he gotten her up so she could go with him?

Jonah looked up. "A friend of yours arrived asking for him. Apparently, he needed help. Morgan went with him to assist," he said.

Red frowned. "A friend? What did this friend look like?" Her stomach tightened, strangling a hunger pang before it had a chance to turn into a growl.

"He was wearing a white protective suit," Jonah said. "Here, see for yourself." He pressed a button and a vid popped up of Morgan and Demery. They were talking low, but the outpost recording devices still picked up the majority of the conversation. Demery and his blood had somehow escaped the Sand Devils. The vid ended with Red still staring at the screen. Her apprehension grew.

"How long have they been gone?" she asked, glancing at her watch.

Jonah scratched his head. "Can't rightly say. Morgan did tell me that he wanted you to man this device." He pointed to the mess on the table. "Said he was expecting to hear back from the Eye of God."

"The Eye of God?" As if on cue, the receiver crackled and a voice tried to emerge from the static.

". . . Hunter? Eye . . . God here. . . . can't hear. . . . might . . . you."

"Ah," Jonah said. "That would be him now."

Red raced toward the transmitter. "What do I do?" she asked, staring at the mess. It looked nothing like the equipment she was used to dealing with at work.

"Press that button," Jonah said, pointing to a black button in the middle of the tangle of wires.

"This is Morgan's mate, Gina Santiago, over. Can you hear me?"

Static blurred into white noise as Red turned up the volume. "I don't think he heard me," she said.

"Give him a minute," Jonah said. "You're not exactly using state-of-the-art equipment."

A hiss howled out of the machine. "Have news," the garbled voice said.

"Could you repeat that?" she asked, straining to hear.

"Missing . . . vid shows possible . . . abduction," he said.

Red's heart clenched. Who was missing? This damn machine was useless. She reached out to touch the mic and the receiver popped again. She jumped back as the garbled message continued.

"Bad news . . . Robert Santiago . . . missing. Believed . . . kidnapped. Announced . . . min— . . . ago. Blame you. Montgomery . . . reward. Turn . . . yourself in."

Red's throat tightened, cutting off her air. She hadn't heard everything the Eye of God had to say, but it had been enough to piece together. Her grandfather had been kidnapped and they were trying to blame her and Morgan. She looked over her shoulder at Jonah, who was staring at her with empathy in his eyes. The room spun and she barely made it into the chair before her legs gave out.

"I'm sorry," Jonah said. "I take it that man's related to you somehow."

She choked down the lump in her throat. "He's my grandfather. I have to go."

"But he said they think you're behind the kidnapping," Jonah said.

"I know what he said." She ground her teeth until her jaw

hurt. "But I also know who has him. I should've known he'd do something like this when he couldn't find us." Red jumped out of the chair and kicked a nearby cabinet. The metal sound reverberated throughout the room. "So stupid." She clenched her fists.

"You couldn't have known," Jonah said.

Red laughed, the sound maniacal to her ears. "That's where you're wrong. I've been through enough with Roark that I should have known. I have to go get him." Red's mind was already churning over the possibilities. It would take three to four days minimum to get back to the boundary fence. They could do it, if they moved at a fast enough clip. She needed to get packed and make sure they had enough supplies. She'd taken two steps when the alarms inside the building went off. "What's happening?" she shouted over the deafening drone.

"Towers have spotted something," he said, his fingers flying over multiple buttons. "Report!"

"Sand Devils spotted on the feed. Approximately four miles out."

"When was it recorded?" Jonah asked, his bushy brows shadowing his eyes. His face creased with concern.

"Thirty minutes ago," Razor said.

"Are they coming toward us?" Jonah asked.

"No, sir. They don't appear to be."

"Then why did you sound the alarm?" he asked, shaking his head. "Damn guards are always breaking protocol," Jonah muttered more to himself than to Red.

"We spotted something else when we reviewed the feed," Razor said. "Thought you might like to see it."

Red watched as a picture appeared on the screen. Razor was holding some kind of scope in his hands. He placed the camera next to the scope and hit a button. Two tiny figures appeared on the screen. Red couldn't tell what they were until the sun hit Demery's white suit. A moment later the unmistakable flash of a laser pistol blast appeared and the figure without the suit on dropped to the ground.

Her heart stopped and she couldn't breathe. She felt as if

her body was being ripped in two. The pain radiated, causing her limbs to twitch.

It could've been anybody. Morgan would've been too fast to get caught by a laser blast. Possible explanations raced through her mind until black dots appeared in her vision. Red quickly blinked them away. Moments later the feed showed the Sand Devils arriving, then everyone was loaded into the vehicles. They raced off and the recording ended.

"What's happening?" she asked, wanting to see what occurred next.

"Can you tell where they went?" Jonah asked the tower.

"The other feed shows them moving south toward their base camp," Razor said.

This couldn't be happening. Roark had her grandfather and now the Sand Devils had Morgan—thanks to Demery. They wouldn't take a dead man with them, which meant Morgan had still been alive. At least he had been thirty minutes ago. "Where's their base camp?" Red asked, her brain on autopilot.

"They're about a three-hour journey south of here. It's only ten miles, but the terrain is rough going. Of course, it won't take them as long to get there since they're not on foot," he said.

Red thought about her grandfather locked in Roark's prison and her stomach nearly emptied its acids onto the floor. She threw her head back and this time she did scream—a primal piercing sound that brought her wolf to the surface. Her body trembled violently in impotent rage.

How was she supposed to choose between the two men that she loved? She couldn't. Red pictured Morgan's limp form being tossed into a Sand Devil vehicle and her mind splintered.

"No!" she shouted as the alarms died. "Damn you, Demery!" They should never have left him.

Jonah had risen from his desk and backed against the wall. His hands were outstretched, placating. "Calm down. Take a breath. What are you going to do?" he asked softly, almost as if he were afraid to let her know he was still in the room.

Red swung on him wildly, her gaze barely able to focus beyond the crimson haze clouding her vision. What was she going to do? She knew her grandfather wouldn't want her to come after him. And neither would Morgan. Both would tell her to pursue the other.

Her heart was breaking as she took a shuddering breath. Not since the loss of her parents and sister had Red been in so much pain. Was it possible to die from heartache? Red didn't even know she was crying until Jonah held out a cloth. She snatched it from his hands and violently scrubbed her face.

The room flashed before her eyes again, switching from drab beige to rich color. She knew the wolf inside her was fighting to get out. "I have to go," she said, striding toward the door.

"Go where?" Jonah asked.

"To get my mate back." The thought of leaving her grandfather nearly buckled Red's knees, but the truth was that Morgan was closer. She'd just have to pray Roark didn't do anything hasty.

Even as the thought crossed her mind, Red felt what little hope she had die inside.

"That's suicidal," Jonah said. "The Sand Devils number in the hundreds. You are only one woman."

"I'm stronger than I look." *And a lot more deadly.*

"At least let me send a couple of my men with you," he said.

She shook her head. "No, I'll travel faster on my own." Red wasn't about to be responsible for anyone else's death.

A familiar voice whispered in her mind, but she was too far gone mentally to respond. Red changed into baggy clothes, then made her way to the lift. She wouldn't shift until she got out of sight of the outpost. Thanks to the vid the guards had played, she knew just how far that needed to be.

"Give me my guns," she growled. "Now!"

The guards didn't question her. They simply tossed down

the weapons and she quickly scooped them up. Red took a deep breath and howled.

Raphael winced and rubbed his temples as pain flashed behind his eyelids. He swayed and Catherine reached out to catch him.

"Are you okay?" she asked. Her hand moved to stroke her gun. A nervous habit she'd developed over the last few days. It worried him.

"I'm fine," Raphael said, taking a steadying breath. "But something is wrong with Red."

Catherine stopped suddenly and he nearly barreled into her. "What do you mean something is wrong?"

He could see the emotions swirling behind her green eyes. A lovely mixture of panic and something indefinable.

Michael stopped and adjusted his pack. "What's happened?" he asked.

"I'm not sure. She shut me out, but not before I sensed immense torment."

"Has she been injured?" he asked.

Raphael shook his head. "I don't think so. This felt more like mental anguish than physical." What had happened to cause such a severe reaction? He rubbed his arms to ward off the sudden chill. He tried to reach Morgan, but was met with a wall of pain.

"We need to pick up the pace," Catherine said, tightening her pack so she could jog.

"It won't do us any good if we collapse from heat stroke before we reach her," Raphael reminded her. He'd donned his long-sleeved clothing to give him some protection, then lathered on the sunscreen, but still felt the heat saw in and out of his lungs with every breath.

They ran anyway, covering the last of the foothills. Michael stopped at the base of the final one and inhaled.

"Do you smell it?" he asked.

Raphael frowned and breathed deeply. His muscles froze

the second the familiar fragrance hit him. "Morgan." He sniffed loudly, half afraid of what he'd find next. Fortunately, he didn't detect any blood, but he did smell something equally disturbing—another vamp. Demery? And there were others around. More purebloods than he could distinguish.

"Do you have his scent?" Michael asked.

Raphael nodded. "Yes, follow me."

He trotted over the desert floor, stopping every few feet to sniff the air. Morgan's scent remained strong, but it appeared to be leading off into two directions. He squinted and caught a flash of metal in the sunlight.

"There." He pointed.

"I see it," Michael said.

"I'm not sure which way he went," Raphael said.

Michael stepped forward and slowly turned in a circle. "His scent is stronger that way," he said, pointing south. "I also sense something else. Another wolf, perhaps."

"Is it Red?" Raphael asked.

"Can't tell." Michael shook his head in frustration. "Damn heat is distracting me."

Catherine raised her arm. "I vote we follow the unknown wolf," she said, continuing without waiting for an answer.

Raphael looked at Michael and shrugged. "Fine with me."

Michael smirked. "That woman leads you around by your balls."

"You say that as if it's a bad thing," Raphael said, grinning.

chapter twenty-seven

R ed left the safety of the compound, feeling more alone than she'd ever felt in her life. Jonah had given her approximate directions to the Sand Devil campsite. A month ago she would've shot and killed him on sight and now she was depending on him to find Morgan.

She ran, stopping every hundred yards or so to see if she could catch Morgan's scent. His musky fragrance tickled her nose, but it was followed by a more sinister odor of fear. Whether it was Morgan's or someone else's, she couldn't tell.

Red's heart thudded painfully in her chest as she picked up her pace. She glanced over her shoulder, but could still see the towers at the outpost glistening in the sun. If she could see them, then they could see her, which meant she hadn't traveled far enough. Red raced on until the lookout towers could no longer be discerned from the landscape.

She glanced ahead. The swirl of dust from the Sand Devil vehicles had long since faded. Red prayed she was still going in the right direction. Red continued on a little farther, then stopped. She glanced around to make sure she was alone. Nothing greeted her but the warm desert breeze. She inhaled deeply, beckoning the wolf to come forth. It leapt at the chance, no longer timid and shy.

Pain racked her body. Red threw her head back as bones broke and blood splattered the front of her shirt. She cried out, unable to contain the agony as her body reformed into a two-legged shape she barely recognized.

Red closed her eyes as her vision faded to black. She awoke with a start and glanced around. What she'd considered a world of beige now took on new nuances of color. There were golds, reds, and coppers mixed with the beige, giving the desert a glistening effect to her wolf eyes. Red looked at the sky. The sun was still high, which meant she hadn't been out long.

She inhaled smelling the musk of her fur, the coppery tang of blood, and the sharp acidic scent of anticipation. Her jaw snapped shut with a clack as she ground her incisors together. Claws sharp as razor wire and twice as deadly stretched out where short nails used to be. She flexed them, watching them retract and extend.

Red's muscles bunched and she leapt forward, running at speeds that would've been impossible only moments ago. Her claws dug into the earth, leaving deep furrows behind. From the sun's location, she knew she was making good time. She could smell Morgan on the breeze, his male scent mingling with that of others.

Red ran over the uneven terrain, but despite the heat she felt anything but tired. Her mind and body were energized as she took in the world around her. So much to see, so much to do, with only one goal in mind: find Morgan. Red had no time to think about Roark holding her grandfather. She couldn't contemplate the torture he might be enduring or she'd turn around and head back to the boundary fence.

She came upon the Sand Devil compound in the late afternoon. She hit the ground and sniffed, easily locating the guards who watched over the area. Unlike Jonah and his band of men, these men didn't bathe. There were six of them. Out of those six only one appeared vigilant. The rest were distracted by what was happening in the center of the compound. Her mouth watered in anticipation, but she didn't move. First she needed to locate Morgan.

Red worked her way around the encampment until she

spotted Demery's white protective suit. He was seated next to a fire across from the Sand Devil leader, Reaper, and the woman Demery claimed was his blood. Red didn't know who she really was, not that it mattered. Demery had risked everything for Melea, a mistake he would soon regret.

The jingle of chains had Red's ears perking. She followed the sound and that's when she spotted Morgan. His bound arms were outstretched and his chest was bleeding. Chains dangled from his bare neck and waist, binding him to a post.

He wore a makeshift collar. Red had seen those in the history vids. People used to put them on their pets. His amber eyes were closed, but his breathing was steady. She could sense the anger burning inside of him. At least he was conscious.

Red continued making her way in a circle, using small mounds of sand and dried dirt as cover, trying to search for an easy entry. There was none. If she wanted her mate, she'd have to fight her way in. Her wolf raised its head in eagerness. From this vantage point, she now had a better view of Morgan.

She watched as one of the Sand Devils approached him with a long dagger. He sliced a fresh wound on his arm and held a cup under the tear as the blood dripped down. When it started to slow, the man reached up and squeezed his flesh to increase flow. Morgan growled, but the man ignored him, intent on doing his job. The man filled two cups, then brought them to Demery and Reaper, who drank with gusto. Neither one acknowledged Morgan's presence. To them he was an animal to be used for sustenance.

Red's body trembled in fury and her claws ripped at the earth, scoring it with her anger. If they wanted an animal, she'd give them one. The wind shifted and Morgan's head shot up. He looked in her direction before quickly dropping his chin. The glance may have been short, but the warning was clear. He might not be able to see her, but he knew she was there and wasn't happy about it.

For a second, Red questioned her decision. Should she

have gone after her grandfather instead? There was only one of her and at least a hundred Sand Devils. What chance did she stand? She couldn't fight them all. She looked back at Morgan and caught a quick head jerk. Did he think she'd just leave him here to slowly bleed out? Surely he wasn't that naïve.

Red thought about Roark and what he was doing to her grandfather while she hesitated to act. Her resolve solidified. Both she and Morgan would get out of here together or no one would get out alive.

She began to stalk the nearest guard. Everyone was so busy celebrating the capture of Morgan that no one noticed when Red took the first guard down with a swipe of her claws across his carotid artery. The blood from his neck wound showered the ground as he dropped to his knees.

The only sound came from a gurgle as he attempted to speak, his mouth opening and closing like a fish exposed to air. She'd been worried about Demery scenting the blood until she saw him drinking from the cup. He wouldn't be able to smell anything with blood in his mouth and Morgan bleeding nearby.

Demery laughed at something Reaper said, then held out his hand for Melea to come to him. She did—in a rush. Not that Red could blame her. Melea was trapped between two powerful men, neither of whom truly cared for her. Red had only been around the Sand Devil leader for a few hours, but in that short period he'd proven himself a ruthless bastard. She wouldn't feel bad when she killed him. He deserved far worse for what he'd done.

The second guard was harder to take down. He kept shifting positions, which made it difficult to sneak up on him without alerting him to her presence. In the end, Red leapt fifteen feet, landing on his chest and knocking the wind out of him.

He punched her repeatedly to try to dislodge her. The blows hurt, but Red refused to release him. When punching didn't work, he inhaled to scream, but turned blue in the attempt. Red reached out and snapped his neck, letting it stay at the odd angle as she moved on to the next man. The thrill of the kills left her head spinning. The wolf was out for blood.

The third man seemed more interested in what was happening inside the encampment than in what was going on outside. His mistake, Red thought as she sliced open his abdomen, gutting him. He didn't make a sound when he spotted her, his eyes wide with shock and disbelief as he saw his intestines lying on the ground at his feet. Red growled softly as she fought the urge to taste her kill.

"Later," she hissed softly.

There were only three guards left. Red saw Morgan cocking his head left and right, listening. Was he following her progress? Her wolf mind couldn't decide. It was too focused on the next hunt, the next kill.

Red snuck up on the final three by crawling on her belly. One man was looking around and had finally noticed that the other men were gone. Red surged forward before he could sound an alarm. Her jaws clamped down on his throat while she impaled the other two with her claws. Like knives, they slid in deep, under their rib cages, filleting their hearts as she flexed her fingers.

The men dropped, while the guard in her mouth whimpered. His Adam's apple bobbed against her tongue. Red's jaw locked to prevent him from escaping. She squeezed until his windpipe caved beneath the pressure. Red tasted his hot, sticky blood and quickly swallowed a few gulps, then licked her lips as he joined his friends in death.

With the guards down she rose, knowing she'd only get one chance at this. She raced toward the leader of the Sand Devils. Reaper's reactions were slower than she'd anticipated, or maybe she was just faster. Melea screamed as Red stretched out her claws and swiped at him. Reaper stumbled back and she missed delivering a fatal blow. He was bleeding from where her claws raked his chest. There was no time to try again, so Red spun on Demery.

"I trusted you," she snapped, her jaws closing with an audible click.

Anger and outrage erupted from her. He'd trapped her mate. Sliced him. Bled him. And drunk from him. For that he would pay. She hunched, preparing to leap.

Before she could attack, Reaper rushed her like a maglev tank. "You bitch!" His big hands locked around her as he squeezed her against his chest.

Morgan struggled, pulling at his chains. He shifted and the chain holding his right hand twisted and snapped. The air rushed out of Red's lungs. Reaper was going to break her ribs. She kicked out, connecting with his shins, but his grip didn't loosen. Her vision swam from lack of oxygen. If she didn't break free now, it would be too late.

"Hold her," Demery shouted, trying to get close.

She kicked a boot at his face and the vamp backed away. Red opened her mouth wide and bit down as hard as she could, breaking Reaper's arm and severing tendons. He bellowed and released her, shoving her away. Red gasped, trying to catch her breath. Her lungs burned as she rose, preparing for the next attack. Some people watched, fascinated by the creature that would dare attack their leader. Others ran, terrified by what they'd witnessed thus far.

Red's claws clacked as she brushed them together. "No one bleeds my mate and lives," she barked. The garbled words were followed by a deep growl. She felt the hair on her neck and legs rise as she and Reaper circled each other.

Reaper was favoring his wounded arm, but he'd pulled a knife from somewhere and now held it out, swiping at the air.

Red bared her teeth, snapping at him as she circled slowly in search of an opening.

He jabbed.

She dodged, sucking in her stomach. The blade barely missed the tender flesh of her abdomen. She could hear Morgan pulling at his chains, clanging them as he fought to get loose. Red knew soon he'd be free. But this man would be dead long before that occurred.

"Come on," she shouted. "What are you waiting for?"

"Patience, love. I'll get to you in a moment." Reaper never took his beady eyes off her when he addressed Demery.

"You were holding out on me. You told me there was only one."

"You only asked for one," Demery said, moving toward Morgan. "Let me show you how to end this."

She growled out a warning, which Demery didn't heed. "This is your last chance," she shouted as Demery pulled out a laser pistol.

Red didn't think. Didn't hesitate. She swung away from Reaper, her arm arcing wide as she caught Demery across the chest with her long claws, tearing his suit. She heard him gasp, but knew it was more out of surprise than out of pain. The leader of the Sand Devils took the moment her back was turned to charge.

"Drop!" Morgan yelled.

Red hit the ground. Reaper had so much forward momentum that he ran right over the top of her and straight into Demery, burying his blade deep into the vamp's chest. Demery clenched the knife in shock. The leader of the Sand Devils was so surprised that he didn't try to grab the knife back.

Red jumped to her feet and rushed forward, her claws sinking into Reaper's sides. She twisted, slicing his organs. Her jaws clamped onto his thick neck and she shook her head, shredding arteries and muscle. Reaper dropped to his knees, still facing Demery. Red released him and stepped back. She spread her claws and swiped, decapitating him in two blows. Reaper's head rolled off his shoulders toward Morgan before coming to a stop.

Red looked at the knife sticking out of Demery's chest and the wound she'd inflicted, then met his eyes. The chocolate color had started to glaze.

"I'm sorry, mon. I didn't mean for any of this to happen."

"I know, but it did." Red's jaw clenched and tears burned her eyes. "You turned my mate over to these animals. I-I saw you drinking his blood."

He laughed, but the sound quickly faded to a cough. "I'm a vampire. What did you expect?"

Red sniffed. "I trusted you." Her body began to turn back into its human form.

Demery looked pained, whether from the wound or from her words she didn't know. "I would've never let them have you," he said softly. "I've seen what they can do to a woman." His gaze sought Melea. She was whimpering on the ground, rocking back and forth, her cheeks wet with tears.

"Did you make her the same promise?" Red asked.

He flinched, but didn't answer. "I know I don't have the right, but I have to ask," Demery said, his face looking fuller than it had moments ago. His body began to swell, slowly filling up his protective suit.

Red watched horrified. The adrenaline in her veins had yet to subside.

"Not much time. You need to leave now." Demery gritted his teeth against the pain. Blood spattered the inside of his face plate. "Please take my blood back with you. Fulfill the promise I made."

"Get back!" Morgan shouted.

Red turned to look at him in confusion.

"He's becoming a weapon." Morgan pulled at the remaining chain. It finally snapped.

Red grabbed Melea and yanked her to her feet. She was weeping silently, trying to go to him.

"Let me go!" she cried.

Red pulled her away from Demery and ran toward Morgan, who met them halfway.

"I don't understand," Red said, forgetting all about the stories she'd heard. "What's happening to him?" She glanced back. Demery was even bigger now. The protective suit ripped at the seams and spread like butter away from his body. His flesh had turned from dark brown to a strange red as blood pushed to the surface, forming geysers across his skin.

"He's reacting to the sunlight," Morgan said, tugging them away.

Demery was unrecognizable beyond his mocha eyes, which had started to bleed crimson tears. "I'm sorry," he said, a second before he exploded.

Fleshy shrapnel shot out in all directions, catching a few of the Sand Devils as they tried to flee, killing them instantly. Morgan pushed them to the ground behind a dune, then covered them with his body. When the last of the hardened skin had fallen from the sky, they rose. Morgan led them in the opposite direction of the screaming Sand Devils, who were running into the desert.

Red looked back at the spot Demery had occupied. All that was left was bits of hair and bone. Her stomach lurched and she dropped on all fours and vomited.

"It'll be okay." Morgan rubbed her back. "We have to get out of here before the rest of them decide to come after us," he said. They rounded the first low mound of sand and ran straight into Raphael, Michael, and Chaos.

"Fancy meeting you here in this paradise," Raphael said. He gave them a once-over, then picked a hardened piece of flesh off Morgan's shoulder. He flicked it away with his fingertips. "I take it we missed all the fun."

"Not quite." Red stepped forward, balled her fist, and punched Michael squarely in the face. "How could you do this to me, you son of a bitch?"

chapter twenty-eight

"What in the hell are you doing?" Raphael asked, helping Michael off the ground.

Gina rounded on him, but Morgan stepped between them and grabbed her by the waist. "Why don't you ask him?" She stabbed a finger in Michael's direction.

Raphael turned to Michael. "Do you know what she's talking about?"

"No idea." Michael, brushed off his clothes. "Perhaps the sun has gotten to her."

"It's not the sun, you asshole. It's my grandfather," she cried.

"What about him?" Morgan pulled her close and stroked her hair. "Does anyone know what's going on?"

"I have no idea," Raphael said, looking to Catherine and Michael for answers.

Catherine shrugged and shook her head. Her hand moved restlessly to her weapon. She stared at Gina for a moment, her body tense, then looked away.

All eyes fell upon Michael.

"Don't ask me. I have no idea why she hit me," he said, wiping the blood off his mouth and licking it from his fingers.

"I'm surprised to see you here," Morgan said.

Michael frowned. "Why?"

"I heard your screams," he said quietly. "How are you feeling?"

Michael flinched and his dark eyes squinted. "As you can see, I'm better now," he said.

"How could you?" Gina hissed. "He's an old man." Her voice cracked and tears clouded her eyes. The fight had drained out of her.

Morgan stared at him, looking for any sign to contradict his words. He looked like the old Michael, albeit a little sunburned, but he couldn't forget those screams or Roark's glee. They'd address his concerns later. First he had to find out what had happened.

"Gina, honey, calm down and tell me what's going on," Morgan said, pulling her back until he could look in her face. Her eyes were red and filled with unshed tears.

"I heard from the Eye of God before I left the outpost," she said, sniffling. "But he couldn't hear me. I tried, but the static . . ."

"It doesn't matter now," Morgan said, brushing the hair away from her cheeks, now wet with tears. What he'd found in Kane's audio journals was far more damaging to Roark Montgomery than anything the Eye of God could've located.

"I was about to sign off when he said there'd been a worldwide announcement made. He said," she choked. "He said Robert Santiago, leader of the International Police Tactical Team, had been kidnapped. Roark is blaming us for his disappearance." She buried her face in his chest. "He has him, Morgan. The bastard has my grandfather."

Morgan's gaze burned through Michael. "Is this true?" he asked.

Michael scowled. "How the hell should I know? I've been in no-man's-land for several days. The last few with Raphael and Catherine."

Morgan looked at Raphael, who gave him a curt nod, confirming Michael's story. "Roark has fooled us before. Maybe he's at it again," Morgan said.

"Do you think so?" Gina asked, wiping her face with the back of her hand.

"Only one way to find out." Morgan looked at Michael while he rubbed Gina's back. "I'm sure Roark sent a communications device with you. Get on it and find out if this latest transmission is true or another one of his carefully orchestrated lies."

Michael nodded. He reached into his bag and pulled out a navcom. "This may take awhile. We're not exactly close by."

Morgan's ears perked at the sound of engines roaring to life. "Save it until we get back to the outpost."

Gina raised her head. "What about her?"

Morgan turned to the woman standing a few feet away. He'd forgotten all about Melea. The woman's dark skin was pale and her eyes looked too big for her face, hollowed from the horrors she'd witnessed at the hands of the Sand Devils. She trembled and Morgan could smell her fear. It burned his nostrils, making him sick.

"Don't worry, we will not harm you," he said.

"She killed Demery," Melea said, her voice barely above a whisper. "He would've died from the wounds she inflicted, even if Reaper hadn't finished the job."

He tensed. "That was unfortunate, but unavoidable given his actions," Morgan said.

Melea wrung her hands. "He was only trying to help me," she said, barely holding herself together.

"Had he asked, we would've gladly assisted him, but he chose to betray us. Given our situation that is something we cannot tolerate. Even when it's done for the *right* reasons. I hope someday you'll understand."

Tears streaked down her cheeks and she shook her head, slowly backing away. Her fearful gaze remained locked on Gina.

"You have a choice. You can either go back to the Sand Devils or you can come with us. But if you come with us, know that we will not tolerate betrayal. Take Demery's death as a warning." Morgan knew he was being extremely harsh on the woman, given what she'd been through, but he had little choice. Roark had just upped the stakes exponentially. They didn't need any more surprises. He began walking north. Morgan kept his arm around Gina and didn't bother to see if anyone followed. He knew they would. What choice did they have?

"I will come with you," Melea said, her voice desperate.

"Smart choice," Morgan said. He hoped she wouldn't regret her decision.

It was dark by the time they reached the outpost. No one had said much on the slow walk back and for that Red was grateful. She hadn't been in the mood to talk. She couldn't get the look on Demery's face out of her mind. She'd seen the surprise, regret, and eventual acceptance of his impending death. The sadness lingered, haunting her.

Jonah was waiting when they returned. The guards disarmed everyone before allowing them to enter. She could've told them it was pointless, but she didn't bother. It made them feel like they were in control. There was no need to shatter that illusion.

"Glad to see you're back in one piece. More or less," he said. "Want to introduce me to your friends?"

"This is Raphael Vega, Michael Travers, Melea, and Catherine Meyers," Red said by way of introduction. "Everyone, this is Jonah. He runs this outpost and has been kind enough to help us."

He shook their hands and showed them to the spare rooms so they could freshen up.

"Let's meet back here in . . ." Red glanced at her watch. ". . . forty-five minutes. You need to send that transmission and find out what's going on," she said to Michael.

Thirty minutes later Michael was pressing several buttons on his navcom. His normally placid expression looked strained as he thumped the device a couple of times.

"What's wrong?" Red asked.

"It must be the sand. It's working intermittently," he said, shaking it.

"Can you hail, Roark?" Red's stomach knotted. She needed to know what was happening with her grandfather. Was Roark playing mind games or did he really have him? And if he did, what would she do? She had no problem exchanging her life for his, but would that be enough to appease Roark?

"This is Travers reporting in," Michael said. "This is Travers, do you read?"

Static filled the air.

"Home base, this is Travers. Please respond."

More pops and crackles blasted the silence. Red felt so helpless. What if he couldn't reach Roark? She'd have no choice but to return to the Republic of Arizona and hope that was enough to garner his release.

"Travers report," Roark barked.

Red jumped. "Ask him."

Michael nodded and held up a finger. "I've received a broadcast claiming the commander of IPTT has been kidnapped," he said.

There was a pause. For a moment Red thought they might have lost him. Then he spoke.

"Are you alone, Travers?" Roark asked.

Michael looked at Red, then at Morgan. They both nodded at him.

"No, sir. That's negative."

"Hello, Ms. Santiago. Mr. Hunter." His smug voice grated on Red's nerves. He was gloating. "I see you received the message I sent."

She snatched the navcom from Michael's grasp. "Where's my grandfather, asshole?"

Roark chuckled. "You mean the commander?"

"You know very well who I mean," she said.

"He's here, keeping me company in your absence," Roark said. "I had to ensure you'd comply to my demands."

A strained voice as familiar as her own came onto the line. "Gina? Is it really you?"

"It's me Grandpa," Red said. "Don't worry. We'll get you out of there. Stay strong."

"Don't make promises you can't keep," Roark said.

"Gina?" her grandfather repeated, sounding weaker. There was a scrape, then a loud moan.

"What have you done to him, Roark?" Red asked.

Roark chuckled. "Had to soften him up so he'd cooperate. Old fool actually thought he could come here and threaten me."

Red brought the navcom to her mouth. "Grandpa, can you hear me?" Damn it! He had to hear her. He had to know she was coming for him. Had to know how much she loved him. "I'll be there soon. Don't worr—"

"Save it, "Roark said. "I'm afraid it'll be too late. I haven't forgotten what you did to me in that cell."

Fear's cold fingers enveloped her. There was some shuffling, then Red heard the hum of a laser pistol as it began to charge. "Roark, what are you doing?"

"What I should've done a long time ago," he said.

A shot rang out over the connection, cutting off her words. The sound was followed by a frightened male shriek and a loud thud as something hit the floor. They heard a gasp, then a sickening gurgle. "Gi-na? help—" There was another shot, then silence.

Red's heart pounded. For one painful moment she thought it'd exploded in her chest. She gasped and forced air into her lungs. Her fingers trembled as she shook the navcom. "Grandpa? Grandpa? Answer me this second! Damn you, Roark! What have you done?"

"Sorry, the commander is permanently indisposed." Roark laughed long and hard as Red crumpled to the floor. "One problem down, two to go. Come back so we can finish this once and for all."

This would never have happened if she'd stayed in the Republic of Arizona. She'd been selfish to run. Hadn't thought about what would happen to the ones they left behind.

Red choked back her cries until an eerie calm replaced the pain. "I'll kill you for this," she vowed, clutching the navcom. Did you hear me?"

"Save your breath," Roark said. "You'll need it for your defense. That is if you make it back to the republics alive."

She cursed loudly, clutching the navcom. It did little to alleviate the pain coursing through her, the sheer agony of losing the last member of her family. Red didn't know how she'd survive or if she'd survive. A piece of her heart had shattered as the second shot was fired. Her limbs went numb as her mind retreated to safety. She clasped her hands around her knees and started to rock back and forth, seeking comfort where there was none.

"You've lost, Roark. You just don't know it yet." Morgan pulled Red close. "This time we're dealing with more than our word against yours. We now have the proof to destroy you. One tiny broadcast and your political career is over," he said, leaning into the navcom. "In the end, you may get your wish, but we're going to take you down with us."

"You'll never get the message out," Roark said, but his voice wavered a bit. "I've made sure of it."

"We'll see about that," Morgan said.

Red glared at the navcom. "You just shot your only bargaining chip."

"Travers?" Roark barked.

"Yes, sir," Michael said.

"Remember your duty," Roark said. "Here's a reminder in case you forgot."

Michael screamed as the chip in his brain sent shock after shock through his body. He fell to the floor, clutching his head, writhing in pain. "Make it stop. Please make it stop!"

"Finish your job and I will."

Red tossed the navcom against the wall, cutting off Roark's transmission. Michael's pain had temporarily jerked her out of the shock that had set in. She'd done the first thing she could think of to kill the signal.

Michael stopped thrashing, his breath coming in deep gasps.

"How is the chip doing that?" Red asked, hugging herself.

"I don't know," Morgan said. "I've never heard of a chip that could do that to a man."

She frowned. "Can we scan him to assess the damage?" Red asked.

Raphael picked up the device. "I think you broke the navcom when you threw it."

Red ran a trembling hand through her hair, "I didn't know what else to do. I was afraid it was going to kill him."

"I might be able to get the navcom working again," Morgan said. "Give me awhile. In the meantime, get him into a bunk. Try to make him comfortable."

Michael struggled to his feet. "I'm all right," he said. He blinked to clear the shadow people from his vision, but they refused to leave.

He blinked again, this time keeping his eyes shut for a few seconds longer. Michael cracked one lid and saw a gray shadow race across his line of vision. He opened his other eye and knew he wasn't alone.

The shadows stood like sentries, waiting. For what, he did not know. They'd always been quick to dart out of the way, but not anymore.

"On second thought," he said, swaying. "A short rest might do me some good."

Michael allowed Raphael to help him down the hall. His brother's face was pinched with worry, but he said nothing. What was there to say? Michael glanced over his shoulder as he entered the area that housed numerous bunks. The shadows waited, their ghostly faces filled with glee.

"What happened back there?" Raphael asked.

He tried to shrug, but couldn't. "It was just Roark sending a reminder of who's in charge," he said.

Raphael grabbed his hand. "We'll figure out a way to fix this."

Michael smiled. "You worry too much, brother."

Raphael's voice to cracked. "Somebody has to. Now get some rest." He pulled the blanket up.

Michael's chest clenched. "I will," he lied.

Morgan stared at the broken navcom, unable to focus. He couldn't get Gina's cries out of his mind. Her tears had scorched his soul and no amount of shifting to his wolf form would repair it. The calm she'd shown after listening to her grandfather's murder had been worst of all. She'd shut down before his eyes as if someone had flipped a switch. Morgan still didn't understand how Montgomery had gotten the drop on Robert Santiago, but there was no denying what they'd heard. Someone had died at Roark's hand. Someone who sounded exactly like the commander. Roark would die for his multitude of sins. Determined, he picked up the device. If he could manage to fix it, they might be able to broadcast.

He thought about the recording sitting next to him. If Morgan sent out Kane's message, there would be no hiding for the Others. Questions would be asked. Answers would be sought. This journey wasn't just about him and Gina anymore. Something far greater was at stake. Could Morgan risk the lives of the people of Nuria and the Others around the world for revenge and their freedom?

Freedom—what a joke. He and the Others had been living in self-imposed exile from the rest of society for decades.

Morgan had spent so many years in hiding that he wasn't sure if he could live out in the open. And what if the same people who'd hunted them down before tried to come after them again? The men behind the experiments were dead, but their successors were still around, watching, waiting for the Others to pop their heads up so they could blow them off their shoulders.

He thought about the Nurian trainees. The Other tactical team was nowhere near ready for that kind of altercation. With Demery's death, they'd lost one of the most promising cadets. Morgan knew his mate mourned the vamp's death. She hid her grief well, but he'd still noticed. It was his fault he was dead. They should've never left Demery behind.

As if her grief for the vamp wasn't bad enough, she'd now have to deal with the presumed loss of her grandfather, Commander Robert Santiago. He pictured her tear-stained face when the shots were fired. She'd shattered before his eyes, while Roark Montgomery cackled triumphantly. Morgan hoped like hell he never heard anything like that again.

Morgan took out the tools Jonah had loaned him and

pulled off the back of the navcom. It didn't look good. In fact, it looked like a mess—thanks to Gina's impromptu rage. He moved a few wires to get to the crystal keyboard that fueled it. At least the crystal was still intact, which was something. Morgan set the tools down on the table.

He brushed a hand over his chest and winced. He was still tender from the stun blast and the knife wounds, but thanks to a quick shift they had stopped bleeding and sealed tight. By tomorrow, the discomfort would be gone. In a week, it would look as if nothing had occurred.

He fiddled with the navcom. Everything was about to change. Morgan hoped the Nurians would forgive him. Hell, he hoped they wouldn't have to. He lowered his head and went back to work.

Red came upon Melea standing in the giant greenhouse. "Amazing, isn't it?"

The woman jumped in surprise. "I'm sorry. I didn't . . ." Her gaze roamed the room for another exit, but she quickly realized that Red blocked the only one.

"It's okay. I like it in here, too. It's a good place to think," Red said. "Especially now."

The woman nodded, but didn't relax.

Red looked at her. "Can I ask you a question?"

"Go ahead," Melea said.

"Why did Demery call you his blood? I know you weren't his mate. If you had been, he would've challenged Reaper long ago."

The woman gave her a sad smile. "I reminded him of his little sister. The fact that I had her name helped. Obviously he didn't treat me as such, but he did look after me, or at least tried to. Demery was a good man, but he had his faults." Melea shrugged. "I loved him like a brother, but he gambled. And when he lost . . ." her voice trailed off.

"He lost you to the Sand Devils?" Red asked, trying to imagine the woman's terror. She shuddered at the thought.

Melea nodded, then quickly looked away. "He didn't

mean to, but Demery learned the hard way that you can't beat Reaper. He promised to return to get me and he did, even if his rescue was cut short." Her voice turned bitter.

"If he viewed you as his little sister, how did you become his blood?" Red asked, steering the conversation away.

The woman laughed, but there was no amusement in her soft voice. "It was an accident. Demery had a little bit too much to drink one night. Thought it'd be funny to see me swallow his blood. I'd been traveling with him for awhile, so I didn't think much of it. It wasn't until the next day when Reaper forced me to . . . that I found out it could also harm Demery."

Red thought about Raphael. Could he feel her pain now that she'd tasted him? And what of Morgan? Raphael had fed him his blood to save his life.

"How much blood did you drink?" Red asked.

"Several mouthfuls. I ended up vomiting," Melea said.

Maybe the amount mattered. She'd have to ask. "I'm sorry things turned out the way they have," Red said. "You probably won't believe me, but I really liked Demery. I don't take my part in his death lightly."

"You kept your promise to him." Melea sounded surprised. "Why?" she asked.

Red couldn't blame Melea for being surprised. Everyone in her life had either lied or used her. Most did both. "Because he asked."

The woman brushed her face, wiping at the tears that had started to silently fall. Her shoulders shook. "That's it? No other reasons?"

"He was my friend." It was a stark admission, but no less than the truth. Red wanted to comfort Melea, but she didn't know how when they were both in so much pain. "I will make sure you get to the Republic of Arizona," she said instead.

"Because of guilt?" the woman asked, eyeing her suspiciously.

Red leveled her with a sharp gaze. "Does the reason matter?" she asked.

"I guess not," Melea said. She slipped deeper into the greenhouse, disappearing behind the fruit trees.

Red left her to grieve and went to find Raphael. He was standing in the control center looking at all the buttons. His back was to her, when she walked in. "I haven't seen one of these places since the war," he said softly. "It looks so ancient now, but back then it housed so much destructive power."

"How are you holding up?" Red asked.

Raphael turned. "I could ask you the same thing. You look like you've lost weight."

Red laughed, despite the pain. "Wandering around the desert does wonders for the diet."

He smiled, flashing fang. "Yes, I suppose it takes some getting used to."

"How are Michael and Catherine?" she asked.

"My brother is not well. The chip inside him is causing him pain. He blocks me so I can't tell how bad it's gotten. I fear for his health. Perhaps if Morgan can get the navcom working, we'll have a better idea of what we're dealing with." He sighed. "Catherine." Her name brightened his features, lighting his eyes. "She is still in shock over Roark's transmission, but she is strong and will get through this."

Red rubbed her bare wrist. She missed her navcom, Rita. She'd always found comfort from its nasally voice, even though it wasn't real. "Roark's caused so much pain and misery. If he gets elected, I fear for our people. I fear for *all* people."

Raphael met her gaze with his black doll-like eyes. "No matter what happens, he will be dealt with. You have my word."

"I hope you're right." Red rubbed her arms. "I better check on Morgan," she said, noticing Catherine at the door.

Chaos watched Gina Santiago leave, then slipped into the room. She hadn't been able to talk to the woman alone. It seemed like every time she tried someone appeared. Chaos had never been good at waiting. "I don't know what to do," she said, glancing at Raphael.

He frowned. "About what?"

"I promised the commander I'd bring her back." She pointed at the doorway. "If he's truly dead, then there's no one there to return her to. All she has left is Morgan."

Raphael slowly shook his head. "That's not true," he said. "She has me and several of the townspeople of Nuria to lean on."

"I see." Chaos' face flushed. "I suppose as long as she has you that's all that counts."

Raphael's eyes twinkled. "Is that a problem?"

"No, why would it be?" Chaos asked through a snarl. "We have no claims on each other. Our agreement was quite clear. Help each other to reach our mutual goals. You've found your brother and I've found Red. We're sorted."

Raphael let the smile spread across his face, exposing his fangs. "Liar," he purred.

Chaos' body responded like Pavlov's dog to a dinner bell. "Knock it off."

"Knock what off?" he asked, his footsteps silent as he closed the distance between them.

She gave him her shoulder. "You know very well what I'm talking about," she said.

"Yes, I do." Undaunted, Raphael tilted her chin and kissed her tenderly. "You have no need to worry, little storm. I care about Red, but not in the way you've implied. She has chosen her mate. I respect her wishes."

Anger fueled her blood. "So what you're telling me is that I'm a default pick. Couldn't get what you wanted, so you're settling for second choice. Nice. I feel so special," Chaos spat. She needed to leave before she embarrassed herself.

"Hardly." Raphael slid his hands up her arms. "You have held my attention from the moment I laid eyes on you. I find you infinitely more fascinating than the she-wolf." His gaze raked her, simmering with intent.

Emotions welled within her, despite her efforts to keep them tamped down. As much as Chaos would like to deny it, she was starting to fall hard for Raphael Vega. He'd gotten under her skin literally and she'd allowed it with nary a whimper. She stared at his face, wondering not for the first time what she was going to do with him. He'd come into her life like a tornado and turned her world on its ear. The thought of parting left her bereft, but she couldn't exactly take him with her to IPTT.

Chaos had always been a loner, trying to fit in without standing out. It had worked for a while, until her *gift* raised its ugly head.

Now Chaos wasn't sure if she'd even return. What would be the point now that the commander was gone? No doubt she'd already been replaced, especially if Bannon had taken over. She looked at Raphael. His black eyes shimmered with emotion.

"You'll be the death of me," she said.

"No." He shook his head. "I will bring only light into your life."

She gave him an incredulous look.

"You shall see. Just give me a chance," Raphael said, kissing her again. He deepened the embrace, running his tongue along the seam of her lips until she opened for him. Raphael swept in, exploring, imploring, and demanding her capitulation. Her head spun.

Chaos clasped her hands behind his neck and said yes the only way she knew how—by kissing him back and hanging on for dear life as the world dropped out beneath her feet.

Red found Morgan sitting in front of a desk. "How goes it?"

"I may have the navcom working. It was locked so it couldn't broadcast everywhere, but I changed its setting."

She hugged him. "That's great. Now you can contact the Eye of God and see if he can help us."

Morgan sighed. "I found something while you were sleeping." He reached into his pocket and pulled out one of Kane's audio journals. "Jonah kept this safe while I was detained."

"Did you finally listen to them?" she asked, knowing how

hard it would've been for him to do so. He still mourned the loss of his cousin.

"Yes, and there's something you need to hear," Morgan said, then pressed play.

Red stood dumbfounded as she listened to Kane and Roark. She couldn't believe what she was hearing. "Can you play it again?" The order to have her killed left Roark's mouth with ease.

Morgan reached for her hand. "I'm sorry."

"What does this mean?" Red asked, her mind racing to comprehend. The implications were overwhelming.

"It means our nightmare is almost over," Morgan said. "At least once we broadcast this to the republics."

Red nodded as she replayed the words in her mind. "Wait a minute. If we do that, then everyone will know about the Others," she said.

Morgan grew silent, his expression grim. "I know."

"There has to be some other way," she said.

He ran his hand over his stubbled chin. "There isn't."

"We can't just send this to the satellites for everyone to hear. You've kept these people safe all these years. They're counting on you to continue."

"I know," Morgan said, his expression growing apprehensive. "But it's the only way we'll stop Roark for good and gain our freedom. The proof on this recording will seal his fate."

"And the Nurians?" Red asked. "What will become of them?"

He sighed. "They will have to learn to adapt. Just like I will. We've survived worse. Hopefully people will be more forgiving this time around."

Red didn't want the death of the Nurians on her head. "You can't count on that," she said.

Morgan rose from his chair. "What do you want me to do? We have run out of options. You know that as well as I do. And we can't stay here. Jonah has been kind, but he doesn't have the means to support all of us. We have to end this before Roark comes after Nuria, if he hasn't already."

"Now that the commander is out of the way, there'll be no one to stop him." She choked on the pain, clogging her throat. "He may already have control of IPTT by now." The thought was truly terrifying. Nuria had no hope against a well-trained tactical team force.

"We don't know anything yet. Let's not speculate," Morgan reminded her. He picked up the device. "Now the bad news. I don't think this navcom will broadcast out of this valley. I've checked its signal strength and it's weak."

"I swear we can't catch a break." She began to pace. "Is there any way to boost it?"

"Possibly," Morgan said. "But we'll need to get someplace much higher to try."

Red sighed. "Okay, so we climb one of the mountains."

"There's something else." Morgan touched her hand. "We'll probably only have one shot at this before it fries the crystal."

"Can we still do a scan on Michael?" she asked. Red wanted to get the message out, but not at the cost of another life.

Morgan turned the navcom over. "Yes, I think it'll still work. But even if it does find something, we don't have the equipment to do surgery here. I already asked Jonah. In all likelihood, we'd kill Michael trying to help him."

"We have to do something. We can't just leave him like this. He's in so much pain," Red said.

"I know." Morgan stopped her and pulled her into his arms. "How is Raphael holding up?"

Red shrugged. "He is hurting, but he hides it well. You know Raphael."

"Yes, I do," Morgan said. "For his sake, I hope there's something we can do for Michael."

"Me, too." She could tell by Morgan's expression that he was thinking about Kane. He didn't want Raphael to lose his only surviving close family member, too.

They walked into the barracks where Michael was lying on a cot. "Are you awake?" Red asked.

"It's rather hard to sleep when your head is splitting in two," Michael said, opening his eyes. His skin was paler than usual and his black hair was disheveled.

Morgan put his hand on Michael's shoulder. "We think the navcom has been repaired enough to run a scan on you," he said.

Michael laughed. "It doesn't matter."

"Don't say that," Red said. "We want to help."

Michael met her gaze and shook his head. "You truly are special, but there's nothing to be done. The chip in my head has A.I. capabilities that seem to have taken over. Roark doesn't need to be near for it to activate."

Red gasped. She hadn't meant to, but she didn't realize the situation was so dire. "At least let us try," she said. "For Raphael's sake."

His cheeks flushed at the mention of his brother's name. "Suit yourself," Michael said.

Raphael walked into the room as Red placed the navcom on Michael's wrist. He was followed by Catherine, whose lips were kiss swollen.

"Ah, I see we're having a party," Michael said, his gaze sweeping Catherine. "And you obviously started early, Raph."

"Your sense of humor has always been off-color, brother," Raphael said.

Red pressed scan. The navcom beeped, then began to hum. It beeped again five minutes later. She lifted the navcom off his wrist and read the results. "The chip seems to be lodged in the frontal lobe area of his brain. I thought perhaps it had been attached to the bone."

"I told you that nothing could be done," Michael said.

"We have to get it out," Red said. "It's amazing you've made it this far without dislodging it."

Michael shook his head. "You can't remove it without killing me. It's been burrowing in my brain. I've felt it. It's like a continual itch that cannot be scratched."

Red bit her bottom lip as she considered the possibilities. "There has to be a way to block the signal," she said.

Everyone looked at Morgan, who shook his head slowly. "If there is, I don't know about it.

Raphael reached for the navcom so he could read the results for himself. "It's in a bad spot; sensitive," he said. "If we try to remove it, he could become psychotic."

"We can't leave it in there," Red said. "It's hurting him. Hell, for all we know it's killing him while we argue about what to do." She began to pace. It was easier to think when she was moving.

"Gina," Morgan said. Red stopped midstride. "Even if we wanted to, I told you we don't have the equipment to take it out. The only hope is to get him to an emergency care center before he dies."

chapter twenty-nine

"**W**ill you be able to travel?" Red asked Michael.

"That depends," he said. "Where are we going?" Michael tried to sit up in the cot, but slumped back down.

"Morgan has found the proof we've been looking for to nail Roark and prevent him from winning the election and taking over the republics," she said. "But we can't send it from here. The reception is too bad. We have to get higher. We're thinking that the top of one of the mountains might work."

Michael lay very still in the bed, his expression unreadable. "What kind of proof?" he asked.

Red looked at him, then at the others in the room. Raphael and Catherine leaned forward, eager to hear what she had to say. No one seemed to notice Michael's lack of reaction but her. She debated whether to continue, but in her excitement, she'd already said too much. "It appears Kane recorded one of the conversations he had with Roark," she said.

"What did it say?" Raphael asked.

"Who's Kane?" Catherine asked, looking around in confusion.

Raphael gave her a quick shake of his head, silencing any further queries. "I'll explain later," he said.

Red's gaze met Michael's once more. "The message will help clear our names, but it's not all good news," she said. "At least not for the Others."

Raphael crowded her. "Okay, now you have me worried. What did the message say?"

"The message was Roark ordering a hit on me. Unfortunately, the recording inadvertently reveals the existence of the Others. So if we send it out, there will be no more hiding," Red said, letting the magnitude of her statement settle in. "For any of us." Her gaze swept Catherine.

"I'm not an Other," Catherine said in a rush.

"That may be, but you're definitely not a pureblood."

Catherine flushed.

It was Raphael's turn to grow silent. He knew it would happen someday, but not so soon. He considered the ramifications. Was the world ready for the existence of Others? They hadn't been before. Sure, they'd been living side by side with purebloods for over a century, but he could still remember the dark days. When most people heard that term, they thought he was talking about the war, but he wasn't.

The dark days came after the war ended, when their status as war heroes disintegrated and they were hunted like vermin. He could still remember the fear, the pain of discovery, and the years of torture that followed. He and the rest were lucky to escape with their lives. Lucky? He laughed to himself. The dead were the lucky ones. At least their pain had ended. He couldn't go back to that way of life. And he wasn't sure that enough had changed in the world to avoid repeating past mistakes.

Raphael looked at Morgan and Red. They knew the risks. He could see it on their faces, along with the hope they tried to hide. "What do you plan to do?" he asked.

"Morgan might be able to come up with more proof if he can reach the Eye of God, but it won't be enough on its own. We need this recording to ensure victory," Red said.

"And what if that chance you speak of brings down hell onto Nuria's head?" Raphael asked.

Red met his eyes. "We've considered everything carefully. The truth is, if Roark gets away with what he's done there won't be a Nuria left to go home to. His goal is and has always been to get rid of the Others. He doesn't care how he accomplishes this goal, only that he does. If you think otherwise, then you are only fooling yourself."

Catherine stepped forward and ran her hand down the length of Raphael's arm. Raphael knew he was trembling. He couldn't help it—the memories of the past were still strong. "And what of my brother?" he asked.

Red's expression turned grim. "We'll get him back to the Republic of Arizona and into the emergency care center. They should be able to get that chip out before Roark realizes what's happening."

"And if they don't?" Raphael asked.

"Brother," Michael said, drawing his attention away from Red. "I have lived through much. I'm sure I can make the journey back to the republics and through a little surgery."

Raphael frowned. What choice did he have? His brother would die if they didn't return. Nuria's existence balanced on a razor's edge and someone would have to bleed. He nodded his assent.

Michael turned to Red. "I don't suppose you can let us hear this recording."

She looked uneasy, then slowly shook her head. Raphael stared at his brother. Michael gave him a sad smile and something inside of him crumbled.

"The journal is safe with Morgan for now," Red said. "If you're up to it, we'll leave tonight."

"I'll be ready," Michael said.

Although he had not heard the recording, Michael had no reason to believe what Red had said was untrue. Unfortunately for her, he couldn't allow that recording to reach the mountaintop. Contrary to her beliefs, Michael knew Roark was the only one who could remove the chip in his brain. The only one who knew what it was capable of, if it remained buried inside him.

Deep down Raph knew the truth, too, although he refused to see it. His concern was a valid one. Michael didn't have to read his mind to sense the fear rolling off him. He remembered the dark days. All the Others did. Red had not been born. She never went through the terror of such things. She never had to live through a hunt. She had never been feared.

His head throbbed, but it was no longer from the chip. Realization of what he must do weighed heavily on his shoulders. The shadow men nodded in agreement. If Michael could avoid harming them, he would, but he doubted that would be the case. They were natural fighters. Red and Morgan would do what they must to protect the recording and he'd do what he must to destroy it. It was his only chance.

In the end they'd understand. They'd have to. Michael knew they'd do the same if they were in his situation. Red and Morgan would sacrifice themselves if they thought it would save the Others. Michael knew he was not so noble. He wanted to live. He had so much to live for now that he'd found his brother. They'd only begun to build new memories and catch up on the years they'd lost.

Michael's gaze automatically went to Raphael, who was firmly ensconced in Catherine's arms. He wasn't even aware Michael was still in the room. Witnessing the love shining in Raphael's eyes was hard to take. *Please stay out of this, brother. I wish you no harm.*

Michael listened to the sounds of the missile silo creak around him, but it was quiet in comparison to Raphael's and Catherine's hearts beating. The rhythm was eerily similar. He'd probably matched hers on purpose. Raphael always was a romantic, at least while he was fucking a woman. He'd tire of Catherine eventually and when he did, Michael would be there to help him move on.

A quick flash of the future shined before him. In that second, Michael saw what life held in store. His path became clear. He hoped in the end Raphael would forgive him. . . .

* * *

The night rolled in and the small band gathered their packs for the journey ahead. Michael looked tired and gaunt, but was otherwise in good spirits. Red still couldn't help feeling that something was wrong. He wasn't the same man she'd encountered on the streets of Nuria. He'd been somehow diminished.

Jonah gave them their weapons back, along with a few extra knives. Red tucked one into the waistband of her pants and the other beside her ankle. She watched Raphael and Morgan do the same. Michael walked past the weapons, which evoked a curious glance from Jonah.

Red knew Michael didn't need any weapons to kill and that's what worried her the most. Her senses told her to be ready for anything given his physical condition, but what defense did they have against a man who could kill them with a thought? None.

Morgan shook Jonah's hand. "I really wish you'd reconsider coming with us," he said.

"I have found my Eden. You have to find yours," Jonah said, smiling. "But I would appreciate it if you could get me the supplies I asked for when you get back," he added. "And the credits."

"If we make it, you'll have your supplies, along with the other things we promised," Morgan said. "You have my word."

"You are welcome back to partake of the shower anytime," Jonah said.

"Thank you."

They stood on the platform and waited for Jonah to hit the button. The lift began to rise. Red gave Jonah one last wave, then looked up. No longer would she be able to stare at unknowns without seeing their faces and knowing what they've been through on this side of the boundary fence. If they lived through the next few days, she would do everything in her power to get the laws changed.

"One thing at a time," she murmured to herself. *You have to make to the top of the mountains first.*

Morgan grabbed her hand in the dark and held it to his

chest. The lift came to a stop in the round room they'd first entered only a few days before. They made their way toward the door, taking care to avoid all the piles of debris. Razor threw open the door and stepped aside for the group to exit.

The other guards were still in the towers. They'd learned there were ten men total, though they'd never seen them all. The men took turns watching out for enemies and lived in a section of the silo Red hadn't explored. She'd never really made it past the showers and the greenhouse. Memories of sharing the water with Morgan came back in a rush of warmth.

"We'll be back," he said, whispering in her ear as if he'd read her mind.

"We have to make it out of no-man's-land first," she said, staring at the imposing peaks in the distance.

His amber gaze met hers. "We've made it this far."

"Yes, but we didn't have quite as many obstacles," she said.

His expression grew somber. "Like all the rest, we'll get over this one, too. Now come on." He pulled her forward so they could take the lead.

Morgan gave Raphael a look and he immediately dropped to the back to bring up the rear. Catherine followed. Michael stayed in the middle with Melea, floating between the group.

"How long do you think it'll take us to reach the mountains?" Red asked.

"A few hours," Morgan said. "We won't start climbing them until dawn. It's too dangerous to attempt in the dark."

"How do you plan to send the signal out?" Michael asked.

Morgan glanced over his shoulder. "Your broken navcom."

"It's only good for contacting Roark," he said.

"Not anymore."

Red saw a look of uncertainty cross Morgan's features. He wasn't sure it was going to work, but he didn't want her or the others to worry. The thought sobered her.

Whether it worked or not, she couldn't wait to get back to civilization. It had its faults, but scavenging for days had left her adrift on the sand. Red couldn't live without the order she'd been brought up with. And this place made order of any kind impossible.

They reached the base of the foothills and snaked their way higher before finding a place to camp for the rest of the night. It wasn't perfect, but at least no one would fall off the hill and die before dawn. And it was out of reach of the predators hunting on the desert floor.

Red glanced up at the black mass of mountain peaks, searching for any sign of movement. They might be away from the low-desert predators, but they were in big-cat territory, so they'd have to remain sharp. With food scarce, the cat wouldn't think anything of coming into camp and trying to kill one of them and drag them away.

"We should be safe for the night," Morgan said. "The Sand Devils have remained to the south since the death of their leader. Jonah had the tower guards watching out just in case they decided to move their base."

Red nodded. "I was looking for animals."

"I haven't sensed any nearby. Raphael, you take the first watch," Morgan said. "Catherine, you take the second. Melea and Michael get some rest. I'll take the third watch."

"What about me?" Red asked.

He brushed her hair away from her face. "You rest, too. You had a very busy day yesterday."

She snorted. "So did you, as I recall."

"Yes," Morgan said. "But my body is used to the fatigue of combat and shifting. I don't need a lot of sleep and I've learned to recover quickly from injuries."

He had her there. The shift had healed the wounds the Sand Devils had inflicted. Only red scratches remained. Red ran her hand over his arm where they'd bled him.

He pressed his hand to hers. "I'm all right," Morgan said, his voice lower, more intimate.

"I know. I just needed to see for myself," Red said, then pulled off her pack to bed down for the night.

Red slept fitfully. Thoughts of the Sand Devils attacking

them while they camped turned her dreams into nightmares. Twice Morgan had to shake her awake to stop her cries. He'd held her until she'd fallen back to sleep, promising to stay with her until his watch shift. After being shaken awake for the third time after a bad dream, exhaustion took over and she didn't dream at all.

The dawn brought more heat. Red's eyes were crusted shut and her skin held a thin sheen of sand. She rose, scratching her head and rolling her stiff muscles. She doubted she'd ever get used to sleeping on rock. They ate a quick meal, then packed the gear.

"I'll be right back," Raphael said.

He led Catherine away from their prying eyes and softly pressed his lips to the rapid pulse beating in her dainty neck. She didn't question him, only tilted her head to give him better access. His fangs extended and he sank them deep, relishing the sweet taste of her blood.

His whole body hardened as he held her in the intimate embrace. Under different circumstances, he'd take her right here. To hell with anyone in earshot. But they needed to get moving. An unspoken urgency rode the group, making him nervous.

Raphael didn't like it, because he knew part of the sensation was fueled by Michael's precarious health. He swiped his tongue over the wounds, closing them before pressing his lips to her skin.

"I wish we had more time," he murmured.

"Me, too," she said, her voice breathless.

"The others are waiting." Raphael rested his forehead against hers.

Catherine frowned when their gazes met. "What's wrong?" she asked.

Raphael shook his head. "It's nothing," he lied.

Her eyes narrowed to jade slits. "I know when you're lying. I can see it in your face. Something is wrong."

"No," Raphael denied. He didn't want to worry her. "I'm tired. And like you, I long to be back in familiar territory."

That much was true. He'd feel a lot better once they crossed the boundary fence into the Republic of Arizona and got Michael to the emergency care center. At least then he wouldn't be jumping at shadows.

chapter thirty

Michael came upon them behind the boulder as Raphael leaned in to kiss Catherine.

Raphael stopped midmotion. "Brother, you startled me," he said.

"Sorry for the interruption. I thought perhaps I could ask you for some nutrition," Michael said, his gaze straying to Catherine. Her neck was still raw from Raphael's bite. He could smell her coppery blood and it made his fangs ache.

Raphael stiffened and stepped in front of her, blocking her from Michael's view. "I'm afraid that is not possible," he said, the warning clear in his voice. "But I would be more than happy to offer you sustenance." He pulled up his sleeve, exposing his wrist.

Michael's expression betrayed none of his emotions. "I suppose I have no choice but to accept." He stepped forward and gently took Raphael's wrist in his hands, then raised it to his lips and drank. Catherine's eyes widened and her skin paled, accenting her freckles. She took a step back as if he were about to leap on top of her.

Michael considered it for a moment, then quickly dismissed the idea. He didn't think his brother would approve. The urge to act was strong, fueled by the electrical impulses coming from the chip.

Raphael looked at Catherine. "Return to the camp. I will be there in a moment."

Had his brother suspected? If Raphael did, his expression gave nothing away.

She nodded, but kept her eyes on Michael. "I'll be close by if you need me," Catherine said.

Raphael smiled. "Thanks."

"She watches over you like a mother hen," Michael said, licking the blood from his lips.

Raphael waited for her to leave, then rolled up his other sleeve, holding his forearm out to his brother.

"Are you sure?" Michael asked.

"Just do it," Raphael said. "It should aid you enough to make it the boundary fence."

Michael released his wrist. "You must really love her if you don't want me to feed from her," he said casually, then encircled Raphael's forearm before pulling it to his mouth and sinking his fangs in deep.

"I do," he said.

Michael stopped feeding and raised his head. "I'm surprised you'd admit it," he said, then went back to drinking.

"Not half as surprised as me." Raphael groaned as Michael drew his blood into his body. "She has a way of getting under your skin."

Michael didn't let the pain from Raphael's declaration show on his face. Somehow he'd managed to lose his brother, along with himself on this journey. The salty tang of Raphael's blood rushed over his tongue and down his throat. His brother had always tasted good. Michael had wondered throughout the years if they tasted the same since they were brothers, but he doubted it. Raphael had always been different, even when they were kids. The women had loved him right from the start and he'd loved them back.

Women had always been frightened of Michael. He'd tried many times to make a connection, but he'd always screwed it up by saying something inappropriate. In the end, Michael had settled for the occasional fuck. There hadn't been many—nothing like his brother's track record with women. But it seemed now that Raphael had settled down. He'd found something far greater than instant physical gratification. And as much as Michael hated himself for feeling it, jealousy ate at his soul. The A.I. chip rewarded his negative feeling with a rush of endorphins.

"Enough," Raphael said gently. "Or I'll have to feed from Catherine again and I don't want to weaken her. We still have far to go."

Michael ran his tongue over his brother's wrist and forearm, sealing the wounds. "Sorry, I guess I was hungrier than I thought."

"With all the blood you were carrying when we met up, I'm surprised you're able to eat a thing," Raphael said.

Michael didn't rise to his bait. He'd known Raphael would sense the blood he'd had on him when they met up several days ago. It would be impossible for a vamp to miss. He wouldn't apologize for taking the nomadic tribe's blood. This was survival. Raphael of all people should understand that.

"It's not here now," Michael said, wiping his mouth with the back of his sleeve. "Is it?" Blood didn't last long in this heat.

"How are you feeling? Well enough to reach the boundary?" Raphael asked. His arm had already started to heal.

Michael nodded, even though his hunger hadn't even begun to be sated. "Fine, thanks to your generous gift. I'm used to going days without feeding. I'm sure I'll have no trouble making it to the fence now." A shock jolted him, causing Michael's hands to twitch.

"Are you sure?" Raphael asked, noticing the movement. "We could turn back. We haven't gone too far."

"Positive," Michael said, fighting back the pain. He had to get to Roark soon. The chip's interference was definitely getting worse. The blood took the edge off, but it wouldn't last long.

Raphael squeezed Michael's arm. "You are a better man than I, my brother. I wouldn't make it an afternoon without a taste of that glorious elixir." It was a lie and they both knew it.

He met Raphael's eyes and for a moment they connected.

"No, I'm not," Michael said seriously. "You've proven that you are the better man time and again. Our parents would be proud of the man you've become."

"Michael, I didn't mean you any disrespect," Raphael said. "I was . . ."

He touched him with trembling fingers. "It is not a point of contention between us. I'm simply stating the truth. You are the better man and I love you for it. Please remember that always. Now we had better go, before they leave without us. Wouldn't want to miss the big transmission."

Raphael stared at his brother's retreating back. He wasn't sure what just happened, but his gut was twisting with worry. How could words so tender leave him feeling so much pain? He swallowed hard and rushed to catch up.

Red, Morgan, Catherine, and Melea had already started to climb the mountain. They'd settled on a peak the night before, declaring it tall enough to broadcast the recording. That's if the navcom was still working. Raphael had seen Morgan fiddling with it the night before. He hadn't looked happy.

He'd considered reading his thoughts, but chose not to, since it wouldn't change their circumstances. Now Raphael had wished he had. Morgan's expression was grim and Red kept glancing back to check on Michael. Not that he could blame her. He found himself watching his brother, too. He'd been unnaturally quiet since the feeding and his skin had grown pale under the sun's rays.

Raphael had hoped the blood would help his brother. At the very least alleviate some of his pain. But if it did help, Raphael couldn't tell. He began to climb. He'd covered his skin with the balm he'd gotten from the border crossing store, which would allow him to move without the use of a protective clothing at least until the sun rose high in the sky. The sun's rays didn't seem to bother his brother today. In fact, nothing seemed to be bothering Michael. Concern ate him; they had to hurry.

They reached the top of the peak an hour later. There weren't many places to stand, so each member of the group had to find his footing carefully. Raphael glanced over his shoulder at the drop behind him. It might not kill him, but he'd be in no shape to travel if he slipped. Catherine stood closest to Red and Morgan. She tried to look casual, but Raphael knew it was a tactical move. He still wasn't sure what kind of deal she'd made with the commander of IPTT—not that it mattered now, the circumstances had changed for everyone.

Morgan pressed a button to power up the navcom. The screen glowed, which was a good sign. At least it was receiving some juice from the crystal. He reached into his pocket and took out the small digital recorder Kane had used to tape Roark, then looked at the group.

"I'm only going to get one shot at this before I drain the power out of this navcom," Morgan said.

"Then you'd better hurry," Raphael said. The words had barely left his mouth when he saw a blur of movement. There was only one creature that he knew could move that fast—his brother, Michael.

Michael's arms snaked around Catherine. In the next heartbeat, he'd pulled her knife and held it to her throat. The sharp blade glistened in the sunlight, its deadly teeth threatening to shred the soft flesh protecting her esophagus.

"No one move," Michael said, his voice a harsh rush of air and panic.

"Brother, what are you doing?" Raphael asked, judging the distance between them. He shifted his feet and rocks tumbled down the mountainside, crashing below.

"I wouldn't," Michael said. "Unless you want to lose your woman."

Raphael raised his arms and stepped back. "We're trying to help you."

"I can't let you send that message," Michael said to Morgan, ignoring Raphael.

Morgan's gaze shot to Raphael, who shook his head in warning. "We have no choice. It's the only way Gina and I will ever be able to return to the republics." Morgan went to push the button, but his hand froze above it. "Damn it!"

"It's Michael," Red said, then attempted to rush the vamp.

"He's using his telekinesis to stop us." Her body shook as she tried to break free.

Raphael focused his attention on Michael. Catherine hadn't moved, although he could hear her thoughts and she was planning an attack. "Don't!" he cried out.

Michael and Catherine jumped, which caused the knife to nick her throat. The smell of her blood filled the air and Raphael saw Michael's eyes lock on the slow, steady drip. The moment Michael's fangs extended, Raphael's heart tripled its beat in his chest.

"Michael, no!" he shouted.

Michael tore his eyes away from Catherine's throat. "You are in no position to make demands, brother." He licked his lips.

"Why are you doing this?" he asked.

"You know why." Michael pulled Catherine closer.

Raphael shook his head. "No, I don't."

Michael tapped his brow. "It's in there. It's always in there. It's keeping the shadows at bay. Roark can get it out. He promised if I brought Red and Morgan back he'd take it out. He's the only one who can. Don't you see? I can't let you destroy him."

Raphael frowned and looked around in confusion. "What shadows?"

He glanced around, his eyes wild and unfocused. "They think I don't see them, but I do. I really do. They've been following me, keeping just out of sight. I'm surprised you didn't notice that they're waiting for me, when you put me on the cot."

Cold enveloped Raphael. His brother was mad. Morgan and Red tried to warn him, but he hadn't listened. He'd been too focused on getting help. How could Raphael have missed the signs? They'd been there. The subtle clues in his behavior and the not-so-subtle ones like him wiping out an entire nomadic tribe. He had no doubt now who was behind the murders. And Raphael had ignored them all. Made excuses for him as . . . as anyone would do for someone they loved.

The realization that he was partially responsible for this situation struck Raphael. Fear came on the heels of that discovery, numbing him. He shuddered. Catherine was in the hands of a madman and there wasn't anything he could do about it, unless he wanted to get them both killed.

Raphael looked at Morgan and Red. Red's eyes had started to turn amber and claws had sprouted from her nail beds. She hadn't even cried out, but he knew she was in pain. It was a show of sheer willpower. Soon the change would be complete and there would be no reasoning with her.

Please don't, he pleaded with her and Morgan using their mental connection. *Michael is not well. The chip has left him paranoid. I believe he will kill Catherine if he feels threatened. I cannot lose them both.*

We can't stop the broadcast. It's our only chance. The only chance we'll have to prevent Roark's blood war, Red said.

Give me a moment to talk him down. I believe I can reach him. If I fail, then . . . you know what needs to be done, Raphael said.

The navcom won't last much longer, Morgan said. *Even now I can see the power draining.*

He is my brother, Raphael said softly. *My only family. And Catherine, well, she holds my heart.*

Morgan nodded in understanding. *You won't have long,* he said. *This thing only has about three minutes left in it before it dies. He won't let me reach the controls to shut it off.*

Thank you for allowing me to try, Raphael said.

"Let me go," Catherine said, but she didn't try to struggle.

Be still, Raphael told her, but it was too late.

He felt her power building a second before she released it. Morgan, Red, and Melea clutched their heads and dropped to their knees. Michael swayed, then his eyes clouded before quickly snapping back into focus. The power washed over Raphael, harmlessly passing through him.

"I forgot about your little trick," Michael said, leaning down to lick the blood off her throat. "You try it again and I'll widen this slit until you bleed out."

A growl rumbled in the air. It took Raphael a second to realize that it was coming from him and not the wolves. "Don't touch her again, brother. You test our bond with your actions. You know I love her."

Catherine's eyes widened, then filled with tears. Raphael forced his gaze away. He couldn't chance being distracted.

"In another minute, it'll be a moot point because the nav-com will be dead. Already the screen is beginning to dim," Michael said.

"Has Roark given you so much that you're willing to sac-rifice everyone else for selfish gains?" Raphael asked.

Michael's eyes locked on him and he felt pressure build around his throat, threatening to cut off his air. Raphael didn't give Michael the pleasure of seeing him grasp at in-visible fingers.

"Selfish gains?" Michael hissed. "How dare you? You know nothing of what I've had to put up with over the years."

"And yet, here you stand still doing your master's bidding," Raphael said. "Seems to me that you've learned nothing."

"My life is worth more than a few Others. Our time to-gether is priceless to me." Michael's grip tightened on the knife handle. "Would you like to see what Roark taught me, brother?"

"No!" Raphael rushed forward as the knife began to slice Catherine's throat. The movement distracted Michael and he dropped his hold on Morgan's hand.

Raphael grasped Michael's arm, stopping him from cut-ting Catherine any further. Her wound was bleeding badly. He pulled the blade a few inches away from her throat and she grasped her neck with her free hand. Michael had to release her to get a better grip on the knife. When he did, Raphael shoved her, sending her sprawling onto the ground. Melea rushed forward to help her. Raphael stood face to face with his brother in a desperate struggle to disarm him.

"Michael, stop this foolishness. No one wins," Raphael grunted out between clenched teeth. Kane's voice rang out from the recording as Morgan sent the message, but it was Roark's voice that nearly caused him to drop the weapon.

The recording was short and direct. It ended almost before it began. "Please let me help you."

"It's done," Morgan said.

Michael looked around, his black eyes growing wider. "It's too late. They're coming for me. There is no escape." He struggled to break Raphael's grasp. The fact that he didn't use telekinesis to fight spoke volumes. The knife slipped, cutting Michael's hand. "Keep them away."

Tears stung Raphael's eyes. "Please, brother. Do not do this. Give me the knife. We *can* help you. We just need to make it to the emergency care center."

Michael's gaze met his and softened. For a moment the world dropped away and they were children again, playing cowboys and Indians in the backyard with sticks and water guns. "Remember what I said. You are the better man," Michael whispered softly. "Now allow me to help you with what needs to be done."

The words had barely registered in Raphael's ears when the pressure Michael was exerting on the knife ceased and the blade flipped over. Raphael was still bearing down hard. Without his brother's resistance, the knife slammed into Michael's throat and came out the other side.

Blood sprayed over Raphael's face and down the front of his shirt. He shrieked and removed the knife, pulling Michael into his arms before falling to his knees onto the rocks.

"No, damn you! No!" Raphael cried, rocking Michael in his arms. "Why did you do this?"

Michael opened his mouth, but was unable to speak. Blood bubbled out of his wound. Raphael pressed a hand to Michael's throat to stem the flow, but the blood just kept coming. His fingers were covered in crimson.

"Make it stop," Raphael said, shaking Michael. "You have the power. Make it stop."

Words flowed into Raphael's mind.

Please do not feel any guilt. It was the only way. The only way I could escape once I realized I wasn't going to make it, Michael said.

But we could've gotten you help, Raphael said.

Then what? I'd spend the rest of my life waiting for an assassin to find me? That is no way to live. I tried to make it easy on you.

His words stilled Raphael's breathing. *You set this whole thing up.*

Not initially. Only when I realized it was too late.

Why, brother? Raphael asked.

You wouldn't do it otherwise. I knew the threat to the Others wasn't enough, but your love for Catherine would be. I knew you wouldn't let her die.

Raphael brushed his face and cooed softly to soothe his passage. *No, I couldn't.*

Michael choked, spitting up blood. *I swear on our mother's grave I would never have killed Catherine. The chip made me cut her. I didn't want to. I know how much she means to you.*

You mean a lot to me, too, Raphael said. Crimson tears flowed freely down his cheeks as he rocked his brother in his arms.

Remember me as I once was.

I will, Raphael said, holding him tighter, as if that would stave off death. It didn't.

Raphael threw his head back in anguish. He raged at the heavens. A century of pain erupted in guttural growls. His brother was gone, leaving only emptiness.

It took several minutes for him to notice the warm arms encircling him, comforting, even as the pain threatened to crush his heart. He felt moisture on his back and realized that Catherine was crying with him. Or maybe she was crying for him. He didn't know. And it didn't matter. All that mattered was that she was there doing everything she could to remind him that he wasn't alone.

Raphael didn't know how long he sat there. His muscles were stiff by the time he released Michael and attempted to stand. He stumbled, but Catherine steadied him.

"Did you get the message out?" he asked Morgan.

Morgan shook his head. "I don't know. We only got to

send it once, then the navcom died. I guess we'll find out when we reach the boundary fence. I'm sorry for your loss."

Raphael nodded, then wiped the tears from his face.

They carried Michael back down the mountain and buried him deep under the sand. Raphael stood over the mound, swaying on his feet. The rest of the group surrounded the makeshift grave. Red, Melea, and Catherine had never experienced a funeral. They'd been done away with long before any of them were born. Outdated on the dead world, bodies were now recycled like any other biodegradable object and used as mulch to feed the plants in the hydroponic chambers.

"Do you want to say a few words?" Morgan asked.

Raphael shook his head slowly. "No, we said all we needed to say on the mountain. I hope he found the peace he so desperately sought."

"Amen," Morgan said. "Let's go end this."

chapter thirty-one

It took three days for the group to clear the last of the dunes. They could see the boundary fence glowing in the distance, its sight both welcome and foreboding. What if the transmission hadn't made it out? What if no one knew what Roark had done? They might be walking into a trap, but they wouldn't know until they got a little closer.

Red couldn't think about that now. They'd made it over the mountains and through the endless dunes without any more trouble. For that she was grateful. There'd been enough death on this journey. It was time to put this conflict to rest. On the other side of the fence the Republic of Arizona waited for them.

They stopped so she and Morgan could put their registered chips back into their necks. It was a risk. A big one. If anyone was tracking them, they'd know exactly where they were with the chips in place. But it didn't matter—they were done hiding.

Morgan brushed the hair away from Red's face. "Are you ready?" he asked.

"Don't have much of a choice," she said, smiling. "Let's go. Nothing changes if we put this off."

The five of them continued on. It was easier going now that they'd left the deep sand behind. Red brushed the dust off her clothes as she scanned the fence line. The blue boundary crackled, the sound carrying on the dry desert breeze. Something flashed behind the fence.

"Did you see that?" Red asked.

"Yes," Morgan said, moving closer. "Did you catch what it was, Raphael?"

Catherine stopped, along with Melea. Raphael squinted, then drew to a halt. "It's a laser sniper rifle. If I'm not mistaken, International Police Tactical Team issue," he said.

"Everybody down!" Morgan shouted.

Red's heart slammed painfully into her ribs. Their signal hadn't made it. Their journey back had been for nothing. She took out a monocular and scanned the fence line. A blond head stood out from the rest.

"Bannon," she whispered.

"Are you sure?" Morgan asked, scanning the horizon.

Red lowered the monocular. "I'd know that shorn head anywhere," she said. "It looks like he's leading the teams."

"Teams?" Catherine asked. "As in plural?"

"Yes, there are at least three of them there. And that's just the ones I can see," Red said.

"What are we going to do?" Melea asked, her eyes wide with fright. She searched desperately for a place to hide.

Red and Morgan looked at each other, then slowly nodded. "You guys are going to make your way toward the crossing. Morgan and I will turn ourselves in."

"No way," Raphael said. "We didn't walk all this way to have you imprisoned now."

"They don't know about you," Red said. "I'd like it to stay that way. There's a tunnel off to the left. Stomp on the ground to find it. Melea, if you wait until dark, you should be able to make it across with no problem. Raphael will come and get you at midnight."

"I'm not waiting out here by myself," she said. "I'm un-armed."

Red took her pistol out of its holster and adjusted the weapon so Melea could fire it, then handed it to her. "Now you'll be safe."

"I'm not going to let you walk into a firing squad," Raphael said. "We can't clear your name if you're dead."

Red sighed. "You said there's a sniper rifle trained on us."

Raphael nodded. "There is."

"Then they've already spotted us. We could probably convince IPTT that we took you hostage," Red said. There had to be a way to protect their friends.

He arched a brow.

"It's worth a shot," she said.

"Not from where I'm laying," Raphael said.

"I hate to break up this argument," Morgan said. "But I just spotted three tanks moving in. I believe the decision has been made for us. We'll have to proceed before they blast us with the heat seekers."

"It's me Bannon wants," Red said. "Maybe if I turn myself in, he'll take me and leave."

Morgan shot her a look that said this conversation was over.

"Fine, have it your way," Red said. She stood and started forward slowly.

The closer they got to the fence the greater her dread grew. There were more than three squads lined up along the boundary fence. Bannon had brought half the teams. Roark must have really been threatened by the information they held. Too bad no one but them and Roark would ever know the truth.

"Who is Bannon?" Raphael asked.

"He's a commanding officer at IPTT headquarters," Catherine answered. "Bit of an asshole, if you ask me."

Red laughed. She couldn't help it. "I see you've had an encounter."

"He was with me when I visited Roark's office," Catherine said. Her eyes widened a moment later as if she realized what she'd said.

Red stopped. "And just what were you doing at Roark's office?" she asked.

"It's a long story," Raphael said. "One that perhaps is better shared later."

"Are you vouching for her?" Morgan asked.

Raphael stepped forward. "I am."

Morgan held his gaze and the tension inside the little group rose.

"For you, my friend, I will do this once—and once only," Raphael said, before slowly lowering his eyes in respect for Morgan's position as alpha.

Morgan looked stunned. "I never thought I'd see the day," he said.

Raphael grinned. "I figured since we may not be alive in the very near future it was the least I could do."

The men laughed, sharing an easy camaraderie that Red didn't think she'd ever witness between them.

"Come forward with your hands up where we can see them," Bannon shouted, shattering the moment.

Red's hands shook as she raised them high. Bannon shouldn't be here, leading the teams. Her grandfather should. He was the rightful commander of IPTT.

Bannon was a bully as a lieutenant, and she couldn't imagine the power trip he'd be on as commander. The tactical team would lose a lot of good men and women under Bannon's command. Red forced her feet forward. Morgan still kept his body between her and the teams, but it would do little good if Bannon ordered them to open fire.

"Lower your weapons," Catherine shouted. "It's Private Catherine Meyers. Team member 11174." She pulled out her I.D., but her hand continued to rest on her weapon.

"I'm afraid we can't do that, Private," Bannon said. His face was grim as they neared the fence. "We have orders to neutralize the threat."

Catherine's gaze locked on Red.

The time to move was now. Once she's in custody, I won't be able to touch her. I shouldn't have waited so long. I should have jumped at the opportunity to take Gina Santiago down when I had the chance.

I felt panic hit. My orders were clear. I must kill her.

I glanced around at the tactical team members. All eyes were upon me, waiting to see what I'd do next. They'd bear witness to my sacrifice.

My nerves were jumping beneath my skin, caught somewhere between fight or flight. No time to back down. I was doing this for the team. My hand brushed my weapon.

Gina stood a few feet away with her head held high. Pride radiated from her. It fueled my anger. How dare she act like she's innocent. If she were smart, she'd have recognized the threat that has been with her all along.

My fingers wrapped around the handle of the laser pistol. The weapon recognized my thumb print and began to charge. In a few seconds, it would be ready to fire.

My hand trembled as I fought the urge to draw the pistol from its holster, but the compulsion to kill was too strong. It drove all logic away, leaving only savage impulses behind. Red had to die. She was ruining the tactical team, tearing apart what it stood for by creating that abomination in Nuria. Didn't she understand that this was my home?

There was only room for one tactical team and it had been in existence for more than a hundred years.

Must kill her.

She needed to get closer. I couldn't take the chance that someone might stop me. I took a deep breath. It was now or never.

Red's stomach clenched as she saw Catherine grasp her laser pistol. A muscle ticced in Bannon's jaw. She'd seen that more than a dozen times. It meant that he was furious. That didn't bode well for them. One wrong move and he'd give the order to kill them. Red knew she needed to do something. She glanced back at Catherine. Their eyes met and Red shook her head in warning, but the private's aggressive stance didn't ease. If anything, it got worse. Catherine was going to get them killed.

She walked forward briskly, keeping her arms raised. "It's me you want," Red said.

"Gina, get back here." Morgan tried to stop her.

"I said hands in the air," Bannon shouted.

Morgan stopped midmotion and raised his arms once more.

"Gina Santiago," Bannon yelled. "You are wanted for crimes against the republics. You will be taken into custody the second you cross the boundary fence. If you choose to run, you will be shot." He spoke the last sentence with anticipation.

Bannon wanted her to run. Red had no doubt that he'd take great pleasure in killing her. "I will surrender without resistance," she said. "Let the others go."

"Nice try," Bannon said. "But Morgan Hunter is also wanted. The others will be detained under the conspiracy law."

A dust trail rose in the distance as a vehicle approached from the north.

The power in the fence went down. One by one, Red and her traveling companions stepped forward, only to be knocked to their knees. Power cuffs were placed on Red's and Morgan's wrists, then they were ordered to stand. The vehicle Red had been watching had nearly reached them. She could see now it was a turbo shuttle. IPTT rarely used them because they required so much power.

"Roark," she muttered. It had to be Roark.

Bannon followed her line of sight and smirked. "Just in time."

"In time for what?" she asked.

"You are a disgrace to the uniform," Bannon hissed.

Red flinched. "I did what I had to do in order to save my people and clear my name."

He snorted. "Your name will never be clear." Bannon's large hands closed around her throat and began to squeeze. "Must stop you," he said.

"What are you doing?" Red kicked out, connecting with his groin, but all it did was make him more determined. Spots swam before her eyes and the world turned scarlet. She gasped, but no air came in. "Bannon stop."

She could hear Catherine and Morgan struggling beside her, but someone was holding them down. "Why are you doing this?" She choked.

His blue eyes were wild and glassy. He was looking at her, but Red didn't think he could see her. "Why won't you die?" Bannon shouted.

"Stop . . ." Red gurgled as she tried to breathe. Her vision dimmed.

"That's enough, Lieutenant. Stand down," a baritone voice boomed from behind Bannon's broad shoulders.

He ignored the order.

Red recognized that voice, but even as the thought passed through her mind, she knew it wasn't possible. She must be dying. For that voice had been taken from her in two deafening shots. Bannon turned, giving her a clear view of the approaching tactical team member.

"Let her go or we'll be forced to open fire," the man said.

"No," Bannon bellowed, squeezing tighter. "You can't stop me. My orders are clear. I'm protecting IPTT."

A flash from a laser blast nearly blinded her. Red felt Bannon's grip ease. She coughed, then blinked several times forcing her eyes to focus. A gaping hole smoldered where Bannon's abdomen used to be. He tumbled, landing beside her. Red turned in time to see Melea lower the weapon she'd given her, a power cuff hung from one of her wrists.

Shaking, the woman dropped the gun on the ground and slowly raised her hands. "He was going to kill you," she said. Her dark eyes were haunted by the violence she'd been forced to commit.

"Thank you," Red said as Melea started to cry.

The tactical team members raised their weapons.

"I said stand down. That's an order."

"Grandpa?" Red asked. She blinked as tears filled her eyes. "Is it really you?" She had to be dead. Either that or she was seeing a ghost.

Robert Santiago rushed forward and pulled her into his arms.

The hug felt real. Red inhaled, taking in the slightly musty odor that clung to her grandfather from handling his book collection. "I can't believe it. You were dead. I heard the shots. I'll never forget that sound of you gasping for breath," she said, tears streamed down her face.

"I know" he said, trying to push her back so he could look at her. "We found the body of an unknown and the recordings when we searched Roark's office. The audio reproduction was very convincing. It took the tech people a couple of days to figure out he'd hijacked our security feed so he could record my voice. From there it was a matter of editing the right phrases together."

Red burrowed deeper. She didn't allow the power cuffs to stop her. She snuggled into his shirt, breathing in his scent, savoring it. Robert Santiago gave up trying to move her and glanced over her shoulder at Morgan Hunter.

"What in the hell was going on here?" he asked. "Why was Bannon choking Gina?"

Morgan's jaw was covered in a short beard and his hair had grown to the middle of his shoulders. If it wasn't for his eyes, Robert wouldn't have recognized him.

"He was trying to kill her," he said.

"So I saw," Robert scowled. "But why?"

Morgan shifted, his gaze growing wary. "I don't know, but I'm sure Roark has something to do with it. He always does."

He snorted. "That's ridiculous. Bannon lives and breaths IPTT." Robert glanced down. "At least he did."

"Do you have a better idea?" Morgan asked.

Robert brushed his granddaughter's back with his palm and said nothing.

"I didn't think so." Morgan dropped his gaze.

Robert looked at the fragile young woman who'd shot Bannon. Her eyes were round with fright and she couldn't seem to stop trembling. He'd considered charging her, but that was before he got a good look at her. There'd been no malicious intent in her expression, only fear for one woman from another . . . who'd seen far too much violence in her short lifetime.

"We tried to send out a message that could prove our

innocence, but I see now it didn't reach you," Gina said, looking around at the teams.

"Nonsense." The commander kissed her forehead. "Why do you think we're here?"

"But I thought . . ." her voice trailed off as she held up her cuffed hands. "Bannon said . . ."

Robert Santiago's gaze shot to Bannon Richards' body. "I don't know what got into Richards. He asked to lead the team. I didn't see a problem with it given his rank. I had no idea it was so he could get his hands on you. I'm so sorry, Gina."

"It's not your fault. It was like he was possessed," she said.

"I'll have the dissecting lab run tests on his body to figure out why. I'm not sure what he said to you, but we're here because we received your broadcast. The republic leaders asked IPTT to personally meet you and escort you in without further incident."

Gina's brow creased and she shook her head. "What are you saying?"

"I'm saying that everyone heard Roark put that hit out on you. They heard it from you and from your navcom, Rita. We were able to piece together the recording you made in the shuttle. Even without your evidence, we had enough to go to the republic leaders. They are holding an emergency tribunal about Roark's actions and the discovery of the Others. You are both expected to stand before them and tell your side of the story. They are eager to listen."

Red looked over her shoulder at Morgan, who wasn't smiling. "It's going to be okay," he said, even though his expression said otherwise.

She heard the words, but still couldn't believe it. The message had gotten out. Somehow the broken navcoms had come through for them. She choked and began to cry harder, this time with happiness. This whole ordeal was over. They'd done it. They had beaten Roark.

"What about Montgomery?" she asked, remembering the election. "Did he win?"

"Yes," Robert said.

Red deflated a little.

Her grandfather's expression clouded and his dark eyes glittered with anger. "Don't worry. We'll find him."

"What do you mean, you'll find him?" Red asked.

"He won the election," Robert said. "But before he could celebrate his victory, your broadcast went out around the world. He knew I planned to send someone for him. I'd already informed him of the physical evidence I had against him," he said.

"What evidence?" Red asked, more confused than ever.

"Thanks to Private Meyers, we were able to examine the shuttle Roark claimed was attacked by Morgan. She found it hidden in the sand."

Red turned to Catherine. "I guess I owe you an apology," she said.

Catherine shook her head. "No, you don't. I didn't exactly come after you out of the goodness of my heart." Her gaze strayed to Raphael, then to the commander.

Red arched a brow, but Catherine didn't elaborate.

"I gave her permission to find you," Robert said. "I needed to know you were okay. Not that I didn't trust Morgan to take care of you, but I wanted to know firsthand that my special one was all right."

Red smiled. "Thank you," she said. "Thank you both." She nodded to Catherine, who responded in kind. "So do you have any idea where Roark might have fled?"

Robert shook his head and a shock of white hair fell onto his forehead. "No, we've checked his office and his home. We even found that cell under his building. Nasty place."

"Yeah, I know," Red said. "Morgan and I received a private tour."

Her grandfather's gaze searched her face. "You're safe," he said more to himself than to her.

"So what happens now?" Red asked, glancing once more at the teams.

"We have to take you in. Don't want it to look like we do not follow protocol. You'll be processed and held at IPTT.

You won't be kept in a cell, but your rooms will be guarded. In two days' time, you'll meet with the republic leaders. From there," he said, "it's only a matter of e-filings."

Red still couldn't believe it. They'd traveled so far. Lost so much. And now it was almost over. She thought about Demery and Michael as they were loaded into her grandfather's transport. Robert Santiago sat on her left and Morgan sat on her right. There was a low hum as the maglev shuttle started rising slowly off the ground.

"Where do you think he's hiding?" she asked, her voice so low that only Raphael and Morgan could hear her.

Morgan shook his head. "Don't know. He could be anywhere. Someone might even be hiding him. He has a lot of allies."

"Why would anyone do that?" she asked, horrified at the prospect of someone harboring Roark.

"He's a powerful man with a lot of powerful friends. It's not out of the realm of possibility," Morgan said. "You forget, people put us up knowing we were wanted."

Red thought about Jonah and the Sand Moles. Morgan was right. Roark may be an asshole, but that didn't mean everyone believed he was in the wrong.

Do not worry yourself, Raphael said, using their mental pathway. *I have no doubt I could find him. His stench permeated my brother's flesh. The odor stays with me to this day. He will not escape justice.*

I've been meaning to ask you something. Do you feel pain when I do? Red asked.

He frowned. *No, why do you ask?*

Melea said something about Demery being able to feel her pain.

Ah, you mean a blood bond. You and I have not experienced such a thing, Raphael said.

But you drank my blood and I drank yours, Red said.

There's more to it than that. A sexual element. We'd have to exchange blood multiple times for it to occur.

Why didn't she say that? Red asked.

She might not remember. Memory grows fuzzy with blood loss.

Oh, she said.

You sound disappointed, Raphael said, glancing at Catherine. His gaze warmed.

Not at all. More like relieved.

Raphael laughed.

Morgan's amber eyes met Raphael's black ones, then he looked at Red. He knew they were talking and if his expression was any indication, Morgan wasn't happy about being left out of the conversation.

Roark is ours, he said mentally, slamming the thought into Raphael's mind loud enough for Red to hear it.

Morgan is right. I know you hurt over what he did to Michael, she said.

He destroyed my brother, Raphael said. Gone was the humor. It had been replaced by anguish.

I know, Red said. *And he will pay. I promise. But first we have to get through this.* She raised her cuffed hands in reminder.

Raphael's expression soured, but he eventually nodded. *I will not harm him—much—if I find him. I'll make sure there's some left to chew on.*

As reassurances go, it wasn't the greatest, but Red knew it was the best she could hope for under the circumstances. The trip back to IPTT was long and uneventful. One of the few shuttle rides she could say that about as of late. She was having a hard time keeping her eyes open, so she stopped trying. It wasn't until the vehicle halted that she realized she'd fallen asleep with her head on Morgan's shoulder.

"Sorry," she said, shaking her head to wake up.

He smiled down at her. "It's okay. It was nice."

"Ready to go?" her grandfather asked.

Red nodded. "Let's get this over with."

Over a hundred tactical team members had turned up at the shuttle lot. She didn't recognize many of the faces, which meant most had just come here to get a look at the hottest news to hit the planet in a few decades. Red straightened her shoulders and held her head high. She wasn't about to cower under their regard. She'd done nothing wrong. And in a couple of days, she'd get her chance to prove it.

Her grandfather and ten armed men led them into IPTT headquarters. There they were processed by more team members. Her grandfather never left her side as images were taken, along with their statements. Morgan turned over Kane's journal. These would be logged into the official compunit banks as evidence. The republic leaders would listen to them and read the files, then conduct the tribunal.

Red had no doubt it would take at least a week before they would hear an official verdict in their case. She hoped that Catherine, Raphael, and Melea were released after they gave their statements. Despite the power cuffs, Catherine was still considered a member of IPTT in good standing. Her grandfather had even discussed promoting her.

As for Bannon Richards, they'd know what had happened to him once the dissecting lab examined him. Red had no doubt he'd somehow become another one of Roark Montgomery's casualties. With any luck, he'd be the last. Red tried to muster sympathy for him, but she was fresh out.

chapter thirty-two

The tribunal was long and arduous. Red and Morgan were interviewed together and separately. The republic leaders were particularly interested in the existence of the Others and what effect they'd have on the community. Once Morgan explained that they'd been living with Others for more than a hundred years, they calmed down. At least most of them did. A few worried about the safety of so-called pure-blood people, but fortunately they remained in the minority.

Red and Morgan reassured the tribunal that a tactical team made up of Others was already being formed and would be available to begin policing the Other community within the month. This quieted the last of the dissenters. Although they did have to agree to allow regular inspections at least until the republic leaders could determine whether the Others posed a credible threat.

Red supposed that was something. Certainly better than the previous policy of shoot first and ask questions later. The next three days were spent testifying about Roark Montgomery's actions. He'd fled shortly after the broadcast of him ordering the hit and hadn't been seen since. The tribunal assured them that they had people looking for him and it was only a matter of time before he was found.

Red listened attentively because she knew that's what was expected of her, but she thoroughly disagreed. Roark wouldn't be easy to find. He was used to slipping through nets. And she had no doubt that he had more than a few friends sitting on this tribunal, even if they weren't actively defending him now.

On day six, Red and Morgan walked into the tribunal to await their ruling. Red had spent the night staring at the ceiling of her old quarters. The place felt foreign compared to where she'd been in the last few weeks.

Nothing smelled right or tasted the same. She'd walked around the room picking up objects that should've been familiar, but weren't. They might as well have belonged to a stranger. Well, everything but the navcom that now encircled her wrist.

She still couldn't believe that her grandfather had resurrected Rita. She rubbed the familiar band, resisting the urge to power up. Red hadn't had a chance to see if she still sounded the same. Her grandfather had assured her she did, but Red wanted to hear her navcom's voice for herself. Unfortunately, that would have to wait until the verdicts were read. She didn't want Rita alerting the tribunal to her elevated heart rate.

Red grasped Morgan's hand. He squeezed hers back, but didn't look over. Instead, he stared straight ahead, his body at attention. He looked so proud and handsome that once again she remembered why she loved him so much. Robert Santiago walked into the room and Red automatically saluted the commander. Ten years of training drilled into her head was hard to forget.

"All rise," the leader of the tribunal said.

The other members stood, scooting back their chairs. Red looked at their faces, attempting to read their expressions, but it was impossible. She inhaled, sifting through their scents. Most gave off clean odors. There were a few that held a slightly sour smell, which could be attributed to nerves or diet. Overall, she didn't sense lies or deception. She hoped that was a good sign.

"Have you reached verdicts?" the leader asked.

"We have, illustrious one," the group said as one.

He nodded. "What say you on the charges of escaping detention and eluding arrest? Guilty or not guilty?"

Red's heart thundered and her ears began to buzz as her blood roared through her veins. She swayed. Morgan tightened his hold on her hand until pain shot through her fingers. The discomfort forced her to focus and the panic receded.

"Not guilty with special circumstances," the group said.

She knew that was a formal way of saying she and Morgan had just cause to flee.

Morgan turned to her and smiled. He pulled her into his arms a second later and kissed her. "Told you everything was going to be okay."

He had, but Red didn't dare hope in case things hadn't gone their way. "We're finally free," she said.

"Yes, and we can go home. I found out they released Raphael, Melea, and Catherine a couple of days ago."

"How?" Red asked.

"Your grandfather told me," Morgan said. "They even gave Melea a chip, so she could stay in the Republic of Arizona."

"He came to see you? He didn't come to see me."

Morgan pulled back. "Don't be too hard on him. He wanted to see you. He just didn't want to do anything that could be perceived as giving you preferential treatment."

That sounded like her grandfather. He always followed the book, even when he disagreed with it.

"What else did he say to you?" Red asked, genuinely curious. How many times had her grandfather visited Morgan? And what could they find to talk about besides her? Suddenly Red didn't like the idea of her grandfather visiting without her present.

"Oh, a little bit of this and that. Mainly guy talk. We had to come to an understanding. If you want to know more, you'll have to ask him, because I've been sworn to secrecy." His lips twitched.

"That's sounds ominous," Red said. What were they up to?

"Now that this tribunal is over, I'm sure the commander will have a lot to say to you," Morgan said, grinning.

"Why does that not sound like a good thing?" she asked. "What aren't you telling me?"

"Nothing, I swear," he said, chuckling.

"You're a terrible liar," Red said, fighting back a smile.

"Only when it comes to lying to you," Morgan said. "Go spend some time with your grandfather. Now that we're free, I need to contact Nuria to have the credits and seeds sent to Jonah. He kept his end of the bargain. It's time for us to keep ours." Morgan strolled out of the tribunal.

Red waited for her grandfather, who was shaking the hands of the republic leaders congratulating them on a job well done. It didn't take him long. He came over the second he finished.

"So how does it feel to be free?" he asked.

"Good," Red said, pressing the power button on her navcom.

A nasal voice came out a moment later. "Gina, where have you been? I've been unable to contact you for . . . My scanners seem to be unable to recall the date. I will have to run a diagnostic on you and my system to see why."

"It's good to hear your voice, Rita," Red said.

"My system detects dehydration and malnutrition. Administering patch fluids now," Rita said. "You really should take better care of yourself," she chastised.

"I was about to ask you if she was working the same," Red said to her grandfather. "But now I have the answer. How did you ever repair her after Roark crushed her?"

Robert Santiago's bushy white brow lowered over his brown eyes. "It wasn't easy. The tech guys called the job impossible, but they gave it a shot anyway. As you can see, it worked."

Red stood on her toes and threw her arms around him. "Thank you, Grandpa."

He patted her back. "There, there, it's all over now."

She held him for a moment longer, then pulled back. Her gaze met his and her expression hardened. "It won't be over until Roark is caught."

"Leave that to the tactical team, special one," he said, half pleading and half warning.

"Which team? Mine or yours?" Red asked.

"So you're going back?" he asked.

Red nodded. "I have some things to straighten out in Nuria." She looked over his shoulder, but Morgan was gone.

"He loves you, you know," Robert said. "So do I, Gina."

"I love you, too, Grandpa. Always."

Red and Morgan returned to Nuria the next morning. Strangely, the town looked the same. Red didn't know why she'd expected it to have changed. So much had changed for them. Juan and Takeo met them in front of the sheriff's station.

"Welcome back," Juan said. "I told Takeo you'd return soon."

"Saw that in a vision, did you?" Red asked, shaking their hands.

Juan blushed. "Something like that."

"He saw it on the viewer like everyone else in town," Takeo said.

"Some psychic." She snorted. "Where's Raphael and Melea?"

Takeo stiffened at the mention of the woman's name.

"Is there a problem?" Red asked.

Juan grinned at Takeo. "Nothing that won't be resolved with time," he said.

"Don't you have work to do?" Takeo asked Juan.

"Nope, my afternoon is clear," he said, then turned back to Red. "We're up to ten team members now, not counting Takeo, Demery, and me."

Red tensed. In all the excitement, she'd forgotten all about Demery. The expression on her face must've shown her pain because Takeo asked what was wrong.

"Demery is dead," she said. "I'm surprised Melea didn't tell you."

Takeo suddenly looked uncomfortable.

"She hasn't said much besides 'keep him away from me,' " Juan said, pointing at Takeo.

Red's eyes narrowed. "You better not be harassing that woman. She's been through hell and she saved my life."

Takeo held his hands up. "I haven't touched her," he said, looking as innocent as possible, but his expression said he would like to. His lovely Asian eyes sparkled with mischief.

She tapped her arm and waited.

"I swear," he said.

Juan laughed. "He's telling the truth—sort of. He might not have touched her, but he's been following her around like a lost puppy for the past two days."

Takeo shot him a warning look. "I have not."

Red pressed her lips together to keep from laughing.

"I wanted to make sure she was finding everything. She's never lived in a town before," Takeo said, as if that was a perfectly reasonable explanation for his behavior.

"Whatever you say," Red said.

Morgan touched her shoulder. "I'm going to head inside. I'm sure there is a mountain of paperwork waiting for me. It'll take time to get reinstated."

"I'll be in, in a moment," she said.

"So what happened to Demery?" Juan asked, turning the jovial conversation somber.

Red didn't know how to break it to them gently so she came straight out with the truth. "The leader of the Sand Devils and I killed him."

The men's eyes widened and they took an involuntary step back.

"What is a Sand Devil?" Takeo asked. "And do I really want to know?"

Juan scowled. "Why would you do that?"

Red hadn't had time to mourn Demery's death. Until now, she'd done her best to forget all about him. But these men deserved an explanation. Demery had been their friend. He had been a friend to them all—at least until things went sideways.

"The trip didn't go exactly like we expected. Life was much harder than we'd anticipated. Demery didn't lie about knowing and trading with several bands of people in no-man's-land. He was known by almost all. He just left out the fact that he'd gambled Melea away and needed Other blood to get her back," Red said. "The leader of the Sand Devils, the group that held her, raped and beat her repeatedly. She's been through so much that I'm amazed she's survived. That girl is a fighter and she deserves our respect." She looked straight at the beautiful Asian warrior standing before her.

Takeo's face morphed into a mask of pure fury. His slanted eyes glistened and his fangs flashed. She heard a hiss. Red had no doubt the viper was restless beneath his trench coat, ready to strike.

Juan looked over at his friend, then asked softly, "What happened?"

Red took a deep breath. Why hadn't Demery told them what was going on? All he had to do was confide in them, but he hadn't. Instead, he'd played everyone and gotten burned.

"Demery kidnapped Morgan and helped the leader of the band holding Melea bleed him," she said. Images of a bloody Morgan strung up at the center of the Sand Devil encampment flashed in her mind. Foolish. They should've never taken her mate from her. She'd have killed them all, if given the chance.

"It's a good thing Demery's dead," Takeo said. *Or I'd have killed him myself* was left out. His voice was so cold Red shivered.

"He paid dearly for his mistakes," she said. "I ripped Demery's protective suit open right before Reaper, the leader of the Sand Devils, tried to knife me. He missed, but nailed Demery in the process."

"So he exploded?" Takeo asked.

"Yes," Red said, reliving the horrifying moment. Her stomach flipped, threatening to empty.

Takeo's jaw tightened. "He didn't pay nearly enough, if what you say about the girl is true."

Red met his gaze. "She was nothing but chattel to this group and they treated her as such."

"I will make sure that doesn't happen in Nuria," Takeo vowed.

Red gave him a small smile. "You do that," she said, then turned to Juan. "Have you been able to locate Roark yet?"

He shook his head. "The man seems to have disappeared off the planet, which means he's found a very good hiding place. I've sent two wolves to his old office to check out the prison under his building. If they can get a scent of his blood, it'll be easier to track him."

"Keep me posted." Red walked to the sheriff's office, but stopped at the doorway. "I want to thank you both for continuing to build the tactical team and taking care of Nuria while we were gone. I won't forget it."

They shifted uncomfortably under her regard. Red thought she spotted Juan blushing, but he turned before she could be sure.

"It's nothing," Takeo grumbled.

"If you hear anything else, let me know," she said.

"Will do," Juan said, but he still wouldn't look at her.

Red laughed and walked into the sheriff's station. She found Morgan standing in his office. It looked like the place had been hit by a sandstorm.

"What happened?" she asked, staring at the mess.

"My guess is either Roark or the tactical team paid the station a visit," he said, picking up an overturned chair.

"Why didn't Maggie clean this after they left?" Red asked, glancing at the open safe door. The yellowed copy of *Little Red Riding Hood* was still inside. It had been Morgan's and Kane's favorite book when they were children. And the inspiration behind Kane's murders.

"She said she didn't want to get in trouble if they came back."

"Right." Red marched out of his office. She'd had enough of Maggie's crap. Morgan might not believe his assistant turned on her when he left, but Red knew the truth. "This stops now!" she shouted.

Maggie Sheppard let out a startled yelp and her eyes

rounded. "I don't know what you mean," she said, hiding her trembling hands beneath her desk.

"I put up with your appalling behavior when Morgan was gone, but it ends now," Red said.

Maggie's eyes turned dark amber as the wolf inside her surfaced. She stood, directly challenging Red.

Red's claws came out and her vision faded, before snapping into a clarity that only came with her Other self. "I will not accept anything less than your full submission," she growled, Tufts of hair covered her arms. Bones broke and her teeth ejected. Red screamed, but somehow managed to keep her feet beneath her. "Do you understand?" Her jaw snapped at Maggie, stopping inches in front of her face.

Maggie whimpered. "Yes." She quickly lowered her gaze to the floor.

"Does anyone else have a problem with me running Nuria with Morgan?" Red asked, her voice nearly unrecognizable. Soon she wouldn't be able to form words at all.

"No," a chorus of deputies shouted.

"Good," she said. "Now get back to work."

Morgan stepped out of his office and surveyed the scene. Pride colored his features. "You heard her," he barked.

Everyone jumped and busied themselves, even the ones who had nothing to do.

She'd finally claimed her spot in the pack—in this town. Red looked at Morgan. His eyes glowed softly, letting her know she'd conquered his heart long ago.

There would be no more defiance as long as they led together. They'd proven ten times over that they were meant to be mates. And no one, not Roark, not Nuria, not even death itself, would ever tear them apart again.

Epilogue

Roark Montgomery stood on the front porch of his stone cabin in the Republic of Utarado. He'd found this place tucked inside a dead forest on the side of a mountain range that used to hold twenty feet of snowpack. He'd killed the recluse who owned it and buried him out back. That had been twenty years ago and no one had been any wiser.

There was a nip in the air. He held the cup of synth-coffee to his lips and blew on it before taking a sip. It was bitter, but the warmth cut the chill from his bones. The woods had seemed eerily calm today. No sounds of scurrying creatures, only the slight breeze that caused the branches to creak incessantly. He raised the cup again and was about to drink when he heard a piercing howl.

It wasn't the first time he'd heard the wolves, but they tended to come at night, not during the day. He squinted at the woods, searching for signs of movement in the branches and among the petrified tree trunks. Foliage deserted the forest long ago, leaving it bare. Nothing caught his eye. He drank the coffee, then put the cup down. A second howl came, this time much closer. Roark reached for his gun. The howl was answered by another and another. The hair on his neck rose. It was the only warning he got.

Roark didn't see the attack coming, but he felt it. Teeth

and claws ripped at his body, tearing pieces of his life away. He saw flashes of amber eyes. Familiar eyes. In that moment the truth shined with clarity: Roark was staring into the faces of death.

His death.

There would be no mercy. No reprieve. For he'd shown none.

Iron jaws clamped onto his bones, snapping them like twigs. Roark screamed until he could scream no more, but there was no one around to hear him. The trees and mountains didn't care, and neither did his attackers.

The world swirled in pools of crimson, then slowly faded to black, taking his dreams of power with it. He gasped, then gurgled. Then Roark did something he'd never done before. He died.

"That about wraps it up," Chaos said to the investigative team. "Did you find anything else?" she asked.

The IPTT members shook their heads and waited for the cleanup crew to gather their equipment.

Chaos walked around to the back of the cabin and up the ridge. The sun dappled the area thanks to the dead tree branches. She was about to turn when she saw a flash of metal on the ground behind a stump. She walked over to investigate.

This would be her last case for a while. She was off to do an exchange with the Nurian Tactical Team . . . and to see Raphael Vega. She ignored the thrill that thought brought and kicked the object with the toe of her boot. It rolled over.

Chaos recognized the object instantly. She glanced around to make sure no one was looking. When she was sure she wouldn't be spotted, Chaos leaned down and quickly picked it up. She shoved the device into her bag and walked back to join the rest of the team.

"Are we finished?" she asked.

"Yes, Lieutenant," one of the men said.

Chaos smiled. "Very well, Private. Let's head back to the shuttles and return to IPTT."

"Yes, ma'am."

The ride to International Police Tactical Team headquarters didn't take long. She couldn't believe that Roark had hid practically under their noses. They would've never found him if the anonymous tip hadn't come in this morning.

She thought about all the havoc the man had wreaked. Chaos had no doubt that he was behind Bannon Richards' attempt on Red's life. It frightened her that it could have just as easily been her, since they were both drugged with influgas. The tox report had come back inconclusive. Raphael had been telling the truth about the gas being undetectable.

They parked the shuttle and Chaos strode into IPTT headquarters. She had one more thing to do. She typed up her report and submitted it before heading to the commander's office. Chaos brushed her hand against the wooden surface of the door and waited for the camera to extend and scan her eye. It did and she was quickly allowed inside.

"Sir, have you read my report?" she asked.

"I'm finishing it up now," Commander Robert Santiago said. "Is this your official finding?" he asked.

"Yes, sir. There was insufficient evidence that a crime occurred," she said, standing at attention.

"Says here that only *animal* DNA was found on the scene," he said.

"That's correct, sir. We did a very thorough sweep."

"Then I suppose this case is closed," he said.

Chaos nodded. "Yes, sir." She watched the commander write "Animal Attack" across the report, then "Case Closed."

"You about ready to head out on your exchange?" Robert asked.

Chaos' stomach fluttered at the thought of spending a year in Nuria. She and Raphael could pick up where they'd left off. She blushed, when she realized *exactly* where that would be. "Yes, sir."

He nodded. "Good. Enjoy yourself," he said.

When she didn't immediately move, Robert Santiago looked at her. "Is there something else to report?" he asked.

"No, sir," Chaos said, taking the navcom out of her bag. She placed it on his desk and went back to standing at attention. "But you may want to return that to its owner. I found it outside Roark Montgomery's cabin."

The commander reached for the navcom and turned it on.

"Gina, where are you? I'm not sensing your presence," Rita said.

He quickly powered down the navcom and shoved it into his desk drawer. "I will make sure the owner gets it. We're meeting for lunch tomorrow. I'm sure she'll be grateful you returned the navcom."

"Tell her to be more careful next time," Chaos said.

Robert Santiago leveled a piercing gaze at her. "Now that Roark Montgomery is dead, I assure you there will not be a next time."

TOR
ROMANCE

Believe that love is magic

Please join us at the Web site below
for more information about this
author and other great romance
selections, and to sign up for our
monthly newsletter!

www.tor-forge.com